To John
Christmas 2014
Love Philo.

CW01639446

The Priest & The Prostitute

To
Mary
Happy Reading
Angelina

Angelina Kelly

ORIGINAL WRITING

ISBNS
Parent : 978-1-78237-575-3
epub: 978-1-78237-576-0
mobi: 978-1-78237-577-7
PDF: 978-1-78237-578-4

A cip catalogue for this book is available from the National Library.

Published by Original Writing Ltd., Dublin, 2014.

Printed by Clondalkin Group, Glasnevin, Dublin 11

Dedicated to Colm, Barbie and Danni

Acknowlegements

I'd like to thank my husband Colm and daughters Barbie and Danni for being my best and worst critics, for giving me the time to write this book and for being patient with me when I was writing instead of being with them. An extra special nod of appreciation to Danni for her expertise and technical advice

Thank you to Maeve McNamara and Mary Farrelly for being my proof readers and for the time they took to go through my manuscript with a fine tooth comb. For their belief in me as a writer and for becoming as familiar, and incensed, with my characters as I am.

To my tester readers, especially Barbie, for their feedback and comments.

To the Irish Writers' Centre for their encouragement and for believing in the concept of the story so much that they sent me away on a writers' holiday to prepare the final draft.

To my therapists Patricia Ravelle and Kay Raymond who were with me at the beginning as the story unfolded and Anne French who was with me at the end and is still with me today. To Adrienne Heeney for keeping my head on straight.

To Garrett, Steven and all the team at Original Writing Ltd. for taking my manuscript and turning it into a book to be proud of.

To Paedur and Elaena for inviting me into their world and for telling me their story, every moment I spent with them was a privilege and an honour. I hope that they will now find the peace they both craved.

And most of all to you, the reader, who have bought this book and will keep this story alive.

This is not a love story, although love is very much its main feature. It is more a story about the destructive force of anger and about possession and how even a genuine love, once it possesses, also destructs.

Contents

If I knew then what I know now this story would have had a very different ending.

I'm eternally grateful to Angelina for listening, for being willing to relive the memory with me and for having the courage to tell my story for me.

Elaena

Chapter One

407 AD

It was a cold, crisp winter's morning; the frost lay heavy on the ground giving everything an eerie blue white glow. The mountains loomed dark and foreboding over the town. The bay, equally dark and foreboding, stretched out to the horizon with gentle waves lapping on the shore. The boats gently bobbed as the sea ebbed and flowed, the only sound was the creaking of the masts on the bigger boats and the sloshing of the waves. Nothing moved, it was the hour before dawn and the town life had not yet begun. There was an air of peace, tranquillity and calmness.

On the hill above the town a lone figure, seated on a sleek black horse stared down on the sleepy town. Wrapped in a heavy dark cloak that completely covered his body, the cowl pulled up over his head covering his eyes, all that was visible were his nose, mouth and chin. The early morning breeze caught the hem of his cloak making it gently flap against his ankles. The horse, reined in, stood patiently awaiting his master's command. The figure made no attempt to move but just sat silently surveying, observing, lost in his own world, his own deep inner calmness matching that of the sleepy town below. As dawn lightened the sky the horse sniffed, shifted gently and shook his head bringing his master's attention back, pulling him out of his pensive state. Gently the figure shook his head and, widening his eyes a little, he surveyed the landscape.

The Oppidum nestled around Conwy Bay, skirted by the rivers Conwy and Gyffin. It was surrounded by grey stone walls with a barbican enclosure and main entrance gate which had twin guard towers, iron gates allowed the town to be shut off in times of siege. To the left of the entrance were the oak grove, forest, brook and a path leading down to the banks of the River Conwy. Along the river bank were the quay, dock and stone buildings used by the fishermen and traders as storage there was also a large level area which was used for parking carts, loading and unloading merchandise and provisions, stacking firewood and tethering animals. The River ran the length of the eastern wall at the end of which was a strong stone bridge which gave the merchants access to the river and the forge access to the town. On the banks of the River Gyffin stood the forge and mill and along the south wall were extensive farming lands, a small Roman garrison took up the western corner. A defensive ditch ran around three sides of the outside of the town, the River Conwy running along the fourth.

Inside the walls to the left of the entrance gate stood stone buildings which served as the granary and store rooms just beyond them, in the east corner of the town, was the wing gate and tower. Along the riverside wall stood the tradesmens' stalls, lower gate, taberna, the merchants' stone booths, craftsmen's workshops, market and postern gate and bridge. Rising above them, in the south corner, stood the hill fort surrounded by its own stone walls, to the left of the fort, along the west wall, were timber dwellings, the millgate and tower. To the left of this, taking up the corner opposite the fort, were dwellings, the upper gate, bridge and tower. Along the north wall, leading back to the Main Entrance, were timber dwellings with thatched roofs. Opposite the granary were stone buildings with terracotta roofs. The large section in the centre of the town was taken up by the Roman temple, bathhouse and administrative buildings, in the street behind it, was the town square. The south corner was taken up with the fort, timber and stone dwellings. In the west section of the town were timber dwellings with thatched roofs. The eastern section of the town was the main trading area with a very wide street and opposite the stalls and market stood substantial stone buildings with terracotta roofs.

The roads were paved with drains along the kerbs leading down to the old Roman sewerage system beneath the town. There were three main streets leading up to the hill fort with three smaller streets crossing them. The town had once been a major Roman fort and trading centre and the current inhabitants, while utilising the old Roman buildings, also maintained their own Celtic ones, The current fort now stands on what was once the old Roman fort and still uses the buildings left behind by the Romans.

At this time of morning all was quiet, the quietness seemed to draw in on him, a far cry from the hustle and bustle of the city life that he was used to. The sights, sounds and smells of Londinium were still fresh in his memory. The room he had occupied and worked from with its books and fighting equipment. He had spent the last few months on Ynys Mon and in his homeland of Snowdonia where he had rested before embarking on this leg of his journey. He had spent most of the night travelling to this nearby Oppidum of Conwy where he was about to begin a whole new way of life. As he observed the town below a wave of tiredness and loneliness descended upon him, his eyes burned with the cold and lack of sleep. As he took a deep breath he felt his journey was over, he felt that this was where he would end his days.

As the sky brightened and the sun peeped over the horizon the first stirrings of movement could be heard. The shuffling of feet the sound of a fire being stoked, water being poured into a pot standing on its hook over the fire. The boats being loosened from their moorings the bakery ovens being put into action, the smithy fires being stoked and the shops being made ready for the day ahead. Slowly life returned to the town as more and more people awoke and began their day. Somewhere a cock crowed heralding the beginning of a new day, it was early January.

The figure gently touched the horse's side with his heels, pulled on the reins and with a gentle whisper, commanded the horse to move. As they walked slowly down the hill the day brightened even more and the sun peeped over the horizon. Travelling along the road he noticed there was a deep grove in the middle suggesting two way traffic, the surface was of hard packed earth with loose shingle on its surface which was heavily dusted with hard frost, high rough grass grew on either side. The air was crisp and cold his breath formed white clouds in front of him. By the time he reached the town the rising sun made the frost glisten, the frost crystals dazzled his eyes. He stopped at the barbican and greeted the guard on duty after speaking with him for a few minutes he was allowed to enter the town. Remaining on horseback he walked slowly through the cobbled streets noticing a raised pathway on each side of hard packed grey stone, smooth and even which made walking safe, bordered by kerbs of grey stone blocks. He took a deep breath and tuned his senses to the town around him bidding the people a good day, bowing in respect and greeting them with the local words "bore da", good morning. The men and boys were dressed in bracae trousers some plain with plaid hip length long sleeved tunics, some plaid with plain tunics. The women and girls wore ankle length tunics similar to the men's, all wore soft leather boots and heavy woollen cloaks, torques bracelets and other jewellery. The people stopped what they were doing and stared at the stranger. They noticed his regal bearing and his voice which was soft and gentle but with a hint of power and strength and the sleek black coat of the horse on which he rode. They wondered who he was and what his business was in their town. Passing the granary he turned right on to the traders' street, a wide street where the business of the day was beginning to be conducted. The traders were stocking their stalls and displaying their goods; the taberna was closed and quiet, the merchants were opening their booths and greeting each other. In the market the farmers were placing their foodstuffs in an appealing fashion so as to attract maximum purchase. Chickens waddled down the street, clucking as they went, their owners following behind them directing them to their designated spots. Women walked along the street checking out who had the best produce at the best prices, while children and dogs ran under everybody's feet getting in everybody's way. Cats sat on walls, some silently observing others grooming themselves. Carts trundled along the cobbled street doing their best to avoid everyone especially the children. The town grew nosier by the minute with everyone greeting each other and the hackers calling out their prices. He adjusted his senses to accommodate the noise around him.

Dwellings lined the other side of the streets some timber with thatched roofs, some stone with terracotta roofs.
The figure made his way past the postern gate and stone bridge, to the hill fort that loomed over the town it was surrounded by a grey stone wall with one single wooden gate which lead into a courtyard. The gate was open so he made his way through; on the other side he dismounted his horse and shook his cowl back. People were at work and a group of warriors lay resting. The great hall was directly in front of him, there were stables on one side and stone dwellings on the other. A large open fire sat in the middle of the courtyard and some women were busy attending to pots and cooking utensils. One of the warriors detached himself from his group and came over to him.
"Bore da, kind sir, how can we help you" he enquired.
"Bore da", replied the figure bowing. "I wish to speak with your leader I believe his name is Násuin"?
"That is correct sir, does he know you", asked the warrior.
"No, but I believe he awaits my arrival", replied the figure.
"In that case I shall take you to him, follow me", the warrior instructed.
The warrior led him into a grey stone outbuilding with a terracotta roof, just inside the gate on the right hand side. The figure noticed that everyone had stopped working and were staring at him; he nodded in their general direction.
"Please wait here, I shall inform our leader that you have arrived" said the warrior.
As the figure waited he observed that the outbuilding was small and round, a fireplace took up half of the far wall opposite the door and was lit with a small fire. Spoils of war hung on the walls alongside a large bronze Celtic cross, the floor was covered with hard packed earth. A wooden table and seats with cushions took up the area in the middle. Flaming torches hung on the walls which had no windows so they and the fire were the only source of light the room had.
As the door opened the figure observed a man approximately five foot ten inches tall with a very striking appearance. His long blond hair fell to his shoulders in cascading curls, his beard

was clipped and neat. His skin was deeply tanned and smooth he was good looking with finely chiselled features and he had ice blue eyes, his body was highly toned. His hands were strong and lean with short nails. He wore plain brown bracae trousers and yellow plaid tunic over which he wore leather armour. Around his waist he wore a thick leather belt which held a sword and dagger etched with Celtic designs. His feet were clad in leather boots with studded soles and around his shoulders hung a heavy woollen cloak. The figure got the impression that this was a man of about twenty-six years old, strong, brave, courageous and wise yet there also seemed to be a gentle air about him.

"Croeso a Conwy, welcome to Conwy, sir, I trust your journey was pleasant", he greeted the figure bowing. Walking across the room extending his right hand he said, "I am Násuin, Chief Warrior and Guardian".

The figure shook Násuin's hand and replied bowing "Bore da, may the peace of the Gods and the blessings of the Goddess Macha be bestowed upon this place and may your guardianship be guided by wisdom and justice".

Násuin observed a tall man, about forty-seven years old, broadly built, imposing and regal, thick dark greying hair falling to just below his shoulders. He was dressed in a dark, full length heavy woollen cloak, fastened at the front with a gold broach. Under this he wore a red tunic with leather belt holding a dagger and sword and green bracae trousers tucked into knee length leather boots soled and studded with nails. He looked as much Celtic as he did Roman; his overall appearance was of dark calm strength. His most striking features were the deeply tanned face etched with lines of wisdom and strength, clean shaven with strong piercing blue eyes that held and captivated. His hands were strong and tanned with long manicured tapered nails. Násuin got the impression that this was a man of authority well used to being in command, a man who was listened to and obeyed, a man who was well capable of ruling with an iron fist if necessary.

"Be seated", he said.

Giving the traveller time to settle himself, Násuin walked over to the fire and scooped out some hot liquid into two earthenware goblets. Walking back over to the table he placed one down in front of the seated figure.

"So sir, who are you and what brings you here?" he asked.

Taking a sip of the liquid and placing the goblet back on to the table the figure replied "I am Paedur Llewellyn of Snowdonia, a Druid of the Order of the Ancient Ones, although schooled on Ynys Mon; I have travelled the length and breadth of Britannia and have served for the last twenty years in Londinium"

Násuin nodded in respect noting the soft, gentle tone of Paedur's voice, like his clothes it was a mixture of Celtic and Roman. "Ah! Ynys Mon, Mona, yes, the home and administrative centre of the Druidic Order", Násuin said. "You are known to us, My Lord, we have been aware of your existence for some time. Mother Superior told us of your arrival and gave us to understand that your presence amongst us would be of great benefit".

Paedur nodded and continued. "Alas, the ways of our ancestors are no longer observed in the south and I have been asked by my Order to return to Cymru to help maintain the old ways. It appears that Scotia and Cymru are now the only parts of Britannia still observing the heritage, culture and language of our ancestors. It is believed that the barbarians have once again attacked and the young Emperor Honorius can no longer hold the empire intact. The Romans are restless and trying desperately to regain control. Therefore I have been appointed as Chief Druid of Cymru and have been instructed to strengthen her against the Romans".

Násuin bowed and replied, "My Lord, you are welcome among us and on behalf of Conwy and her people, I offer you the freedom of the town. Up until recently we have been governed by a Chieftain who unfortunately was slain in our last skirmish with the Barbarians. Since then I have been guardian but I am a warrior not an administrator, your administrative skills and your knowledge of the Romans will assist us greatly, whatever you require you shall have".

"Thank you", replied Paedur, "I need somewhere to live".
"That has already been arranged for you by a good friend of yours who resides with us", Násuin replied. "She has acquired a large room for you above the great hall and furnished it with all your needs. At the edge of the forest you will find a large round house, she awaits you there. In the meantime let me escort you to your room and get you settled in".
"Thank you", replied Paedur, "I would very much appreciate that".
Standing up Paedur followed Násuin out of the room into the courtyard it was more active now. The warriors were attending to their horses and the women were feeding the children sitting around the fire, all stopped what they were doing and stared at both men as they emerged from the room.
"Bore da", Násuin called, "this is Paedur Llewellyn, our new Chief Druid he will reside with us and be at our service".
The people nodded respectfully, some waved in his direction.
"He will be introduced to you formally later for now I am taking him to his dwelling and assisting him to settle in".
He gestured to one of the warriors to join them when he was in ear shot he said "Attend to Lord Llewellyn's horse and have his belongings brought to the room above the great hall".
The warrior nodded, bowed and did as he was commanded.
Násuin lead the way and together they walked across the courtyard,
"This is our administrative centre and focus of our town it is where myself, the warriors and those who attend to us live", he explained. "To our right is the barracks, one half is used to house the single warriors the other we use as a weapons store. In front of these are the stables, inside are stalls for the horses and an equipment area at the back, there is a grooming area in the middle. This one is my dwelling a stone structure painted white with pointed terracotta roof, a wooden entrance door with a small window on either side and a back door".
Turning and pointing across the courtyard, he said, "Over there is the well, and in front of it are the married warriors' dwellings and other storage buildings. In front of them is the bathhouse

and latrines, the fort is served by the old Roman sewerage system with drains that go into the rivers".

Turning to his left and pointing to a large stone building with white painted walls and a pointed terracotta roof, a stone chimney rose out of the left hand wall, "And this is our great hall", Násuin said as he opened the door and allowed Paedur to step through.

The structure was made of black and grey stone; a long room stretched down the length of the building, spoils of war hung on the walls, in the middle of the left hand wall was a large fireplace with grey slate hearth stones. Strong wooden pillars stood at intervals along the room holding an oaken ceiling in place, the cross beams clearly visible, at the left gable wall opposite the entrance stood a raised wooden dais. In the middle of the right hand wall, opposite the fireplace was a wooden door which lead into a corridor, tables and chairs stood randomly around the room drinking vessels lay on the floor, ash lay on the hearth and there was a smell of smoke, evidence of a recent gathering.

"Although it is empty now, we use it for strategy meetings for the warriors and festivities for the townspeople", Násuin explained. "We had a small meeting here last night; the women will tidy up later as the day progresses".

Turning to the right he said, "Your room is upstairs, follow me".

Just inside the door on the right hand side were a set of stone steps. Násuin walked up the steps and Paedur followed him, torches blazed from hanging braziers on the walls lighting their way. At the top was a long corridor with black and grey stone walls, a wooden floor and ceiling, at the end of this there was a heavy oak door with dark hinges. Násuin pushed the door and entered the room, holding the door open; he waited for Paedur to enter, closing the door softly behind him he waited allowing Paedur to get his bearings.

Looking around the room, Paedur noticed that the door opened into the middle of the room the wall opposite had a small fireplace and hearth and a fire blazed in the grate, the yellow, orange and red flames giving the room a warm welcoming glow.

In an alcove to the right was a low wooden platform with a long cushion covered in a blanket. Standing against the right gable wall stood a wooden chest, a pestle and mortar and a golden sickle lay neatly on top of it, to his right just inside the door was an empty space. In the alcove to the left of the fireplace stood an oak writing desk and a cushioned chair. In the middle of the left gable wall was a small window with oak shutters, in the corner stood an oak table and stools, running along the wall behind him was an oak press and dresser. In the centre of the room stood a large high backed chair with a cushion on the seat and another for the back, beside it stood a majestic gleaming, golden harp with serpent designs embossed around its edges. The floor was oaken and overhead strong oaken cross beams held an oaken ceiling in place.

"I trust everything is in order My Lord", said Násuin cutting into the silence.

Nodding, Paedur replied, "It is exactly as I requested".

"We have done our best to provide for all of your needs, however if anything is missing let us know and we will do everything to acquire it for you", Násuin said.

"Thank you", replied Paedur.

Opening the door Násuin said "I will leave you now to settle in, your friend awaits you".

"I will visit her presently", replied Paedur.

Násuin returned to the courtyard to join his men leaving Paedur to get acquainted with his new surroundings. A few minutes later there was a knock on Paedur's door. When he opened it, a woman handed him a basket of provisions and pitcher of water saying "With compliments from our leader, My Lord".

"Many thanks, My Lady", replied Paedur, "be sure to thank him for me."

He took the basket from her and placed it on the floor beside him. A few minutes later the warrior brought Paedur's belongings to the room.

Standing just inside the door, Paedur closed his eyes and took a deep breath, allowing himself to relax after his journey. Slowly he opened his eyes and looked around the room. The walls were constructed of black and grey stone and were unadorned; the hearth was made of black slate and in the fireplace was an iron grill, surrounding the fireplace on either side were strong oak beams supporting an oak mantle piece. The chairs were made of oak with emerald green leather cushions and oaken legs, the press, dresser and table were made of oak, the floor was made of oak wood boards.

Crossing over to the wooden chest he inspected the pestle and mortar, both were made of white ceramic, the golden sickle lay neatly beside them. Bending down he opened the door and discovered that it was empty inside. Turning to his left he looked at the bed which was a raised platform on four wooden legs with an empty space underneath, wooden slats formed the base of the bed and the long cushion was thick and firm. Covering it was a heavy brown woollen blanket.

Walking past the fire he went over to the solid oak writing desk, it was beautifully constructed; it was empty and waiting to be put into use, fat beeswax candles stood on ceramic patterned coasters lighting the desk and the corner of the room. Turning to his left he walked over to the window and opened the wooden shutters. His room looked over the great hall door, Násuin's dwelling and stables, the fort wall, the mill, mill gate and the town.

Raising his head he looked up at the sky, it was clear and bright blue. The air was crisp and cold and outside the walls the frost was beginning to melt on the grass. He breathed in a long and slow breath, held it for a moment and then let it out. Again he breathed in holding the cold air in his lungs for a few seconds and closed his eyes savouring its coolness then he slowly exhaled. Opening his eyes he turned to his left and observed the table, stools dresser and press and crossed over to them, opening the dresser he noticed that it was well stocked with plates, glasses, goblets, cups and cutlery, the press beside it was stocked with towels. Earlier the warrior had placed Paedur's travel bags on the floor in the centre of the room he contemplated unpacking but decided not to, it could be done later. He did however pick up the basket of provisions and placed it on the table. In it were some candles and lighting sticks, bread, fruit, a bottle of olive oil and a small amphora of wine. He contemplated emptying it but, like his travel bags, he decided that it could wait till later too for now he felt it was a better idea to go and have a look around the town and reacquaint himself with his friend at the edge of the forest.

Coming out of his room he walked down the corridor and descended the stairs back to the great hall. Several women had arrived and were in the process of returning the tables and chairs to the side walls clearing the ashes from the fire and hearth and resetting the fire, picking up the drinking vessels into a basket and sweeping the floor with brooms. At the door he greeted them but they were so intent on their work that they merely grunted a reply.

Walking out the door the first building he came to was the one that Násuin had pointed to as his own, it was a long stone structure painted white on the outside with a pointed terracotta roof, a hole allowed smoke to escape from the building. In the middle of the front wall was one heavy oak door which allowed access to the building, a small window on either side of the door allowed the occupant to look out into the courtyard, another door at the back provided a secondary exit.

Walking past this he came to the stables, a long stone building with pointed terracotta roof, wooden stalls housed each horse individually and a generous amount of hay lay on the floor, he checked in on his horse and noticed that he had been fed, washed, groomed and placed in a stall with fresh bedding. Going over to him he rubbed his nose, patted him and greeted him, and reassured that he was alright, he carried on with his tour of the fort.

The next building he came to was the barracks and weapons store. He noticed swords of various sizes, shapes and styles, javelins, sling shots, bows and even a pitch fork and a few sticks, a ballista stood in the far corner. Carrying on he then came to the outbuilding where he had first met Násuin and stopped, looking back in to the fort he noticed the ground was hard packed earth,

the open fire in the centre was lit and several cauldrons were hanging on wire tripods liquid bubbling in all of them. The women were busy clearing up after breakfast, washing some items of small clothing and the children were running around the courtyard their whoops, cheers and laughter filled the air.
Looking across to the other side he observed the buildings Násuin had said were the warriors' dwellings and noticed that they were all constructed of stone with pointed terracotta roofs with a hole in the middle; each had a wooden door front and back.

Turning to his left he walked out the gate and made his way through the town. Just below the fort was the traders' street with stone stalls, booths, carts and the market. In the centre of the town stood a Roman temple, small by normal Roman standards, strong stone columns held the pointed terracotta roof in place and the walls were painted white with statues standing at intervals along them. The bathhouse stood behind it to the right and was similar in appearance to the temple. In a street behind it was a square, a few small streets crossed each other and were filled with a mixture of stone houses with pointed terracotta roofs and timber dwelling houses with thatched roofs. Along the way he noticed that the townspeople observed from a distance some nodded, some waved everyone knew that sooner or later he would be introduced to them. For now they were content that Násuin had allowed him into their town so he was obviously of no threat to them.

He walked past the gate and out into the forest, the rough track was covered with stones which crunched under the soles of his boots as he walked. All around him he heard the twittering of the birds in conversation with each other in the trees, the rustle of the wind in their leaves and he noticed the long grass on either side of the track.

As Násuin had said, there was a large round house just at the edge of the forest, built of grey stone with a pointed thatched roof. It was a strong structure, one single door was placed in the middle of the front wall; a plume of smoke reached to the sky from a small opening in the roof, on either side of it was a track that led down to the forest and to the left of it was the oak grove. In a gap in the trees behind the house he caught a glimpse of the river. Walking over to the door he knocked on it and while he was waiting he noticed the long spike grass and hip high fronds at the edge of the track and the trees towering overhead. He heard the distant sound of the river and the gentle sound of the stream in the ditch. A few minutes later the door was opened by a tall, elegant lady of thirty-five years, slim build with long dark hair. She wore a long robe of dark blue velvet, soft leather sandals covered her feet and her hands were long and slim with manicured nails, her skin was soft, smooth and tanned. She had an oval face with deep dark blue eyes and there was an air of serenity about her.

Paedur bowed saying "My Lady Niwelyn it is good to see you again, I see that you are well and in good health".

"My Lord Paedur, she replied, I have been expecting you, you have arrived safely and you appear to be well".

"And all the better for seeing you", Paedur replied.

Shaking her head she replied, "Your talk is sweet, as always, come in".

Stepping back into the house she waited for him to enter. As he did so he noticed that it had only one room with a hard packed earth floor, in the centre of the floor was a hearth with a small fire burning. Opposite him was a stone wall with a wooden door in the middle to the right of the door stood a large wooden dresser, a wooden press stood on the left side. In the corner, along the left hand wall, was a wooden table with a pestle and mortar, amphorae, jugs and bowls sitting on top of it. An oaken sleeping platform with a long firm cushion covered with a blue coloured blanket took up the rest of the left wall, opposite it along the right hand wall was a long bench with cushions and in the back corner, lying against the wall, were musical instruments. On the walls were bronze plaques, one with a Celtic cross, another with the three legged triskele and another of a serpent. Strings of herbs hung from the rafters drying in the warmth of the room.

Slowly he walked over to the bench and sat down. Allowing him a few minutes to settle himself Niwelyn took two patterned glasses out of the press and filled them with red wine from an earthenware jug standing on the dresser. Slowly she walked over to Paedur and handed him one of the glasses.
"Croeso a Conwy", she said quietly, "it is good to have you with us, I have awaited your arrival, I have missed you".
Nodding and looking up at her he replied, "Aye, I have missed you too My Lady, we have been apart too long, no matter, we are here now, together, at last".
Taking her hand he sat her down beside him and embraced her in a long lingering hug. After a few minutes he pulled away saying "So, tell me, what news?"
"Conwy", she replied "is close to the Cymru Britannia border and is therefore of strategic importance, it is close to the Roman town of Deva and, as it is a seaside town, is important for the transport of goods and provisions; thankfully this means that we are well stocked with an abundance of food and textiles. As you know it is also close to Ynys Mon, Mona as it is called around here, whose major port gives us access to the nearby isle of Hibernia, although we are a well defended town with a strong military presence, we are unfortunately prone to attack. While we still hold close to the Celtic ways we have also adopted some Roman ways and are as Roman as we are Celtic".
Paedur nodded saying "So I should fit in well then".
"Aye, My Lord, it is the perfect place for you", she replied. "I take it Mother has explained your duties to you. We are very much in need of a wise counsellor, administrator and teacher. The warriors require a skilled swordsman with knowledge of Roman battle tactics who can instruct them and help them to play the Romans at their own game. But that is for later, for now it is enough for you to become familiar with Conwy, her people and countryside".
"I will do my best to be of service to you all", Paedur replied,
"I trust your accommodation meets with your approval and that you have everything you need", she said.

"Aye, My Lady, you have provided me with everything I requested and the room seems adequate", he replied.
"Will you stay for lunch?" she asked.
"I would like that, thank you", he replied.
Nodding and standing up she went over to the press and took out two samian ware bowls and deep basined spoons. Walking over to the fire she scooped out a portion of nettle stew into each bowl, handing one to him and keeping the other for herself she returned to the bench and handed him one of the spoons. They ate in silence, comfortable in each other's company. When they were finished they washed the meal down with the remaining wine in their glasses.
After their meal they went for a walk in the forest behind her house. Coming out of the door they turned right along the track, the rough stones crunching under their feet as they walked. As they entered the sounds changed and became muffled, the forest was dark, cool and still. Slowly their ears tuned to the frequency of the forest and they began to hear the rustle of the wind in the upper leaves of the trees as they discussed the day's business, a small fury animal scurried in the undergrowth on its way to find a meal. It squeaked when it realised that it was not alone but food was more important than fright so it carried on its journey.
They noticed strands of grass growing up through the track giving the appearance that a wheeled vehicle had used it several times. Fronds, nettles and long grasses lined the track; a bird flew past their ears almost crashing into them on its way to find some grubs, the trees stood straight and tall the shadows of their leaves giving the ground underneath a dappled look.
They came to the river and stood on its banks listening to the gentle lapping of the water on the shore, the ripples of the water making their way down stream. They listened to the twittering of the birds overhead in the trees. On the far bank they noticed the high trees the rolling hills and green fields. The Beech, Oak and Holly trees stood proud and tall at the water's edge, the reeds rose proudly out of the water lining the river bank. They could hear the distant clinking sound of the boats at the

nearby quay, the boatmen going about their business and the distant sound of the cattle in the meadows. One dead trunk of a fallen tree leaned down into the river another hung in mid air just above the water. On the far bank a group of swans glided majestically oblivious to the bustling activities in the town.
Paedur spoke "I think I would like to meditate here a while if you do not mind".
"That gives me time to collect some herbs", she replied.
They kissed and she walked away back into the forest, as she went she collected nettles, holly, twigs and bark from the trees. Carefully she chose each one making sure that they were strong, healthy and vibrant before picking them.
Back at the river bank Paedur stood at the water's edge and turned his face to the sun, although it was a cold winter's day the sun was now warm in a clear blue sky and its warmth felt good on his skin. Slowly and deeply he breathed in the air holding it in his lungs for a few seconds then exhaling slowly, several times he repeated this then, standing with feet hip width apart he repeated the breathing several more times then, raising his arms parallel to each other above his head pointing them at the sky, he took several more breaths, a calm feeling of serenity descended upon him and he totally relaxed.
Bringing his arms down to his sides and placing his hands against the sides of his thighs he took several more deep breaths. Bowing to the sun, then the river and finally to the trees he prayed "Goddess Druantia, may your strength always be with me, may your wisdom always guide me and may your peace always comfort me".
Taking one last deep breath he turned back to the forest path looking for Niwelyn and found her beside a holly tree removing some branches. When she was aware of his presence she said "Ah! You are finished, let us return, the day is beginning to cool and evening will draw in soon".
They returned to her house and she deposited the herbs on her table at the end of the house, then she took the wine jug back to the fire and replenished their glasses. They sat by the fire chatting then Paedur let out a big yawn, "Thank you, Elyn for

your company, hospitality and a wonderful day, it has been a long one for me and I am really tired and in need of rest".
"Then go and rest, Paedur, we can talk again soon", she advised.
As he stood up to go she looked into his eyes and said, "I am glad you are here, things will be better now".
Nodding and looking back into hers he said tiredly, "I hope so, Niwelyn, I am tired of fighting and fooling around it will be nice to rest and write...and be with you".
Taking a deep breath he bent down and kissed her gently on the mouth then turned and let himself out. He returned to his room and, still in his travel clothes, wrapping himself in his cloak, he lay on his bed and fell into a deep sleep.

Chapter Two

The following day Paedur awoke refreshed and lay on his bed, he was slightly disorientated not recognising where he was. Slowly he pieced together the events of the previous day and realised that he was in his room in his new abode. He got up and walked over to the fire, stoked it and placed some wood on the embers. While he was waiting for the fire to reignite he went over to his travel bags and began placing his things in his room, while he was doing so Násuin came to see him.

"Good morning, Paedur, how do we find you today?" he greeted him.

"Well and rested thank you", replied Paedur putting his clothes into the press.

"The women brought you provisions and you have everything you need?"

"Yes, thank you", replied Paedur, crossing the room he placed his scrolls and writing equipment on the desk, they told me they were compliments of yourself".

"Indeed, and so it shall be for your time here with us, it will be our way of thanking you for your services", replied Násuin.

"I have more than I require. It is my intention to share with those more needy if that is permitted", continued Paedur tidying the table.

"A noble gesture and one that will be welcomed I am sure", replied Násuin nodding. The people are curious about you they want to know who you are and why you are here. I wonder would you agree to stage a mock battle with me...purely for entertainment...a way of introducing you and letting the people get the measure of you?"

Paedur stopped what he was doing and waited a moment thinking before replying then nodded "Yes, I can see how that would be beneficial, he hesitated a moment longer, yes indeed, set that up for us".

"Forgive me, I have interrupted you in your preparations for the day" Násuin said, "I shall take leave of you now and arrange that immediately".

As he opened the door he stopped and looked back at Paedur "Everything is to your liking, and you have met with Lady Niwelyn?" he asked

"Yes, all is well Násuin, thank you", replied Paedur.

Násuin nodded "That is good, she was eager to see you".

"Aye" said Paedur nodding.

Thinking Paedur was going to say something more Násuin waited a moment but he didn't so Násuin nodded, turned and left the room. Paedur crossed the room took his footwear from the travel bag and placed them neatly under his bed.

Crossing the room he went over to the shutters and opened them. The sky was a clear blue with only small white fluffy clouds, the air was crisp, frost covered the grass below. Taking a deep breath he held it for a moment then quickly let it out, his breath formed a white cloud in front of him. Several times he breathed in long slow deep breaths holding them for a few seconds then letting them out slowly. Quickly he took another breath and continued this for a few minutes. Looking to his right he noticed the fire had become a bright warm blaze so he turned to his left, went over to the dresser took out a large clear glass bowl and brought it over to the fire. A cauldron hung on a hook just above the flames with water in it. By now the water was warm so he scooped some into the bowl and carried it carefully over to the table placing it down gently. He went back over to the press and took out a large white towel and placed it on the table. Crossing the room to the chest he selected some items of clothing and a pair of soft dark brown leather boots from under the bed and brought them over to the table. Removing his travel clothes he began to wash; the water was warm and refreshing and when he was finished he towelled himself dry and put on a pair of dark cotton underpants and an ankle length emerald green heavy velvet gown and the boots.

Scooping his dirty clothes up and draping them over his left arm he then picked up the bowl of water and carried it over to the press, he placed it down and opened the door. Picking the bowl up he left the room closing the door behind him with his right foot. He carried it down to the door of the great hall which was open and walked over to the drain. Behind the hall he poured the contents of the bowel into it and walked over to the fire. A woman was tending to a pot and looked up as he approached.

"Bore da", he greeted her.

"Bore da", she replied.

"I have some things here which need to be cleaned", he said holding the clothes and bowl out to her.

Taking them from him she replied, "They will be cleaned and returned to your room presently, My Lord".

"Thank you", he replied bowing.

"From now on you may wash in the bathhouse over there", she pointed. "It is the private bathhouse of the fort and those of us who live in it. You can leave your dirty clothes there and they will be washed and returned to your room".

"Thank you, I shall do that in future".

"Have you eaten?" she asked.

"No, Madam, I have not".

"Sit then, I shall serve you", she said.

He nodded and sat on one of the log stumps around the fire, a few minutes later she brought him a chunk of bread and a cup of boiled water which had now cooled to a comfortable drinkable temperature.

Taking them from her he said "You are most kind, thank you".

"Welcome, My Lord", she replied and turned back to the fire to resume her work, he ate in silence by the time he was finished she had gone.

Later that afternoon Paedur visited Niwelyn, arriving at her roundhouse he found the door closed and a thin plume of smoke emanating from the hole in the roof, gently he knocked and waited.

Opening the door she greeted him "My Lord Paedur, how are you this fine day?"

"Well, My Lady. May I have a few minutes of your time", Paedur asked.
"Of course, my door is always open to you", she replied, "Come in".
Stepping into her house he noticed a cauldron hanging on a low tripod over the fire, liquid gently bubbled in it and a distinct aroma of mint permeated the room.
"Medicines", she said.
Paedur nodded.
"You have eaten?" she asked.
"I have", he replied.
"Wine then", she offered.
"That would be acceptable" he replied.
"Be seated, make yourself comfortable" she said as she made her way over to the dresser. "You seem more rested today I take it you slept well?"
"Aye, that I did", he replied.
"So what can I do for you now?" she asked.
"Your company please" he replied.
"You already have that".
"Sit with me then" he said.
Sitting opposite him she waited, giving him time to gather his thoughts.
"Násuin came to see me this morning" Paedur began, "he wants us to stage a mock battle, his way of introducing me to the people".
Nodding she replied "You are both well matched, it is a good idea".
"I expect it will be soon", he seems eager for me to integrate".
"Aye, that he would", she replied "they are curious, about you their main concern is, are you a threat, the battle will answer that question for them".
"You will be present?" he asked.
"Of course", she replied, "Mother has given me to you as your ceremonial consort; I will be by your side, always".
"That is comforting", he replied, "you were my consort in Londinium, it's nice to know that you are so again now".

"Ah! Londinium", she replied, nodding, such memories. Remember that time in the market when we were dressed in our long hooded cloaks and we stole some apples, they could never prove it was us so we were exonerated".

Paedur nodded "And that time in the park when we lit a small fire for our ceremony which we were forbidden to hold and it grew bigger than we had intended and one of the bushes caught fire. We had to hastily put it out and cover up the damage as best we could".

"Indeed I do", she laughed. "And that other time when you were caught in your room with one of the students who, in anger, slammed her goblet against the stained glass window and broke it showering the people below with coloured glass".

Paedur let out a low growl "Indeed, because of her I was almost relieved of my duties and, when Mother heard about it after wards, she almost excommunicated me".

"Your own fault, we warned you not to tarry with her but you would not listen because you knew better, you said no one would know".

"I hadn't counted on her being quite so....spirited", he replied.

"Well she was", she replied, "and we all learned from your experience, no one made that mistake again after that".

"Good times, good times", replied Paedur as he sipped some wine. "We are here now together and no doubt we have much to experience and many new things to learn".

"No doubt", she replied, "and ceremonies to conduct, speaking of which I have appointed a young maiden called Kerri to assist you in the upcoming celebrations, I trust you will find her suitable".

"As always, you anticipate my needs before I have time to request them", he replied.

"That is my job", she replied.

There was a gentle knock on the door Niwelyn stood up, walked over to it and opened it "My lady", said a young warrior, "Násuin requests the company of our new guest, in the courtyard outside the great hall, now if possible"

Niwelyn looked back at Paedur, standing he nodded "I will join him immediately", he said. Looking at Niwelyn he asked "You will accompany me?"
"As you wish", she replied.
The warrior nodded and headed back to his post, Paedur and Niwelyn made their way to the courtyard.
Arriving at the courtyard they found Násuin surrounded by his warriors all were dressed in long sleeved thigh length cotton vests, plain brown bracae trousers and studded boots. He seemed to be instructing them and they were listening to him intently nodding as he spoke. Seeing them entering, he finished what he was saying, dismissed the warriors to their various posts and gestured for Paedur and Niwelyn to join him at the fire.
"Bore da to you both", he said, "sit with me a while we have much to discuss".
All three sat on seats made from oak tree stumps which were placed around the fire.
"Lady Niwelyn, it is nice to see you", greeted Násuin.
Paedur answered "Niwelyn has been my consort for many years. We served together in Londinium, we have been apart for many months I am very grateful of her presence here with me now".
"Paedur asked me to accompany him today but if you wish to speak with him alone I can go and attend to other duties", Niwelyn replied.
"No, no My Lady your wisdom is always of benefit to us, you are welcome to stay", replied Násuin.
Turning to Paedur he continued "I have been speaking with my men and they are agreeable to our mock battle. Tomorrow afternoon has been suggested, if that is suitable for you?"
Paedur nodded and replied "That is fine by me". Where shall we be staging such battle?" he asked.
"Here in the courtyard, I suggest late afternoon just before our meal and afterwards we can celebrate your arrival", replied Násuin.
"Be it done as you say", replied Paedur.

Turning to Niwelyn Násuin asked "My Lady you will be present?"
"Off course", she replied, the battle has to be blessed and the rules have to be set".
Relaxing a little Násuin asked "So you have both been friends for some time it seems, Londinium I take it?"
Paedur replied, "Yes, at first Niwelyn was my student, and a very good one she was too, when she qualified she became my ceremonial consort and later my... friend".
"Are you hand fasted with each other?", Násuin asked looking from one to the other.
"No", replied Niwelyn, although sometimes it would seem that we are".
Paedur nodded "Indeed, she is my rock, my strength and the voice of my conscience, without her I would sometimes forget myself".
"Mother was very keen to have you both here with us at this time", replied Násuin, "perhaps she knows something?"
"Troubled times lie ahead, it would seem", replied Paedur, perhaps she feels that together we can all offer Cymru some strength, she certainly speaks very highly of you".
"I am in her debt then", replied Násuin bowing, "she speaks equally highly of you both. The people are weary of strangers and even more so of the Romans", he said turning to Paedur. "Your presence among us, and your appearance, has caused them concern, our battle tomorrow is aimed at showing them who you are and reassuring them that you are here to help and support them", he explained.
"I will do my best to put my skills at their disposal and allay their fears", Paedur replied nodding.
Standing up Násuin said "Then we shall meet here tomorrow, for now, good day to you both".
Walking away he left Paedur and Niwelyn sitting by the fire where they remained for a short while before separating and returning to their dwellings.
Paedur spent that night in his room quietly writing at his desk. Before he left Londinium he had begun translating some Latin

texts into Cymraeg so that the people would have access to the knowledge of the Romans. He had also started working on a history of the Romans and Britannia; he continued this work now in the quiet hours of night.

The next day Paedur gathered some fresh clothes and went to the Fort Bathhouse, positioned on the left side of the entrance; it was opposite the outbuilding where he had first met Násuin. It was a simple long stone building with a pointed terracotta roof. Three round stone pillars stood at its entrance and behind them were strong oak, double doors which was the main entrance to the building. The foyer ran the full length of the building with a white tiled floor and walls, six round tiled pillars held the cement painted roof up and statutes stood in alcoves along the walls. It was a small version of a Roman bathhouse and was a place for cleansing not socialising.

To the right of the foyer was an archway leading into the apodyterium and tepidarium to the left were the latrines, one for the women and another for the men. Paedur went into the apodyterium, a simple long room with white tiled walls and floor and cement ceiling. Long wooden benches took up the centre of the room. Small numbered alcoves set into the walls provided a place to put clothes while bathing. There were several large wooden presses filled with towels. He placed his clean clothes in the alcove numbered thirteen and went over to the nearest press where he selected a large white body towel and a smaller one for his hair. Removing his clothes he wrapped himself in the towel and placed his clothes in the alcove along with his other ones.

Walking through an arch he came to the tepidarium which had a comfortably warm air about it. Tan coloured painted walls gave the room a warm feel; a green painted strip at eye level gave the walls an earthy feel. A white painted ceiling and tiled floor gave the room a clean healthy feel. He dropped the towel at the side of the pool and stepped in, the water was warm and soothing and he submerged himself totally. For several minutes he remained beneath the surface wallowing in the warmth of the water then coming back to the surface he swam several lengths

of the pool. After a few minutes he lay on the surface of the water floating, his eyes closed, his breathing calm and relaxed, he was alone and he surrendered to the feel of the water and the quietness of the room. After another few minutes he stood up and swam over to the side. He got out, towelled himself dry and returned to the apodyterium where he dressed in plain brown bracae, yellow plaid tunic and soft brown leather boots. He put on his heavy woollen cloak, left his dirty clothes in the numbered alcove and left the bathhouse.
As he stepped out of the bathhouse the cold morning air contrasted with the warmth of the bathhouse and he pulled his cowl up over his head, walking past the fire he felt its warmth and continued on to the great hall and his room.

Later that day word went round that there was to be a battle between Násuin and the new arrival, everyone was excited and curious and they all worked hard so that their tasks would be completed in time. As the sun began to drop towards the horizon the townspeople left their work and homes and made their way to the courtyard, there was an air of curious excitement about the town. The women had already begun to gather around the fire laden down with provisions for the evening meal. The children ran around the courtyard playing enjoying the freedom they had because the adults were busy. Food was being set out on large cooking plates ready to be placed on the fire. A hog rotated on a spit over a nearby fire being basted from time to time by a burly man bathed in sweat from being so close to the fire. The air was crisp and cold and everyone wore heavy cloaks and leather boots. The warriors were gathered together close to the stables making sure the horses were safely corralled and fed. A smaller group was tending to one particular shield and long sword, making sure that both were clean and gleaming. All wore tan coloured full length bracae trousers, cuffed at the ankles, and plain long sleeved tan coloured vests over which they wore thigh length plaid tunics of various colours, on their feet they were soft leather boots.

Presently Násuin emerged from his large dwelling between the stables and the great hall accompanied by the young warrior who had been sent to summon Paedur the previous day, both walked with a long confident stride towards the group of warriors. Today Násuin was dressed in plain black bracae trousers and an olive green sleeveless vest over which he wore leather armour. A brown leather belt strapped to his waist held a strong leather scabbard which was empty. On his head he wore a metal helmet with ear flaps and another which covered the back of his head down to the nape of his neck, strands of long blond hair rested on his shoulders. On his feet he wore tan coloured leather boots with studded soles. His strong, muscular arms were bare and his skin gleamed with oil, a tattoo of a swirling circular design was clearly visible on his right upper arm.
On arriving at his group of warriors his sword was handed to him, he took it and gripped it securely in the palm of his right hand. The handle was made of bronze and grooved for better grip, extending from the handle was a long blade, double edged and gleaming. He made circular movements with it in the air and as he did so the sun caught the shining metal and the sword seemed to glow. He was then handed his shield which was a circular piece of flat wood covered in thick black leather. There was a circular swirling pattern etched in gold on it, the same one that was tattooed onto his arm. The young warrior made one final check to make sure that everything was in place and securely fastened and then stepped back to the other warriors. Násuin, now ready for battle, turned to face the crowd and, as he did so, they chanted Ná-suin, Ná-suin and clapped.
Just as the applause was dying down Paedur emerged from the door of the great hall dressed in a knee length red cotton tunic over which he wore a thigh length chain mail shirt with shoulder flaps. Strapped to his waist was a brown leather belt from which hung a leather scabbard, the top and bottom were decorated with a strip of patterned metal. A small chain hung from the top and was attached to a metal strip half way down its length. On the left side of the belt hung a dagger, and in the middle a groin guard made of leather and metal hung down to

mid thigh. On his head he wore a metal helmet with side flaps that covered his ears and cheeks, a metal strip attached to the forehead of the helmet protected his nose. His arms and legs were bare and he wore strapped leather sandals with studded soles on his feet.

In his right hand he carried a Gladius, the sword favoured by the Romans, which had a short double edged blade ending in a wooden guard. Coming out of this was a handle made of dark wood with thin bands of metal wrapped around it at six inch intervals; the handle ended with a dark wooden pommel studded with metal. In his left hand he carried a large round wooden shield with a serpent design etched on it. Niwelyn walked beside him dressed in a full length blue velvet gown cuffed and hemmed with a gold pattern. Around her waist she wore a black leather belt from which hung a dagger. She carried a leather broad bottomed case in her right hand. On her feet she wore soft leather boots. Both strode towards the centre of the courtyard. Násuin joined them.

Both men greeted each other with a deep bow, Niwelyn, placing herself between them said in a clear and loud voice, "May Camalus give you strength and may Macha protect you".

Stretching her arms, touching each man on the chest, she said, "Fight with strength, honour and dignity, the first to draw blood ends the fight".

Breaking contact with them she returned her arms to her sides and stepped back placing herself within the ring of people who had gathered around them. An air of hushed expectation descended on the courtyard.

Both men stood for a moment sizing each other up. Both tuned their senses to each other and mentally blocked out the crowd around them. Both assumed a classic battle stance and raised their swords in front of them. Násuin took a step forward and moved towards Paedur, Paedur took up the challenge and stepped towards Násuin. Their sword blades clashed and a metallic sound echoed around the courtyard. Both men circled each other, their foot work defined and sure. As one advanced the other retreated, both lunged, thrusted and parried. Both used cross over steps to keep their balance and watched each other with concentrated focus.

They continued to circle each other, lunging and blocking in turn testing each other's sword skills and footwork. As they circled each other their faces became even more determined as they really began to get the measure of each other's skill. As the duel continued both men began to tire of carrying their shields, the weight of them was restricting their ability to fight. As if it had been planned in advance, the two men dropped their shields to the ground, freed from their weight; both men were now able to press their attacks again, this time with much greater freedom of movement. Their swords crossed many more times and both held their stance, neither one giving any quarter, staring into each other's eyes each willing the other to back down. Neither did. They both moved with grace and strength circling each other with a natural synchronicity. The crowd of soldiers, warriors and townspeople watched in awe of the two men.

Everyone was so captivated by the battle that no one noticed the sun had sunk below the horizon and it had grown dark. Fires were hastily lit around the courtyard so that the duel could continue. The shadows cast by the firelight gave the two men an almost sinister appearance. As they continued to fight with increasingly determined looks on their faces; there was an air of determined competition between them.

For a few more minutes their battle continued, neither besting the other. Paedur lunged forward doing a full three hundred and sixty degree turn, the blade of his Gladius whistled through the air as he spun. Násuin was caught off guard and attempted to block but Paedur was too swift and caught Násuin's upper left arm, with a glancing slice, the blade opened a small gash on his skin. Násuin winched in pain and lost his grip of his sword which fell with a thud to the hard packed earth of the courtyard. He raised his hand to the gash and as he drew back his fingers there was blood on them. The crowd gasped in awe, no one had seen Násuin bested before; they waited in hushed silence to see what would happen next. Both Paedur and Násuin were breathing hard; a fine sheen of sweat covered their brows. As Násuin continued to inspect his wound a tense silence fell on the crowd. Paedur, breathing hard, stood in battle stance and waited.

Násuin, breathing hard, looked over at Paedur and said "It would seem...that you have....drawn blood...as this is not...a fight to the death...I wager that we let this...be the conclusion of our battle".

Paedur took a long, slow deep breath and relaxed his stance and replied "I totally agree".

Bowing deeply to Násuin he said "You fight well, warrior...it is clear that you are...well versed in battle tactics...and have no fear".

Still breathing hard and sweating with a fierce look in his eyes Násuin replied, "I fear no one, Druid...I would rather die...than give in".

Paedur nodded, his breathing much calmer now, and holding Násuin in a focused stare replied "Your people are safe with you at their helm".

Násuin relaxed his stance, his breathing returning to normal, and bowed deeply towards Paedur saying "You are a worthy opponent well versed in battle techniques some of which we do not know...perhaps you could instruct us and improve our skills".

"That I will", replied Paedur, "but I shall leave the fighting to you and your men while I return to my books, from this day forward my sword shall be my pen".

Both men stepped back and bowed. The crowd applauded them, some whooped and some cheered.

Niwelyn, having checked that all was well with Paedur, went over to Násuin. Allowing her to inspect his arm he said "It is but a scratch, I will live. No harm has been done".

Niwelyn replied, "At least allow me to clean and dress your wound so that no infection may set in".

Nodding he stood while she deftly cleaned his wound and covered it with a strip of clean cotton cloth. When she had finished he turned to the crowd and raising his hands in the air

he called "This is Paedur Llewellyn of Snowdonia, a Druid of the Order of the Ancient Ones and now one of us, give our guest the honour he deserves".
He turned to Paedur and led the applause and the crowd joined in.
Paedur first bowed to Násuin and then turned and bowed to the crowd.
"And now, we eat and celebrate" continued Násuin.
Everyone made their way to the great hall hungry and cold looking forward to the feast that they were about to partake in.
Niwelyn returned to Paedur's side and, looking into his eyes, said "You fought well My Lord I think perhaps you do have a place amongst us, you are well matched; perhaps with both of you at our helm we may beat the Romans yet".
"I pray that we do My Lady", he replied.
"Are you hurt?", she asked.
"Apart from a broken nail, no I am not", he replied.
"Then let us join in the festivities, the people are eager to meet you", she said.
Together they walked across the courtyard. Almost everyone was already in the hall. All that were left outside were the people gathering up the cooked food for the feast. Lifting the large trays, they walked ahead of Paedur and Niwelyn bringing the food to the tables. The air was warm inside the hall, a big fire blazed in the fireplace. Tables had been set up along the walls and were filled with food and pitchers of mead. It was noisy, everyone chatting at once. Whoops and cheers came from the top table where Násuin was surrounded by his men clapping him on the back and congratulating him on a fine battle. The ones closest to Paedur and Niwelyn bowed reverently making way for them to pass through the crowd. One woman handed them a plate of food and two goblets of wine and bid them sit at a table while they ate. After the meal some of the men began to sing and all joined in everyone relaxing after a hard day. Paedur and Niwelyn sang a duet and afterwards moved among the crowd meeting and greeting as they went.

Násuin detached himself from his men and went over to Paedur "You fought well today" he said. "May I have a look at your armour? I have not seen such items up close before", he continued.
"Certainly", replied Paedur and took his chainmail shirt off, "I was about to remove this anyway".
Removing his shirt he laid it on the table for Násuin to inspect.
"It is composed of 25,000 individual iron links with dagged edges, it is heavy but flexible and offers good protection from swinging swords", he explained.
Pointing to his chest he continued "Underneath it I wear a stiff leather jerkin which offers good protection from missiles and keeps my undergarments clean and rust free it also has fringes at the base and arm holes".
Fascinated Násuin ran his hands over the garment feeling the metal and inspecting the way the links were held together, "It is of such high quality", he said.
Lifting it up and holding it in the air he felt its weight and twisted and turned it observing its movement. "It is a very fine garment indeed", he said nodding, "a must for every serious soldier".
"Indeed it is" replied Paedur.
"Thank you for allowing me to inspect it", Násuin said and put it back on the table.
"Please do not let me detain you from the festivities any longer", he continued, "you fought well today you deserve to celebrate".
He bowed to Paedur and returned to his men. As the night progressed the crowd began to thin and everyone returned to their homes.

***

The next night while Násuin was inspecting the town's walls and checking their defences he noticed Paedur out walking alone, he watched him for a few minutes and noticed that he was acquainting himself with the town. Having assured himself

that the town was secure for the night and that all was well, he walked over to Paedur.
"Nos da, good evening, Paedur, you are well and none the worst of our battle"?
"Iawn Diolch, I am fine thanks", replied Paedur "and you, none the worst of your scratch?
"I will live", chuckled Násuin, "a minor thing and Niwelyn treated it well. You impressed the people they are no longer afraid of you, you will find that you may move among us quite freely".
"I am pleased to hear that", replied Paedur, "it is always worrying when a stranger comes to town, one does not know what their intentions are, I understand their concern, but they need not worry my placement here is to guide and, if necessary, to guard". "It has turned cold", continued Paedur, shivering, I am returning to my room for the evening. Would you like to accompany me"?
"That I would", replied Násuin, "thank you".
Together they walked through the town towards the great hall. "As you have already seen we are a thriving town, we are built on the remains of the old Roman fort of Kanovium", Násuin explained. "We have kept some of the buildings from that time but have replaced some of them with our own more Celtic ones. Living among us we have builders, plasterers, carpenters and roofers, we also have road builders, stonemasons and chariot makers. There are also vets, doctors, healers and therapists of various kinds, the more artistic among us turn their hands to painting, basket weaving, pottery and glass making and we even have candle and shoe makers. Then there are the bakers, cooks and cleaners, the taberna and restaurant staff. Highest among us are the Roman officials, clerks and civil servants along with the lawyers and judges, each live in dwellings according to their status which is why we have such a difference of styles. The officials live in the dwellings surrounding the Temple, the Roman soldiers live in the garrison just outside the town", he continued.

Paedur nodded from time to time committing this information to memory.

When they got to the great hall Paedur preceded Násuin up the steps to his room, on entering Násuin closed the door and immediately felt a sense of calm strength; the room was lit by candles and a roaring fire, shadows dancing on the walls. Paedur had taken off his cloak and was already pouring two goblets of wine, handing one to Násuin he said "Welcome to my humble home, thank you for allowing me to have use of it".

"It was Niwelyn's choice", replied Násuin, "she was rather persuasive and insistent that you should have this room.

"Aye", that she is", said Paedur, "but always with good intent, I have never seen her do any harm to anyone nor has she any ill intent towards anyone. She has a kind and gentle soul but is a strong and brave woman".

"I have not spoken with her often, she keeps very much to herself, but whenever I have she speaks very fondly of you", replied Násuin. "You say you are only friends but I suspect that friendship is very old and very deep".

"Aye", said Paedur, sipping some wine, "we perhaps should have hand fasted but never did, relationships are sometimes... complicated and life does not always allow us to do what we want".

Staring into the fire and after taking another sip of wine he continued "I once thought that we would hand fast but she was unable to bear children, even though she is a mid-wife herself, and so we settled for friendship and ceremonial consort and developed a much deeper relationship than we perhaps would have if we had hand fasted".

Putting down his goblet he went over to the desk and got his chair, bringing it over to the fire he said, "Sit with me", and placed it close to the fire, Násuin sat on it, Paedur settled himself into his own chair and went very quiet for a while staring into the fire, Násuin sipped some wine and allowed Paedur the time and space to be with his thoughts. Looking around the room he noticed how it had already become a home and relaxed into the chair.

After a while Paedur took a deep breath and let out a long sigh "Forgive me, I retreat into myself sometimes".
"We all do that", replied Násuin, "there is nothing to forgive.
"So, my friend, tell me about you" replied Paedur.
Taking a sip of wine Násuin said "I come from this town; Conwy is where I was born and have lived all my life. My mother died in childbirth having me, my father never hand fasted again. He was Chief Warrior before me and taught me everything he knew, since I was able to walk I was at his side learning from him and helping him. He was killed along with our Chieftain in the recent skirmish with the Hibernians and in spite of my youth the other warriors felt I was the best man to replace him, I have protected Conwy ever since and we have lived in relative peace.
"I am sorry to hear of your parents, do you miss them?" Paedur asked.
Taking a sip of wine Násuin replied "Aye I do, but life goes on and we do the best we can each day".
"They leave us physically", replied Paedur, "that is true, but they remain in our hearts forever. When we listen to our hearts we realise that we are not so far apart, the love they had for us still remains and thinking of them should bring us peace, joy and love. When we are lost and lonely thinking of our ancestors brings us comfort and we one day hope to be with them again".
Násuin nodded quietly, a deep sense of calm descended upon the room and for a few minutes the only sound was the crackling of the fire. Both men stared into the flames both lost in their own thoughts, after a few minutes Paedur spoke "The world should be a happy place and we should all feel that we can go about safe and be secure in our homes".
He raised his head and continued, "The Romans took our lifestyle away from us replacing it with new values, new ways and a new language. They take over every place they go to; they take our women and make our children slaves. They insist on us living our lives in ways that are alien to us and care not for our ways".

As he spoke his eyes took on the reflection of the fire and it gave him a fierce and disquieting appearance. "We must rise up against them, we must stand our ground and we must rid our land of all Romans. We must return to our old ways and bring back happiness to our people", he continued.

He took a deep breath and his passion transmitted itself to Násuin who began to feel a burning need to take up this cause and fight for his people.

"Do you think we are capable of that?" Násuin asked.

"It will not be easy", Paedur said, "but I do believe we can".

"I fear for our people, we lost a lot in the last skirmish, we cannot afford to lose anymore", Násuin said.

"It is not my intention to lose any", replied Paedur. "In fact I intend to make Conwy so strong that it will be impenetrable".

"We are a small band of men, the Romans are a mighty force, we are good in peacetimes but I am not sure how strong we would be in war", Násuin said.

"Do you doubt yourself?" asked Paedur.

"No I do not", replied Násuin.

"Then trust yourself and your men, you have trained them well and they will rise to the challenge when it comes", encouraged Paedur.

"Will you help me then to do just that?" Násuin asked softly. "Will you lead us and guide us?"

"Aye, I will but you will do the fighting I shall negotiate", replied Paedur.

Reaching across to Paedur Násuin touched his goblet to Paedur's and said "Together we shall conquer; we shall return our land to Cymraeg rule"

Both nodded.

"And now", he continued, standing up, "it is late I shall leave you to rest, thank you for your company and wine, I shall see you tomorrow".

"Nos da", replied Paedur.

As Násuin returned to his dwelling that night, the stars seemed brighter, the air seemed warmer and more fragrant, the town seemed more vibrant in spite of the quietness and he carried with him a deep sense of calm and strength. He felt he would remember this night forever.

The next day Násuin summoned both Paedur and Niwelyn to join him at the fire in the courtyard, Niwelyn arrived first, Násuin greeted her, "Bore da, My Lady, you are well"?

"I am Násuin", she replied. "And you, you are none the worst of your injury"?

"Hardly an injury My Lady, a mere scratch nothing more, you have expertly attended to it and I heal quickly", he replied.

"You summoned me", she said.

I did", he replied, "I was thinking it is a good time for us to discuss the welfare of the town".

Niwelyn nodded silently.

Just then Paedur arrived, "Forgive me, I am late", he said.

"No, Paedur, be at peace you are not late we have not started" Násuin replied.

Bowing to them both, Paedur sat down, Niwelyn and Násuin sat with him.

"So, Násuin, why are we here?" he asked.

"I feel it is time to review the town's situation", Násuin replied, "It is clear that we are the makings of a very good administrative team and I wanted to seek your co-operation in setting out a strategy for the welfare of the town in the coming years".

"What have you in mind?" Niwelyn asked.

"My Lady you are good with healing so I feel it would be best for you to take on the health of the townspeople", Násuin replied.

"I already do", she replied.

Násuin nodded, "I know that, but if there is another ambush there will be injuries and perhaps even death and it will be then that we will require your great knowledge and skills".

"They are at your disposal Násuin", she replied, "I will do whatever I can".

Nodding he then turned to Paedur saying "There is no question about your battle skills and after last night, there is no question as to your intentions, you have worked with the Romans you know their ways and their beliefs, you know how they think

and how they operate, would you be willing to share that knowledge with us and be our administrator?"
"I would." replied Paedur, "But I will not do it alone. If we combine our talents together we can, as you say, make a formidable team".
Násuin nodded "Then I suggest, Paedur, that you go about the town freely, get to know everyone, make them comfortable with you, make them feel you are one of them and have their best intentions at heart".
"As you command", Paedur replied bowing.
Násuin stood up saying, "I will inform my men of our decision, we will set out a plan and I will present it to you both presently". Bowing to them both he turned and strode across the courtyard back to the barracks. Paedur followed him with his eyes watching his every move.
Niwelyn, watching Paedur closely, asked "So what happened last night?"
Still watching Násuin he replied "Násuin and I shared a drink in my room".
"And", she pressed.
"And we talked", he replied.
"About what", she pressed further.
"Things", he replied.
Niwelyn closed her eyes and formed the next question. "What kind of things", she asked.
"Oh! Getting to know each other things", he shrugged.
Realising that she was not going to get much more out of him she stood up saying, "Well, I have things to do now, so I shall take leave of you".
She turned and strode out of the courtyard leaving Paedur sitting alone by the fire.

The next day Paedur went down to the courtyard and approached one of the women "Madam, do you think it would be acceptable if I took the children down to the square for a while, I would teach them how to make things, if that would be permitted", he said.

Surprised the woman nodded "I think that would be permitted indeed", she replied.

She turned toward the centre of the courtyard and clapped her hands, loudly she called "Children come to me please", immediately they gathered around her.

"This is Paedur, our new Chief Druid", she said pointing in his direction, "he is going to take you to the square and teach you, you are safe with him and you are to follow his instructions", she explained.

Turning to the children Paedur bowed and greeted them "Bore da".

A little shy they just nodded.

"Go now children", the woman urged shooing them.

Paedur gathered the children around him and together they left the courtyard turning left they walked past a collection of timber dwellings with thatched roofs, they continued on to the theatre and as they walked he explained "The Romans discovered a long time ago how to make mortar out of volcanic ash which allows them to build very strong structures like this. It is made of stone and is white washed and has terracotta slates on the roof, pillars and columns stand at intervals supporting the roof, it is circular in shape and is small by city standards".

The children looked at each thing as he pointed to them.

"Inside there is an auditorium where people can sit or stand and watch plays performed by actors and artists on a stage", he explained.

"Can we go in", asked one of the children shyly.

Paedur nodded and went over to the door pushing it he discovered that it was locked so he shook his head and replied, "Not today, perhaps another day".

The children made sounds of disappointment.

Continuing on they came to the town square, a large open space with stone benches in the centre. He walked over to the benches and sat down, the children gathered around him, some sitting on the other benches, others sitting on the ground. He began telling them stories of heroes, villains, dungeons, dragons and princesses; they hung on his every word and became wrapped up in the wonderful adventures. Then he introduced them to some words of Latin telling them that all educated people spoke this strange foreign language and that knowing how to speak it would help them in later life.

A few children yawned making him realise that they had probably heard enough for today and he walked them back home to the courtyard returning them to their mothers.

The next day he brought them down to the square and showed them how to make dolls out of wood, pretty ones for the girls, warriors and soldiers for the boys. In the days following he showed them how to build toy houses and kites, he showed them how to use whips, tops and hoops and showed them how to paint them to make them look more interesting.

Each day the children eagerly awaited his appearance in the town square and quite often he was seen to have quite a crowd sitting at this feet. The adults welcomed this because it gave them freedom to attend to their duties. In the Roman world he had recently come from he had been a Paedagogus, a teacher and child minder, it was a role he was comfortable with and fell back into here with ease. When the Romans enquired about him, all the townspeople would say was that he was a teacher. Eventually they discovered that he was a Druid but believed him to be of low office and therefore of no importance so they took no interest in him. The Roman priests however, while they did not agree with the Celt's beliefs, begrudgingly recognised him as an equal.

Chapter Three

The Romans celebrated the coming of spring with three festivals. The first was Parentalia where they placed flowers, milk and wine on their parents' graves so that the dead wouldn't be hungry, they believed this would prevent the living from being haunted. Then the youths gathered in the theatre and raced around the grounds dressed in goat skins, as they raced the people gathered around them whipping them with strips of goatskin, it was believed this would promote fertility and so any woman wanting children stood close to them. The festival ended with Caristia where families would gather together and enjoy a large dinner.

The Celts celebrated the coming of spring in their own way, at sunrise in the beginning of February they gathered in the fort around the well. Niwelyn, dressed in a full length midnight blue velvet gown, carried a blazing firebrand from the open fire to the well and threw it into it invoking the Goddess Brighid to bless their well and give it life and healing qualities. Then she presented Paedur, also dressed in a full length midnight blue gown, with a tiny bottle containing three drops of liquid asking the Goddess Cerridwen to bestow upon him the knowledge of the past, present and future. She also requested that the Goddess Mebh bestow upon the town the gifts of fertility and regeneration and asked Goddess Olwen to bestow love and rebirth upon the people. Going back to the fire she presented the Goddess Rosmerta with a cornucopia and a stick with a carving of two snakes entwined around it asking her to bestow fertility and wealth upon the town. To finish the ceremony she presented the river Goddess Sequana with a small amphora of water requesting that she bestow health upon the townspeople.

In March the Romans celebrated the progression of spring with a day of festivities. In Roma this ceremony took up the whole month of March however, here in Conwy, it was just one day. The day began in the Temple at the shrine of Vesta, officiated by the six Vestal Virgins who were selected from the leading

Roman families, with the rekindling of the perpetual fire. After the ceremony horse races were held outside the Temple in honour of their war God Mars. In the afternoon the people had picnics down by the river celebrating their Goddess Anna Perenna; it was believed that they would live as long as they could drink cups of wine. The day finished with a trumpet ceremony to Mars requesting him to grant them success in battle.

One bright warm day in the month of April Paedur, surrounded by children in the town square, became aware of another presence close by. He felt he was being watched. Out of the corner of his eye he noticed a cloaked figure standing on the edge of the group, almost imperceptibly, he bowed to the figure; he was in mid sentence and couldn't stop. Quickly he finished the story, dismissed the children and turned towards the figure, instantly it hurried away. He got the impression of a woman of slim build about five feet three inches tall with head bent and a purposeful stride.

Several days later, in the late afternoon, as he was showing the children how to make garlands for the forthcoming Celtic Bealteinne and Roman Ludi Florales festivities, he became aware of her again standing on the edge of the group silently watching him. He nodded in her direction and, when she realised he had become aware of her, she hurried away. He would never know why but something about her touched him that day and he wondered who she was.

For the Romans April marked the festivals of Ludi Megalenses, Ludi Ceriales and Parilia, again in Roma these were three separate occasions but here they were celebrated as one. The day began with games in honour of Cybele, the Great Mother and in the afternoon more games in honour of Ceres, the Goddess of corn. The farmers brought their sheep down to the river to be purified so that they would remain disease free. The day finished with a large feast and bonfire around which people danced, the priests actually danced in the fire.

In the first days of May the festivals of Bealteinne and Ludi Florales were celebrated, both occurred within days of each other and the town had come to combine the two into one big celebration. The air was sweet and fragrant with the new growth of late spring, young green leaves and bright flowers painted a vibrant picture of dazzling colour. The sun shone brightly, the breeze was gentle and warm and the grass was a lush green soft carpet, buttercups and daisies pin picked the grass with colour. All the women busied themselves preparing the May Tree and the tables for the open-air banquet that night. The children scampered about, there were no lessons today. The women cooked, baked and shooed the children away when they tried to steal some titbits of food. In the middle of the oak grove was a clearing, where old trees had been felled and the ground had been trampled for centuries by feet using the area for ceremonies. In the middle of this stood a stone altar with the triskele, concentric circles and interlacing patterns carved into its sides. Paedur and Niwelyn decorated it in preparation for the ceremonies; the town was a hive of activity, excitement on every face.

As dusk approached the town became more hushed. The fires were lit, the tables were stacked with food and the area around the altar became the focus of attention, the garlands of flowers that the children had made were proudly displayed all around it. Torches flared at each of the corners and several burning braziers stood close by, everyone awaited the arrival of the Goddess Creiddylad, the May Queen, it was every girl's dream to be picked and it was always a girl of beauty and poise.

Standing just beyond the crowd Paedur stood with Kerri, this year's girl, she was very nervous,

"What if I fumble and make a fool of myself", she said shaking. Taking her hands in his Paedur said "Remember your words, relax and speak clearly".

She nodded and took a deep breath and when she had calmed down he escorted her to the altar. He was dressed in a full-length robe of white linen, his belt now holding only a dagger etched with Celtic serpent designs. Around his shoulders he wore a midnight blue velvet cloak with a gold clasp, his hair rested loosely on his shoulders. Around his neck hung a gold pendent with two entwined serpents facing each other, one was green the other was red, with runic letters around them. Kerri, as Creiddylad, wore a long robe of white silk tied with a gold belt; on her hair she wore a garland of flowers. Both wore soft leather sandals on their feet.

Paedur greeted them in a strong voice "Friends, I present to you one of your own whom you know as Kerri, our Creiddylad for this evening".

He bowed towards her and then, turning back to the crowd, he continued, "We come together on the first night of summer to celebrate. May Creiddylad bless us with abundance and may Camalus grant our warriors the strength and courage to protect us from harm".

In a shy shaking voice Kerri intoned, "The time for the festivities has come, join me in song, dance and feasting".

At once the musicians began playing, the singers sang of wonderful tales, the dancers swung into action and the drinking and eating began, this was the first big night of the summer and everyone, Celt and Roman, was out for a good time.

Paedur looked reassuringly at Kerri, "Diolch, thank you for your participation, you did well." he said bowing, "Go now, be at peace and enjoy your night".

"Diolch", she replied and ran over to her friends waiting at the tables.

His duties for the evening done he joined Niwelyn waiting by the fire, the light of the fire reflected in their eyes as they whispered to each other. Taking her hands in his he looked longingly into her eyes "My Lady, you look lovely, stay with me this night and grant me your comfort".

"No, do not tarry, your people need you", she whispered softly.

"I need you", he replied in a low deep voice.

"Later, there is time", she replied reassuringly.

He nodded lingering a moment longer then they kissed and parted. As they both wandered around mingling with the crowd Paedur noticed that the girl in the cloak was nowhere to be seen he wondered where she was and what would keep her from enjoying the festivities of such an important night.

The following morning at dawn as the town was settling down after the festivities Paedur was out on a stroll, he enjoyed this time of day it was so quiet with a gentle dampness in the air and dew on the grass. As he approached the square he saw the cloaked figure, he waved in her direction but she hurried on. There was an air of exhaustion about her and she made no attempt to stop even though it was clear she had seen him. For now he decided not to pursue her but as he returned to his room he thought deeply about her and wondered who she was.

A few days later, as he was instructing the children and beguiling them with stories, he became aware of her presence standing at the edge of the group listening. This time he pretended not to notice but every fibre of his being reached out and willed her to stay.

As early evening drew in the children began to disperse and return to their homes wide eyed and excitedly chattering amongst themselves about dungeons and dragons. As Paedur turned to walk toward the great hall he saw her quietly staring at him making no attempt to move, he bowed but made no approach. Quietly he observed a slim girl; about five foot three inches tall with a round face, full lips and bright blue eyes. Chestnut red hair fell in waves down to her elbows; her hands were slightly wide with stubby fingers and short nails. She had an innocent sad quiet air about her, she reminded him of their Maiden Goddess Elaine.

After a few moments she said "The children love your stories, listening to you makes me wish I was a child again", her voice was soft with a hint of sadness.

"It keeps them amused and gives their parents a break", he replied.

She breathed deeply fully aware of how close she was to him; there was a heavy air of quietness about him which unnerved her, not knowing what else to say she moved away.

"Where are you going?" he asked.

"To work", she replied.

"Where do you work?"

"The taberna", she replied.

"Serving maid"?
"No...Prostitute", she replied.
"Ah! Where I come from we call such people blitidae, may I accompany you?"
"No, I would rather you did not, it is probably not good for us to be seen together" she replied.
"That does not worry me, I am not concerned about what people think", he said.
She took a deep breath and nodded, somehow she realised getting away from him now was not going to be easy.
"If you insist", she replied shrugging.
Together they walked toward the taberna chatting, he noticed her robe was old and worn, the cloak around her shoulders was thin and the sandals on her feet were loose.
"Who are you, I have seen you many times", he asked.
"I am Elaena. I live in a small house beside the mill gate, my family are poor and I work to bring in some money", she replied.
"Is you family big, he asked.
"I have three brothers, my parents are still alive", she replied.
"And they do not work?", he asked.
"No, they are alcoholics, my mother cares for them", she replied.
"I see, and how old are you?"
"Seventeen", she replied.
By this stage they had reached the taberna, "Thank you for walking with me", she said.
"Croeso", he replied bowing.
She quickly turned and hurried into the taberna glad to be away from him.
The taberna, a two storey stone structure, was the biggest drinking establishment in the town. The ground floor had bare brown stone walls and the upper floor had grey stone walls. Its outer walls were plastered and painted white with wooden beams in triangular patterns, there were three windows front and back and a smaller one at each gable end. A pointed terracotta roof with a brick chimney on the left gable wall covered the building. The entrance door was made of heavy oak and opened into the taberna from the footpath. The dark wooden floor was stained

by years of spilt drinks, wooden tables and chairs were placed around the room with gaps between them. A large fireplace and hearth took up the entire left gable wall with a chimney; a large iron grill held a log fuelled fire. The bar was made of heavy dark oak. Amphorae of wine, beer, mead and water were stacked in the left corner behind the bar. A shelf lined the back wall with jugs and jars of sauces, fruits and nuts, in the right corner was a metal sink.

As she entered the taberna she recognised her first client for the night, a young Celt with long blond hair and drooping moustache. He was dressed in bracae and tunic with brown leather boots. She gestured to him to follow her.

At the right gable wall a wooden stairs rose to the upper floor, a short section upwards which came to a large step then turned left up a longer section of stairs on to a long corridor. Three rooms on each side of the corridor were used for private entertainment and lodging. The ones that were used for private entertainment were just painted plain white with a bed and press. The lodging rooms had painted walls decorated with both Celtic and Roman patterns. The beds were finely dressed with satin sheets and fine blankets. All had wooden wardrobes, presses, chairs and a brazier. The only lighting were the windows and candles.

She brought him into the first room and, having fixed a price, commenced business. She took off her cloak and dropped it on the clean swept floor, then she guided him over to the bed and removed his tunic laying him on the bed she gently straddled him and massaged his chest, slowly he relaxed and gave in to her touch. As she worked that night the memory of Paedur invaded her thoughts his presence, his voice and those piercing blue eyes. Somehow she could not get him out of her head. When she was finished and just about to go home she asked the manager "Who is he"?

"He is Paedur, the Druid, recently come to us from somewhere down south", he replied.

"He looks old, how old is he", she asked.

"I am told he is forty-seven", replied the manager.

Taking a deep breath she replied “That is old. What is he doing here?”
“I believe he is our town’s new guardian”, he replied.
“Does that mean we are answerable to him”, she asked.
“Not exactly”, he replied, “he is here more to guide and guard, or so I am told”.
“Do we not have the warriors to do that?” she asked.
“Yes, we do”, he replied, “but he has knowledge of the Romans which we do not have and it is for that knowledge we have him here. I am told he is going to help rid us of them”.
“I do not like him, he frightens me”, she pouted.
“Stay away from him then”, he replied.

As Paedur walked back to the great hall he committed to memory the scent of her, she had a slightly unwashed smell and her clothes were dusty, smoky and alcohol stained. She had a slight frame, long flowing chestnut red hair, dazzling blue eyes and creamy coloured skin. He noted there was an air of defiance about her, she fascinated him deeply. Thinking of her awakened a feeling within him, a feeling he had not had about any other woman so far. He was amazed that, just before he asked her what her name was, she reminded him of Goddess Elaine and then she had told him her name was Elaena.
Being alone that night made him rather restless, something he was not accustomed to feeling. He had difficulty concentrating nothing held his attention for very long. He stood up and paced the room, then returned to his desk, but very soon got up and paced again. After a while he went to see Niwelyn, she greeted him warmly and invited him in. Slowly he walked over to the bench and sat down. Niwelyn quietly tuned her senses to his mood. She took two patterned glasses out of the press and filled them with red wine from an earthenware jug standing on the dresser. Slowly she walked over to Paedur observing him, he was deep in thought. She handed him one of the glasses and then sat down beside him, they sat together quietly drinking, he staring into the fire, she staring at him.
Eventually she asked “What troubles you, Paedur”.

"I have met someone...a woman", he replied.
"So what is the problem", she asked.
"She is young...very young...she is seventeen", he replied.
"Oh", she replied nodding, watching Paedur for hidden meaning behind his words, facial and body expressions.
"Her name is Elaena", he continued.
"I know her", replied Niwelyn, "her mother comes to me for herbs and lotions. She is pretty, works at the taberna, I hear".
"Yes...she is a blitidae" he replied.
"I have heard she is good, she is popular and always in demand. She is paid very highly and much sought after", she said.
"Mmm, I did not know that", he replied.
"How well do you know her" she asked.
"Not very", he replied. "I have seen her many times but only spoke with her for the first time tonight. She is always in a hurry, never seems to be able to stop and talk. Tonight was the first time she stopped; we only had a few minutes together".
"And?" Niwelyn asked.
"And...for some reason...I already feel deeply for her", he answered.
"Does she show any interest in you?" Niwelyn asked.
"No...If anything she seems almost...frightened", he replied.
"Well, you are rather imposing and I imagine the age difference is a major issue for her. She probably sees you as a father figure", she said.
"Mmm, perhaps", he replied, continuing to stare into the fire. Both fell into a companionable silence. After a while Paedur drained the remainder of the wine from the glass then, kissing Niwelyn lingeringly, wallowing in their affection for each other, he left.

The next day Paedur brought small blocks of wood, sheets of papyrus, reed pens and ink pots down to the square and handed them out to each child. He also brought a large wooden easel down for himself. Pinning a large sheet of papyrus on to the easel he began to form letters on the page. He showed them how to hold the pens and dip them into the ink. He asked the

children to copy the letters on to their own page, some of the children had no problem but others needed help. Patiently he sat beside each child and assisted them according to their needs. Elaena stopped on her way to work and watched Paedur; she waited for him to finish, dismiss the children and pack up. While he was packing up he noticed her watching him and greeted her "Ah! Elaena it is good to see you, you are well"?
"Yes, thank you", she replied. "I have been watching you".
"I know, I saw you but I was busy helping the children", he said. Having packed the last few things away he asked "Going to work now"?
"Yes", she replied.
"May I escort you"?
She nodded in silence.
Having placed the things under one of the benches he stood beside her and said "Let us be on our way then".
"Are you not taking your things with you" she asked.
"No, they are quite safe where they are for now", he replied. "They are heavy and hard to carry no one will steal them, I will return for them later".
Nodding she began to walk towards the taberna and he fell in to step beside her. In spite of their age difference she began to feel more comfortable around him. Being in his company made her feel protected, a feeling she had never had. She realised that he meant her no harm and she began to look forward to being with him.
The next night, as Elaena was preparing for work, her father came into her room. He found her just inside the door standing at her wooden table, an enamel bowel filled with hot water and an empty jug stood on top of it. She had just washed and was dressed only in cotton undergarments; she was combing her hair and singing softly to herself. The wooden press on the left side of the table was open, her clothes stacked raggedly on the shelves. He grabbed her making her gasp; roughly he dragged her across the wooden floor to the left gable wall, threw her down on her bedroll, and raped her. Gasping in pain, as he drove himself roughly inside her, she bit her lower lip stifling a

scream. She lay quietly submissively under him waiting for him to stop, his sweaty bloated body and smelly breath disgusted her and she turned her head to one side to lessen the smell.
Breathing heavily he said menacingly into her ear "Work hard wench...bring me home lots of money".
Getting up and adjusting his clothes, he looked at her with disgust then turned and left the room.
Elaena lay on her bedroll for a few minutes staring out the window fuming with anger, an anger she could not express. To do so would have incurred her father's wrath and he would have hit her.
After a few minutes she took several deep breaths and got up. Angrily she crossed the room back to her table and washed herself again mumbling "Someday I will get away from here, away from him and them. Someday I will meet someone who will love me and care for me and then I will be happy".
She dressed in a cream plaid long tunic with brown stripes and went into the kitchen angrily staring at her father sitting at the table. He remained silent, her brothers totally ignored her, her mother handed her a bowl of stew. Quickly she ate and left.

The next morning on her way home she met Paedur in the square. All was quiet, nothing moved, the dawn was breaking but the sun had not risen yet. They greeted each other and spoke for a few minutes.
"Bore da, Elaena, you seem tired" he said.
"It has been a long night and a busy one", she replied shivering.
"I will walk you home", he said.
Taking off his cloak he wrapped it around her shoulders pulling the hood up over her head. It trailed the ground behind her as she walked.
Looking into her eyes he asked "Are you alright?"
She nodded.
He nodded and, sensing she didn't want to speak, he made no further conversation. He linked her hand around his arm and gently guided her home. There was an air of sadness about her.

As she walked beside him she felt safe, protected and respected, it was the first time she had felt these things in the company of a man. As she snuggled deeper into his cloak; she became aware of the woody earthy scent of him and the imprint of him on the cloth. For a brief moment she wished that time could stop. As they reached the wooden door of her timber framed dwelling with thatched roof and a window on either side of the front door she turned to him.

"Thank you for walking me home", she said.

"Croeso, you are welcome, My Lady", he replied bowing.

Softly she said "Nos da, Goodnight".

"Nos da, Godspeed", he replied.

She removed his cloak and handed it back to him with difficulty because it was heavy. As he reached out to take it from her he looked deeply into her eyes. Not knowing what to say, Elaena turned and quickly went into her dwelling closing the door softly behind her. She stood in the timber hallway for a few minutes and leaned against the door with her hands behind her breathing deeply, the smell of the wooden walls and floor seemed to be more noticeable tonight.

She looked to her right and noticed that the door to her parent's room was closed, there appeared to be no movement so she assumed they were asleep. She looked left past her own room to the boys' room, its door was also closed and there appeared to be no movement, so they seemed to be asleep too.

His eyes haunted her.

For a few minutes Paedur stood staring at the door then he turned and put his cloak back on, as he did so her scent invaded his nostrils. He pulled the hood over his head and face, tucked his hands into his sleeves and returned to the great hall.

Taking a deep breath, Elaena pushed herself away from the door, turned left and went into her own room.

***

One afternoon in summer Elaena stopped to listen to Paedur's stories, he noticed her arriving and nodded to her. Quietly watching him she noted how the children hung on his every word their eyes bright and shining, recoiling in fear when he took on the voice of a giant and his voice boomed. She also noted the deep compassion and love in his eyes when a child was sad and upset, and observed the tender way he soothed the child sending them on their way happy and smiling. She wished he could be that way with her.

Paedur dismissed the children and sat on the stone bench waiting, hesitantly she walked over to him, he patted the space beside him and gestured to her to sit down. Slowly she sat several inches away from him on the edge of the seat half turned sideways towards him.

"You are early for work today", he said in a soft voice looking at her.

"Yes", she swallowed, "I came to hear your stories".

He raised his eye brows then nodded and bowed, "Diolch, thank you", he said, his voice had a touch of amusement.

She sat silently apparently lost in thought staring at the ground.

"What are you thinking?" he asked.

"Oh! Just that it would be nice to be somewhere else", she shrugged.

"Where?" he asked.

"Deep in the mountains nothing but green trees all around me, deep rushing rivers and no one to disturb me", she replied.

Paedur nodded. "That sounds like where I come from", he said, his eyes taking on a distant look.

"Where do you come from?" she asked.

"I am from Snowdonia", he said proudly.

"I hear it is lovely", she said.

"Beautiful", he replied. "The mountains are dark, dusky and mysterious, the rivers are clean and the water is sweet. The air is fresh and heavy with the smell of grass and flowers", he continued with a faraway look in his eyes.

"Do you miss it?" she asked looking up.

"Sometimes", he said nodding, "but I am happy here too and Snowdonia is not all that far away if I ever feel like going back".

"Will you ever go back?" she asked.

"I think I will, eventually", he replied.

"I dream that someday I will go there and live a happy life away from here, away from my family", she said.
Both sat in silence for a while then she got up saying "I had better go to work now they do not like it when I am late".
"I will walk with you", he said. He also got up and they walked to the taberna together.

***

The summer Solstice coincided with the Roman Fors Fortuna festival. The Romans celebrated by rowing down Conwy River, their boats brightly decked with garlands, later they held sacrifices to the Goddess Fortuna on an altar in front of the temple. The citizens brought their offerings of sheep, pigs, goats and doves and presented them to the priests dressed in long flowing cotton robes. The Pontifex Maximus, dressed in a long flowing white gown decorated with a gold pattern at the neck and hem, accepted the offerings then he washed his hands and called for silence. When the crowd had grown quiet he sprinkled salt and wine on the animals' heads. He signalled to the other priests who then slit the throats of each animal and placed parts of their carcasses on the fire for the Gods to consume. The rest of the meat was handed to the cooks who brought it to the countryside just outside the town walls where the citizens spent the rest of the day feasting.
In the great hall Násuin and the warriors gathered to discuss the current state of the country,
"It is becoming clear that the Roman Empire is in disarray", Násuin said. "I can see a time coming when extra care will need to be taken to ensure the safety of our townspeople. We will make a stand against the Romans, reclaim our town and then set out to reclaim our country".
One of his men asked, "How do you propose we do that, we are only a small band of men, the Romans are a formidable force we cannot fight them".
Násuin replied, "I share your concern but now we have Paedur who has knowledge of the Roman ways. He has agreed to assist

us to reclaim what is rightfully ours and it is his intention to make Conwy impenetrable".

Everyone turned to look at Paedur who simply nodded.

All day they discussed their battle plans should the need ever arise. Paedur sat in with them absorbing their knowledge and experience, after a while he left them; he had his own meeting to attend.

Late in the afternoon a group of Britannic Druids began gathering in the oak grove, Paedur and Niwelyn joined them. Paedur addressed the gathering.

"The Roman Empire is crumbling, and when it does, it will be up to us to guide the spiritual needs of the people. The Roman beliefs clash with ours and it is us Druids that they will target first. If the Empire actually does fall, it will be up to us to ensure the law and order of the country, so we must prepare. I have just come from a meeting with the warriors and they intend to fight to reclaim our land and our beliefs, and I think it would be beneficial if we assist them in every way".

All the Druids nodded in agreement.

As evening drew in the Celts gathered around the fire and had their own ceremonies to the sun. Gathering in the oak grove, they placed fresh foods upon the altar and thanked Goddess Danu for her abundance. The farmers presented sheep, goats and pigs to Paedur and Niwelyn. They blessed them and handed them to the cooks who immediately prepared them and cooked them on open fires which the people consumed. Later the Celts and Romans relaxed together in the forest.

Paedur and his Druids took up prominent positions around the fire. They were all tall and imposing men like him, there were also a few women among them slim, elegant and equally imposing. Some of the men were dressed in bracae and tunics and some wore long flowing gowns, all of the women wore long flowing gowns. They began singing and playing some of them used piped instruments and some stringed instruments. Paedur beguiled the adults with stories of princes and princesses, lovers and foes, good and evil and unrequited love. Niwelyn played a haunting melody on a tin whistle.

Because it was mid-summer and the night was particularly hot and dry, the taberna owner decided to conduct business in the open around the fire. Elaena met her usual clients and took them to the more secluded areas away from the crowd. At one point, when she was taking a break, she noticed Paedur, this time surrounded by adults, beguiling them with stories. She noticed the hushed silence around him and found herself becoming captivated by his mesmerizing voice. Listening to him gave her a warm and tingling feeling in the pit of her stomach; his voice seemed to reach into her heart as she pictured the scenes he was describing.

Looking up Paedur noticed Elaena, as usual at the edge of the group, watching and listening. He bowed to her and smiled, her insides turned to jelly, her skin tingled, her legs almost crumpled beneath her and her heart melted. He had one of the serving maids bring a drink over to her with his compliments. As she raised the earthenware goblet to her lips he tilted his own in her direction and bowed. Although he frightened her, she was also drawn to him in a way she couldn't describe. She drank deeply from the goblet then placed it on a nearby table. Drying her lips with the back of her hand she noticed a dark haired woman and a blond haired man sitting close to him, both seemed to be rather friendly with him.

Presently Elaena turned and moved away, Paedur saw her talking to a man and, as they walked away together, he had the impression that a deal had been struck. That night in the forest, as she pleasured her client, Paedur's eyes and voice haunted her. She had difficulty concentrating on what she was doing and had to shake her head several times to clear her thoughts and bring her back to what she was doing.

As the festivities drew to a close and the taberna staff were clearing up Paedur noticed Elaena, this time alone, and walked her home.

"Thank you for the drink", she said.

"Croeso, My Lady", he replied bowing.

"Your stories were amazing; it seems you can captivate adults as well as children".

"Something I learned a long time ago", he said.
This reminded her of their age difference; she shook herself and carried on,
"Who were those people you were with tonight?" she asked.
"Druids", he replied.
"What were you doing with those strange folk?" she asked.
"I am their leader", he replied.
She shivered, remembering tales she had heard as a child about the spells and horrible things the Druids would do to you if you were bold. She had difficulty getting a grip of herself this time.
"Why are they here?" she asked.
"A meeting", he replied.
"About what?", she asked.
"Druid things", he replied.
"Does that mean you cannot tell me?" she asked.
"Exactly", he replied.
"The blond man, he is not Druid is he", she asked.
"No, he is our chief warrior. His name is Násuin", he replied.
"And the woman, is she Druid", she asked.
"Yes, she is", he replied. "Her name is Niwelyn; she is my consort and friend".
Elaena shivered. Taking off his cloak, Paedur wrapped it around her. His closeness disturbed her but she was tired and appreciative of the company.
"Looking forward to getting home", he asked.
"No", she replied.
"Why?"
"It is dark, dusty and my father rapes me. He beats me when I do not bring home enough money", she replied.
"How much is enough", he asked.
"As much as they can get", she replied.
"As much as you can get, you mean", he said.
"Mmm", she replied.
"Is that likely to happen tonight?" he asked.
"No, they will be asleep, she replied, perhaps tomorrow, when they want to go drinking. Why do you ask"?

"I will stay with you and try to prevent it if you want", he replied.
She looked at him, "You would do that for me?"
"Not just for you", he replied. "I would do it for any woman, but especially for you".
"Why?", she asked.
"Because I like you and I know you would not hurt anyone", he replied.
"How do you know that?" she asked.
"Good judge of character", he shrugged.
"And what else do you know about me that I have not told you?" she asked.
"That you are soft, gentle, kind and loving underneath a brazen, defiant, rebellious exterior", he replied.
"No I am not", she said, defiantly shaking her head.
"Yes you are", he nudged her shoulder with his. She moved slightly away.
"Tell me about your family", he asked, trying to draw her out.
"Mum is kind", she replied. "She helps everyone and works hard trying to keep the boys happy, which is impossible. She keeps the clothes clean and cooks the food, when we are sick she gets us stuff to make us better".
"What kind of stuff", he asked.
"I do not know", she shrugged, "drinks that smell awful and taste even worse, all I know is I hate them".
He smiled knowingly to himself and nodded.
Elaena continued, "I like her, she tells me stories, some are nice which make me dream of far off places and of being someone else", she said with a distant look in her eyes. "These stories make me happy. Some are scary, they frighten me", she said cowering. "It makes me sad when I see her crying because of the boys being rude and unloving to her. She worries about us but they do not seem to care".
"And your Father", Paedur asked.
"My Dad's name is Medwyn he drinks, sleeps and rapes me, he does not do anything", she replied. "He roars when he is angry and his face turns red and he dribbles. He is smelly and sweaty.

He used to be well but then the Romans came and they took his job away and then he started drinking".
"What did he do", he asked.
"I do not know, I was too young", she replied. "All I know is he worked", she shrugged.
Paedur nodded there was a few minutes silence between them allowing Elaena time to catch her breath.
Then he asked "And the boys".
"Ioan is my oldest brother, Gruffudd is the next one and Dafydd is the youngest, they just drink and eat", she replied.
"Did they ever work", he asked.
"No", she replied.
By this time they were standing outside Elaena's dwelling and, with a look of concern, he asked, "Do you want me to wait"
"No, thank you", she replied.
"You are sure?"
"Yes, thank you", she replied, looking down at the ground.
Paedur nodded and gently, taking his cloak, he said, "Nos da, sleep well". He stepped back
Elaena stood at her door a moment and looked up saying, "Thank you for walking me home".
He nodded, turned and walked down the road. Breathing deeply, Elaena watched a moment then turned and opened the door.
"You are late", her father hissed standing on her right at the closed door into his room.
"I was busy" she said, brushing past him in to the kitchen, the hem of her dress swishing.
"Who was he?" he asked following her.
"Who was who?" she asked innocently, opening the wooden kitchen door at the end of the hallway.
"That man, the one you were talking to outside", he asked coming in to the room behind her.
"Oh! Just a man from the taberna", she replied shrugging and walked across the room to the wooden dresser on the right side of the window opposite the kitchen door.

"He looks old, what does he want with you", he asked standing at the kitchen door.
"He is a client", she lied as she took a glass from the dresser and poured some water into it from an earthenware jug.
"I hope he pays good, show me what you got", he said crossing the room.
Placing the glass on the dresser shelf she took her cloak off, dropped it on the ground and reached into the small bag tied around her waist, pulled out some coins and handed them to him. Roughly he took and counted them. Elaena waited.
He looked up "not enough", he said.
"I did my best", she said picking up the glass and taking a sip from it.
He came over to her and sniffed, "You have been drinking", he said.
"I had one", she said taking another sip.
"You are not allowed to drink", he said.
"The man gave it to me" she said, defiantly.
"One what?" he asked.
"Beer", she replied taking another sip of water.
"Beer is for adults", he said sneeringly.
"I am an adult", she said taking another sip.
"No you are not, you are a child and you will do what you are told", he said.
She stood defiantly in front of him glass in hand and shook her head her hair falling around her shoulders as she did so.
"I am an adult and I will do what I want", she said, "and right now I want to go to bed".
She put the glass back on the dresser shelf and brushed past him, passing the wooden table and stools along the right hand wall of the room.
"You will do what I say", he said following her and hissed into her face, "get me more money".
"I cannot, I got as much as I could" she said, defiantly going over to the kitchen door.
The look in her eyes angered him; he lashed out and hit her several times on the face, knocking her to the ground in front of

the bench on the left of the door. She curled up in a ball on the hard packed earth floor, shielding her head and face with her arms to prevent further damage from any more blows.

Her father stormed off down the hallway breathing heavily, Elaena lay on the floor sobbing. She crawled over to the dying embers of the fire on the left gable wall and stared into it. The remains of a fire smouldered in the free standing iron grill. The iron wall behind it, which protected the timber wall of the room, was black from years of smoke. The iron hearth was strewn with ash from the fire; wooden logs were stacked in a basket on the left of the fireplace. In the corner of the room a poker, hard brush and ash bucket stood beside it. Silently she stared into the fire and eventually fell asleep.

The next morning her family found her asleep on the kitchen floor in front of the fire. Ioan kicked her in the ribs, "Get up, bitch" he said, with a look of disgust as if she were a heap of rags.

She moved slowly feeling the pain.

He kicked her again, "I said get up, bitch".

She sat up rubbing her eyes, her hair was dishevelled and her dress was crumpled and stared hardly at him rubbing the places he had kicked. After a few minutes she got to her feet heavily, she was still in pain, and stumbled out of the kitchen down the hall to her room. She fell down heavily on her bed roll and lay there alone listening to the sounds around her. Eventually she fell into a painful sleep.

Later when she awoke she lay quietly, afraid to move, listening, the house was quiet apart from her mother moving about humming to herself. She moved, instantly the pain coursed through her, she winched, slowly she got up and washed. Her mother knocked on the door and when Elaena opened it her mother handed her a clay pot with lotion in it and said nothing. Closing the door Elaena opened the pot, "*this one smells good*", she thought. She put the lotion on her bruises, put on a fresh dress and brushed her hair. When she was happy with her appearance she went in to the kitchen to the kitchen table and sat down. Her mother was working at the wash bowl, in the right hand corner close to the table, washing cups; she put them on the shelf of another wooden dresser, along the right gable wall. Going over to the wooden press, in the other corner of that wall, she took out a cloth and returned to the dresser and dried them leaving them there. She then crossed the room to the fire and scooped out a measure of hot stew into an earthenware bowl and, crossing back to the table, she put it in front of Elaena. Silently Elaena ate then left the dwelling.

In the taberna that night Paedur sat by the fire with a group of people. He looked up and immediately noticed the bruises, a look of concern passed over his face. Elaena quickly hid her face from him avoiding eye contact, grabbed her client and rushed up the stairs with him. Working that night was uncomfortable, she was in pain and had to fight hard within herself to remain calm and concentrate on her clients. At the end of business she quickly left the taberna and hurried home hoping to avoid meeting him.

When Paedur left the taberna that night he went to Niwelyn, there was a light shinning in her house so he knocked softly on the door and waited, after a moment it opened and he stepped in.

"You seem troubled", she said.

"It is Elaena", he replied. "I saw her tonight in the taberna, she is badly bruised. She hurried away when I looked at her. She was gone by the time I left".

Niwelyn sighed, "What are you thinking?"

"I have to do something", he said shaking his head, "but I do not know what. She does not want me to defend her", he said shrugging.

"So what are you going to do?" she asked.

"I do not know", he replied. He fell into silence staring at the floor.

Niwelyn went over to the fire and scooped out a ladle full of liquid into a clay goblet. Going over to Paedur, who was now seated on the bench, she stood in front of him and handed it to him.

"Drink", she said.
"Diolch", he said. Taking it from her he raised it to his lips and drank; the liquid was hot and the chamomile taste pleased him. He drank deeply remaining silent.
Niwelyn sat with him for a moment realising that he didn't want to talk. After a few minutes she got up and moved around tidying the already tidy room. She tried to be as quiet as possible so as not to disturb his thoughts. Eventually she went to bed leaving Paedur staring into the fire. By morning when she awoke he was gone.

Chapter Four

As summer progressed into autumn Paedur and Elaena became quite friendly. Most nights he was waiting for her after work and walked her home. One night as soon as she saw him she exploded angrily.

"Look at me, just look at me, my tunic is stained and smelly, my hair is wet and matted and my cloak is stained too".

She paced angrily up and down the pavement pointing to her long blue canvass tunic and lightweight plaid cloak.

"What happened?" Paedur asked quietly.

"There was a fight", Elaena said angrily, her eyes wild. "The Roman Marcus insulted my brother Ioan; Ioan insulted him back. The Romans sided with Marcus, everyone else sided with Ioan, they all got angry and started a fight and drink got spilled all over the place. I was sitting on a client's knee, we were minding our own business, Marcus poured a jug of beer over us", she made angry gestures with her hands, "my client jumped up knocking me to the floor and punched Marcus, who threatened to kill him, all three were thrown out and I was left to fend for myself".

Angrily she paced up and down; Paedur watched silently, allowing her to express her anger, a smile touched the corner of his lips and glistened in his eyes, he thought she looked breathtaking.

Quietly he asked "Do you want to go and wash?"

"Where", she asked angrily.

"Down at the stream in the forest", he replied.

"No I do not, who knows what is down there I could get eaten or something", she said waving her hands in the air.

Paedur hid a smile by rubbing his chin and mouth and, taking a deep breath, said "I will guard you and keep you safe".

Elaena exploded even more her eyes wide and angry.

"I am no safer with you than I would be alone" she said, shaking her head defiantly. "I am going home I will wash there and change my clothes" she said, pouting.

"Then at least allow me to walk you home" Paedur said quietly, bowing.
The next night Elaena was surprised that Paedur wasn't waiting for her so she began to walk home alone. Finding him in the square sitting alone on his bench she walked over to him and sat down silently beside him. Neither spoke. It was the early hours of the morning and the day was still in the grip of night, there was a heavy air of silence and peace and Elaena sank into it relishing the quietness after the noise of the taberna. Paedur reached up with his left hand to the sky and made a clutching movement then, forming a loose fist, brought his hand down and put it in the pocket of his cloak. Several times he did this silently offering no explanation.
After a few minutes Elaena asked, "What are you doing?"
"Picking stars", he replied.
She looked at him quizzically.
"Do you not pick stars?" he asked.
Elaena shook her head silently.
"I do this all the time, I thought everyone did", he said innocently, shrugging.
Again Elaena shook her head. "I had better go home now", she said quietly, getting up.
Paedur also got up saying "Yes, I will walk with you I think I have picked enough stars for one night".
"What do you do with them?" Elaena asked, thinking it was a stupid question.
"I use them to cheer me up...I also include them in medicines", he replied.
Reaching up and picking one more star he handed it to her and said, "Make a wish...for something that cannot possibly happen.
Feeling very stupid but taking the star from him she wished, "*Someday I will find a man who will love me and take me away from here*".
Paedur, looking down at her, smiled and nodded, Elaena shook her head and asked no more.

Around mid-autumn Paedur found Elaena sitting in the village square alone in the place where he usually sat with the children. Before approaching her, he observed that she seemed more exhausted than usual, her shoulders were hunched and she had a definite air of despondence about her. He wasn't sure if she was crying but he knew she was very much in need of comfort. Quietly and gently he approached her, she wasn't even aware of him until his shadow fell across her.

She looked up and saw those eyes gazing at her intently and sagged even lower into herself. He sat down beside her and waited. Eventually she took a deep breath and turned to look at him saying, "I can tell you anything, right"?

Quietly he nodded.

Taking another deep breath and shaking her head she said, "I cannot do this anymore".

"What can you not do", he asked quietly.

"Prostitution, I cannot bear the feeling of all those drunken men falling all over themselves and falling all over me. The noise of the taberna and the fights upset me", she replied.

"Why do you not stop then?" he asked.

"I cannot", she replied.

"Why not?" he asked.

"Because of my family", she replied. "If I stop working, my brothers and my father would have no money and my mother would have nothing. My father would rape me, beat me and send me back down to the taberna again. No, it is no good", she said shaking her head. "I have to continue".

Paedur quietly took her hand in his and sat with her enfolding her in the deepest sense of peace that he could transmit to her. Eventually she got up slowly and heavily saying, "I had better go home now and have some rest".

She sighed deeply.

"I will bring you home if you would like me to", he said softly.

"Please", she replied, looking down at the ground her voice shaking.

Together they walked home in silence. When she quietly entered her room her father was already waiting for her. Taking off her clothes she lay on her bedroll and quietly submitted to him. As he drove himself into her, she thought of Paedur.

***

Although Paedur was busy attending to duties over the next few weeks he thought of Elaena. One night, as he was alone in his room charting the course of the stars, an idea came to him. He stopped his work and thought the idea through, his room was dark apart from the light of the fire and the candles, he pulled his cowl up over his head and eyes and soon became lost in his thoughts.

In the taberna, in the middle of entertaining a client, Elaena sighed.

At dawn, having spent a sleepless night thinking, his plan firmly in his mind now, he got up and went to Niwelyn, he found her sitting outside her house breathing in the cool early morning air. He sat down beside her, "I have a plan", he said.

She waited.

"I will take her into my custody as my apprentice".

"By her I take it you mean Elaena" she said.

Paedur nodded.

"And her family?" Niwelyn asked.

"I will provide for them", he replied.

"Do you think they will agree?" she asked.

"Why would they not?" he asked shrugging.

"Because she is their only means of survival", she replied.

"I will provide for their every need, they will want for nothing. In exchange I will take her into custody and teach her everything I know", he explained haughtily.

Niwelyn looked at him quizzically "Everything"

"Yes, everything", he replied.

Niwelyn remained silent.

"Did you not learn anything from Londinium?" she asked quietly.

Both sat in silence, both staring ahead.

"Elaena is unhappy she wants to leave her family, I can give her the means by which to do that", he said eventually.
"At what cost", Niwelyn asked.
"No cost, what harm can come of it. She wants to leave her family, I want an apprentice, both of us win", he replied.
Niwelyn sat quietly for a few minutes then nodded saying, "She is seventeen and you are forty-seven".
Paedur nodded quietly.
"You have learned nothing", she sighed.
"Nevertheless", he said, "it is what I am going to do; now all I have to do is convince Elaena.
Niwelyn nodded and said no more.

For the next few days he searched the town for Elaena but couldn't find her anywhere. In the taberna he asked several of the townspeople and the owner and was told that she had not reported in for several nights. He called to Násuin's dwelling and saw lights shining through the window and a plume of smoke coming from a hole in the roof so he knocked on the door.
Násuin called out "It is open, come in".
Paedur pushed the door gently and stepped into the house and found Násuin, sitting on an oak stool in front of the open fire in the middle of the room, cleaning his sword, a small fire was burning in the hearth. Along the right hand wall, was a long wooden bench with cushions, over the bench, painted on to the wall, was a picture of a Roman gladiator. In the right hand back corner of the room was a press, in front of it was a wooden table and stools, a door cut into the middle of the back wall. In the left hand back corner stood Násuin's weapons, some leaning against the wall others lying on the floor. Taking up the left wall was a long wooden sleeping platform, over the platform painted on the wall was a picture of the Goddess Branwen dressed in a cream tunic and brown leggings tucked into brown leather knee high boots. Her brown hair flowing loosely around her shoulders, she had a smouldering look in her eyes. In the left hand front corner stood an oak press. The room was lit by two

small windows on either side of the front door, candles and the fire. The floor was of hard packed earth.
"Welcome to my humble home, Paedur", he said, pointing to the bench in front of him. "Sit with me".
He allowed Paedur a moment to make himself comfortable.
To what do I owe the honour" Násuin asked.
"Have you seen Elaena lately?"
"No", replied Násuin, "I have not". Is she not in the taberna?" he asked.
"No, they have not seen her for some time it seems", he replied.
"Nor I", said Násuin. "Are you concerned for her?" he asked.
Nodding Paedur replied, "I am". It is not like her to miss work", he frowned.
"I am sorry I cannot be more helpful", replied Násuin. "If you like I shall go and search for her".
"No", replied Paedur, "perhaps it is nothing. I am sure she has a good reason. I will find her myself".
"Do you want me to accompany you?" Násuin asked.
"No", replied Paedur. "I do not want to draw attention to her if there is no need to do so".
"As you wish", replied Násuin. "If there is anything I can do, let me know".
"Thank you, I will" said Paedur.
Looking around the room Paedur said, "You have a fine house here, simple but sufficient and very cosy".
"Thank you", nodded Násuin. "It is an old Roman house which has been returned to Celtic style. Originally it had separate rooms with partition walls but it was dark and cold so when I took over possession I took the inner walls down, covered the mosaic floor and built the hearth. I live alone so I have no need for separate rooms; I have no use for fancy objects or comfort".
Paedur nodded. "I see I am keeping you from your work, I will not detain you any longer. Thank you for your time".
He stood up and began walking towards the door, stopping in mid stride he turned back to Násuin and asked, "Would you be willing to help me change the furniture around in my room" I

am planning to ask Elaena to live with me and, if I do so, I will need to make adjustments to accommodate her".
"Has she agreed to this?" Násuin asked.
"No...I have not asked her yet", replied Paedur.
"Should you not do so before making any changes?" Násuin asked.
"Perhaps I should", replied Paedur, "but I was hoping she would readily agree".
"I do not frequent the taberna so I do not know her", replied Násuin, "but my men tell me she is a firebrand and very defiant and does not respond well to being told what to do".
Paedur nodded, "This is in her best interests".
"Be that as it may", replied Násuin, "it is best that she feels it is her choice, and not your command", he advised.
Paedur nodded. "Given that she...will agree...will you assist me"?
"Of course", replied Násuin.
"Can we do that now"?
Closing his eyes, sighing and nodding Násuin replied, "As you wish".
Together they left Násuin's house and went to Paedur's room.

Over the next few days Paedur passed by Elaena's dwelling but, having no reason to call in, he carried on. His concern for her grew and eventually he decided to call and enquire about her, he knocked on the door, after a moment Ioan answered bleary eyed and half dressed.
"Bore da, Sir", Paedur greeted him bowing. "I am enquiring about the Lady Elaena, she has not reported for work for some nights now, is she well"?
"She is away", Ioan answered abruptly, and slammed the door in Paedur's face.
He waited a moment contemplating whether to enquire further but decided not to. As he began to leave he thought he caught a movement behind the window out of the corner of his eye but, when he looked back, there was no sign of movement.

A few days later he met her coming across the square, he sighed with relief and closed his eyes to calm himself.
He greeted her, "Where have you been, I have been looking for you for days. Ioan told me you were away".
"I have been ill", she replied.
"He raped you again", Paedur said.
She nodded looking down at the ground.
A genuine wave of concern coursed though him, he wanted to hug her but knew it wasn't appropriate, instead he asked, "Can you talk about it"
She shook her head silently, being close to him made her feel strange. She wanted to be hugged by him, to feel his arms around her. She wanted to cry, but thought he'd see her as a baby, so she stayed silent biting her lip.
"You are early for work, will you walk with me a while" he asked.
Silently she nodded and fell into step beside him. He guided her to the forest, watching her step all the way, helping her gently over the fallen trees and around the stumps. Tears stung her eyes but she wouldn't let them fall. In the oak grove he stopped, spread his cloak on the ground and gently assisted her to sit down. He noticed her movement was heavy. They sat quietly together for a few moments listening to the heavy silence of the forest broken only by the sound of a scurrying animal.
Eventually the silence and his presence got to her, she sighed deeply and shifted. He waited, allowing her to make herself more comfortable.
"After you left me that night", she began, "my father beat me. He said I had not made enough money and he wanted more. I told him that was as much as I could make and I could not do any better", she took a deep breath. "He was unhappy that I had been drinking and told me I was a child so I should not be drinking and that I should do as I'm told...what he tells me".
She breathed deeply then continued, "Since then he raped me again and I became ill, I had an infection", she looked at him sadly. "I know you called to our dwelling but they would not let

me see you, I have been so weak". She shook her head catching her breath and breathing with difficulty.
"Are you well now?" he asked quietly.
"No", she said shaking her head. "My mother has been giving me stuff to heal me but it has taken a long time to work and I am still not fully well".
Leaning against him she let the tears flow, hot tears flowed down her face, and for a few minutes she cried quietly. Silently he held her in his arms. Several minutes passed, she desperately trying to control her tears, he waiting, allowing her to take the time she needed.
Slowly her tears stopped and once she had calmed down a little he asked, "Elaena, would you live with me, give up the taberna and become my apprentice?"
He waited for her reply.
Her mind went into a spin; she couldn't believe he had just asked her to live with him. She thought about it for a moment contemplating the possibility then, silently, she shook her head. "No", she whispered.
"Why not?" he asked gently.
Inwardly she was afraid of him, but she didn't want him to know that, so instead, looking up and shaking her head in gentle defiance, she replied, "My family would never agree to it".
"Because of the money?" he asked.
"Yes", she nodded, "and..."
"And?" he pressed.
Taking a breath she continued, "...because you are old".
She waited for his reaction. There was none.
"If you become my apprentice", he said, "I will see to it that your mother has food, clothes and everything she needs and that your father and brothers have enough money for drink. I will take you into my custody and they will be under my protection. They will have everything they need for as long as they live and..."
"How will you do that", she interrupted.

"as Chief Druid I am entitled to provisions from the town", he continued. "Usually I give away what I do not need; from now on I will give most of my allowance to your family".

He waited, allowing his words to sink in.

Elaena took a deep shuddering breath, turned and looked at Paedur with big round eyes. She thought he was joking, but the serious look in his eyes convinced her he meant what he was saying.

After a few minutes she said, "I cannot, my family would never agree".

"Let me talk to them", he said quietly, "I will convince them".

Mindful of the time she got up, he stood up too and steadied her. This time his nearness really unnerved her and she felt fearful. Realising that he was not easy to get rid of, she nodded. "All right", she said, "but I do not think that even you will get anywhere with them. I am going to work now".

"Can I walk you there?" he asked quietly.

She nodded.

Falling into step beside her they walked silently to the taberna. At the door he held her hands and looked deeply into her eyes and said, "Work well, Elaena, I will be waiting for you".

She nodded, turned and went into the taberna, Paedur stood outside the door for a few minutes then turned and walked away.

Working that night was really difficult for her because his words kept coming back to her, "*come live with me...become my apprentice...I will take you into my custody*". The thought of it frightened her and yet, somewhere deep inside her, something suggested that it was the right thing to do. "*At least I would not have to work anymore*", she thought, "*And right now I would welcome that. Perhaps he is the one I wished for, perhaps he is the one who will take me away from here and make me* happy". This thought took the edge off her fear. Work was a blur that night but somehow she got through it.

Paedur immediately went to Elaena's family, it was still early in the evening and he figured they'd still be there. The dwelling was a long wooden structure its interior divided up into separate

rooms by partition walls. When he arrived Medwyn opened the door dressed in brown bracae and short-sleeved tunic.
Good Evening, Sir Medwyn, may I be permitted to enter your fine dwelling" Paedur asked bowing.
Medwyn stared at him but continued to block the doorway.
"I mean you and your family no harm, I come in peace", Paedur continued.
"You are that old man Elaena speaks off" Medwyn said.
"Yes, Sir, I am", replied Paedur bowing.
"Go away, you have no business here" Medwyn said, shooing him away.
"I have a proposal to put to you that will be to your advantage", said Paedur quietly.
Medwyn looked suspiciously at Paedur, hesitated a moment longer, then stood back and permitted him to enter. Stepping into the house he stood in a hallway with one large room on the right hand side and two smaller rooms on the left hand side. He was led down a timber hall into the kitchen at the back, a long room running the width of the house, everything was neat and tidy.
Ioan, Gruffudd and Dafydd were sitting around the table, Elaena's mother rushing about attending to their needs.
Paedur embraced them all with a hard stare and gently asked her mother, "Will you sit with us a while and rest, Madam"
Reluctantly she agreed, having first set a cup of hot brew down in front of him.
"Diolch, thank you", he said and raised it to his lips.
"What are you doing here?" hissed Medwyn.
"I have come to seek your help", Paedur replied.
"What help can we be to you?" Medwyn asked sulking.
"I have come to know your daughter Elaena and I wish to take her into my custody", replied Paedur.
"What would you want with her", her mother asked with a concerned look on her face.
Paedur turned towards her and bowed respectfully asking, "Madam, what is your name".

Demurely, looking down at the floor, she replied, "I have no name".

"Everyone has a name", Paedur replied.

"Branwen", she whispered.

Paedur nodded and continued, "Branwen, I wish to make her my apprentice and train her in the ways of the old ones".

"NEVER", roared her father, jumping up out of his seat, "SHE BELONGS TO US", he continued.

Her brothers shifted in their chairs. Paedur waited silently, he could feel the tension between them and the many questions they wished to ask him so he gave them time to come to terms with his words.

Eventually Branwen timidly asked, "But what would we do, Elaena is the only one who works here, without her we have nothing".

Paedur embraced her with a compassionate look and replied, "Branwen, as Chief Druid of Cymru..." at that the boys gasped and recoiled into themselves; they'd heard the stories too,

Ioan remembered hearing how a Druid had turned a man into a mouse and sent him scurrying through the fields for food for the rest of his life.

Gruffudd remembered a tale where a Druid had given a man a drink and he had broken out in oozing boils all over his body that no one could heal.

Dafydd recalled hearing how a Druid had thrown a man across a room slamming him against a wall and he had died. Medwyn, breathing heavily, stepped back a few paces and pictured in his head being turned into a dragon and being left that way for ever.

Paedur momentarily stopped, noting their reaction, then he continued, "As Chief Druid of Cymru, Branwen, I am entitled to a share of all things produced and sold in Conwy. I propose to give your family most of my share providing you all..." he looked at each one in the room, "with all your needs, and in return I will take Elaena into my custody. For as long as you live you will be provided for, you will have everything you need".

He stopped and waited silently.

The boys shifted, Medwyn shuffled around the room. Branwen stared at the floor wringing her thin worn hands in her lap, eventually she looked up at Medwyn saying, "It is a good idea perhaps we should allow it".
"NEVER", roared Medwyn, spittle drooling down his chin his face turning red. "I will not hear of it". Pacing restlessly around the room, he continued, "She is mine", I will not let her go", he was visibly distressed now.
"She is seventeen, by now she should be married with children and living in a place of her own" replied Branwen, "all her friends are married".
"SHE HAS NO FRIENDS", roared Medwyn.
"Because of you", said Branwen.
The boys shook their heads fear in their eyes; they wanted nothing to do with this strange man.
Patiently Paedur waited observing each one in turn, their distress was mounting and he knew that his presence was playing on all their fears.
Medwyn paced around the room muttering "Never, never, never".
Branwen got up and went to him pleadingly she looked at him saying, "Please allow this it is best for her and we will benefit from it too".
Impatiently he snapped at her, "Be gone from me, woman", and shoved her roughly across the room.
Paedur got quickly to his feet and stood between them staring at Medwyn, behind him Branwen cowered welcoming his calm quiet presence, the boys were wide eyed with fear.
Medwyn roared, "NO, I WILL NOT LET HER GO, SHE IS MINE".
Paedur stood silently waiting eventually; quietly he said, "Your every need will be provided for, you will want for nothing", he stared at Medwyn who shook his head.
Paedur took a deep breath and quietly, raising his head a little, drawing upon his full height and the depths of his character, he turned his gaze toward Medwyn's empty chair and mentally

willed it to move. Slowly at first it shifted, then, it shot across the room barely missing Medwyn before it stopped.
All eyes were on him now; fear in each one.
In a hard voice Paedur said, "I could command it", and in a softer voice he continued, "but I would rather you would let her go willingly".
The air in the room was tense; Branwen fidgeting nervously, the boys shifting wishing they could run. Medwyn stood still breathing heavily staring at Paedur who held him in a hard glare. Eventually, unable to hold the stare any longer, he looked down at the floor and slumped into himself. He remembered hearing how a Druid had taken a man, who had disobeyed, and made him a sacrifice at one of the ceremonies, where he was burned alive on the altar, in front of all his neighbours. He most definitely did not want to suffer that fate, he was disgraced enough as it was, that kind of thing would be talked about and remembered for ever, his family name would never recover from that. He took a deep breath then nodded silently.
Instantly the tension in the room eased, Paedur stood silently waiting.
With great difficulty and in a strained voice Medwyn, still looking at the floor, said "All right, do as you will", he let out a long shuddering breath.
Paedur looked at him compassionately and asked quietly, "Does that mean I have your permission to take Elaena into my custody".
"Yes", Medwyn whispered, he seemed drained now.
"Diolch", Paedur said. "I will make arrangements immediately", he continued.
He bowed to Medwyn and turned to look at Branwen, he walked over to her, took her hands in his and looked deeply into her eyes noticing the pleading look in them, and silently nodded, "You need have no fear, Madam", he said, "Elaena will be cared for and you shall have whatever you need".
She raised his hands to her lips and timidly kissed them replying "I know, thank you, Sir".

Medwyn shifted running his hands through his hair, Paedur was well aware of the feelings of loss of control, fear, intimidation and perhaps even loathing that he was probably experiencing. He turned to look at the boys who fled from the room glad to be away from him. A few seconds later they heard the front door closing and the boys hurried footsteps going down the road. Medwyn excused himself and followed them leaving Branwen and Paedur alone in the kitchen, he gently guided her over to the table; she leaned heavily on his arm and sat down.

Slowly he walked over to the fire where a pot of water was simmering. Reaching into a canvas bag hanging on his shoulder inside his cloak, he pulled out a handful of dried Camomile leaves, scooped out a ladleful of water and put both into an earthenware goblet. Cradling it in both hands and swirling it, he quietly said, "Airmid, Goddess of Healing, may this bring peace and calmness to our sister Branwen who is about to drink it". He carried it over to the frightened woman and as he placed it into her hands he bid her, "Drink".

She took the cup silently and, with shaking hands, raised it to her lips doing as he commanded. He waited silently for her to compose herself, the room was silent, it was as if time had stopped. She looked up into Paedur's face and saw a look of pure compassion, unable to speak silently she pleaded, "*Take care of her*".

He nodded and gently rested his hand on her shoulder, softly he replied, "Have no fear, she will be safe. I will take care of her, I will train her and teach her to read, write and heal. One day she will be a great woman and a force to be reckoned with".

Finding her voice Branwen asked, "She has been abused all her life, will you abuse her too"

"No, Madam, I will not", Paedur replied. "I will make her my equal in every way. I will love her and provide her with all her needs, I will also provide for you. What are your immediate needs"?

"I need clothes, these are worn through", she replied, pointing to her dress which had holes in it and frayed edges. "I also need food; I have only enough for two more days".

"Both will be brought to you immediately", he said.
Branwen took a deep breath, looked into his eyes and nodded saying, "Thank you, Sir, you are a kind man, thank you for taking an interest in Elaena, no one else has so far".
Seeing that she had calmed down and was now reassured, he left.
Immediately he made his way to Niwelyn. Sitting in front of her fire drinking wine he told her about the evening's events so far.
"Does Elaena know yet" she asked.
"No", replied Paedur. "I am going to the taberna now to tell her. I am taking her home for her belongings and then I am taking her home with me tonight. I am not giving her family a chance to change their minds, this way, by the time they do, it will be too late".
"What if Elaena does not agree", Niwelyn asked.
"The only thing stopping her is her family" he replied.
"Be gentle with her", she said quietly, she is young and probably afraid of you. Let her adjust in her own way. Remember what you were like when you were her age? Remember how you felt when you were taken from your family and put into training".
Paedur nodded the scene came back to him now, sitting on the grass outside his parents' mountain home distinguishing the difference between the Elm, Larch, Beech and Oak twigs. He recalled the strange hooded figure speaking to his parents, his father negotiating and his mother crying. He then remembered the figure coming over to him, looming over him and telling him to get his belongings. He remembered being afraid but the figure appeared to be calm and seemed to pose no threat. Shaking himself back to the present he nodded and, placing the goblet on the floor in front of him, he said, "Yes, I remember, I will be gentle with her".
Niwelyn nodded and looked deep into his eyes saying, "Please, Paedur, go easy with this one. I do not think she is the one, train Kerri instead she is a far better choice".
Paedur remained silent.

Niwelyn, realising that Paedur had already made up his mind and that nothing she said would change that, nodded and said no more. A few minutes later Paedur left.

He made his way straight to the taberna, it was almost closing time and he had promised Elaena that he would be waiting for her. As he approached the door Ioan, Gruffudd and Dafydd came out stumbling, recognised him and fled. A few minutes later Medwyn came out, also recognised him and stopped, drunkenly he said, "You, big scary man, the one who wants to rob me of my daughter".

The people around them stopped and listened, wondering what was going to happen next.

Paedur stood staring at Medwyn.

Medwyn continued, "You probably want her for yourself and think that because you are the great and powerful Druid, you are entitled to her".

Paedur said nothing, the crowd grew bigger.

Medwyn, realising now that they had everyone's attention, continued, "What does an old man like you want with a child like her anyway"?

Paedur continued staring at Medwyn.

Medwyn went on, "You come in here, from who knows where, you eat our food, you take over as if you have always lived here and now you take our children".

He lunged at Paedur and raised his hand, with lightening speed Paedur grabbed his arm and held it in a fierce grip, Medwyn winced in pain. The crowd increased and one of the warriors detached himself from the crowd and ran towards the fort. Paedur held Medwyn in a firm grip and stared into his eyes; Medwyn kicked out and caught him on the shin. Paedur drew a deep breath and dug his nails into Medwyn's arm, blood oozed from the cut and Medwyn cried in pain; Paedur dropped his arm and stepped back.

Loud footsteps rang on the pavement as Násuin and the warrior approached, the crowd parted and loudly Násuin said, "Stop... blood has been drawn...this goes no further".

He stood between the two men glaring at them both and said, "Both of you, go home and come to your senses". Looking at the crowd gathered around them he said, "Everyone, go home, there is nothing here of interest to anyone".

The crowd dispersed and Medwyn shuffled down the street mumbling.

Násuin stared at Paedur and asked, "What was that about".

"A drunken rant", replied Paedur.

"Well he is gone, I suggest you go too", said Násuin, holding Paedur in a hard stare.

"I cannot", replied Paedur, "I promised Lady Elaena that I would be waiting for her and escort her home".

"You should know better than to pick a fight with a drunken man", Násuin said.

"I did not start it, I was merely defending myself", Paedur replied.

One of the last onlookers said "He is right, Medwyn started it, Paedur was just protecting himself".

Násuin nodded, "Be that as it may, let that be the end of it".

Just then Elaena came out, saw them and stopped; both men held each other in a steady stare.

"What is going on?" she asked.

Paedur stood silently still staring at Násuin who answered, "Nothing, all is well,"

Holding Paedur in a long stare he continued, "I will leave now; see to it that there is no further disturbance this night".

Paedur nodded silently, Násuin bowed to Elaena and returned to the fort. Turning to Paedur she shivered, he unclasped his cloak and wrapped it around her, his hands lingering on her shoulders and with deep concern; quietly he said, "You seem tired".

She nodded.

"Walk with me", he said and took her hand.

Together they walked through the town the last of the revellers were stumbling home; soon the streets became quiet and hushed. The ground was dry and their soft leather boots made no noise as they walked. The air was still quite warm for early autumn but there was a slight chill, the scent of flowers hung in the air. Neither of them noticed the buildings around them both were lost in their own thoughts.

Acknowledging the guard at the entrance, Paedur stopped and spoke quietly to him for a few minutes then beckoned Elaena to join them; taking her hand again he walked her out of the town and into the surrounding countryside. They were now truly alone. He led her to the oak grove and bid her sit beside him; he waited for her to catch her breath and settle herself.

When he was sure she was settled he quietly said, "Elaena, I called to your family this evening, I have spoken with them and they have agreed to release you".

Quickly she looked at him her eyes wide with disbelief, "How, why, what did you say", she asked.

"I explained that they would be taken care of", he replied, "and that all their needs would be met and in return they would release you into my custody for training".

"And they actually agreed?"

He nodded.

She went silent digesting his words.

"Did you threaten them?" she asked.

"No" he said, inclining his head, "though your brothers are afraid of me, and Medwyn did not take too kindly to not getting his own way but...no...I did not threaten them", he replied.

"My mother, how did she take it?" Elaena asked.

"Naturally Branwen is concerned for you", he replied, "she wants you to be safe and cared for, I promised her I would take care of you and teach you to be my equal. I have her blessing, once the decision was made and the terms agreed, the boys left her alone with me, she actually thanked me".

"Branwen...you call her Branwen"? "No one calls her that".

Paedur nodded and stared at Elaena.

Elaena sat silently thinking, aware of his presence beside her and their aloneness. She couldn't believe what she'd just heard and looked at him several times for any hint of untruth, but there was none.

Silently Paedur sat and waited, watching, giving her time to adjust. He remembered Niwelyn's advice, "*be gentle...she is young and probably afraid of you*".

Elaena's mind was in a daze, her body exhausted, right now this was too much for her to take in; his words "*decision made... terms agreed*" rang in her head.

Quickly she looked at him and a new energy coursed through her and said, "So in effect you have bought me, that means I am your slave". A new defiant look came into her eyes and she tossed her head, her hair falling around her shoulders.

Paedur could see her eyes shining; quietly he said, "No, Elaena, I bought your freedom. You are Cymru and that makes you a free person..."

"...But now I belong to you", she interrupted. "I still have to do what I am told, and training, what does that mean, what kind of training?" she flashed at him.

"Training as a Druid", he replied. "Reading, writing, healing, sighting, negotiating, fighting, everything I know I am willing to teach you".

She got up and paced the ground in front of him rubbing the small of her back, which ached. She felt dizzy but held herself together; pride wouldn't let her show him she was in pain. She tossed her head, her hair falling like a cloak around her shoulders, breathing deeply she walked up and down, her body begging her to rest but she wouldn't give in.

Defiantly she looked down at him and stopped pacing and, holding him in a steady stare, she asked, "And what if I do not agree".

He remembered Niwelyn and Násuin asking this very question only hours beforehand. He remembered his own hesitation and how he had wanted to refuse and he replied, "I cannot make you do anything you do not want to do...but do you really want to go home"?

His words hung on the air. At this she stopped short, instinctively her hand rose to her ribs and she rubbed them. Paedur watched silently, he knew it had to be her own decision; he couldn't influence it in any way, his presence alone was doing that.

She raised her head and blew out a long slow deep breath. The thoughts of living with this man, old enough to be her father and little more than a stranger, frightened her...but the thoughts of going back home pained her...deeply. Her father's words, his expressions, the rape and beatings, her mother's tears and her brothers' abuse cascaded down around her. She stumbled and almost fell but corrected her stance, Paedur made no attempt to help her.

Eventually she looked at him steadily and replied, "No...I do not want to go home".

He waited for her words to become part of her.

She shook her head and breathed deeply and again said, "No...I cannot go home".

Paedur sat silently transmitting as much peace and reassurance as he was capable of to her and waited.

Eventually she asked, "What do you want me to do"

"Come with me to your dwelling", he replied, "collect your belongings and come home with me, now, tonight".

All the exhaustion she had been hiding took over; she slumped into herself and nodded.

Slowly, silently, Paedur rose to his feet and walked over to her, he took both her hands in his and looked deeply into her eyes asking, "Are you sure?"

"No", she replied, "but it is better than going home".

"And the taberna, are you prepared to give up that too?"

Again she nodded, this time more definitely, "Yes", she whispered.

He held her gaze for a moment longer then nodded. Gently he guided her back into the town acknowledging the guard as they walked through the gate. Together they walked, both silent, both thinking, digesting the night's events. As dawn broke they reached the square and Elaena said, "So here we are again, we keep meeting here".

Paedur smiled, "Is that not what town squares are for", he asked, then, more seriously, he asked, "Are you ready".

Taking a deep breath she replied "As ready as I will ever be".

Together they walked to her home. Elaena remembering all the nights he had taken her there, remembering how loved and protected she'd felt then and, taking a deep breath, she snuggled into his cloak.

When they arrived they entered quietly so as not to wake her family however they were already up and breakfasting. The boys looked up as Paedur and Elaena entered the kitchen, instantly fear sprang into their eyes. Medwyn sat mumbling to himself at the table, his arm now cleaned and neatly bandaged. Branwen was the only one who had the presence of mind to greet them.

"Croeso, My Lord", she greeted, "Bore da, Elaena".

"Good morning, Ma", Elaena replied quietly.

Paedur bowed to Branwen and embraced the boys with a stare, to Medwyn he said, "I have come for the Lady Elaena".

Instantly Medwyn jumped up and crossed the room to Elaena; his hand raised, Paedur stepped between them and held him in a steady stare. The room darkened and the air became heavy, the boys cowered and Elaena shrank behind Paedur's back. Medwyn stopped half way across the room; hand still raised, Branwen shot him a hard look silently reminding him of the agreement made yesterday.

Gently but firmly Paedur said, "Elaena, get your belongings, NOW".

She hurried out of the room. Paedur stood between Medwyn and the door blocking it. A few minutes later Elaena returned carrying a bundle, in her hand were several coins which she placed on the table saying, "I won't need these now, they are yours".

Paedur looked at Branwen and bowed, he held the boys and Medwyn in a firm stare, he took the bundle from Elaena and, holding the door open for her, together they left the kitchen. Branwen followed them out and stood at the door watching them, she noticed the tender way he helped Elaena and steadied her so that she wouldn't stumble, inwardly she smiled, outwardly she looked concerned.

Later that day a basket of clothes, food and money was delivered to Elaena's family and, from that day onwards, every week, a basket of provisions was sent to her home.

Chapter Five

Arriving at the hill fort they entered the courtyard, some women were placing cauldrons on the fire and the warriors were going about their early morning exercises for training. Some small children were sitting on the hard packed earth eating some bread, the women bringing them drinks, in the stables the horses and other animals were being attended to.

As Paedur and Elaena entered the courtyard everyone stopped and looked up, Elaena lowered her head, the hood covering her face completely; she snuggled deeper into Paedur's cloak and moved closer to him tightening her grip on his arm. Paedur guided her towards the great hall, all his concentration on her. He was aware that they were being watched and understood everybody's natural curiosity; he also felt her tiredness and shyness and decided that introductions could wait till later. For now it was more important to get her washed, changed and fed. Gently he guided her over to the door and opened it for her, just inside the door on the right hand side were a set of stone steps. He preceded her up the steps and, gathering the hem of his cloak up in her hands, she followed as they climbed the stairs the darkness closed in around her. Torches blazed from hanging braziers on the walls lighting the steps, she tread carefully trying not to stumble. At the top Paedur waited for her to catch up when she joined him he walked down the corridor in front of her. She was breathless and it took her a moment to catch her breath, walking behind him down the stone walled corridor with wooden floor and ceiling she noticed a heavy wooden door with dark hinges. Paedur pushed the door and entered the room, holding the door open; he waited for her to enter. Closing the door softly behind her he waited standing on her left side allowing her to get her bearings. He remembered the first time Násuin brought him to this room and how it had taken him time to take it all in.

Looking around the room she noticed that the door opened into the middle of the room. On her right was a high backed chair with a cushion on the seat and another for the back. Behind the chair, taking up the full corner, was a wooden writing desk and chair with cushion, papers and others things were lying on the desk. Beside the desk stood a majestic gleaming golden harp with serpent designs embossed around its edges, beside the harp was a wooden chest, a pestle and mortar and golden sickle lay neatly on top of it. In the centre of the opposite wall was a fireplace, wooden mantelpiece and hearth. In the alcove to the right was a low wooden platform with long cushion covered with a blanket; Paedur's belongings were neatly placed around it. On the left, in the corresponding alcove, was another low wooden platform with long cushion covered with a blanket, a small wooden cupboard stood beside it. In the middle of the left gable wall was a small window with wooden shutters, in the corner on her left side was a wooden table and stools. Running along the wall behind her, between the table and the door, was another wooden dresser and press. In the centre of the room, painted on to the floor, was a large circle with a triangle in the middle and strange markings. The room was lit by candles and the fire.

Walking quietly across the room Paedur placed Elaena's bundle down beside the bed and then went over to the fire and stoked it, a cauldron hung on a tripod over the fire with water in it, he stirred it. While his back was turned to her she slowly walked over to the left alcove and looked down on the bed, folded neatly on top of the blanket lay a square of dark cloth, she rubbed her right hand over it noticing the softness and raised fibres.

In a voice shaking a little, she asked "What is this"

"Velvet" he replied, looking at her, "pick it up".

Elaena picked it up and discovered that it was a full-length robe the colour of the midnight sky; she had never held anything so soft before. Looking back at the bed she noticed a square of white cloth, placing the velvet robe back on the bed, she picked it up and it opened into a long thin tunic so fine it felt almost like cobweb; she was afraid she would tear it just by holding it. Paedur, watching her intently, seemed to hear her thoughts and said "It is stronger than it looks".

Elaena, wide eyed, asked, "Are these for me?"
Paedur nodded.
She looked down at the two beautiful garments and shook her head. Her voice shaking she said, "I cannot wear them they are too fine".
"They are my welcoming gifts to you", Paedur replied, continuing to watch her every move. He could feel the struggle within her.
Turning toward the fire, he took a large bowl from the hearth, filled it with hot water and carried it over to the table. From the press he took out a large white towel and a smaller one and placed them beside the bowl on the table.
Quietly he said, "I will leave now and let you wash, when you have done so put on the garments, I shall return".
He left the room and waited for her in the courtyard, the thought occurred to him that she might attempt to run and he was giving her no opportunity to do so.
Alone in his room Elaena took off her old clothes and began washing, the water felt warm and good. Having dried herself she timidly put on the new clothes, the undergarment felt soft and light, the over garment felt rich and heavy, she was glad of its warmth, winter was approaching and the air was cooling down rapidly. She noticed a pair of soft leather boots on the floor next to the bed and put then on, they fitted like a glove.
In the courtyard Násuin came over to Paedur and greeted him saying, "She has arrived then. I take it she is now in your custody and under your protection?"
"Yes" Paedur replied, nodding.
Násuin nodded, "She came of her own free will?"
"With a little persuasion", Paedur replied, nodding. "Her training will begin in a few days I will need your help with the fighting and weaponry".
"Whatever help I can give I will give freely" Násuin said. "I cannot speak for my men however; they may not be so co-operative".
"I am sure they will obey your command", Paedur said. "Her safety is paramount, make sure that she is left alone but protected

at all times. Make sure that they treat her with respect, she is my woman now and therefore must be treated as a lady".

"I will see to it that they do", replied Násuin bowing. "I will leave you now you have much to do today".

He walked back over to his men and Paedur saw him speaking in earnest to them.

One of the women around the fire brought some food and drinks over to Paedur, "For you and the lady" she said.

"Diolch, you are most kind" he said, bowing.

Reckoning he had given her enough time, he returned to his room.

After washing and dressing Elaena moved slowly around the room acquainting herself with it. She felt the wood of the table; it was smooth even and scrubbed, the wood of the chests was slightly rougher but they were solid and well made. Above the fire and hearth she noticed a sword with a serpent design coiled around the handle, there were also other markings which she didn't recognise. Above the sword was a staff, with a serpent head, and a javelin. Paedur's corner was neat and tidy, there were strange implements resting on his desk.

The door opened and he walked in, he stood for a moment looking at her dressed in the clothes he had given her. He hardly recognised her she looked so different, he caught his breath at her transformation, what was a scruffy girl a few minutes ago was now a beautiful young woman.

After a few moments he brought the food over to the table and placed it down beckoning for her to join him. He opened the wooden shutters and light flooded into the room, as the sun rose in the morning sky they eat breakfast.

"The women and children are curious, they want to meet you", Paedur said.

"They already know me", Elaena replied sullenly.

"Aye, they do", he replied. "But now that you have come to live with us, they want to get the measure of you and find out what you are like, away from your family and the taberna".

"I do not want to meet them", she said obstinately. "The way they looked at me disturbed me".

"They are just curious", he said, reassuringly. "They mean you no harm".
"And those horrible men, do they mean me no harm either", she asked. "I know them from the taberna and their intentions are definitely not good", she said sullenly.
"I have their leader's promise that they will do you no harm" he replied.
"Hmm, and they will obey?" she asked sceptically.
"If they know what is good for them they will", he replied. "Now let us go for a walk".
"No, I'm tired, I have not slept since yesterday", she said sullenly.
"Nor have I", he replied. "I think it is important for us to do so, you do not want a formal introduction to the people. In this way we can introduce you quietly and informally and the people will see that your status has changed and you are my wom...apprentice now".
"I do not want to go; I want to go to sleep". She said even more sullenly.
"A short walk then, it will clear your head after the events of last night and make it easier for you to sleep later. But first I must change so you can have a short rest while I do so".
He walked over to his chest and took out a long flowing brown velvet gown changed into it and turned back to her.
"Ready?"
Nodding she said, "Alright".
Together they walked down the corridor and stairs, Paedur stopped at the bottom and walked into the great hall, in spite of the early hour it was neat, tidy and swept. The tables and chairs were placed neatly along the walls and the centre ones were arranged in a neat tidy line with the chairs placed beside them. The fireplace had been swept and cleaned and new logs placed on the grill ready for the next fire. The dais at the end of the room was clean and tidy. Spoils of war hung on the walls, a testimony to past battles and victories. New candles had been put into the holders and the torches were filled, some with fresh oil and others with kindling ready for their next use.

"It is cold and dark in here", Elaena said moodily, "and it smells smoky, just like the taberna".
"At night the women and some of the men gather in here for company after the day's work is done. They like to be close to the children in case one of them needs help and...the women do not really like the taberna", Paedur replied. "It is also used by the warriors for meetings and by our people for festivals and ceremonies".
Nodding Elaena said, "Yes, I think I have been in here as a child but since I started working at the taberna I have not been in here. Not everyone attends the ceremonies so I usually work those nights".
"Ah! That explains why I have not seen you on such occasions, I wondered about that", he said nodding.
"All the wood you see in here is oak, it is strong and supports the ceiling well. It lasts for a long time, not quite as long as the Roman stone ones, but for a long time nevertheless", he explained.
"Come; let me show you the fort".
He walked out into the courtyard and Elaena followed, the sunlight hurt her eyes and she shaded them with her hands for a few minutes.
"Not used to sunlight?" Paedur asked.
"Not at this hour of the morning I am not".
Putting her hands down she looked around her.
"This first building you see in front of us is the Chief Warrior's dwelling, Násuin; the blond man you asked me about at the summer festivities, I will introduce you to him later".
Walking on he pointed out the stables, barracks and weapons store, "Would you like to see inside" he asked.
"No, I do not", she said sullenly.
"Then we shall move on", he said.
He brought her over to the round out building, "This is our reception; it is where we first greet new comers to the fort".
"Why was I not brought here first then?" she asked.
"Because you were with me", he replied matter-of-factly.

Crossing back over to the open fire he said, "This is where the women cook our food, and most of us eat here too. The children play around it so that the women can see them while they work and the men gather sometimes to chat".
Several women were at work around the fire; they stopped and looked up but Paedur shook his head when they looked questioningly at him. He did however greet the children, "Bore da children".
"Bore da Paedur", they relied. "Are we doing lessons today?" one of them asked.
"No, perhaps tomorrow", he replied.
Walking past it he went over to the well and explained, "This is a holy well used for many years, it is said to be extremely clean and some claim it heals. We use it ourselves for our own use and, if the town is ever under siege, we can lock down the fort and provide the whole town with water if necessary. We sometimes hold ceremonies here too".
Then he walked past the dwellings explaining, "These dwellings are where the married warriors and their families live. And this large building here is the bathhouse; I will bring you in there tomorrow.
Walking out the gate he brought her through the town past the merchants' booths; business was in full swing, the streets were full of people going about their daily tasks. Carts rattled down the cobble streets, people calling to each other, the hawkers calling out their prices. On the other side of the street the people in their dwellings swept their verandas and pathways, hung clothes out to dry and attended to their gardens. They walked past the taberna; it was closed and quiet. The people didn't exactly stop what they were doing, but they did slow down and observed the couple walking. Paedur took Elaena's hand in his and held on tightly to it. They carried on past the traders' stalls and turned left along the granary and store rooms. They past the timber dwellings of the townspeople and, at the end of the street, they turned right past the upper gate and bridge and more timber dwellings. They carried on to the mill gate and the cluster of timber dwellings where Elaena lived.

"Do you want to go in?" he asked.
"No, I am tired, I want to rest now", she said grumpily.
Nodding, he said "Then let us go rest".
As she passed her dwelling she looked back and remembered all the times he had walked her home. All the times her father had beaten and raped her and her brothers had taunted her. She shivered, stumbled and clung on to Paedur's arm. Together they entered the hill fort and were greeted with a hive of activity. The warriors were training just outside the barracks. Some men were coming out of the bathhouse; the women were bustling around the fire cooking and cleaning. The children were running around playing games and the horses were being groomed. They all stopped and looked, Elaena moved closer to Paedur's side.
Paedur called out, "This is Elaena, my new apprentice. She will be introduced to you later, for now she is tired and must rest".
Everyone nodded and resumed their work; Násuin stood and stared at the couple then turned back to his men and resumed training. By the time they got back to their room Elaena was absolutely exhausted, she had not walked so much in years and her feet were tired. She slumped down on to her sleeping platform and was asleep in minutes. Paedur sat at his desk and resumed his writing.

The next day Paedur gathered some fresh clothes for both of them and brought Elaena to the Fort Bathhouse. Walking towards the simple long stone building Paedur explained to her that it had a pointed terracotta roof.
"This entrance is held up by three round stone pillars; behind them are strong oak, double doors which are the main entrance to the building".
"The foyer runs the full length of the building and has a white tiled floor and walls, six round tiled pillars hold the cement painted roof up. The statutes you see in the alcoves along the walls are, in the middle, Boann, the Celtic Goddess of Rivers, and Nechtan, her husband, the God of the Seas. That one over there, he pointed to the left, is Cyhiraeth, the Celtic Goddess of

streams. To the right is Llyr, the Cymru God of waters and the sea and, beside him, is Sequana, the Celtic Goddess of health. This is a small version of a Roman bathhouse and is a place for cleansing not socialising".

"To our right in the foyer is an archway leading into the apodyterium, the changing room, and tepidarium, the bath room. To our left are the latrines, one for the women and another for the men".

Paedur went into the apodyterium, Elaena followed and observed a simple long room with white tiled walls and floor and cement ceiling. Long wooden benches stood in the centre of the room and small numbered alcoves were set into the walls, some of them had clothes in them. Paedur put their clothes in the alcove numbered thirteen and noticed that a painted tile with a serpent design had been placed beside the number with his name on it. He then went over to one of the large wooden presses filled with towels and took out two large ones and two small ones.

"Wait here," he commanded.

Walking through an arch he went into the tepidarium and found two men bathing, quietly he explained to them that he had a young woman companion of a shy temperament with him. He asked if they would leave so that she could bath alone, readily they agreed and stepped out of the water wrapping themselves in large towels. A few minutes later all three men went back into the apodyterium and while her back was turned they hastily dressed and left.

When he was certain that they were alone he removed his clothing, wrapped himself in a towel, and gestured to her to do the same. Shyly she copied what he was doing and, when she was tightly wrapped in her big towel, he brought her into the tepidarium which had a comfortably warm air about it. The tan coloured painted walls gave the room a warm feel; a green painted strip with a leaf pattern at eye level gave the walls an earthy feel. The white painted ceiling and tiled floor gave the room a clean healthy feel.

He dropped his towel at the side of the pool; stepped in and gestured to her to do the same, shyly she did so. The water was warm and soothing. He submerged himself totally while Elaena stood transfixed. She had never been in a bathhouse before though she had heard others talking about such places. For several minutes he remained beneath the surface wallowing in the warmth of the water then, coming back to the surface, he swam several lengths of the pool. Elaena tried to walk and found that it was difficult to do so she then bent her knees and allowed the water to come up to her shoulders. The warmth of the water caressed her skin and the warm air of the room made her feel weak, she clung to the side wall and held on. After a few minutes Paedur lay on the surface of the water floating, his eyes closed his breathing calm and relaxed. Although he was not alone he surrendered to the feel of the water and the quietness of the room.

After another few minutes he stood up and swam over to Elaena and looked down at her, she had a frightened look on her face. Gently he assisted her to get out and covered her in her towel, he towelled himself dry and assisted her back to the apodyterium and sat her on one of the benches. He dressed in plain brown bracae, yellow plaid tunic and soft brown leather boots. Elaena, having now calmed down somewhat, stood up and dried herself off. Paedur assisted her to put on white cotton underwear, gossamer under tunic, a long brown velvet gown and soft leather boots. He folded their dirty clothes neatly and left them in his named alcove and together they walked back to the entrance.

As they stepped out of the bathhouse the cool morning air contrasted with the warmth of the bathhouse. Elaena shivered and huddled into herself slightly; Paedur took a deep breath of air and stood up straight and tall.

"I think perhaps some breakfast would be a good idea, we will sit by the fire, the women will feed us today", he said.

Together they walked over to the fire and sat on the oak logs immediately a woman handed them both a bowl of porridge and a spoon, both ate in silence grateful for the food. The woman

busied herself around the fire watching out of the corners of her eyes. When they had finished eating Paedur put his bowl and spoon on the ground at his feet and turned to Elaena.
"You did not enjoy that experience", he stated.
Shaking her head she replied "I do not know how to swim, I have never been in a bathhouse before and I have never been in a bath".
"Most people do not know how to swim", he said. "Most, like you, just stand in it and refresh themselves. This particular bath is more for cleansing rather than swimming".
"Are you ready to meet the children now?" he asked.
"Do I have to?" she asked.
"Sooner or later you do", he replied. "They are good children and eager to meet you".
She sighed "Alright perhaps I will".
Paedur called "Children".
Suddenly children came from the dwellings, some from the stables and some from the far side of the fort, all ran to Paedur and stopped in front of him.
Looking up at them he pointed to Elaena and said "This is my new apprentice Elaena, she will be working with us from now on".
In chorus they all said, "Bore da Elaena".
"Bore da", she replied shyly.
"What say you all that we go to the square and prepare some things for the forthcoming festivities?" Paedur asked.
Eagerly the children nodded and made noises of excitement; some headed straight for the entrance and started down the road ahead of the others. Some followed them more slowly and some hung back to walk with Paedur and Elaena. Making their way through the streets to the square they appeared to be a happy bunch, Elaena walked close to Paedur unsure of herself, he looked at her reassuringly and quietly said, "Relax, you are doing well".
She nodded.
When they got to the square Paedur settled them down and began with a story. Elaena remembered all the times she had

passed by and heard him telling these stories, today she was a part of the group and not just at the edge of it. It felt strange to her but also...it felt right.

As the sun began to sink and the air cooled down, Paedur lead the children back to the fort and ate with them. Elaena was tired so they returned to their room and again she was asleep in minutes, Paedur resumed his writing.

The next day the harvest began. The adults and children went to the farms to assist with the collection of the crops. Paedur and Elaena stayed behind in the fort to prepare the storage facilities, Násuin had all his men and horses sent to the fields to carry back all the produce. There was a great air of excitement and co-operation about the town, everyone picked as much as they could. By the end of the day all the horses returned to the town pulling carts laden down with apples, pears, wild berries, corn, barley, oats and rye. Cattle had been rounded up and selected for slaughter and quantities of salt and brine were provided by the merchants to preserve the foodstuffs for the winter.

The Romans celebrated their feast of Ludi Romani with games and plays for their God Jupiter. A cow was sacrificed in his honour and the representatives of the Senate and the magistrates celebrated with a banquet in the temple. The statues of Juno and Minerva were dressed in fine clothes especially for the occasion.

After all the foodstuffs had been treated, bagged and stored the Cymru gathered in the courtyard that evening to celebrate and feasted on the left over scraps. Wine, beer and mead flowed and everyone congratulated themselves on another fine harvest. Some bragged that they had gathered more than their neighbours. All cheered and sang and danced around the open fire.

Paedur contemplated formally introducing Elaena on this occasion but, she was reluctant to have attention drawn to herself so he decided he would just let her join in and become comfortable with the people in her own way. The children stayed quite close to both of them and kept her company when she was alone.

After the festivities the winter began to draw in, the nights became longer and colder, the days became shorter and greyer. All around the town people began preparing for the cold dark months. The goods were stock piled in a small roundhouse in the courtyard for distribution later. The animals were made more comfortable with extra warm hay, blankets and foodstuffs, some of them were slaughtered to provide food throughout the winter. The warriors strengthened and repaired the town's defences. The Romans adopted the Celtic way of dress. This was not their favourite time of year. Britannia and, Cymru in particular, were cold, wet and dreary. Their thin linens were no good to them here so they adopted the plaids and woollens of the Cymru.

The Celtic feast of Samhain arrived coinciding with the Roman feast of Ludi Plebii. For the Romans this was just a day of drama, games and races. For the Cymru this was their New Year and therefore the most important festival of all. This was a time of great magic. It was believed that the veil between the worlds of the dead and the living were thin at this time and so communication between them was easier. This was when they honoured their dead and appeased the spirits; it was a time of great strength and power. It was also Paedur's forty-eighth birthday. The festivities began on 31 October and continued for three days. After the animals were attended to and the food was ready the people set about preparing the great fire.

Paedur and Elaena went down to the forest and found Niwelyn outside her house gathering sticks and wood.

"Bore da, Niwelyn. How are you today?" he greeted her.

"Ah! Bore da, Paedur, I am well", she replied dropping an arm load of sticks on to the ground.

"May I present my new apprentice Elaena", he said. "She will be assisting me from now on".

Turning toward Elaena Niwelyn observed a round faced young woman with dazzling blue eyes and long flowing chestnut red hair, there was an air of innocence about her and she reminded her of the Maiden Goddess Elaine.

"Bore day Elaena", Niwelyn greeted her bowing.

Paedur turned to Elaena and said “May I present my ceremonial consort and friend Niwelyn”.
Shyly Elaena nodded to her.
Niwelyn looked at Paedur and shook her head; Paedur looked back at her and nodded.
Just then the children started arriving and Paedur, Elaena and Niwelyn set up a small fire especially for the children just outside her roundhouse. They went into the forest to collect chestnuts, when they had a basket filled they brought them back to the small fire and roasted them until they burst; a prize was given to the child whose chestnut took the longest to burst. Laughter filled the air and the children’s’ excited voices carried on the gentle breeze. Niwelyn then set up a large samian ware bowl with clear spring water and placed apples into it. Paedur and Elaena gently tied the hands of the children participating, they had to put their faces into the water and grab onto an apple with their teeth and take it out of the bowl. The children not participating cheered and encouraged the ones who were, their excited voices cheered the hearts of everyone close by preparing the evening festivities. Each child who had been successful got to keep and eat their apple.
As evening drew near the children dressed up in costumes that Paedur had helped them to make, Elaena and Niwelyn assisted. Some dressed as witches, others dressed as animals, some blackened their faces with soot and turned their clothes inside out and back to front. All laughed when they tried to walk and kept falling over but they soon got the hang of it and quite enjoyed the experience. When the children were ready Paedur and Niwelyn lead them into the oak grove to join the adults. Elaena followed closely behind.
That night all gathered around the great fire in the oak grove, the Druids had been arriving all day and met with Paedur and Niwelyn in the grove briefly just before the ceremonies. As darkness descended upon the town, Paedur and Niwelyn took up their positions at the altar. Násuin, at the edge of the crowd, dressed in tan coloured bracae and tan tunic, loaded his bow with an arrow. One of his men touched a lighted firebrand to

its tip, he then shot the arrow into the fire stack and it burst into flames. The crowd cheered and clapped and some danced with glee. Paedur called the crowd to attention and when all eyes were on them and the crowd quietened he gestured to Elaena, standing at the edge of the crowd dressed in an emerald green velvet gown trimmed in gold with a full length cloak to match. Slowly she walked through the crowd carrying a plate of food in one hand and a glass of red wine in the other. All her concentration was on getting to the altar without faltering or spilling the wine. Successfully she reached the altar and handed the food to Niwelyn and the wine to Paedur.

Bowing to her he placed the glass on the altar and then in a loud voice he called, "Tonight I introduce to you my new assistant Elaena, she is one of your own and has agreed to go into training with me". He gestured to her to join him and, taking her hand in his, he presented her to her people. After a few minutes he turned to her and gestured to her to stand beside him at the altar.

The ceremonies began with Paedur making sacrifices and offerings to the Gods, with a strong clear voice he said, "We give thanks for the summer abundance".

In an equally clear voice Niwelyn requested, "Mother Cerridwen, bless us throughout this winter and provide us with enough food to see us through the cold months".

Paedur continued, "We honour our dead and ask that you keep the souls of all who have gone before us safe and close to you. Give each one comfort and rest according to their needs".

He then turned to Elaena and nodded; taking a deep breath she said loudly, "Join us in feasting, song and dance".

The ceremonies done, the Druids readied themselves for a special treat.

The musicians took up positions close to the fire while the Druids formed a circle around it; they were an imposing sight and as the music began everyone became hushed. Led by Paedur and Niwelyn the Druids began to dance, they created geometrical formations swirling and twirling, dipping and bowing. On and on they danced casting a magical spell upon the watchers; the air cracked around them. One by one the townspeople fell into their power and, for a while, it seemed that time had stopped and all that existed was the dance of the Druids. There was a calm relaxed atmosphere around the town and everyone in their own way felt it. Presently the Druids and the music slowed down and stopped, for a moment a heavy air of silence hung over the crowd then, as one, everyone clapped and cheered.

Paedur joined Elaena and, taking her hand, walked with her over to Násuin who was sitting by the fire. "Násuin, may I present my apprentice Elaena". Násuin stood up "My Lady", he said nodding and bowing with respect.

Turning to Elaena he said "May I present our Chief Warrior and my protector Násuin".

Not knowing how to react, shyly she nodded and drew closer to Paedur.

"Elaena will be assisting me from now on but forgive us, we have interrupted you, Násuin", Paedur said, "I must introduce Elaena to some other people, if you will excuse us please".

"But of course", Násuin replied and turning to Elaena again said, "My Lady".

Paedur took Elaena by the elbow and guided her over to the fort women and introduced her to them. After a few minutes he turned to Elaena and said, "I have some more duties to attend to, I will return shortly".

Leaving her with the women he rejoined his group of Druids and had a short meeting with them. The Druids' duties done for the evening, they mixed and mingled with the townspeople some singing and playing, some telling stories and some dancing.

Niwelyn took Paedur aside and said, "Happy Birthday, My Lord, you have made it through another year".

"Aye, that I have", he replied, "and this time I get to spend it with you" he said, looking into her eyes. "Will you celebrate privately with me this night"?

"If that is your wish, so be it", she replied.

Quietly and unnoticed they slipped away to her roundhouse.

Later when Elaena noticed Paedur was missing she became distressed, Násuin, close by, noticed her distress and went over to her asking, "Is something wrong, My Lady"?
"It seems Paedur has disappeared", she replied looking around. "He does not want me to be unattended but I seem to have no one to escort me home", she continued.
Bowing Násuin asked "May I have the pleasure of doing so?"
"No I am used to walking home alone I have done it all these years", she replied.
"Ah! but that was when you were a...Professional", he replied. "You are now a...Lady and ladies do not walk unaccompanied".
Elaena looked at him, seeing him for the first time, his tall strong body, long blond hair, neat beard and bright blue eyes. His tan coloured tunic fit him perfectly and his tan coloured bracae were a comfortable fit, they were cuffed at the ankles and his feet were covered by soft tan coloured leather boots. She was unsure of him but Paedur had introduced him to her as his protector so she believed that she would be safe with him.
"Yes, that would be nice, thank you", she replied.
Walking beside him back to the great hall she felt a strong confident presence emanating from him, she was shy in his company so she didn't speak. He was very aware of her walking beside him, her slight frame, her long wavy chestnut red hair, her round face and innocent large round bright blue eyes. She seemed vulnerable and shy and very quiet, he decided not to engage her in conversation.
When they arrived he left her at the bottom of the stairs saying, "I think you are safe now. Nos da, My Lady, sleep well".
Shyly she replied, "Nos da, thank you for escorting me safely home".
She turned and walked up the stairs; he stood for a moment waiting; the lavender smell of her hung in the air. After a few moments he turned and returned to his quarters.
Sitting alone in his dwelling that night he committed her appearance to memory and the feelings he had as he walked her home. He had heard his men talk about her when she worked in the taberna. They seemed to have no regard for her but, from

the few brief moments he had spent with her; he felt she was a woman of hidden beauty and talent. He wished he could get to know her better, being Paedur's woman and now apprentice, there was probably very little hope of that.
After Samhain the town became quieter and settled in to surviving the winter months.

***

As mid-winter approached, the preparations for the Solstice celebrations began. Paedur and Elaena hung garlands of ivy and holly around the great hall which the children had made. From time to time their hands would touch or they'd bump into each other, for her it was like electricity shooting through her body, for Paedur he found himself enjoying her company and assistance. He was very aware of the changes he saw in her; he noted the fuller figure and the clear complexion. All bruises gone now, her skin was soft and there was a fresh lavender smell about her, he breathed the scent of her deeply into his soul. Sometimes Elaena saw him gazing at her and, seeing the look in his eyes, turned her insides to jelly.
As night fell the great hall door was opened leading into the long room. A large table stood to the right of the dais at the end of the hall, Násuin and his men took up their positions around it. Smaller ones were placed around the hall, chairs and stools sat around the tables. The fire brightly blazed, it was the only light in the hall.
Slowly people began arriving and when everyone was in and seated Paedur stepped up to the dais and raised his hands. Drawing attention loudly he said, "Let the ceremony begin".
The crowd quietened and there was a quiet movement at the door, everyone turned to see what was happening.
Niwelyn stood at the door dressed in a full length heavy blue velvet gown trimmed with gold, a leather belt holding a dagger hung around her waist. Behind her stood Elaena dressed in a full length emerald green velvet gown trimmed with gold, both wore soft leather boots on their feet. Niwelyn looked at Paedur

and he nodded. She began to walk up the length of the hall followed by Elaena carrying a lighted candle. As they walked each of the sconces burst into flame lighting the hall as they progressed towards the dais.

When they arrived Niwelyn bowed to Paedur then stepped aside. Elaena took one more step and stopped in front of Paedur. She bowed and handed him the lighted candle, he bowed and took the candle from her.

Raising the candle up he said loudly, "Cerridwen, bring your light into our hearts and souls and sustain us during the cold months".

Niwelyn gestured to Elaena to step on to the dais with her, one on each side of Paedur.

Turning to face the townspeople all three said together, "Cerridwen bless us and protect us".

Paedur placed the candle on a stand in the centre of the dais; all three bowed to each other, and then stepped down.

Násuin, surrounded by his men, watched the ceremony intently. He stared at all three in turn and lingered on Elaena. Taking a long deep breath he drank in her appearance and noted the changes in her. When she had first come to the courtyard she was a scrawny girl, now she was a woman.

The festivities went on till the early hours. Singers and musicians played and sang, the Bards beguiled everyone with stories and everyone danced. Niwelyn played a haunting tune on a wooden whistle. Paedur played a wonderful lament on his golden harp; the sound of the strings created a magical atmosphere, the rich deep tamber of his voice reaching into every soul. Elaena watched his hands gliding over the strings, the expressions on his face and in his eyes, and fell under his power. Every note, every word seemed to course through her soul colliding, crashing and spinning. In an effort to block out these feelings for him she drank too much. Násuin watched her from a distance, watching her every move.

....

For the rest of the winter Paedur and Elaena became comfortable living together, he made sure she was well fed and dressed in warm clothes. He gave her new dresses, cloaks, boots and gloves. As promised he made sure her family were provided for and they celebrated her birthday quietly in the middle of December together.

As the Roman year 407 AD drew to a close he was forty-eight, she was eighteen.

Chapter Six

408AD

In the cold months of winter Paedur began Elaena's training by introducing her to his equipment and tools, instructing her in their uses. As a Romanised Druid he made use of many Roman things that the Celts were unaccustomed to. As a warrior he was trained in the use of the javelin and the sword, for now both hung over the fire. Watching her from his desk Paedur noticed Elaena straining to look at the sword more closely. Standing up and walking over to the fire, he reached up, took it from its cradle and handed it to her. It was too heavy for her and fell to the floor with a clang. Slowly he bent down, picked it up, and held it so that she could touch and inspect it.

"What are these strange markings?" she asked, pointing to the handle.

"They are Runes, an ancient form of writing", he replied. That is my name. This sword was specially crafted for me in Londinium".

Rubbing her hand over the serpent she asked, "Does this have a purpose"?

"It helps me to grip the sword and gives me a stronger hold", he replied.

"Does it not hurt when you are using it?" she asked.

"In fierce battle, yes it does", he replied.

"But your hands do not look injured", she said.

"I heal quickly when I have to and I have not used the sword for some time", he explained.

Taking the sword in his right hand he stepped back a few paces and, striking a warrior pose, he brandished it in the air. Watching him struck terror in Elaena's heart and she made a mental note to herself never to make him angry.

He saw her expression and relaxed and gestured her to come over to him. Keeping the sword in his hand and with a relaxed

version of the warrior pose he said, "Stand between me and the sword with your back to me". She did so.
"Now, put your right hand over mine and hold the sword". She did as she was instructed.
"Now move with me". He made the same movements he had done a few minutes ago she moving with him.
"This is how you use the sword in battle", he said. "You watch your opponent's every move, you watch for them to make a mistake and when you see an opening you strike".
He lunged gently forward as if slashing at someone, the movement startled her and she gasped. She realised that he was practically wrapped around her; his strength and presence unnerved her. She took her hand off his and stepped away from him and took a few deep breaths.
After a few minutes she asked, "What do you wear in battle?"
"Were you not at the battle between myself and Násuin recently?"
Elaena shook her head, "I was working that night".
"A knee length red cotton tunic over which I wear a thigh length chain mail shirt with shoulder flaps", he replied. "Strapped to my waist I have a brown leather belt from which hangs a leather scabbard, the top and bottom are decorated with a strip of patterned metal. A small chain hangs from the top and is attached to a metal strip half way down its length. On the left side of the belt hangs a dagger, and in the middle a groin guard made of leather and metal hang down to mid thigh. On my head I wear a metal helmet with side flaps that cover my ears and cheeks, a metal strip attached to the forehead protects my nose. My arms and legs are bare and I wear strapped leather sandals with studded soles on my feet", he explained.
Pointing to his belt she asked, "Why do you always carry a dagger?"
"It has many uses, here it helps me to cut paper, sharpen my equipment and even stoke the fire", he replied. "I can cut food with it and cloth when I need to. In the forest I can cut wood for a fire so that I can keep warm and I can cut open an animal

so that I can have food to eat. In battle I can use it to hurt and, if close enough, to kill".

Elaena sighed and, noticing that she was losing interest, Paedur returned the sword to its cradle.

Going over to the press he took out a deep coloured glass and golden cup, from a drawer he took out knives, spoons and red pottery bowls and plates. Placing them on the table he said, "This is samian ware, a type of pottery which the Romans are fond of using, these are cutlery".

He picked up the knife, "This is a knife it is used to cut food. This is a fork and these things are prongs, it is used to pick up food to put into your mouth" he continued, showing her how to do that.

"This is a spoon, used to pick up small amounts of liquid" he explained. "Liquid is stored in large pots we call amphorae and poured into jugs for serving into glasses or cups", he pointed to both on the table.

Elaena shook her head, "I know all these things we have them in the taberna. We eat our food by hand and I know how to drink out of a cup or ladle when I have to", she said impatiently.

Paedur continued, "In Roman society we lay out the table this way". He put the knife down on the right hand side, the fork on the left hand side, a plate in the middle between them and a glass on the right hand side at the tip of the knife. We sit at table", he sat down, "and we take our time eating while we discuss matters of the day".

Elaena shook her head again saying, "We do not have time for such things, those of us who work eat quickly standing up and then we go to our jobs. We do not have time for sitting around talking".

Paedur, taking two golden cups, walked over to the fire and poured some wine into them from a jug resting on the hearth. Walking back over to her, he handed one to her saying, "You do not work now so you do have time for these things".

He tipped his cup to hers and drank from it watching her as he did so. Slowly she copied his action and drank from her own.

Nodding he said, "You are a lady now, that which you did before is no longer appropriate".
He went over to the table prepared a meal for them and together they ate. When they were finished he asked her to help him clean and put everything away.
Taking his cup in his hand he gestured to the fire, "Enough", he said. "Come sit with me, I am in need of your...professional company.

***

One day, while he was at his desk writing Elaena asked, "Celts do not write, why do you?"
"I come from the Roman world where writing is very important and all learned men are expected to write everything down. As a Priest I am expected to make lists and keep records and chronicle events", he replied.
Coming over to stand beside him she asked, "What are these strange things you write with".
Picking up a square shaped object with many pieces held together with clasps, he answered, "This is a wax tablet, onto this I write and record things.
"These", he said, picking up long skinny things, "are reed pens". Picking up a similar object, he continued, "This is a stylus, it is dipped into ink and used for writing, Celts are more inclined to use a quill". He picked up a large feather with a pointed tip,
"I know a quill, I have seen them before", Elaena interrupted impatiently.
"This", he continued, pointing to a small round container with a hole in the top, "is called an ink well".
Dipping the quill into the ink well he showed her how to form words on the tablet.
She was amazed when she saw the words forming, she didn't know what they were but it filled her with awe just watching it happen. To her this was magic, she had never seen such things before and she picked each one up inspecting them in turn. She dipped her finger into the ink well; the liquid made her finger

turn black, a puzzled look came over her face as she inspected her finger.
Paedur smiled and explained "It is made from soot and iron gall".
He handed her a damp cloth which she used to clean her finger.
Handing her the quill he said, "You do it".
Putting the cloth down on the table she said, "I do not know how".
Taking up another quill he dipped it into the ink well and formed the letter *A*.
"Just copy what I have done", he said.
Grabbing the quill in her left fist she formed the letter A
"Not as good as your one", she said.
"No, but very good", he nodded.
"It is my first time to write", she said.
"In that case it is very good", he said. "Try again", he encouraged.
Again grabbing the quill in her left fist she formed the letter A
Nodding and smiling he said, "Good. Now take the quill in your right hand hold, it between your thumb and first finger and try again", he instructed showing her again how to form the letter *A*.
Putting the quill in to her right hand, as he had shown her, she bent down and shakily formed the letter A
"Still not as good as your one", she said.
"No but much better" he nodded.
"Try again", he encouraged.
Again, slowly and with great concentration, she formed the letter A
"Very good", he nodded.
Then he formed the letter *B* she copied what he did and formed the letter B
He nodded "Now try this", he said.
On a sheet of papyrus he wrote *E L A E N A*. "This is your name", he said.
Standing beside him, bending down over the desk, with a fierce look of concentration, on the same sheet of papyrus she wrote

ELAENA

"It hurts my hand", she said, putting down the quill and rubbing her hand.
"Yes, at first it does but it gets better with practice, try again", he encouraged.
"No, I do not want to", she said sullenly and threw the quill down on the papyrus, some ink splashed on to it across her name as she did so.
"Alright, we will try again another day" he said, nodding.
Putting down the quill he reached over to his right hand side and picked up some long thin things standing on the floor.
"This", he said, "is papyrus, it comes from Egypt and is made from very thick sheets of reed pressed together. It is used as well as wax tablets for writing on, it is lighter and easier to carry and can be rolled up for storage".
Picking up an already rolled one he said "This is a scroll, these wooden pieces at the top and bottom are called rollers". Using the rollers he opened it out then closed it again and put it back down beside him.
"What are you writing", she asked.
Picking up another square object, this one had two pieces of leather with several thin sheets between them bound with clasps, he said, "This is a codex, a book. I am transferring the words from the papyri into the codex, the Romans are using these more now because they can be carried easily and stored on shelves. In Londinium they have whole rooms and even buildings full of these which they call Libraries", he explained.
"The words look strange to me" she said, leaning over his shoulder aware of the woody earthy scent of him and his nearness.
Equally aware of the soft lavender scent of her he replied, "This is Latin, the language of the Romans".
Pointing to other words he said, "This is Greek, it is the language of the people from Greece..."
"Never heard of it", Elaena interrupted abruptly.

Paedur took a deep breath and continued, "...and this...is Cymraeg, your own language".
"I did not know we had one", she said quickly.
Seeming to lose interest she walked away and lay down on her bed and rested.

***

At the beginning of February, as the grip of winter began to lessen, the Celts celebrated Imbolc. This was the lambing and cheese making season, everyone was involved and had their part to play. It was also the Celtic celebration of the start of spring.
In the first days of February just before dawn, while the day was still in the grip of night, they gathered in the fort around the well in a circle holding hands. With heads bowed Paedur and Niwelyn, hooded and cloaked in black with soft brown leather boots, began a chant. The people joined in and a heavy air of serenity descended upon the group. Some women placed unlit candles and tapers around the fire.
As dawn began to lighten the sky Niwelyn, dressed in a full length midnight blue velvet gown, gently detached herself from the group. Taking a blazing firebrand from the open fire, she carried it over to the well and threw it into it.
"Goddess Brighid", she called, "bless our well and give it life and healing qualities".
Then, taking a small bottle from a leather bag hanging on her belt, she presented it to Paedur, also dressed in a full length midnight blue velvet gown; it contained three drops of liquid.
"Goddess Cerridwen", she said loudly, "bestow upon Lord Paedur the knowledge of the past, present and future".
He took the bottle from her, raised it to his lips and solemnly drank then handed the bottle back to her.
"Goddess Mebh, bestow upon the town the gifts of fertility and regeneration. Goddess Olwen, bestow love and rebirth upon these people", she requested.
Going back to the fire she placed a cornucopia and a stick with a carving of two snakes entwined around it beside the hearth.

"Goddess Rosmerta, bestow fertility and wealth upon this town", she requested.

She placed a small amphora of water on the other side of the hearth.

"River Goddess Sequana, bestow health upon these townspeople", she requested.

As the sky became light Paedur called out, "Virgin Mother Goddess, enter and grace us with your presence".

Elaena, hooded and cloaked in black, entered the courtyard followed closely by Násuin in full battle gear on high alert. As she walked towards the open fire some women approached and whispered their requests into her ears. When she got to the fire she stopped and stood, Násuin gently removed her cloak. Dressed in a light green coloured velvet gown with soft brown leather boots and her hair unbound, she held a dish of flowers set with a candle which she had hidden under her cloak. Niwelyn lighted a long taper from the fire, lit Elaena's candle and escorted her over to the fire. She took several tapers and lit them from the ceremonial candle, handed them to the women who in turn lit the candles and tapers around the fire.

Paedur approached her and, taking the dish from her, he bowed deeply and said, "Welcome Virgin Mother".

There was a quiet snigger from the warriors which Násuin silenced with a cold stare. The women also looked at them with cold distain; there was no further comment from his men.

"Thank you Lord Paedur", she replied, "it is an honour to be here".

Paedur leaned toward her and kissed her on the forehead, Niwelyn kissed her on the cheek.

The sun rose and bathed the courtyard with brilliant light.

Turning to the crowd Paedur called, "Let us celebrate the return of the light with a feast". Instantly food was brought from the warriors' dwellings and placed on the tables in the great hall. Everyone filed into the great hall and consumed the food.

Standing behind her Násuin gently put Elaena's cloak around her shoulders, his hands lingering while she fastened it with a clasp.

"You were absolutely amazing this morning", he said with admiration.
"Thank you, I was so nervous", she replied.
"It did not show", he said.
"Paedur prepared me for this ceremony", she said.
"Then he is a good teacher", he stated.
"It seems Paedur and Niwelyn are already in the hall".
Walking around in front of her, holding his right arm out palm upward he said, "May I have the honour of escorting the Goddess into breakfast"?
Smiling and bowing she said, "You may, Warrior, thank you".
She placed her right hand in his and together they walked into the great hall and joined the feast.

Later that day Paedur took Elaena down to the farm just outside the town on the banks of the River Gyffin. It was on a large plot of land with a collection of stone buildings painted white on the outside with pointed terracotta roofs, some walled off with the same white paint and some fenced off with wooden fences. The farm was divided up into sections each dedicated to some product or activity.
He showed her the ploughs, explaining "Some are made of oak, some made of ash."
"In each section is grown barley, wheat, spelt, leeks, onions, beans, cabbage, lettuce, carrots". He handed her each one and allowed her to inspect them and keep each one for herself.
"Sheep are kept in a pen and sometimes allowed to roam in the fields outside the farm, their milk is a popular drink and their wool is used for clothing", he explained. He allowed her to stroke the fleece and gave her a small piece of wool.
Moving on to the next section he explained, "Pig meat is called pork and is a popular food. Cattle are used as working animals to pull trailers and sometimes used for meat and milk. The most important animal on a farm is the ox because it is the one that is most used for pushing, pulling and transporting, donkeys and mules are also used for this purpose".

Moving to yet another section he explained, "Chickens are kept for their eggs and meat, ducks and geese are also used for meat. Horses are bred mainly for the army and as a means of transport. Goats provide milk and their hair is used to make rope and sacks".

He gave her a little strand of goat hair and a sack to put all her samples into.

He then brought her over to the dovecotes and explained that, "Pigeons are used as food in the winter when other meat is scarce".

Then he brought her over to another part of the farm to see how the lambs were born and cared for.

In the dairy he allowed her to see how the cheese was made, she was delighted when she was handed a small block of cheese that was made especially for her.

"I do not like all these smells they are making me feel unwell", she said turning up her nose and rubbing her belly.

"Then it is time for us to go", he said nodding, and guided her out of the farm.

As they walked back through the town he showed her the dwellings, "These ones", he said, "are made of timber, they are efficient and warm".

"These are like my house", she said.

He nodded, "Exactly".

In the square he walked her around the temple and explained, "We build our great halls with timber walls and columns topped with beams of wood and thatched roofs. The Romans build theirs with stone walls and either columns of wood or stone".

"Like our hall", she asked.

He nodded, "That is correct", he replied. The Romans copied their architecture from the Greeks. they use only the finest materials because they want their buildings to be strong and safe and last for a long time. The roof is made from terracotta slate, the walls are made of concrete and columns are used to hold the building together. Each column is topped with a design, as you will notice some are different than others and

that is because some of them are Ionic, some are Doric and some of them are Tuscan".
She shook her head, "Words, strange words, you fill my head with strange words", holding her head in her hands she said, "Enough I cannot hear any more".
She strode off heading towards the great hall.

***

In March as the days became warmer longer and brighter, Paedur began instructing the children again. He showed them how to read and write, he taught them how to remember things and made them act out plays.
One day he told them, "We need to collect stones and pebbles and form a large circle."
The children were delighted and immediately set off around the courtyard collecting as many stones as they could. One child hurt himself when he dropped a stone on his foot; Elaena immediately rushed over to him and soothed him drying his tears. Another scraped her knee and became very distressed so Elaena hugged the child and comforted her. Both Paedur and Elaena helped the children to form the circle making sure that it was perfectly round.
He then brought them down to the glass maker in the town to collect broken pieces of coloured glass; Paedur gave Elaena some money and got her to pay for them. The glass maker winked to her as she handed him the money and gave her an old worn basket to help them carry the pieces back to the fort. When they got back to the fort Paedur drew out pictures of the zodiac signs, broke the children up into teams, and set them about forming the signs around the circle with the pieces of glass. He took half the group and Elaena took the other half. For hours they worked forming the signs singing, chatting and laughing as they worked. By evening their task was complete and Paedur made them stand and admire their work. That night everyone went home happy and satisfied.

In March the Romans again celebrated the progression of spring with a day of festivities. The day began early in the Temple at the shrine of Vesta officiated by the six Vestal Virgins with the rekindling of the perpetual fire. After the ceremony horse races were held outside the Temple in honour of their war God Mars. In the afternoon the people had picnics down by the River Conwy celebrating their Goddess Anna Perenna. They believed that they would live as long as they could drink cups of wine so the youths and men set up a competition to see who could drink the most. The day finished with a trumpet ceremony outside the temple to Mars requesting him to grant them success in battle.

The Celts celebrated their Spring Equinox where the days and the nights were of equal length. On the morning of the 25th of March at dawn they gathered in the courtyard facing east around the Zodiac circle. Paedur and Niwelyn, dressed in emerald green velvet gowns, black cloaks and soft brown leather boots, placed themselves inside the circle at a small temporary altar. They began a chant holding hands and chanted for twenty minutes as the sky lightened.

Niwelyn then called, “People, present your gifts”

The farmers presented their seeds and corn, the women presented spring flowers and the children presented wild flowers. The men presented items according to their profession and the warriors presented weapons.

When all gifts had been placed on the altar Niwelyn called, “Goddess Olwen enter and accept our gifts”.

Immediately Elaena, dressed in a brown velvet gown with spring flowers sewn onto it, her hair wild and loose with a crown of wild flowers on her head and soft brown leather boots, entered the courtyard.

Paedur greeted her, “Welcome Goddess Olwen, join us”.

Elaena walked towards the group and a gap was made for her to walk through to the altar.

Niwelyn greeted her, “Goddess, accept our gifts and grant our town, and its people, your blessing”.

Elaena took the basket of seeds and mixed it with the basket of corn saying, "I bless these with health and strength, they may now be planted and will yield good crop".
Paedur and Niwelyn bowed. Then Niwelyn called, "The Goddess needs a champion who will volunteer?"
A voice replied, "I will".
The crowd turned toward the voice, Násuin emerged from his dwelling dressed in bright yellow bracae and a long sleeved matching thigh length tunic with soft brown leather boots. His long blond hair hung loosely to his shoulders, in his right hand he held a spear and again repeated, "I will champion the Goddess".
He made his way towards the circle and danced around each zodiac sign before presenting himself at the altar.
"Welcome Beli Mawr, Sun God. Go now into the world and fight for the Goddess and speak on her behalf".
Násuin bowed to Paedur and Niwelyn. Taking Elaena's hand in his, he escorted her out of the courtyard, as he did so the sun rose and bathed the fort in brilliant light.
Niwelyn then called, "Join us now in breakfast to celebrate the spring".
Everyone made their way to the great hall and partook of a grand feast. Outside the fort gate Elaena and Násuin, no longer in their roles as Goddess and Champion, shook themselves, stamped their feet on the ground several times and swung their arms in the air. As Elaena and Násuin they re-entered the courtyard and joined their people in the great hall. Immediately they made their way to Paedur and Niwelyn and after hugging each other mixed and mingled.

***

One day in April Paedur brought Elaena down to the bay and showed her the boats.
"These are called coracles, they are mostly round but some are oblong with rounded corners", he explained. They have

wickerwork frames with animal skins stretched over them to make them water proof".
He showed her how they were sewn together.
Pointing to the boats he explained, "The coracles are very light and can be picked up and carried but in the water they are very strong and they are used for short journeys. For longer journeys boats made of wood are used with long wooden poles called oars to help them move. Long poles rise up from the floors with long strong strings attached to sheets to catch the wind, these are called sails and are used to help move and steer the boats. The bigger boats you sometimes see further out are called cargo ships. These bring in oil, grain and wine from other countries and bring back clothes, jewellery and artistic objects of gold, bronze and enamel made by your people to far off lands".
"Would you like to get into one?" he asked.
"No", she replied, "I would probably fall out and drown".
"I assure you they are quite safe, no harm will come to you" he assured her.
Taking a deep breath she said, "All right, as long as you are with me perhaps I will be safe".
He brought her over to one of the boat men and negotiated the hire of one of the coracles for a short while. Helping her in to the boat he settled her down and they went a short way along the river. After a while he stopped and said, "Touch the water, feel it on your fingertips".
She did so.
"Now, turn your face to the sky and feel the heat of the sun on your skin".
She did as he instructed.
"Feel the air around you and the coolness of the breeze. Now close your eyes and breathe", he instructed
She did so but opened them quickly because the boat gently moved and broke her concentration. She looked around her.
Gently and quietly Paedur said, "Close your eyes, you are quite safe, no harm will come to you".
Slowly she closed her eyes again and in a soothing voice Paedur continued, "Now, close your eyes, listen to the sound of the

water...listen to the masts clinking on the boats...listen to the sound of the cart wheels on the dock...listen to the sound of the gulls overhead...now take in a deep breath and hold it in your chest...now slowly let it out. Now breathe in again and hold... and hold...and now let it go. Immediately breathe in again quickly and hold...and hold...and let go. Now this time, draw in a deep breath quietly and hold...and as you breathe out slowly and quietly...let go of all fear and pain and coldness".

Elaena shivered and opened her eyes looking around her with a startled look in her eyes. Paedur realised that she had experienced enough for now and brought her back to shore, thanked the boatman and lead her away.

They walked through the forest and he showed her the different trees, the Elm, the Larch and the Beech.

"My favourite one", he said, "is the Quercus robur, Oak. To Druids it is the most sacred of all trees; we use it in our medicines and ceremonies. It is a tree of great strength, stability and endurance".

Taking a leaf from each of the trees he allowed her to feel the difference between them and showed her how to distinguish each one.

Elaena, fed up listening, said indignantly, "What does it matter whether it is beech, elm or querysomething, one tree looks much the same as another to me".

Paedur took a deep breath and closed his eyes calming himself and replied, "Because, like people, they all have their own personality, strengths and weaknesses and are used for different things".

"Trees do not have personalities", she said stubbornly, "that is nonsense".

"No it is not" replied Paedur, patiently. Larix deciduas, Larch, has great confidence and we use it to help people overcome fear of failure and be more willing to engage in life. Ulmus procera, Elm, helps people who are overwhelmed by responsibility and helps them to be more confident and self-assured. Fagus sylvatica, Beech, is intolerant and tries to control the other trees around it. As a medicine we use it for people who control others to help them be more tolerant, lenient and understanding. Pinus sylvestris, Pine trees, are used to help people to overcome guilt and self-reproach and helps them to have a more balanced approach to life. Aesculus carnea, Red Chestnut, is used to help people overcome anxiety and helps them to be calm. Aesculus hippocastanum, White Chestnut, is used to help people who constantly worry to have a calm mind. We also use trees to make furniture and boats.

Shaking her head and striding off she said shrugging, "Elm, Oak, Beech, they all look the same to me, they are just trees, who cares".

Paedur remained standing where he was, he bowed his head and shook it letting out a deep sigh saying to himself, "Why do I bother, she is so exasperating, her attention span is so short and she quickly becomes bored. He remembered Niwelyn's words, "*be gentle with her...she is very young*". He smiled and his patience returned.

He set off in search of her and found her in the clearing outside the oak grove lying on her cloak resting. Taking off his cloak and lying down on it beside her, they lay in the sun together. They breathed in the air, as he had previously instructed, enjoying the warmth of the sun and watched the clouds.

Elaena said, pointing to one in particular, "Oh! Look, there is a horse".

Paedur pointed out another one saying, "There is a boat".

"No it is not", replied Elaena, "it is a cow".

"How can you possibly make out a cow in that cloud?" he asked amused.

"Because it is", she replied indignantly. "How can you see it as a boat"?

"Because it is", he replied matter-of-factly.

"Well I do not see it as such", she said defiantly.

"It seems we see things very differently", he replied, exasperation returning.

"So it seems" she replied. "I see things and think nothing of them; they are there and have always been there. You see things

and there is always something to know about them, something to learn from them".
Abruptly she got to her feet and smoothing down her burgundy velvet dress she said angrily, "This dress is too warm; it makes me wet and sticky".
She walked off with an arrogant stride.
Paedur took a deep breath and let it out with a low deep growl. Closing his eyes, he gritted his teeth and clenched his fists. In his head he heard the words, "*be gentle with her...she is very young*". He shook his head and got to his feet, picking up their cloaks, and followed her back to the great hall. The next day he brought her two ankle length light thin tunics, which he called stolas, a long light veil which he called a palla, and two pairs of light leather sandals with straps.
One day in late April Paedur and Elaena were sitting in the courtyard relaxing. All around them the people went about their business attending to their duties. Paedur began telling her a little about history.
"The Celts were once a great and powerful people", he began, "they once ruled all of Britannia and most of Europe. We do not have a ruler like the Romans have but we do have a common language. The Romans call us uncivilised because we wear our hair long and we wear bracae instead of tunics and paint our bodies when we go to battle. We are called the iron people because most of our tools and weapons are made of iron, we have always been fighters. Many years ago we defeated the Romans in a great battle in a place called Allia and defeated them, since then they have been determined to conquer us and wipe us out".
"The Romans first came to Britannia around our year 48 and the first thing they did was to go to Ynys Mon and kill most of my people, the Druids. We have since rebuilt our numbers and our Order but have not recovered fully".
"Around our year 60 they again made a bigger effort to control us and our Warrior Queen Boadicea, of the Iceni tribe, fought hard against them. Unfortunately she and her army were defeated and the Romans have been controlling us ever since".

"After Boadicea's defeat Londinium became the administrative centre for the Romans in Britannia and it is there that their rule is strongest. Scotia, Hibernia, and here in Cymru, we are less influenced by them but we still have a lot of Roman things in our town. Our current town is built over the old Roman fort of Kanovium and we are a relatively rich town because of this".
"Where did the Celts come from?", she asked.
He nodded, "There were two groups and both very different in nature", he replied. "The first group were called the "lowland Celts", who hailed from the middle of Europe and were agriculturally oriented. They spread across Europe many years ago and integrated with the indigenous peoples of the countries they came across and settled in them contributing very much to the economy. They were a matriarchal people and burned their dead".
"The second group are referred to as the "true Celts" who came from the mountainous areas of Europe. They were a military type of people and love fighting and even sacked Roma and Delphi before coming to Britannia. They are inclined to bury their dead in the ground and are more patriarchal. It is from that group that we are descended which is why we like to fight and have such good warriors. It is also why the Romans are so intent on crushing us and making us take on the Roman ways. However, in spite of their martial prowess, they are also a sensitive people and appreciate music, stories and philosophy".
"The Romans have tried to crush us but are finding us harder to conquer than our brethren in Europe. We are on the fringes of the Empire and have had a very strong culture of our own, and still have", he continued.
"The Celts are a free people and believe that even a poor person can become rich with hard work and sponsorship. The Romans believe that they are the rulers of the world and that all the people they conquer should be their slaves and serve them", he went on.
"Can their slaves never be free", she asked.
"Not really", he inclined his head, "although they do allow the military to earn their freedom after many years of service, he

replied. There were many ranks within the military but there was always a Commander-in-chief", he replied.
"Do we have one of those?" she asked.
"Yes we do, we have Násuin", he replied.
From the shelter of the stables Násuin observed the lesson and listened intently to Paedur's recounting of Celtic history.
Elaena yawned and looked around her; she got up and walked away. Paedur, realising that she had heard enough, decided to end the lesson and continued resting. Násuin returned to the stables.
A few nights later Elaena seemed tired, after dinner she excused herself and lay on her bed, within minutes she was asleep. Paedur quietly left their room and went to visit Niwelyn; he had not seen her for some time.
She greeted him and handing him a glass of wine asked, "How goes it, is Elaena progressing well"
Paedur quietly growled, gritted his teeth and clenched his fists saying, "Sometimes she exasperates me, her attention is short and she is easily distracted and becomes bored very quickly. She refuses to listen when I explain things to her and she walks off shrugging. Sometimes I wonder why I bother".
Niwelyn nodded and opened her mouth to speak but Paedur interrupted, "I know...be gentle...she is young". Niwelyn closed her mouth again and looked at Paedur.
"And your friendship, how goes that?", she asked.
"We are good friends, I think, I certainly enjoy her company and she appears to enjoy mine. She has changed much and is more confident, her bruises are gone and her skin has become soft and fragrant. She has filled out somewhat and has a more rounded figure, she looks well; sometimes I do not recognise her. I remember the skinny girl I took on a year ago, now she is a woman and a lady", he replied.
"And love?", Niwelyn asked.
"That is the next set of instructions", he said, staring into the fire, the flames reflecting in his eyes. "But first I would like you to instruct her in the use of herbs, I hope she will listen to you better than she does me".

"I will do what I can", she replied.
He remained with Niwelyn for a while and lay with her, together they rested and when she fell into a deep contented sleep he gently left and returned to the great hall.

***

A few days later Elaena, dressed in a long green plaid gown, trimmed with a gold pattern at the hem and soft leather boots, knocked on Niwelyn's door, when it was opened she said, "Paedur told me to come to you for instruction".
Niwelyn smiled "Come in, you are most welcome". She nodded and held the door open for Elaena.
Stepping into the roundhouse Elaena noticed the open fire in the middle of the room with a cauldron hanging on a tripod over it, something was bubbling gently in it. She also noticed twigs and leaves hanging from the rafters. Niwelyn stood back and allowed her to observe in her own time. There was a heavy air of fragrance that Elaena could not identify and she wrinkled her nose.
"I do not like the smell in here", she said, "it reminds me of the things my mother gives me when I am sick, they smell bad and taste worse".
Niwelyn nodded, "Some do, some do not but they all help to heal in their own way, let me show you".
Walking over to the fire she scooped out a small amount of liquid and brought it over to a small table at the end of the house.
Elaena followed her and looked over her shoulder.
"Aine, Goddess of herbalists and healers and Airmid, Goddess of medicinal plants, bless our work here today and grant us the gift of healing", Niwelyn requested.
Niwelyn took a jar of honey and scooped out a small amount in to a bowl; she then poured a small amount of the liquid into it and mixed them.
"This is Symphytum", she said. "It is used to heal wounds".

When she had finished the mixture she put it into a small jar and handed it to Elaena.
Next she took out a big bottle of liquid and poured a small amount of it into another small bottle. When it was half full she stopped and put the big bottle down on the table, took a jug of wine and poured it into the small bottle filling it up.
"This is Solidago Virgaurea mixed with red wine; it is used for kidney infections".
Elaena sighed, "Strange words, you are as bad as Paedur all I hear is strange words".
She shook her head.
Niwelyn nodded and patiently she explained, "Symphytum" is also called Comfrey and Solidago is also called Golden Rod".
"Then why can we not use the easy name", Elaena asked.
"Because", explained Niwelyn,"these are medicines and therefore we always use their Latin name. The common name is for the common people who have no training in medicine".
Elaena nodded.
Taking another big bottle Niwelyn again poured out a small amount into a small bottle like she did before and explained, "This is Silybum Marianum, Milk Thistle, it is used for liver problems. Those who drink a lot of wine and beer are much in need of this herb".
Repeating the process she explained, "And this one is Mentha Piperita, Peppermint, we use it to help people with sick tummy.
Elaena walked away shaking her head, "Strange words, I grow tired of strange words".
Quietly Niwelyn asked, "Are you tired of red wine"?
"No I am not", replied Elaena.
"Then drink with me, our lesson is over for today".
Taking the three bottles she brought them over to Elaena and handed them to her saying, "These are for you".
Taking them Elaena replied sullenly, "Diolch".
She sat down on the bench and put the bottles and jar on the floor.

Niwelyn poured out two glasses of wine and handed one to Elaena, sitting down opposite her she asked, “How goes it with Paedur?”

Elaena pursed her lips and answered sullenly, “He is all the time teaching I cannot do anything without him explaining what it is, what it does and how to use it. He is very neat and tidy and insists that everything be done right; he does not let me relax for a second”.

Niwelyn nodded and said, “You know that he has your best interests at heart”.

Elaena sighed and nodded, “I do not know what I know” she replied. “But I do know that I feel safe and protected when I am with him”.

“Do you miss the taberna?” Niwelyn asked.

“No, I do not”, replied Elaena. “I am happier with Paedur in the great hall”.

“And your family?” asked Niwelyn “Do you miss them?”.

“Certainly not”, replied Elaena.

Both fell into a quiet silence staring into the fire.

After a few minutes Elaena put her glass down on the floor and stood up saying, “I had better go now. I have been away for some time, Paedur will be worried about me”.

“I very much doubt that”, said Niwelyn, picking up the jar and bottles, “he knows you are safe with me. Here”, she said handling them to Elaena, “these are for you”.

“Diolch”, said Elaena, taking them from her.

“Godspeed”, said Niwelyn quietly as she opened the door.

Elaena left and returned to the great hall.

Chapter Seven

Paedur's appearance had changed since he came to Conwy; he had grown a beard which he kept clipped and very short, although his hair was still long and quite dark, his beard was white. The lines on his face and around his eyes were a little deeper; his eyes more intent and his presence stronger, he was becoming more Celtic looking and mostly spoke Cymraeg. He continued his writings and translations and the whole town benefited from his presence among them, he was completely accepted and the children adored him.

One day when they were in their room together Elaena asked him about the pendent he always wore. She had noticed it in their early days and had meant to ask him about it but there was so much to learn that she never got around to it. She accepted it as part of him and noticed that it was the only jewellery he wore.

It was rather large, approximately two inches wide and made of gold, there was an inner circle surrounded by an outer circle; between the circles were markings. Inside the inner circle were two serpents joined at the tail and rising up forming a circle facing each other at the top, the scales on their bodies were clearly visible, one was red, the other dark green enamel. It was an impressive piece of jewellery and somehow looked right on him, it hung around his neck on a heavy golden chain.

"What is it?" she asked.

"It is a Caduceus, the herald's staff" he replied, the traditional symbol of the Greek God Hermes. It has many meanings and is associated with commerce, eloquence, trickery, negotiation, alchemy and wisdom. It has been described as possessing the ability to charm the eyes of men".

"It is also believed to symbolise creative energy, the markings is my name written in Celtic runes. The red serpent is male and associated with our God Dewi, the green one is female and associated with our Goddess Rosmerta, both are joined at the base symbolising the things they have in common. They rise

separately symbolising the differences between them and their independence, at the top they face each other as equals", he explained.
"Is it Roman or Celtic?", she asked.
"Both, the serpent is sacred to both Roman and Celt", he replied nodding, "To the Romans it symbolises the Empire, Red for the west and Green for the east, to the Celts it is a symbol of wisdom, in this way it symbolises the two different cultures, peoples if you will, both equal, both separate, both with things in common".
"Is it magical?" she asked, looking at it more closely.
"To the Celts and the Greeks it is because of its association with alchemy and wisdom", he replied.
"You said it has many meanings, what are the other ones?" she asked.
"Later in your training I will tell you", he replied.
"Why not now?" she asked.
"You would not understand however, now that you have asked, I think you are ready for the next level of training", he replied.

***

While the townspeople were preparing for the Bealteinne Festival Elaena was receiving her first instructions in Druid lovemaking. As a prostitute she thought she knew all about sex but soon she discovered she knew nothing.
Paedur explained that "A gentle touch of the lips can be far more sensual than a full kiss. More passion can be packed into a touch of the cheek than a night of rampant sex. Feeling loved is much more important than being loved and if a person has both they are truly lucky. The idea behind Druid lovemaking is exactly this because it is what you are thinking and feeling while making love that influences the magic created".
To help her understand he demonstrated what he meant, to Elaena this was a strange experience. To learn about something she had once made a living out of was weird yet, with Paedur it was like nothing she had ever experienced before. During this

part of her training she felt like a little girl and this made her feel very uncomfortable.

In May the festival of Bealteinne/Ludi Florales was celebrated and there was much excitement in the town. The days had become quite long and warm, the birds sang loudly and the flowers were in bloom. The Romans danced around the area outside the temple decked in floral garments. Their Goddess Flora was decorated with flowers and all around her statue tables were piled high with flowers.

Early on the morning of the festivities Niwelyn brought the children into the forest and showed them the sweet-scented hawthorn which was bursting with blossom.

"This is the flower of the May", she explained. "It is usually thought to be unlucky but today you may each take a branch of it into your homes but it must be gone by tomorrow".

She carefully cut off branches and gave one to each child then she cut several more and asked the children to place them in a basket which she had brought with her.

"We will use these branches later for our festivities; they will be placed on the altar."

The children were delighted that their work would be seen by everyone in the town

Carrying the basket she brought them in to her roundhouse and showed them a simple light green garment which she had laid out on the bench.

"This year, Elaena is our May Queen", she told them. "We are going to decorate the garment with flowers for her to wear at the ceremony later".

The children squealed with excitement and watched as Niwelyn put the first few flowers on then copied her and covered the dress with flowers.

At this time the Druids sanctioned and blessed marriages or hand fasting as they called it and this particular year three couples presented themselves. It was a very romantic time and couples that had been together for many years reminded themselves of the love that had brought them together. Younger

man and women began to watch and choose who their partner would be next year and dream of when it would be their turn.
At mid-morning Paedur and Niwelyn, both dressed in green gowns with soft brown leather sandals on their feet, began the parade at the Fort Gate. This year, representing the May Queen Creiddylad Elaena, dressed in a light green gown covered with flowers, a crown of flowers on her head and a basket of flowers and hawthorn in her hands, rode through the streets on a flower decked cart pulled by Násuin on his horse. The children glowed with pride as she made her way through the streets.
Násuin, dressed in dark brown bracae with a dark green thigh length tunic and soft brown leather boots, his hair hung loosely to his shoulders, this year represented the Green Man, the God of Nature.
As she passed, the people followed behind the cart. When they arrived at the altar in the oak grove, it was bedecked with flowers and the hawthorn branches that the children had gathered earlier in the day. All the children had very proud faces. Making their way to the altar and facing south-east Paedur and Niwelyn began the chant. One by one each person joined in and after a few minutes the forest rang with the sound of their voices.
When the chant stopped there was a moment's silence. Násuin dismounted his horse and assisted Elaena down from the cart. She handed him the basket of flowers and accepted his help, when she was steady he handed her back the basket and accompanied her to the altar. He looked longingly on her but, knowing she was Paedur's woman, he knew he hadn't a chance. He was standing right behind her but she wasn't even aware of him, her whole attention was on Paedur. When she arrived at the altar she carefully placed her basket in the centre and bowed to Paedur and Niwelyn, they returned the bow and she joined them standing at the altar. The women approached the May Pole and each one tied a coloured ribbon around it, Paedur nodded to Elaena and she danced around the May Pole. Násuin stood close by on alert with his left hand loosely on the top of his sword watching everything.

Paedur then stepped away from the altar and lit the bonfire. He nodded to Násuin who ran towards Elaena and chased her into the forest. Under the branches of the hawthorn he caught her and led her back to the altar. Together; hand in hand, they jumped over the fire.
Niwelyn called, "Goddess Creiddylad, bless us with abundance and health this year".
Paedur nodded to Elaena.
"Join me in song, fest and dance", Elaena replied.
Immediately the women dished out the food, the musicians played their instruments and sang and the children played.
After the ceremonies Paedur kissed and hugged Niwelyn, "Thank you for your participation in the ceremonies" he said, caressing the smooth skin of her face.
"I am your ceremonial consort" she said, looking lovingly into his eyes relishing the touch of his hands.
"You are also my friend...and my strength", he continued.
"You have strength a plenty of your own, Paedur", she said.
"Aye, I have that", he sighed, "but you keep me grounded", he said affectionately.
"Someone has to", she replied smiling.
"Forgive me, Niwelyn, I must take leave of you now, there is something I have to do" he said.
"Elaena?" she asked.
"Yes", he nodded.
"Go then, do what you must", she replied nodding.
He kissed her again and then, turning, he walked over to Elaena, taking her hand, he led her to the edge of the grove out of sight of the celebrating people. Quietly they stood together leaning against an oak tree; Paedur felt its strength course up through his spine filling him with energy.
Slowly, quietly he drew Elaena to him, her full body leaning against him; he held her face between his hands and kissed her full on the mouth. Elaena's head spun and she broke out into a sweat, her breath caught in her throat, her legs and insides turned to jelly. She felt she was going to collapse; she clung to him so that she wouldn't fall and waited for the kiss to end.

Pulling quietly away from her he gently sat her on the ground against the tree; once he was sure she was safe, he walked away. He knew exactly what he had done and how he had made her feel but he wanted her to feel the after shock...alone.

Unable to move and barely able to breath, Elaena lay against the tree totally devastated, every nerve, cell and fibre of her being tingled; she shook from head to toe. She had never experienced anything so deep, so profound and so soul shattering in all her life. Taking several deep breaths, she closed her eyes and willed herself to calm down. Once her breathing had slowed and she felt stronger, she got to her feet unsteadily and returned to the fire.

Paedur looked up and smiled, he could see the state of mind she was in, he brought over a cup of wine to her and she drank it in silence grateful of its strength.

Niwelyn watched from her position close to the fire and knew exactly what had happened. Násuin had found himself a willing maid and looked like he was enjoying her company. Paedur and Elaena returned to the great hall alone, when she was safe in bed and asleep he sat into his chair watching her. He was well aware of how cruel it would seem he had been to her earlier that night. He wanted her to know the difference between sex and love, only when she had fully grasped this would he be able to train her in the sexual arts.

Her former life as a prostitute, and her own tempestuous nature, were exactly why he had chosen her as his apprentice, she reminded him of himself as a trainee Druid so many years ago. He too had been arrogant in his own way and equally unwilling to learn, however, he had a great teacher who eventually brought him round and turned him into a Druid of formidable power, which he had put to good use in Londinium. He wanted to harness her fiery passion and defiance and show her how to turn it into creative magic for the benefit of all. A Paedagogus he may be, but he was also a master of the magical sexual arts. Realising how tired he was he lay down and slept.

***

Elaena's training continued with the finer arts of Roman hygiene, Paedur presented her with a set of implements.
"They look like hooks and spoons", she said.
"These are strigils", he explained. "The Romans cover their bodies in oils and then scrap them off with the strigils. A large part of every Roman's day is spent bathing, their bathhouses are dedicated entirely to socialising, bathing and massage. Our one here in the fort is tiny and extremely basic compared to such buildings in Londinium and even the bathhouse in the town is small compared to the ones in Londinium".
Going over to the press he took out some small bottles with strong smelling oils and mixed them with a base oil,
"Some oils are used for injury, some are used to heal, this one, Anthemis nobilis, Roman Camomile, is for relaxation", he explained.
Bringing her back to her bed he gave Elaena a full body massage, by the time he was finished she was asleep.
Under Paedur's tutelage Elaena blossomed, now very confident and self-assured, she responded to his questions and completed her tasks, she became radiant and beautiful. Her chestnut red hair was vibrant and her skin was now tanned, soft and smelt of lavender. Her slim frame had filled out a little and she had a tight firm body which she covered with tight fitting long tunics accentuating her natural curves. Her defiance showed in her strong purposeful stride and the way she flicked her hair back.
The warriors cat called and whistled as she walked by, some of them making rude remarks, Násuin would silence them with a stern look and work them harder but when he was sure he was not being watched, he devoured her with his eyes. The Romans too began to notice her and behaved much the same as the warriors, their General would silence them too but he also kept a close eye on her, watching.

***

One day in mid May she returned from an errant rather flushed and annoyed and she explained to Paedur, "They are very rude".

"Who are?" he asked.
"The warriors and the Roman soldiers", she replied. "They call me slut and harlot", she said pouting. "They make rude suggestions and try to grab at me".
"Well, if you do not mind me saying so...My Lady", he said bowing, "you do look rather...attractive and they could be forgiven for wanting to grab at you".
"Well I do not like it", she said sullenly. "It makes me feel bad and reminds me of the taberna".
He held her in his arms kissing her softly, comforting and reassuring her; she instantly calmed down then he sat her at the table and gave her some writing to distract her from her upset.
One day in late May Elaena returned from a task, her pale blue stola was stained with grass and dried earth; she had been picking herbs for Paedur. As she approached the great hall she felt triumphant that she had found the correct ones and picked them in the correct way. As she entered the courtyard the warriors heckled her; Násuin was away that day so they had no restraint and blocked her path.
"Where are you going little one", one of them leered at her.
"Going back to daddy, are you", another said.
"Come with us, little one, we will show you a good time", another leered.
They all pressed closer.
Cupping his hand around his crotch another one leered, "I have something here for you little one".
"You will not want to go back to Daddy after you have been with us", leered another.
Breathing deeply she tried to run but they closed in around her circling her, taunting, jeering and leering in her face. She felt dizzy and began to shake, she looked around for a gap but there was none. She became fearful; they were so close now she could smell their stinking breath and sweat. Just as one of them made a grab for her a horse and rider entered the courtyard, with a roar Násuin dismounted and dispersed his men. Elaena dropped her basket of herbs and stood shaking breathing heavily.

Going over to her he took her hands in his noting her dishevelled appearance and distress and, looking into her eyes said, "My Lady, forgive them, they sometimes forget themselves".
Are you alright?", he asked.
Shaking from head to toe she was unable to answer.
Turning to his men he roared, "GET BACK TO WORK. THERE IS NO TIME TO WASTE. YOU HAVE THINGS TO DO".
Turning back to Elaena he said, "My Lady, sit with me a while and catch your breath".
Gently he led her over to the fire, she leaned heavily on his arm as he walked her across the courtyard. He was acutely aware of her hand on his arm and relished the feeling. Gently he sat her down on one of the oak logs and sat down beside her, facing her watching her intently.
"Did they hurt you?" he asked.
She shook her head.
"Have they harmed you in any way", he asked concerned.
Again she shook her head.
He breathed a sigh of relief and continued, "My Lady, please forgive them, when I am away they are not as attentive to their duties as they should be and get distracted", he explained. "I am truly sorry that they have upset you and I will see to it that this does not happen again".
Elaena took a deep breath and gathering herself said, "Diolch, Násuin, I am grateful for your concern. No harm has been done, no injury has been sustained, they frightened me and I did not know how to react."
Násuin, assured, said "Thank the Gods for that".
Relaxing he asked her, "How goes it with you and Paedur?"
"All is well", she replied. "He is good to me and I feel safe with him", he takes care of me and teaches me things".
Nodding Násuin asked, "Are you happy with him?"
Watching her intently he awaited her reply.
Nodding she said, "Yes, I think so. Sometimes he frightens me but most of the time I am content in his company. At least he

does not beat me or rape me like my father used to do, so, yes, I think I am happy with him".

Silently Násuin drank in her appearance, her tanned skin, her round face and classic cheekbones, her full lips and bright blue eyes, her chestnut red hair tumbling down her back in waves. Her closeness to him and the lavender scent of her, the sound of her voice and the innocent look in her eyes. Her breathing had returned to normal now and she seemed calm and relaxed. Wishing he could hold her and keep her locked in this moment, he said, "I think you are calm now, My Lady, perhaps I should return you to your quarters".

"Diolch, Násuin, there is no need to", she replied. "I think I can find my own way back, now that those horrible men are gone. I think I will be safe now".

Standing up and taking her hands in his he looked deep into her eyes saying, "Well if you are sure then I shall take my leave of you, good day, My Lady".

He bowed deeply and, holding her hands in his for a moment longer, he released them and allowed her to walk away. As she walked across the courtyard and picked up her basket of herbs he watched her every step, her every move and committed this moment to memory.

Mumbling to herself Elaena climbed the stairs. Breathing heavily, she strode down the corridor, pushed the door open and flung the basket of herbs on the floor. All triumph now gone, angrily she said, "Those men, those horrible men".

Paedur remained writing at his desk and quietly asked, "What men".

"The warriors", she replied angrily. "They blocked my path when I came in to the courtyard and circled me leering at me trying to grab at me".

She breathed heavily.

"Did they get hold of you?" he asked.

Still breathing hard she replied, "No, just when they were about to Násuin came in and dispersed them".

"Ah! So that was what I heard, I wondered what was happening", he said nodding.

"But you did not offer any help", she said angrily.
"No, I did not, I did not need to, Násuin took care of the situation expertly", he said. "No harm has come to you so all is well", he shrugged.
Angrily she picked up the basket of herbs and flung them at him saying, "There are your precious herbs, next time, pick them yourself".
She strode over to her bed and flung herself face down on it breathing hard.
Paedur quietly stood up, put the herbs back into the basket and walked over to the table. Putting the basket down, quietly he said, "I am going out now; when I come back I want this room tidy and swept clean".
Turning to face him, "What do you think I am", she shot at him, "a slave".
A smile curled around his lips and a gleam came into his eyes, "I bought you, did I not", he replied, laughter just barely hidden in his voice.
"You told me I am a free person", she replied angrily.
"And now I am asking you to tidy up. Have it done by the time I return", he commanded leaving the room.
Standing up and staring angrily at the door, with her hands on her hips, shaking her head, making a funny face, in a funny voice, she repeated his words, "Have it done by the time I return".
Then, in her own voice, she continued, "I will show him tidy".
Immediately she opened the press and threw the towels on the floor, crossing the room she threw his pens on the floor and swept some papyri off the desk. She kicked his boots apart, scattered his tunics and flung his blanket on to the floor. She threw his pestle and mortar on to the floor and flung the sickle across the room. She poured red wine on to the hearth stones and racked some ash out of the fire and threw it on to his magic circle.
Her anger spent, she stood in the middle of the room breathing heavily, her hair dishevelled, her stola dusty with ash and a wild

look in her eyes. She looked around her at the complete mess she had created and said out loud, "Now there is tidy, Paedur". The door opened and he walked in, closing the door behind him, he stood staring at her. He looked around the room taking in the state of it.

"Is this what you call tidy" he asked, in a restrained voice barely hiding his anger.

"What is the meaning of this", he asked, his voice hard, his eyes angry.

"I have had enough, I am tired of doing what I am told. I grow weary from endless tasks and lessons" she replied, angrily shaking her head.

"It was your choice" he flashed back at her, his face turning red.

"I HAD NO CHOICE", she roared back at him.

"Look at my tools, look at my bed", he said scanning the room, "HOW DARE YOU VIOLATE ME" he roared, his eyes narrowing.

Elaena stood staring at him defiantly.

"I do not believe you could do this after all I have done for you", he continued.

"After all you have done for me", she replied hotly. I was better off at home and in the taberna, at least I got paid there".

Inwardly she was frightened, this reminded her of home and her father, but she couldn't let Paedur see this, so she continued defiantly, "I would be better off back there".

"Return to it then, you are more trouble than you are worth", he replied angrily.

He stepped back and opened the door for her; she brushed past him angrily and rushed from the great hall. Stumbling through the streets crying no one taunted her, her distress was plainly visible. They guessed she had exchanged angry words with Paedur and inwardly felt pity for her. A wonderful person he may be, but when he was angry, in his presence was not the place to be.

Násuin saw her leave and followed her at a distance. She ran down to the beach and curled up at the water's edge crying, deep sobs racking her whole body. After a while she calmed down and stared out at the bay in front of her. Although the incident had frightened her and reminded her of home, she had to admit that there was one very big difference between Paedur and her father. Even in his anger, she still felt loved by Paedur, with her father, all she felt was fear and disgust.

Násuin stood at a discrete distance watching her, he had heard their altercation, and although he knew she was quite safe, he used the incident as an excuse to pretend that he was guarding her; at least that is the story he would tell Paedur later. He wished he could go to her and calm her down, like he did before, but felt this time, it was inappropriate so he just watched and waited.

A few minutes after Elaena left the room Paedur also left, breathing hard and with a purposeful stride, furious and mumbling to himself with a fierce look of anger on his face. Everyone got out of his way, even the children shrank back from him.

In the forest Niwelyn was softly playing a stringed instrument and singing quietly to herself. When she saw Paedur approaching she stopped and waited. Once he was in ear shot he exploded, "That woman how dare she violate me, who does she think she is"?

"I take it you mean Elaena", she replied calmly.

Paedur nodded and continued, breathing hard, "I ask her to tidy up and she makes a complete mess, scattering everything all over the place", he said making angry gestures. "Truly she is more trouble than she is worth", he continued angrily.

"Did she say why she did it", asked Niwelyn.

"She said she was weary and tired of lessons and tasks", he replied.

"Well she has had to learn rather a lot in a very short space of time", said Niwelyn. "It is a lot for a young girl to take in, be gentle, she will come round", she advised.

"Be gentle...right now I feel like killing her" he said, gritting his teeth and clenching his fists.

"Remember when you were a young Druid", she asked. "Were you always a model student, did you always obey your master" she asked quietly, watching Paedur.
He stopped, closed his eyes remembering and relaxed, after a few minutes he smiled patiently, "No," he replied, taking a deep calming breath. No, I used to think my master was quite stupid actually" he replied, running his hands through his hair.
"Well there you are then, imagine how Elaena feels about you right now" she said intently, watching Paedur.
He stared back at her and smiled affectionately, "Elyn, Elyn, always the voice of reason and wisdom" he said, gently shaking his head. "Thank you, My Lady" he continued, bowing.
"You are busy, I have disturbed you, I am sorry" he said quietly. Taking a deep breath he turned and walked away, as he did so Niwelyn noticed that all anger was gone from him. She picked up her instrument and resumed playing.
Calm now Elaena returned to the great hall, Násuin followed her keeping his distance and stayed behind her until she started to climb the steps. Quietly she entered their room, it was now completely tidy and Paedur sat writing at his desk, his back turned to the door.
She put her hands on his shoulders and timidly said, "I am sorry".
Taking a deep breath and standing up, he turned to her, took her in his arms and hugged her, "It is all right, My Lady" he replied, a look of love coming over his face.
"I should not have messed up your things, forgive me", she said. Taking a deep breath and nodding he said, "You are already forgiven; I should not have got so angry, forgive me".
"There is nothing to forgive" she said.
He bent down and kissed her tenderly, Elaena snuggled into his shoulder leaning her full body against him wallowing in his arms wrapped around her. She drew in the woody earthy smell of him, his strong solid presence and was grateful of his forgiveness.
He wrapped himself around her feeling her leaning against him and the soft lavender smell of her skin and clothes. He

was grateful that she had come back to him and gave himself totally to the experience. Again they kissed and spent a pleasant evening together by the fire drinking wine.

The next day Paedur found Násuin in the courtyard quietly cleaning his sword while the warriors were attending to the needs of their horses.

"Bore da, my friend", he greeted.

Násuin stopped what he was doing and looked up at Paedur, "Bore da", he replied.

"You are well this day?" Paedur enquired.

"I am indeed", replied Násuin.

"Thank you for helping Elaena yesterday when your men frightened her", said Paedur.

"You are most welcome, she is well", Násuin enquired.

"A little angry, very frightened, but yes, she is well, thank you", replied Paedur.

"I am glad to hear that" said Násuin. "I had words with my men and confined them to barracks last night, such an incident will not occur again", he said.

"Since the taberna incident with Medwyn I regard you as my protector", said Paedur. "It seems now you are also Elaena's protector".

"That I am most willing to do," said Násuin bowing, glad that he no longer needed an excuse to be in her company.

"I am in need of your help", said Paedur.

"All you have to do is ask", said Násuin.

"I would like you to teach Elaena the art of fighting and weaponry", said Paedur.

Násuin took a deep breath, closed his eyes and calmly replied, "It would be an honour and a pleasure to do so".

"Good, then I shall send her to you presently", said Paedur.

"I am free of duties today, I can take her now if you wish", said Násuin.

"Perfect I will send her down to you" said Paedur.

He returned to the great hall and found Elaena resting.

"Get up", he commanded. "Násuin is going to teach you to fight".

"I do not want to learn", she replied sullenly.
"Nevertheless, learn you shall, it is part of your training".
He went to his press and took out a pair of brown bracae and a cream tunic, handing them to her he commanded, "Put these on and report to him immediately".
She looked at him sullenly, "No, I will not", she replied defiantly.
"Put them on and report to him immediately", he ordered staring at her.
She opened her mouth to reply but the look in his eyes silenced her, standing up and taking the clothes from him she replied angrily, "As you wish...Master".
She changed into the clothes and then asked, "Where am I to report".
"The courtyard, he is waiting for you", Paedur replied.
She strode across the room staring at him angrily, opened the door and marched down the corridor leaving the door wide open.
Elaena found Násuin in the courtyard; two wooden swords lay on the ground at his feet, his back was turned to her.
"I am to report to you for training" she greeted him angrily.
Taking a deep breath and closing his eyes to calm himself he then opened them and turned around, "You are most welcome, My Lady" he said bowing, "I prefer to call it fun".
"Do you know how to fight at all?" he asked.
"No I do not, nor am I interested in learning", she replied defiantly.
"Interesting! A woman of your...profession does not know how to defend herself" he said tauntingly.
"In the taberna I know well enough, but this is not the taberna and you are not a...client", she replied.
"No, indeed I am not", he said. "You are correct, this is not the taberna, any idiot can take down a drunken lout. True fighting requires skill, patience and finesse, none of which you possess... My Lady", he continued, bowing.
"Patience and finesse has no place in the taberna" she said sullenly.

"Indeed they do not", he agreed. "It also requires the desire to fight...which clearly you do not have. "Why then are you here", he asked.

"I am here because my...Master told me to and...I have to do what my Master commands...he gets angry when I object", she said, sullenly.

"I am your master now...here you will do what I tell you, when I tell you, how I tell you and you will not object", he said commandingly.

"No I will not", she said defiantly.

"Then you will not survive" he said. "Someday you will be put upon and because you have not learned to fight properly, you will be taken advantage of".

Furious now, here was another man claiming to be her master and telling her what to do, Elaena lunged toward him and struck out but before her punch connected he grabbed her wrist and, twisting her arm behind her back, he held her against him restraining her.

With a gentle laugh he replied, "Nice to see you have some fight in you, I can work with that".

Breathing hard she became aware of his taut body against hers and his strong arms encircling her. The slight smell of metal and grease, dust and earth, the brush of his hair against her skin and his breath on her neck, she tried to break free but he held her tighter.

"Going somewhere, girly", he taunted.

"Far away from you", she replied, angrily.

"And how do you propose to do that?" he asked.

She moved but he pinned her even tighter, she raised her right foot and stamped him hard.

Winching he said, "I thought you said you do not know how to fight".

"I know how to protect myself", she replied angrily.

"So it seems", he said. "But do you know how to release yourself now?" he asked.

She moved but the more she did the more he pinned her against him. Her full body was against his now, the scent of her intoxicated him. He wanted this moment to last forever but knew it would not.

Almost imperceptivity he eased his hold and said into her ear, "I could have my way with you, right here, right now, and you would not be able to stop me and no one else would either".

Breathing hard she replied, "Paedur could".

"Yes he could", he said, "but he will not".

"Why not?" she asked angrily.

"Because he will see this as a training exercise and believe that I am teaching you how to get out of a nasty situation", he replied.

"I do not need your training or his", she said defiantly.

"That was not the case yesterday when my men circled you", he said. "Then you were a scared rabbit caught in a trap".

"A scared rabbit I am not, I can get out of this if I choose to", she replied defiantly.

"Do it then", he taunted.

Furious, she tore at his arm and dug her nails into his skin, winching in pain he released her. "Cat has claws and will scratch, perhaps we can turn that anger into something and make a warrior out of you yet...maybe even a great Druid", he said staring at her intently.

Bending down and taking one of the wooden swords in his right hand he stepped back a few paces and, striking a warrior pose, he brandished it in the air. After a few moments, he gestured her to come over to him. Keeping the sword in his hand and with a relaxed version of the warrior pose he said, "Stand between me and the sword with your back to me".

Hesitantly she did so.

"Now put your right hand over mine and hold the sword".

Again hesitantly she did as he said.

"Now move with me".

He made the same movements he had done a few minutes ago, she moving with him.

"This is how you use the sword in battle", he said. "You watch your opponent's every move, you watch for them to make a mistake and when you see an opening you strike".

He lunged gently forward as if slashing at someone, the movement startled her and she gasped. She realised that he was practically wrapped around her; his strength and presence disturbed her. She took her hand off his, stepped away from him and took a few deep breaths.

Breathing deeply she glared angrily at him saying, "I grow tired of this, I have had enough".

"But we have only just begun", he said innocently.

"I have had enough for today" she said.

"Then perhaps another day, My Lady" he said, bowing.

She turned and strode across the courtyard her head held high, Násuin stood watching her. Still feeling her leaning against him, he opened his mouth and took a few long deep breaths. His arm stung, raising it to his mouth he licked the pin pricks of blood, taking one last look at her; he turned, picked up the swords and strode back to his quarters.

Chapter Eight

At the beginning of June Paedur called to see Niwelyn, they walked in the forest together enjoying the quietness and savouring the energy of the trees. Coming out of the door they turned right along the track, the rough stones crunching under their feet. As they walked, the grass was lush and green, buttercups and daisies grew in among the grass. As they entered the sounds changed and became muffled, the forest was dark, cool and still. Slowly their ears tuned to the frequency of the forest and they began to hear the rustle of the wind in the upper leaves. A squirrel scurried in the undergrowth on its way to find a meal, it squeaked when it realised that it was not alone, stopped and pondered what it should do, but food was more important than fright so it carried on its journey.

They noticed strands of grass growing up through the track, hip high fronds, nettles and long grasses lined the track. A bird flew past their ears almost crashing into them on its way to find some grubs. The trees stood straight and tall, the shadows of their leaves giving the ground underneath a dappled look. Pine cones and dry leaves crackled under foot as they walked, tree roots protruded through the dry earth

They came to the river and stood on its banks listening to the gentle lapping of the water on the shore, the ripples of the water making their way down stream, and listened to the twittering of the birds overhead in the trees. On the far bank they noticed the high trees the rolling hills and green fields. The Beech, Oak and Holly trees stood proud and tall at the water's edge, the reeds rose proudly out of the water lining the river bank. They could hear the distant clinking sound of the boats at the nearby quay and the boatmen going about their business, the distant sound of the cattle in the farms, the clang of the hammer in the force and the creaking of the wooden wheel in the mill. One dead trunk of a fallen tree leaned down into the river, another hung in mid air just above the water. On the far bank a group of swans glided majestically oblivious to the goings on in the town.

Niwelyn sat on a knee high grass mound at the water's edge looking into the river.
Standing beside her, also looking into the river, Paedur said quietly, "I think Elaena is ready for first initiation".
Niwelyn waited for him to continue.
"At the Solstice ceremonies I will initiate her", he continued.
"Is this wise, is it not too soon?" she asked.
"No, she has the basics, to teach her any more she needs to be initiated", he replied.
"But that is only three weeks away, will there be enough time to prepare her?" she asked.
"She is prepared enough; I will make her a gift of new clothes for the occasion", he replied.
"What kind?" she asked.
"I have chosen a long white tunic, red veil and red shoes", he replied.
Niwelyn's eyes opened wide, her mouth shot open and she turned to Paedur saying, "No, you cannot, does she know"?
"Know what?" he asked innocently.
"That they are the wedding clothes of a Roman lady", she replied.
"No", he replied flatly.
"And do you plan to tell her?"
"No", he replied.
"Why not?" she pressed.
"If I tell her she may rebel..."
"...Rightly so" interrupted Niwelyn, staring at him. "She has a right to know, you have to tell her".
"No, I have decided this is the way it will be" he replied, decisively.
"And do you plan to include sex in this ceremony?" she asked.
"Yes", he replied.
Niwelyn's eyes widened, "In front of everyone"?
"No, in private, alone", he replied.
"No, Paedur, I forbid it", she replied quietly. "As your friend and ceremonial consort I absolutely forbid it".
"Why?" he asked.

"Because it is not the time of year for hand fasting and well you know it, it is unlucky", she replied forcibly.
"It is in the Roman calendar and considered to be exceptionally lucky", he replied sullenly.
"We are Cymru...not Romans", she reminded him forcibly.
Turning toward her and looking deeply into her eyes he replied, "Usually, Niwelyn, I would accept your advice, but this time I do not".
Niwelyn searched inside herself for some piece of convincing information; several times she opened her mouth to say something and closed it again. Then she remembered something.
"Technically, she is already married", she said.
"To whom?" he asked.
"Násuin", she replied.
"How"?
"The Bealteinne festivities...when she jumped the fire with him", she replied.
"That was an...enactment...of a ritual", he replied.
"Still, to those who know, it could be seen as a true ceremony", she said.
Paedur remained silent.
Eventually she asked, "And what if Elaena becomes pregnant".
He remained silent.
Her eyes widened and her mouth opened, "That is it; that is the whole purpose of it", she said with insight. "You are very much aware of your age, you want a child and she is the perfect age to give you one".
Paedur remained silent.
"I do not believe you could be so devious", she said shaking her head. "If any of us tried this you would be the first to talk us out of it, and yet you do this yourself and expect me to agree"?
Paedur turned his back to her.
She stared at him for several minutes.
"Oh! Paedur, please do not do this", she pleaded. "It will bring ill fate upon you, please rethink this", she pressed.
He didn't answer.

"At least wait until next Bealteinne, she will be older and more ready, the time will be right and more luck will come of it".

"I will be older too" he replied sullenly, turning back to look at her.

She took a deep breath to calm herself.

"Paedur, I have never discouraged you from doing anything, I trust your judgement in all things".

She took his hands in hers and looked up beseechingly into his eyes.

"But I beg you...reconsider".

Slowly he shook his head and looked down sadly into her eyes.

"No, Niwelyn, I have decided to go ahead".

Realising there was nothing more she could say, she nodded.

"All right", she sighed. "But I still do not approve", she said resignedly.

"I will not make it look like a hand fasting..."he said.

"...You will not need to, her clothes will say it for you", she interrupted.

"I will be discrete", he continued, inclining his head.

Niwelyn shook her head and became very silent. She got to her feet and walked away from him. He stood at the water's edge for a few minutes more on his own then followed her. At the door of her roundhouse he kissed her and said, "Thank you for listening".

She turned and went in to her house closing the door behind her.

After a moment Paedur returned to the great hall.

***

The summer Solstice arrived and the excitement grew, the days had become very long and warm. The children decked the altar with garlands of summer flowers; they were very proud of themselves because these garlands they made themselves without Paedur's help. The altar was a blaze of colour and looked very impressive; the fire was prepared and stood ready and waiting.

The Druids began arriving and gathering in the great hall. The warriors checked the town's defences making sure they were secure. The tables were stacked with mouth-watering foods and everyone chose their best light summer clothes to wear. The sky was clear blue, a heavy scent of flowers in full bloom hung in the air and there was a real festive atmosphere.

In their room Paedur and Elaena also prepared. He had given her a complete new set of clothes earlier that day and she was very excited about wearing them that night. They were the finest he had given her yet and she was looking forward to showing them off later at the fire. Paedur wore lightweight cream linen bracae and sleeveless tunic, his cloak that night for the ceremony was red silk, the same colour as Elaena's veil and his hair flowed loosely to his shoulders.

When they were dressed and ready they walked through the town, hand in hand, down to the grove for the ceremony. Niwelyn was already there waiting, her eyes opened when she saw them approaching. Elaena was wearing an ankle length white tunic, red veil and red shoes; her hair was braided. Niwelyn shook her head and sighed.

At mid-day the Druids gathered around Paedur and Niwelyn at the altar and, facing south, began a chant. The deep voices of the men blended perfectly with the high sweet voices of the women and together their voices created a perfect harmony. One by one the townspeople joined in and the grove rang with the sound of their voices. The trees joined in too and a deep sense of calm and peace hung in the air, the forest hummed with energy and everyone felt its effect.

When quietness returned Paedur lit a candle in the centre of the altar and called, "Beli Mawr, thank you for gracing us with your presence this fine day".

Niwelyn called, "Mother Danu", thank you for bestowing abundance upon our town this year".

She then gestured to the people in the front row; the farmers approached the altar and presented baskets of fruit. The women approached and presented flowers and the tradesmen presented tokens of their professions.

Elaena stood close by observing and waiting. Násuin also stood close by, on alert, watching.

Paedur then nodded to Elaena.

With a small candle in her hand she approached the altar and lit her candle. Carefully shielding its flame, she walked over to the fire and lit it from her candle. As the flames began to form she returned to the altar and placed her candle on it beside the main one.

Niwelyn called, "Mother Danu, we present our gifts to you in appreciation for your abundance".

Then, looking at the crowd, she raised her hands and called, "Join us now in thanksgiving and celebration".

The Druids bowed to each other, left the altar and joined the crowd.

When the ceremonies were over the singing and dancing began. Paedur went over to the closest table and poured two goblets of red wine. Discretely he removed a tiny glass container from a pouch hanging from his belt and poured the liquid into one of the goblets, he returned the empty container to his pouch.

Behind him, looking over his shoulder Niwelyn said in a level voice, "So you mean to go ahead".

Picking up the two goblets he turned and stared at her, the firelight reflecting in his eyes, his pendant glowing, also reflecting the light.

He nodded silently.

"And what have you put in her drink?" she enquired.

"Something to keep her calm", he replied.

"What is it, Paedur", she pressed.

"Kava Kava" he replied, realising he couldn't hide from her.

"Ah! The herb of ceremonies, used to relax the anxiety of the participant", she said knowingly. "No doubt you have used enough to keep her just about on this side of consciousness", her voice becoming hard.

Paedur remained silent, staring intently at Niwelyn,

"Do you not think that what you are doing is unethical?" she asked.

"No, herbs are used all the time in initiation ceremonies..." he said innocently.

"...Usually the participant has an idea of what they are doing and are somewhat willing" she interrupted. "Elaena does not and therefore it is unethical".

Paedur remained silent, breathing evenly and calmly.

"Please, Paedur, do not proceed with this initiation tonight", she pleaded. "Wait until Bealteinne".

"No", replied Paedur sullenly and walked past her over to Elaena.

Niwelyn turned and watched as he handed Elaena the goblet, saw her drink and being lead away by him linking his arm. She shook her head and, looking down at the ground, in a low voice to herself she said, "Druantia, protect her".

She looked up and saw Násuin watching her intently. She knew he had witnessed her conversation with Paedur. She also knew that he knew exactly what was happening.

She stared back at him.

"He bothers you", he said.

"No man or person bothers me", she replied, shaking her head.

"I do not think that is true, My Lady", he replied quietly.

"What do you mean", she asked frowning.

"No one bothers you, that is true...however...one person has your heart...and it is a man", he replied.

"I give my heart to no one", she replied, shaking her long black hair the firelight reflecting in her eyes.

"You give your heart to no one, that is true...because it has already been given...and it is to a man", he replied continuing to stare at her.

"I have no idea what you mean", she shrugged then walked away mingling with the crowd.

Násuin stood for a while watching her smiling and talking as she moved among them, he shook his head and smiled then joined his men and drank a little too heavily that night.

***

Paedur led Elaena down to the beach, close to the water's edge he had set up a small fire on a wooden tripod; a smaller version of the ceremonial fire used earlier that night. In a boat at the edge of the water was a wooden crate, leaving Elaena at the unlit fire, he walked over to the boat and retrieved the crate, carrying it over to the fire he laid it gently on the sand. Taking off the lid he took out two goblets, a covered jug of wine, some food, tinder for the fire and his winter woollen cloak. Having lit the fire, he poured some wine into the goblets and handed one to Elaena. Taking it from him she was acutely aware of the silence around them broken only by the gentle sloshing of the waves and the distant sound of the revellers.

A strange calm feeling had come over her since they left the ceremonial fire and she felt extremely relaxed.

Looking deeply into her eyes he touched his goblet to hers and then raised it in her direction saying, "My Lady", he bowed.

Not knowing how to reply, she remained silent.

Gently he assisted her to sit on his cloak, fed her some small pieces of food and encouraged her to drink some more wine. He held her hand and talked softly with her watching, waiting. Slowly he leaned toward her and kissed her on the cheek, she responded by returning his kiss. Slowly he put his arm around her shoulders, drawing her closer to him, this time he kissed her full on the mouth, his lips covering hers. Deeply, passionately he kissed her and she responded, pulling herself right against his body, she felt him wrap himself around her.

Gasping a little she pulled away from him and looked into his eyes, he returned her stare his eyes intent. She drew closer to him again, this time kissing him, slowly lightly at first, then deeply, passionately. They pressed together totally wrapped up in each other and together lay down on the sand. Their bodies moved as one, each aware of the other but also aware of what was happening inside them.

For Paedur, as their passion grew, he heard the waves pound on the sand and he felt the sky tremble. He was aware of the pale moon shining down on them and felt they were on the edge of forever. He knew what he was doing was right; he knew they could not fail and he gave himself totally to the experience.

For Elaena it was like nothing she had ever experienced, she felt her body go on fire; rainbow colours swirled around her and her head spun. Her breath became gasping and rapid, her body arched and her head pressed firmly against the sand. Their passion grew and she was dimly aware of his hands stroking, caressing, searching and probing. He covered her with his body, his own breathing becoming less controlled. She heard him moan softly close to her ear and gasped. They clung together two hearts, two minds, two souls, one body.

As he entered her he felt his body was like a naked wire, he silently implored, "Druantia, grant us a soul which combines Elaena's passion and fire and my wisdom and knowledge".

As she reached her climax Elaena felt her whole body turn to liquid, she felt she was floating. There was a loud noise in her ears which she couldn't describe, behind her closed eyes her head burst with a dazzling shimmering white light blocking everything out. The light grew brighter and suddenly all became silent, she felt nothing and sank into total oblivion.

Their passion spent, they lay together wrapped in each other's arms. Paedur breathing very hard, fighting to control his breath, Elaena had passed out and lay in his arms barely breathing. He covered them with his ceremonial cloak and lay beside her, waiting for his breath to calm down. Above them the moon shone, the stars twinkled and the waves sloshed quietly close to their feet.

After a few minutes he gently shook Elaena and spoke softly to her waking her up, when she was awake enough to respond to him he gently sat her up. Retrieving the things from around the fire and returning them to the crate and the boat, he returned to Elaena, she had lain back down and fallen asleep. Again he woke her and assisted her to her feet, she was dimly aware of his arm around her urging her to walk with him, she clung tightly to him allowing herself to be led by him.

In the great hall he had difficulty getting her up the stairs to their room, but, after much effort, he managed. Gently he laid

her on her bed covering her with his woollen cloak, she was already deeply asleep.
Standing over her for a few minutes he watched her then, walking over to his own bed, he lay down and slept.

***

For the next few days Elaena lay sleeping on her bed, completely exhausted and moved in and out of consciousness. Paedur kept vigil by her side keeping her temperature even in spite of the summer heat. From time to time he gently raised her to a half seating position with one arm around her and fed her sips of water and broth.
Day turned to night, night turned to day and Elaena was not even aware of it, on and on she slept totally oblivious to everything. Paedur opened the shutters making sure she was not disturbed by the light, he kept the room aired and comfortable and he kept watch over her.
The day after the ceremony Paedur went to see Niwelyn; she wasn't in her house when he arrived so he figured she was probably in the forest and went looking for her. He found her dressed in a light weight dark blue tunic and brown leather sandals picking herbs. Her long black hair was tied up with a thin hemp strand, her oval face tanned and slightly damp from the exertion on such a hot day.
"Bore da", he greeted her quietly.
Still concentrating on picking herbs she replied, "Bore da", and continued working.
"It is done", he said quietly.
Niwelyn nodded and sighed.
She is resting today; she seems to have had a bad reaction to the herbs", he said quietly.
"I am not surprised", Niwelyn said. "She was just about conscious when she left the fire and I have heard that you practically carried her home later".
"Who told you that", he asked.

Continuing to pick the herbs she shrugged, “I have my sources”, and continued working.

“I would like to know who”, he said.

“It is not in your best interests to know”, she said, continuing to work.

“Niwelyn, please do not be angry with me. I can take anger from everyone, but not you”, he said quietly.

Sighing she replied, “It is too late for that. I am more angry with you today Paedur than I have ever been since we met”.

She walked off with her basket on her left arm and her dagger in her right hand.

Paedur stood silently watching her as she walked away. He contemplated following her and pleading with her but, having trained her, he knew how she thought and felt and he knew he would get nowhere with her that day.

The following day he went down to the courtyard with a big basket of towels and gathered up the children. He walked them down to the River Conwy and set up a play area for them and allowed them to swim and play at the water’s edge. The squeals of delight as the children felt the cool water on their skin, it was a hot day and they were grateful for the coolness of the water. Some of the children found some rabbits nesting under a bush and chased them for a while; Paedur became aware of the rabbits’ distress and encouraged the children to take an interest in something else. Once all the children had been dried off and clothed again he sat them down and gave them some water and fruit. Inwardly he was thinking of Elaena and was slightly concerned about her so the laughter and chatter of the children cheered him up.

After their snack he got the children to fold the towels neatly and put them back into the basket, he assigned two of the larger stronger boys to carry the basket between them each taking a handle. As they were passing Niwelyn’s house they found her outside at a wooden table cleaning her surgical instruments, immediately they gathered around her and watched what she was doing.

“These are surgical instruments”, she began.

Picking up long thin pieces of metal she said, "These are needles".
Picking up things that looked like knifes she said, "These are scoops, and these are scalpels". "This is a tongs and this large one is a forceps and these are hooks".
The children were fascinated and she allowed them to pick each instrument up and inspect it.
She opened her wooden pill box and explained, "Medicines are made from plants, herbs, trees and flowers and are added to wine and sometimes boiled water to be drunk by sick people. Parts of the plants are put into this bowl which we call a mortar and ground down with this pestle into a dust, it is then either put into liquid and drunk or made into a pill with paste and swallowed".
One of the girls took a pill and began putting it into her mouth but Niwelyn gently took it from her and said, "Do not take any pill unless it is given to you by a healer or a doctor".
The child hung her head in shame but Niwelyn patted her on the head saying, "No harm has been done, do not be ashamed".
Paedur looked at her and said, "Thank you, for your patience and your time, we will not detain you any longer".
She nodded silently.
Paedur clapped his hands and called, "Come now children, it is time to go home. Say thank you to Lady Niwelyn for her instruction".
"Thank you Lady Niwelyn", the children said in chorus.
"You are most welcome children", she replied smiling.
He bowed to Niwelyn and walked off. The children made sounds of disappointment put the instruments back on the table and followed him.
As they walked away the girl who had almost taken the pill said, "Someday I will be like her".
Niwelyn smiled and took all the instruments and cleaned them again.
When they arrived back at the courtyard he dispatched them back to their families and went to check on Elaena, she was still

sleeping. After attending to her needs he spent the rest of the evening writing at his desk.

The following day, having checked on Elaena, he decided he would keep the children close to home so that he would be on hand if she woke up. After attending to her needs and having some breakfast he went down to the courtyard.

"Bore da, children", he greeted them.

"Bore da, Paedur", they replied.

One of the children asked, "Where is Elaena?"

"She is unwell, she will not be with us today", he replied.

"Can we see her?"

"No she is resting", he replied.

The children made noises of disappointment.

"However, today we are going to the weapons store".

He walked them across the courtyard Násuin was there checking the weapons and was delighted to show and explain everything to the children.

"The most common weapon is the spear or javelin", he explained. "It has an iron head and is fixed onto a wooden handle. It is thrown at your enemy but can also be used like a lance to stab".

He made a few moves to show the children what he meant then threw one over to Paedur who deftly caught it in mid air. He allowed the children to hold it and touch it, the older ones tried to imitate the moves they had just seen.

Picking up a bow he explained, "This is a bow, this particular one, is a long bow. It is made of yew wood and the arrows are made from ash wood or birch, and some are made from oak and beech. He loaded it with an arrow and shot it into a pile of sacks at the end of the room, the arrow whistled through the air as it flew and startled the children.

"Do not be afraid", he told them, "you are quite safe here".

He then allowed them to pick it up and inspect it, again the older ones tried to copy his movement.

"We also use sticks made from oak, beech and any other wood that comes to hand", he explained. "Pretty much anything can be used as a weapon, the aim is to hurt your opponent worse

then they hurt you and if you can prevent them from hurting you at all that is even better".
"What about killing", one of the boys asked.
"We try not to kill if at all possible", answered Násuin, "but in battle it does happen. The army with the most men standing wins but it is better to negotiate first and only do battle as a last resort".
"Can girls fight too?" asked the girl who had earlier almost taken the pill.
"Yes they can and do", replied Násuin. "We do not have women warriors here but in some of the other towns and village they have a few".
"Our favourite weapon is the sword", he continued. "We have two types, the short one similar to the Roman Gladius and the long sword which we Cymru prefer", he said and showed them both.
"Be careful with the swords", he advised. "They are very sharp and do a lot of damage".
Patiently and calmly he showed them around the store room and allowed them to get the feel of the weapons.
One of the women called the children to the open fire for lunch so they thanked Násuin and ran off to get their food.
As they left the boy who had asked about killing said, "Someday I am going to be like him".
The girl who had asked about girl warriors said, "I will be a warrior someday too".
"I thought you were going to be healer", said the boy.
"I am going to be both healer and warrior", she replied.
"That is silly, you cannot be both", the boy said.
"Yes she can", said Násuin behind them. "Scathach is the Goddess of healing, fighting, magic and prophecy. If this young lady wishes to be healer and warrior there is no reason why she cannot".
The girl smiled, the boy huffed and ran off. The girl looked at Násuin, he looked back at her and held her stare then nodded and bowed to her.
"Go, they are waiting for you", he said quietly.

Still staring at him she said, “Thank you”, and ran off to join the other children.

When they were gone Paedur standing just inside the weapons store door, looked at Násuin and said, “Thank you for your patience and time”.

Násuin, watching the girl as she ran across the courtyard nodded, “Croeso, it is always nice to pass on knowledge”.

There was a heavy air of silence between them; Násuin busied himself returning the weapons to their places.

“Is Lady Elaena well?” he asked.

“Yes, why do you ask”, Paedur replied.

Continuing to tidy the weapons Násuin said, “She did not seem to be so well in the early hours of the morning a few days ago”.

Paedur nodded, “Ah! It was you who saw us then”.

Násuin continued tidying.

“It is true that she is....tired...but she is otherwise well”.

“That is good to hear”, Násuin said quietly. “Give her my regards”.

“I will”, said Paedur. Bowing he continued, “Again, thank you for your time and patience”.

“Croeso”, Násuin replied.

Paedur left the weapons store and returned to his room, Násuin closed his eyes took a few deep breaths and then returned to his quarters.

On the fourth day after the Solstice Elaena woke up weak, pale and frightened, she had not realised how much time had passed and couldn’t remember getting home. Gently Paedur sat her up in bed and handed her a bowl of hot stew, slowly she ate in silence relishing the heat and nourishment. While she was eating Paedur gathered fresh clothes for both of them, large towels, their summer cloaks and some food.

For a few minutes she watched him silently, her eyes big and wide, then asked, “What are you doing”.

“We are going on a picnic, My Lady, you need air and sunlight... and a wash, we will wash in the stream and eat some light food afterwards”, he replied.

Once he had the provisions together he walked over to her bed and assisted her to her feet, unsteadily she clung to him then moved away tentatively testing if she could stand alone. Assured that she was OK, Paedur led Elaena gently out of the room and down the stairs. As they entered the courtyard everyone stopped momentarily and looked towards the couple. They noticed how heavily Elaena leaned on Paedur's arm and how protectively he held and guided her. He was aware of the interest being afforded them but he was intent on getting Elaena out of the courtyard safely and into the forest.

Násuin watched them leave, staring at their backs as they walked out of the courtyard. As they walked through the town they were greeted by the townspeople, both nodded silently.

In the forest Paedur laid his cloak on the ground by the side of the lake, he removed his own clothes and assisted Elaena to remove hers. Gently he guided her into the water and allowed her to immerse herself in its cool goodness, slowly her head cleared, her skin woke up and she began to breathe more deeply. After a short while they got out, dried themselves off, put on the fresh clothes and lay in the sun, Paedur fed her some small pieces of food and cool water and then had some himself. Elaena dozed relishing the warm sun, Paedur watched her closely. As the day turned to early evening Paedur gathered everything up and assisted Elaena to her feet. Unsteadily she walked beside him, protectively he assisted her.

Over the next few weeks Elaena regained her strength and energy. Paedur returned to lessons with the children and Elaena assisted. He kept a close eye on her, Násuin kept a close eye on them.

One day Paedur gathered them in the courtyard and announced, "Today we are going on a trip".

The children looked at him quizzically.

"We are going down to the river".

The children squealed with delight and jumped up and down. As they walked through the town he pointed out the terracotta roofs, the thatched roofs, the timber houses, the stone houses, the cobbled streets and pavements. The children danced around them as they walked some of the smaller ones holding on to Elaena's hands and tunic.

When they got down to the river he showed them the reeds growing along its banks.

"Conwy is built on the old Roman Fort of Kanovium, the Place of Reeds", he explained. "Today we are going to take some reeds out of the river and make papyrus".

Carefully he went over to the water's edge, selected several reeds and pulled them out of the river. He shook them and dried them with a cloth and allowed each child to hold them in their hands. He then gathered them up in a bundle of cloth and led the children back to the square, they danced and sang as they made their way back through the streets. Everyone smiled as they passed by, they had not seen the children so happy ever. Some of the traders waved to them as they passed by, some of merchants saluted Paedur and some of the hackers gave them some fruit. Some of the men whistled at Elaena, she stopped, and with her hands on her hips, she wiggled her pelvis at them and raised the hem of her tunic just a little to reveal her perfect ankles. They cheered and whistled even louder, Paedur smiled and hurried his group along a little faster.

When they got back to the square he opened the bundle and laid the reeds out on the ground, he drew his dagger from his belt and with it removed the outer rind of the reeds, cut the core into strips and soaked them. The children looked on amazed Elaena took each strip from him and laid it down carefully on the ground.

When all the strips were cut he then formed a sheet of two layers of strips at right angles to each other and pressed them together. He then took a wooden mallet and beat the sheet and left them to dry. While they were waiting he and Elaena assisted the children to make their own sheets. When a few were dry Paedur glued them together to form a longer sheet which he then rolled into a scroll, the joints were hardly visible on his one. He then took two wooden rollers and put one at the top and one at the bottom. When the rest of the sheets were ready they assisted the children to make their scrolls, some of them were rather

messy at the end, some of them were quite acceptable. When they were all finished Paedur cut them up into squares and gave one to each child, they were delighted with their work and very proud of their achievement. Then he handed each child a reed pen and got them to write their name on their sheet.
The rest of the summer passed pleasantly, the days were long, warm and bright with only very gentle breezes. Light tunics, stolas and sandals were the order of the day and some of the men adopted the Roman short tunic.

***

Paedur and Elaena became lovers, he delighting in pleasuring her and being pleasured by her. Elaena grew stronger and enjoyed his instructions, all fear of him now gone, she thoroughly enjoyed his company. She noticed the warriors no longer jeered her, when she entered the courtyard they greeted her with respect, opened doors for her and assisted her if she was carrying something. The Romans also no longer jeered her; instead they treated her with the same respect they gave to the women of their own Priests and Generals. Both recognised how she had been dressed at the Solstice and knew that she was as good as being a married woman, even if it wasn't official. The women watched her more closely and engaged her in conversation, walking with her when they met her in the town, the children delighted in having her back with them and played around her. Násuin watched her from a distance.
As the Summer turned to Autumn and the leaves turned from green to brown, gold and russet and the gathering of the harvest began, the adults and children went to the farms to assist with the collection of the crops. Paedur and Elaena stayed behind in the fort to prepare the storage facilities, Násuin had all his men and horses sent to the fields to carry back all the produce. There was a great air of excitement and co-operation about the town everyone picked as much as they could and by the end of the day all the horses returned to the town pulling carts laden down with apples, pears, wild berries, corn, barley, oats and

rye. Cattle had been rounded up and selected for slaughter and quantities of salt and brine were provided by the merchants to preserve the foodstuffs for the winter.

The Romans celebrated their feast of Ludi Romani with games and plays for their God Jupiter. A cow was sacrificed in his honour and the representatives of the Senate and the magistrates celebrated with a banquet. In the temple the statues of Juno and Minerva were dressed in fine clothes especially for the occasion.

After all the foodstuffs had been treated, bagged and stored the Celts gathered in the courtyard that evening and feasted on the left over scraps. Wine, beer and mead flowed and everyone congratulated themselves on another fine harvest. Some bragged that they had gathered more than their neighbours all cheered and sang and danced around the open fire.

Paedur and Elaena realised that she was with child; Paedur became even more protective of her and more watchful. He made sure she was well fed and rested, when she was ill he acquired the necessary herbs to help her and when she was tired, he allowed her to rest. Násuin kept a close eye on them both watching everything they did but not interfering.

As Autumn turned to winter and the trees became bare Elaena's pregnancy became noticeable. The townspeople became more protective of her and the women increased Paedur's provisions even sending Elaena clothes, boots and warm cloaks.

Niwelyn and Násuin watched, not getting involved and keeping their dealings with Paedur strictly professional.

As the town was preparing for the Samhain celebrations Niwelyn, watching Násuin closely said, "You know Elaena is with child".

Násuin nodded, "Aye! I do", he replied. "All goes well with her"?

"Paedur is managing her progress well, it is in his best interests to do so", she replied.

Násuin nodded silently.

On the morning of Samhain Paedur, Elaena and Niwelyn set up a small fire for the children just outside her roundhouse and went into the forest to collect chestnuts. When they had a basket filled they brought them back to the small fire and roasted them until they burst, a prize was given to the child whose chestnut took the longest to burst. Laughter filled the air and the childrens' excited voices carried on the gentle breeze. Niwelyn placed apples into a large samian ware bowl with clear spring water. Paedur and Elaena gently tied the hands of the children who had been selected to put their faces into the water and grab onto the apples with their teeth. The children not participating cheered, their excited voices cheered the hearts of everyone close by preparing the evening festivities.

As evening drew near the children dressed up in costumes assisted by Paedur, Elaena and Niwelyn and when they were ready they were lead into the oak grove to join the adults.

That night all gathered around the great fire in the oak grove and as darkness descended upon the town Paedur, Niwelyn and the Druids took up their positions around the altar. Násuin, at the edge of the crowd, dressed in tan coloured bracae and tan tunic, loaded his bow with an arrow. One of his men lit its tip with a lighted firebrand and he shot the arrow into the fire stack, immediately it burst into flames. The crowd cheered and clapped and some danced with glee.

Paedur called the crowd to attention and when all eyes were on them and the crowd quietened he gestured to Elaena, standing at the edge of the crowd dressed in an emerald green velvet gown trimmed in gold with a full length cloak to match. Slowly she walked through the crowd carrying a plate of food in one hand and a glass of red wine in the other, when she reached the altar she handed the food to Niwelyn and the wine to Paedur and joined them at the altar.

The ceremonies began with Paedur making sacrifices and offerings to the Gods, with a strong clear voice he said, "We give thanks for the summer abundance".

In an equally clear voice Niwelyn requested, "Mother Cerridwen, bless us throughout this winter and provide us with enough food to see us through the cold months".

Paedur continued, “We honour our dead and ask that you keep the souls of all who have gone before us safe and close to you. Give each one comfort and rest according to their needs”.
He then turned to Elaena and nodded loudly she called, “Join us in feasting, song and dance”.
Immediately the feasting began, the musicians struck up their instruments and the entertainers performed for the crowd. Niwelyn and Násuin sat together by the fire watching and drinking wine.
Niwelyn stared at him and said, “Secretly you yearn for her”.
He nodded silently and closed his eyes.
“Then it seems we have something in common, both of us yearn for someone we cannot have”, she said.
“So it would seem”, he replied.
Paedur and Elaena acknowledged his birthday quietly together by the fire.
Holding her glass of wine in her right hand and placing her left hand on her slightly extended abdomen she said, “I think this wine is making me unwell”.
Paedur nodded, “That is because of the child within you, perhaps it would be best to drink boiled water instead”.
She made a sound of distaste, “Boiled water, it tastes bad”.
Smiling he said, “We can flavour it with herbs”.
Making another sound of distaste she said, “Herbs, smell bad, taste worse”, and she shuddered.
“We can find you nice ones; Camomile is pleasant and will help you to feel better”.
Looking at him quizzically she said, “Is this true”.
“Would I lie to you”, he asked, a hint of a smile on his lips.
“Hmmm”, she replied.
She put her glass down on the ground, stood up, yawned and stretched and said, “Take me home I am tired”.
Putting his own glass down he too stood up and bowed saying, “As you wish, My Lady”.
Together they walked off hand in hand leaving the party in full swing behind them. Elaena remembered the many times they

had done this before but this time they were walking towards their shared home.

***

As Winter closed in around the town the air turned cold and the frost set in, the people prepared for the harsh months. Paedur continued his writings and his lessons with Elaena but he was mindful of her pregnancy and lack of concentration and was extremely patient with her. Their love for each other grew and they became comfortable living together.

As Mid Winter approached the preparations for the Solstice celebrations began, Paedur and Elaena hung garlands of Ivy and Holly around the great hall assisted by the children. Paedur watched her lovingly and protectively very aware of the chances he saw in her. She was radiant and glowing with pregnancy, her fuller figure suited her and she looked round and happy. Elaena saw him gazing at her and seeing the look in his eyes turned her insides to jelly.

As night fell the great hall door was opened leading into the long room, Násuin and his men took up their positions around the large table to the right of the dais at the end of the hall. The people took up whatever places they could find around the smaller ones placed around the hall, the fire brightly blazed in the fireplace; it was the only light in the hall. When everyone was seated Paedur stepped up to the dais and raised his hands drawing attention.

Loudly he said, "Let the ceremony begin".

Niwelyn, dressed in a full length heavy blue velvet gown trimmed with gold, a leather belt holding a dagger hung around her waist, walked up the length of the hall. Behind her Elaena, dressed in a full length emerald green velvet gown trimmed with gold, carried a lighted candle. As they walked each of the sconces burst into flame lighting the hall as they progressed towards the dais.

When they arrived Niwelyn bowed to Paedur then stepped aside. Elaena took one more step and stopped in front of Paedur, bowed and handed him the lighted candle. He bowed and took the candle from her.

Raising the candle up he said loudly, "Cerridwen, bring your light into our hearts and souls and sustain us during the cold months".

Niwelyn and Elaena stepped on to the dais, one on each side of Paedur.

Turning to face the townspeople all three said together, "Cerridwen bless us and protect us".

Paedur placed the candle on a stand in the centre of the dais; all three bowed to each other, and stepped down.

Násuin, surrounded by his men, watched the ceremony intently; he stared at all three in turn and lingered on Elaena watching her every move longingly. Taking a deep breath he drank in her appearance and noted the changes in her. When she had first come to the courtyard she was a scrawny girl, now she was a pregnant woman.

The festivities went on till the early hours, singers and musicians played and sang. The Bards beguiled everyone with stories and everyone danced. Niwelyn played a haunting tune on a wooden whistle. Paedur played a wonderful lament on his golden harp; the sound of the strings created a magical atmosphere. Afterwards he returned to Elaena and sat with her, his arm protectively around her shoulders.

Niwelyn watched noting the way Násuin looked at Elaena and how Paedur and Elaena were absorbed in each other. She caught Násuin looking at her and they both stared across the room at each other.

Elaena yawned, stretched and stood up Paedur stood up also and, taking her by the elbow, he assisted her out of the hall back to their room. They celebrated her birthday quietly with food and mulled wine delighting in each other's company.

As the roman year 408AD drew to a close Paedur was forty-nine, Elaena was nineteen.

Chapter Nine

409 AD

In the opening days of January Conwy, in the grip of winter, was quiet, everyone remained indoors as much as possible the only activity was in the warriors' and Romans' enclosures, both continued to exercise and train in spite of the weather. At night the taberna was a sanctuary for the men, the women stayed at home tending to the needs of the children. Elaena, now seven months pregnant, was adjusting to her ever-increasing body size, her movement had become heavy and climbing the stairs made her tired and breathless. She needed to rest more and seemed to be more sensitive to the cold. Paedur kept an ever watchful eye over her, feeding her, keeping her warm, soothing her fears for the coming months and comforting her when she was low.

One morning, having attended to her needs, he left her resting and, so as not to disturb her; he went down to the hearth in the courtyard. One of the women gave him a bowl of hot porridge and a cup of hot brew, although he had just eaten with Elaena he accepted the food gratefully and began to eat. The woman, seeing his pensive mood, went about her business leaving him by the fire.

Násuin, from the shadows of the stables, watched Paedur; he sensed that his friend was troubled, he presumed about Elaena; however it was time to consult with him about the town's defences and he knew now was a perfect opportunity.

Walking over to Paedur at the fire he greeted him, "Bore da, My Lord", his voice was quiet but strong. "I do not wish to intrude upon your thoughts, but I would have a word with you if I may", he said.

"Bore da, Násuin, suit mai, how are you", Paedur asked looking up.

"Iawn Diolch, I am fine, thank you", replied Násuin.

Paedur gestured to him to join him. Taking a cup of hot brew from the cauldron hanging over the fire Násuin sat down with Paedur.

"Is the Lady Elaena well?", he enquired.

"Yes", replied Paedur, "though her size annoys her and the tiredness depresses her, more and more she needs to rest and the cold makes her irritable",

"Give her my regards", Násuin said.

"That I will", replied Paedur.

Giving Paedur a moment to adjust to his company, Násuin took a deep breath and continued, "I fear the coming year could be a troublesome one", he said watching Paedur closely. "The Roman Empire is on the verge of collapse, the barbarians continue to attack Roma, Stilicho was executed recently and Honorius has withdrawn to Ravenna in the north of Italy".

He stopped, allowing Paedur time to comprehend; Paedur turned toward the warrior and watched him nodding silently.

Násuin continued, "Constantine can no longer hold the Empire and civil war among the Romans is causing chaos", he drank from his cup, pressed his lips together, licked them and continued. "The Hibernians continue their assaults from the west, another fleet arrived at our shores just days ago, and the Saxons are invading us from the east".

His eyes bright with intent, he waited for a reply, there was none.

"There is talk of the Goths invading Roma and their leader Alaric is gathering an army around him as we speak", he continued.

"I hear the Vandals intend to invade Hispania", said Paedur, almost distractedly.

"I have heard that too, My Lord, Násuin replied nodding.

"Constantine has made Christianity the official religion of the Empire", said Paedur. "Its Priests are filling the peoples' heads with strange thoughts and beliefs", he said now staring into the fire his eyes wide. Shifting on the oak log he sat up straight and, looking intently at his friend, he asked, "What do we do, what is your advice".

"We strengthen our own defences, secure the borders and fight if necessary", replied Násuin strongly.
"And the women and children?" asked Paedur quietly.
"We protect them as best we can", replied Násuin levelly.
"Do you have a battle plan?" asked Paedur.
"I can command the respect of the warriors, they will do what I tell them to, you can command their belief", Násuin answered determinately. "Together we prepare the troops, watch the progress of events and be ready to strike if necessary".
"Let it be done", replied Paedur nodding.
Putting his empty cup and bowl down on the hearth he stood up, stretched and, turning to Násuin who was now also standing said, "Keep me informed, I will contact my Order later and see what news they have.
"Certainly, My Lord", replied Násuin bowing.
Returning to his room Paedur had the feeling that not only was the Roman Empire falling...but so too was the Celtic one. The spread of Christianity disturbed him, their Priests were strong in their convictions and even stronger in their conversions and their ways were beginning to take hold. Breathing deeply and closing his eyes he prayed, "Druantia, Queen of the Druids, give me strength and guidance, Camalus, God of Battle, give the warriors the ability to protect us all".

***

A month later at Imbolc the townspeople began to move around the town and, in the great hall, celebrated the passing of another winter, all had survived and the animals had fared well.
In the first days of February, just before dawn, while the day was still in the grip of night, they again gathered in the fort around the well. In a circle holding hands with heads bowed, Paedur and Niwelyn, hooded and cloaked in black with soft brown leather boots, began a chant. The people joined in and a heavy air of serenity descended upon the group. In the time honoured way some women placed unlit candles and tapers around the fire.

As dawn began to lighten the sky Niwelyn, dressed in a full length midnight blue velvet gown, gently detached herself from the group. Taking a blazing firebrand from the open fire she carried it over to the well and threw it into it.
"Goddess Brighid", she called, "bless our well and give it life and healing qualities".
Taking a small bottle, from a leather bag hanging on her belt, she presented it to Paedur, also dressed in a full length midnight blue velvet gown; it contained three drops of liquid.
"Goddess Cerridwen", she said loudly, "bestow upon Lord Paedur the knowledge of the past, present and future".
He took the bottle from her, raised it to his lips, solemnly drank and handed the bottle back to her.
"Goddess Mebh, bestow upon the town the gifts of fertility and regeneration. Goddess Olwen, bestow love and rebirth upon these people", she requested.
Going back to the fire she placed a cornucopia and a stick with a carving of two snakes entwined around it beside the hearth.
"Goddess Rosmerta, bestow fertility and wealth upon this town" she requested.
She placed a small amphora of water on the other side of the hearth.
"River Goddess Sequana, bestow health upon these townspeople", she requested.
As the sky became light Paedur called out, "Virgin Mother Goddess, enter and grace us with your presence".
Elaena, now eight months pregnant, was large and felt cumbersome, hooded and cloaked in black, she entered the courtyard followed closely by Násuin in full battle gear on high alert, watching her every move ready to assist her if necessary. As she walked slowly and carefully towards the open fire some women approached and whispered their requests into her ears. When she got to the fire she stopped and stood, breathing slightly heavily, Násuin gently removed her cloak. Dressed in a light green coloured velvet gown with soft brown leather boots and her hair unbound, she held a dish of flowers set with a candle which she had hidden under her cloak.

Niwelyn lighted a long taper from the fire and lit Elaena's candle. Gently she escorted her over to the fire where she took several tapers and lit them from the ceremonial candle. She handed them to the women who in turn lit the candles and tapers around the fire.

Paedur approached her and, taking the dish from her, looked into her eyes, bowed deeply and said, "Welcome Virgin Mother". Again there was a quiet snigger from the warriors which Násuin silenced with a cold stare. The women also looked at them with cold distain; there was no further comment from his men.

"Thank you...Lord Paedur", she replied catching her breath, "it is an honour...to be here".

Paedur leaned toward her, and placing his hand on her shoulder, kissed her on the forehead. Niwelyn, also placing her hand on her shoulder, kissed her on the cheek.

The sun rose and bathed the courtyard with brilliant light.

Turning to the crowd Paedur called, "Let us celebrate the return of the light with a feast". Instantly food was brought from the warriors' dwellings and placed on the tables in the great hall. Everyone filed into the great hall and consumed the food.

Standing behind her Násuin gently put Elaena's cloak around her shoulders, his hands lingering while she fastened the clasp, "Are you well, My Lady?" he enquired.

"I am, Násuin, thank you", she replied.

"May I make a request of you?" she asked.

"Anything at all", he replied.

"Could you please stop calling me My Lady and call me by my given name?" she asked.

Násuin smiled and nodded, "Of course, Elaena, if that is your wish", he replied.

"Yes, it is", she said tiredly.

"How goes it with you", he asked.

"Most days I am fine, sometimes I get tired and irritable but Paedur is patient with me and we get along well enough".

"I am glad to hear that", he said levelly.

"Násuin, please excuse me, I am hungry and tired, I think I shall go have something to eat and then go to my room for some rest".
"Shall I escort you?"
Smiling and bowing she said, "You may, Násuin, thank you".
Walking around in front of her, he held his right arm out palm upward; she gently shook her head and linked his arm instead. Together they walked slowly into the great hall, Elaena leaning slightly heavily on his arm grateful for its strength. Seating her at a table, he gestured to one of the women to bring some food, he sat with her and they eat breakfast together.
Across the room Niwelyn, breakfasting with Paedur, asked, "How is Elaena coping being with child?"
"Well enough though she gets irritable at times especially when she is tired but for the most part she is well", he replied.
"That is good", said Niwelyn. She has not got much further to go now; you have prepared her for what lies ahead"?
"As much as it is possible to do" he replied.
"Hmmm, we will see about that when the time comes", she said.
Having eaten as much as she could, Elaena yawned and caught Paedur's eye across the room and gestured to him that she was returning to their room. He quickly finished his conversation with Niwelyn, kissed her and joined Elaena.
Slowly and heavily she stood up, Násuin stood up also and helped her, Paedur looking into her eyes asked, "Are you ready to leave"?
"I am", she replied, "I need your assistance with the stairs".
"Of course, he replied and taking her by the elbow escorted her out of the great hall.
When they were safely in their room Elaena, gasping for breath, said, "The stairs frighten me...climbing up exhausts me... coming back down is dangerous...my belly is so big it is difficult to see the steps. Several times I have almost tripped...because my hems catch under my feet...and I have to cling to the rail to stop myself falling down", she continued, trying to calm herself down.

Paedur's patience increased towards her, "It will be over soon, My Love," he said encouraging her. "The baby will be birthed and you will return to your normal slim size" he continued, consoling her.

"I grow weary of not being able to do things and always having to adjust the things I can do", she cried.

Taking a small piece of white cotton he gently dried her frustrated tears, "Come now, show me that beautiful smile", he said patiently.

"I look like a big fat cow", she said sullenly.

"No, you look like a Lady" he replied, lovingly kissing and hugging her gently.

"I do not like being fat", she pouted.

"There is more of you to love", he replied reassuringly, "and besides, you are not fat...you are with child", he continued.

In the month of March Elaena gave birth assisted by Niwelyn. Paedur made sure that everything needed was easily to hand and concentrated on keeping Elaena calm so that Niwelyn could do her work as mid-wife. In the days immediately preceding the birth Elaena was irritable, restless and exhausted. Sleep was difficult due to her extended abdomen and she had to sleep propped up on pillows. Breathing was difficult and she didn't feel much like eating. Not having experienced pregnancy before she feared the birth, she had heard of women who died giving birth and as the hours drew closer her panic increased. She began to sweat more in spite of the coolness of the season. Her chest became constricted, the pain in her lower back and pelvis became more annoying and the baby, kicking inside her, disturbed her. Paedur patiently instructed her in breathing to help calm her emotions and thoughts, Niwelyn gave her herbs to ease the pain. Together they watched her night and day fearful that her fiery nature might cause her to do something stupid, Násuin was quietly on alert ready to respond to any command. One day after climbing the stairs Elaena collapsed on the floor of their room completely breathless and shaking, sweating from head to toe and panicking...her waters broke. Paedur and Niwelyn immediately rushed to her side, assisted her to remove

her long clothes replacing them with a short tunic and prepared her for birth.
Niwelyn had a deftness of movement that was elegant and graceful, her presence kept things under control as she worked with confidence. She tied her hair up in a bun and, taking an apron out of her beg, she put it on.
Paedur supported Elaena physically crouching down on the floor with her supporting her weight and steadying her so that she wouldn't fall. Guiding her with breathing he mopped her brow and cooed softly in her ear allaying her fears.

Elaena panicked, she tried to follow Paedur's breathing instructions but found that she could not keep control or concentration. Niwelyn handed Paedur a potion of Helianthemum nummularium (Rock Rose) to help alley her fears, at first it seemed to help but then the pain grew worse and there was a heavy disturbing feeling in her pelvis. Her eyes wide, her breathing short and her hair matted with sweat, she completely lost control. All her childhood fears of dying rushed at her and she became almost delirious. Desperately Paedur worked to calm her, comfort her and sooth her. Several times Niwelyn had to stop working and move away so that she wouldn't be kicked.
Taking a small bottle, out of her bag tied to her belt, Niwelyn handed it to Paedur, "Artemisia Vulvaris" (Mugwort) she said. "Give it to her it will help her to calm down and ease the pain". Nodding Paedur took the bottle from her, it was difficult administering it to Elaena but eventually he tipped it into her mouth.
All sense of reason gone, Elaena went into shock, she shook from head to toe, sweated profusely and felt like her insides were being torn out of her. Niwelyn handed Paedur another potion, this time Ornithogalum umbellatum (Star of Bethlehem). At the height of her panic a strange wave of peace and calm engulfed her and she lay against Paedur breathing hard. He wrapped his arms around her holding her gently but firmly, Niwelyn asked

her to push and showed her a panting breathing, while Elaena was engaged in doing that she resumed her work.

A half hour later Elaena gave birth to a baby girl, deftly Niwelyn cut the cord, scooped the baby up and brought her over to the table where a large white towel was lying waiting. She checked the baby and cleared the mucus from her nostrils, when she was sure that the baby was in no danger she brought her back to Elaena. Paedur gently allowed Elaena to lie against him to catch her breath, slowly her breathing returned to somewhat normal. Quietly he checked her for vital signs and when he was sure she was in no danger, he wrapped her up in a blanket and brought her over to her bed. Earlier he had covered it with large white towels, now he lay her gently on the bed and made sure she was comfortable.

Elaena, breathing hard and drenched with sweat, lay against Paedur; his solid strength supporting her, his quietness comforting her, there was no sense of panic in the room. Realising she had survived the birth she allowed herself to completely relax, a wave of relief swept over her, there was still pain but it had eased greatly. Her heart thumped heavily in her chest and she tried to control her breathing like she had been instructed. Slowly her breathing began to calm down and she became aware of Paedur wrapping her in a blanket and encouraging her to stand. Heavily she got to her feet assisted by Paedur; he stood to her left, wrapped his right arm around her shoulders and guided her with his left hand to the bed. She allowed him to assist her leaning heavily against him, she felt him gently laying her on the bed and making her comfortable. Niwelyn brought the baby over to them and lay her on Elaena's chest, standing shoulder to shoulder with Paedur, they both looked down on mother and baby.

Paedur's eyes shone brightly, his face, tired and drawn, made the lines around his eyes and mouth seem deeper, quietly he watched them both inwardly calming himself. Although he had not shown it he had been deeply concerned for Elaena during the birth, because of her panic he feared she wouldn't make it. Now, seeing his lover holding his only child, he was filled with a deep sense of relief...and love. Niwelyn, aware of Paedur's strong, quiet presence beside her, looked down on Elaena and her baby. She too had been greatly concerned during the birth, Elaena's panic seemed over exaggerated and she knew that when a woman lost control during birthing things quite often went wrong. Her calmness during the birth came from experience, seeing now that all was well, she allowed herself to relax. Watching Elaena holding her baby, seeing her cooing softly to her and running her fingers around her head and face, she smiled. Beside her Paedur knelt down beside the bed, kissed Elaena softly on the forehead and turned his attention to his baby. Together they became acquainted with her stroking, caressing and kissing her. Niwelyn looked down on them and a wave of emotion swept over her, a wave of...jealousy.

While Paedur and Elaena were busy acquainting themselves with their baby Niwelyn deftly began to clean Elaena up and make sure that she was not going to experience any after birth problems. Somewhere deep inside her she knew that Paedur would blame her if something went wrong and she didn't want to incur his wrath. Firmly but gently she worked until she was sure that Elaena was in no danger. When she was absolutely certain that all was well she went over to the fire, scooped some hot water into a blue painted glass with a gold Celtic cross design on it, and lay it on the heart stones. Crouching down she took another bottle out of her bag, this time containing Anthemis nobilis (Roman Chamomile) and tipped it into the hot water, swirling it around she got to her feet. Bringing it over to Elaena, she bid her drink, when she had done so she returned to the hearth and washed the glass. Turning her back on Paedur and Elaena she sat down by the fire, scooped some hot water into the glass for herself and put some Chamomile into it, slowly, quietly, she drank. Very much aware of their presence, but allowing them their time together, she waited, allowing the herbs to work on Elaena. Presently Elaena began to grow drowsy, handing the baby to Paedur; she sank down into the bed and totally gave in to the feeling of exhaustion that was beginning to sweep over her. Her breathing had returned to normal and she felt calm inside, as a wave of pure exhaustion completely engulfed her, she sank into a peaceful sleep.

Holding the baby cradled in his arms he gently kissed Elaena, covered her with a soft pink blanket and slowly, carefully, he got to his feet. The baby's head was lying in the crook of his elbow, her feet resting in his palm. He kissed her softly on the forehead; her skin felt like silk. Walking over to the table he took up a soft white blanket and wrapped it around her; holding her in his arms made him feel strange, this was a feeling even he couldn't describe. Not having personally experienced this before, he had no words, in any language, to accurately express his emotions at that moment. Seeing that she was becoming drowsy, he gently placed her in a cot beside Elaena's bed and stood watching them both for a few minutes...sleeping peacefully.

Going over to the fire and pouring himself a glass of red wine, from a samian ware jug resting on the hearth, he sat down beside Niwelyn. His presence seemed to fill the room, power and strength emanated from him. Silently she watched him out of the corner of her eye as he stared into the fire. Together they sat in silence, the flames reflecting in their eyes, the serpents on Paedur's pendent seemed to glow matching the colour of the flames. Presently Niwelyn said, "Go wash and change, I will stay and watch over them".

Silently Paedur nodded exhaustion clearly visible on his face. Slowly he got to his feet, went over to the press and selected some clothes, a heavy blanket, a large towel and, wrapping his cloak around his shoulders, he left the room. Everyone stopped when he entered the courtyard and waited, in a quiet voice infused with exhaustion all he said was, "A baby girl, mother and baby are well".

A wave of relief swept over everybody, the women clapped, the children danced and the men ran their fingers through their hair or beards nodding. Násuin closed his eyes and took several deep calming breaths.

Without another word Paedur walked down to the stream and bathed, he gave himself totally to the coolness and freshness of the water, although it was only March the sun was warm and bright that day. Raising his face to the sun he drank in its warmth and strength, the water cooled his body and cleared his head. His emotions were all jumbled up; he couldn't remember when he last felt this mixture of emotions, if ever. He searched in his head among the several languages he spoke fluently and wrote but could find no appropriate words; eventually he gave up and gave in to the experience. Presently he got out, towelled dry and dressed, wrapping his cloak tightly around him with his hood up over his head and face he lay down on the blanket... and slept.

Niwelyn, sitting by the fire, continued her vigil, she too was feeling emotional, relief that all went well during the birth and appeared to be still, the fear of Paedur's wrath, no longer appropriate, she let it go. His presence seemed to fill the room even though he was no longer in it, she felt his presence inside her and she felt jealous. She had not realised, until that moment, just how much he meant to her and she had also not realised just how much Elaena meant to Paedur. She realised that Paedur and Elaena were now together two years and she knew, no matter what she thought of him or how she felt for him, that they would only ever be friends. By the time Paedur returned to the great hall the town was alive, excitement evident on every face. The children busied themselves making things for Elaena and the baby, the women cooked up food. The men went to the taberna congratulating themselves and the warriors double checked the town's defences.

Násuin watched his men at work, dressed in brown bracae and a long sleeved cream tunic his hair tied back in a high pony tail, he became aware of his own feelings. He shook his head "*Warriors do not have feelings and commanders have even less*", he thought, yet still he felt very strange. For several minutes he pondered deeply quietly trying to put a word to what he felt, eventually only one word came to mind...jealousy. Seeing Paedur coming into the courtyard and cross to the great hall he looked at him observing, he seemed preoccupied; not seeing anyone at that moment. Násuin almost hated his friend, he narrowed his eyes and emitted a low growl, then he shook his head and returned to his men barking out orders.

The light was fading the night was drawing in and he wanted to make sure the town was secure before nightfall. He also knew that Paedur would blame him if they were attacked that night and he knew it was a perfect night for attack. Assured that all was well, he released his men and returned to his quarters.

Coming in to his house he closed the door and noticed that a small fire had been lit for him, walking past his bed and hearth he felt the warmth of the fire as he passed by. Going to the press he took out a glass and filled it with red wine from a samian ware jug sitting on the table, carrying the glass over to the fire he sat on his bench facing the fire. He thought over the events of the day and especially Elaena giving birth to Paedur's child. He knew that she fascinated him and being in her company intoxicated him but, until this moment, he didn't realise that he actually loved her and he didn't know why. What was it about her that stirred up these feelings for her? He had been with many women and felt nothing for them; they were just a quick moment of pleasure but nothing to be taken seriously. Yet here was this young woman who had lived in his town all her life and he hadn't seen her until recently. Oh, he had passed her on the street, he knew her and her family, he had met her in the taberna and knew what she did but, until now, he hadn't fully realised that, through Paedur, he had actually fallen in love with her.

He took a sip of wine and drew in a big deep breath; he stared into the fire and saw her face looking back at him. He remembered the day she had first come to him for training and how he had pinned her against him, he remembered her defiance and her unwillingness to learn and he remembered the intoxicating smell of her.

This time he took a large gulp of wine. Only for Paedur he would probably never have "seen" her and would probably never have taken any interest in her but, through his friendship, he had come to know her and see her as a person and not just a face on the street and in the taberna. He had seen her change from scruffy gutter rat to beautiful woman and now he wanted that woman for himself but he knew he could not have her. She was Paedur's woman, and now the mother of his child, and that meant she was out of his reach and at best they would only ever be friends. His one consolation was that Paedur had made him her protector and as such it would allow him to be close to her and in her company officially. He could still harbour his feelings for her but could never let them show.

He took another large gulp of wine and stared into the fire and then a thought struck him...

"*What if the Romans did make a concerted effort to win over the town? What if the governor came and put the Druids to death? What would become of Elaena and her baby, would they take her for themselves*", he had recently heard rumours that they were interested in her, "*or would they put her to death with the other Druids?*

He thought about this for a few minutes and remembered his conversation with Paedur just after he had arrived about their plan to rise up and rebel against the Romans.

"*What if something bad did happen to Paedur, what would Elaena do, who would she turn to and who could she depend upon*". He knew if something did happen to Paedur his men and the Roman soldiers would regard her as fair game. He knew that they would make use of her given that before she had become Paedur's woman she had been a prostitute and some of them had made use of her services.

He took another large gulp of wine and took a very long slow deep breath. He stared into the fire...and then another thought struck him...if something did happen to Paedur, "*What if I were to take her on as my woman...it would certainly take her out of the reach of my men... and the Romans would not touch her either...it would afford her some protection and keep her status high among the townspeople*".

He drained his glass and went back over to the table to replenish it; he returned to the bench and sat down again staring into the fire. "*What if I were to take her on as my woman...how would I present that notion to Paedur...what would his reaction be...*

and what would become of their baby...if I take on Elaena I will have to take on her baby too...Paedur's child...how do I feel about that?."
He took a very large gulp of wine and his head spun.
"Oh God", he growled, "What has become of me?"
He stared into the fire. The more he thought about it the more he saw the sense in it...but he also saw the difficulty he would face. He suspected Paedur would not let her go and even asking would probably damage his friendship with him and perhaps even Elaena herself.
Again he took a large gulp of wine and an even bigger deep breath. He thought the idea through again and the thought of somehow making her his grew more attractive to him. He knew that the only way he could convince Paedur to let her go would be under the guise of protection. He didn't know if he would succeed but he did know that he had to try.
He drained the contents of his glass in one large gulp and stood up, as he did so he stumbled and had to check his footing. Slowly he steadied himself and walked back to the table and put his glass down, he didn't even attempt to wash it he suspected one of the women would do it for him tomorrow. He took several deep breaths and then returned to the courtyard to make a final check before closing the gate.

Paedur quietly entered the room; Niwelyn was quietly sitting by the fire writing, Elaena and the baby slept peacefully, there was an air of calmness and serenity in the room. He crossed to the fire, Niwelyn stood up putting her work on the stool, he took both her hands in his, raised them to his lips and kissed them saying, "Druantia bless you this night". Shaking his head and looking deeply into her eyes he continued, "Thank you, Elyn, we are forever in your debt".
"Croeso, Paedur", she replied bowing.
"Go now wash, change and rest, I will keep watch", he advised.
"Diolch", she replied.
Together they looked at the bed. Quietly Niwelyn asked, "What shall you call her"?

For several minutes Paedur remained silent, looking at both mother and baby, eventually he replied affectionately, "Elaena". He helped Niwelyn gather her things then walked her to the door holding it open for her. When she reached the courtyard she found Násuin standing by the fire, he looked up, their eyes locked and they held each other in a long, empathetic stare. She went over to him and for a few minutes they stood together staring into the fire.

Taking a deep breath he asked, "How goes it?"

Nodding she said, "All is well".

"We have lost them" he said.

"Aye, it seems we have", she sighed.

Both looked at each other.

"It has been a long day", he said.

"Indeed it has", she agreed. "I am tired I shall return home now".

"Shall I escort you, My Lady", he asked.

"No, Násuin, diolch, I am safe alone", she replied.

"Nos da then", he said.

"Nos da, Násuin" she said tiredly, turned and left the courtyard. Násuin locked the gate behind her and then returned to his quarters.

Paedur checked the two Elaenas, when he was absolutely certain that they were in no danger, he crossed to his own bed, wrapping his cloak tightly around him with the hood up over his head and covering his face he lay down and slept.

The next day Elaena woke up tired and sore, her insides felt weak, she lay in her bed piecing together the events of the previous day. Secretly she had feared giving birth but once the pains began she had no time to think about it and things seemed to just happen. Now, in the quietness of early morning, she was able to realise that Paedur and Niwelyn had remained calm and relaxed throughout the birth. It would seem that they were happy with how it had gone and that everything happened as it was supposed to. She moved and pain shot through her. She moved again, this time more slowly, to see what parts of her hurt, her belly felt strange, her hips felt stretched and her legs felt weak. She took a few deep breaths and tried to remain calm, she reasoned that if there was something wrong Paedur would already know about it and know how to fix it. She moved again gently trying to work out how she could move without causing herself pain.

Paedur became aware of her movement and raised his head above his pillow to check on Elaena, seeing that she was awake he got up and went over to her. Dressed in a long simple cotton shift he walked bare footed across the floor as he passed the fire he stopped, stoked it and put extra logs into the grate. Coming to the side of her bed he looked down at her, she looked back up at him with wide eyes. She moved and winced.

"Are you in pain?" he asked.

She nodded.

"Where"?

She pointed to her belly, hips and legs.

He nodded, "That would be the after effects of giving birth", he said. "I will have Niwelyn check in on you later to make sure that all is well".

"Diolch", she said quietly.

He walked over to the table and poured some water out of a covered jug into a glass and brought it over to her. Placing it down on the press beside her bed he then gently assisted her to sit up, she moved slowly and cumbersomely and accepted his help gratefully. When she was seated and propped up with pillows he handed her the glass and sat on the side of her bed while she sipped the water slowly.

Out of the corner of his eye he looked for signs of movement from the baby but his whole focus was on Elaena, it was more important to him that she was alright. He took in her appearance her long hair tumbled down her back in a dishevelled mess, her eyes looked tired and fearful, there were dark circles under her eyes. Her face was dry and haggard; her usually full red lips were thin and pink, her hands shook as she raised the glass to them and sipped carefully. The cotton tunic she wore was creased and slightly wet.

"Are you hungry", he asked.
Taking another sip of water she shook her head.
"Nevertheless, it is advised that you eat something, even if it is only something small, it will help to give you back your strength and energy", he said.
Getting up he walked over to the table, took an apple from a large bowl beside the jug, cut it into quarters and brought them back to her bed. Sitting down on the bed again he handed one to her, took one for himself and held the other two in his left hand. Silently they ate, she gingerly. When she was finished the first quarter he handed her a second one and finished the apple himself. There was an air of quietness in the room. When she was finished the apple she took another sip of water then handed the glass back to him.
The baby squeaked and moved and both looked over at her.
"Is that it?" Elaena asked. "Is that the baby?"
"That is her", Paedur replied.
"Is she well?" she asked.
"Yes, it would seem so", he replied.
"What shall we call her?" she asked.
"I was thinking Elaena...after her mother", he replied affectionately.
Elaena quickly looked at him, he looked back at her, both held each other's stare.
Elaena took a deep breath, "If that is your wish, so shall it be", she said.
Paedur nodded.
Baby Elaena moved and gave a tentative cry. Paedur stood up, put the glass back on the table, reached down into the cot and gently scooped her into his arms. She opened her eyes and looked up at him, he looked down into hers and smiled, a wave of love washed over him. Elaena looked at him holding their baby and saw the tender look of love on his face for her. He snuggled her closer against his chest and looked over at Elaena, she held her arms out towards him. Slowly he walked over to her and placed baby Elaena into her arms, she held her close to her chest like

she had seen him do and held her in her arms. Together they sat on the bed drinking in her appearance and presence.

Just then a knock came to the door, Paedur walked over to the door and opened it

"Bore da", said Niwelyn.

"Bore da", Niwelyn, I was about to go looking for you, but you are already here, come in", Paedur said as he opened the door wider for her to step through.

"I thought you would be up and in need of help so I came to offer assistance", she said. "The Elaena's are well?"

Paedur looked down at the floor with a soft compassionate look on his face, "Hum! The Elaenas, I like the sound of that", he said smiling.

Dressed in a long dark blue velvet gown with soft boots, her travelling cloak and carrying her medical bag, Niwelyn put the bag down at the end of Elaena's bed, walked over to the fire stoked it and placed the cauldron filled with water on the tripod, "Open the shutters", she said.

Paedur immediately crossed the room and did as she had instructed. Bright sunlight bathed the room, everyone's eyes hurt for a moment and they all turned their faces while they adjusted to the light. Niwelyn took off her cloak and draped it across the end of Paedur's bed.

Walking back over to Elaena she said, "How are you?"

"I have pain", Elaena replied.

"Where?" asked Niwelyn.

"Here", replied Elaena pointing to her belly, hips and legs.

Niwelyn nodded, "Are you well enough to go to the Bathhouse?"

"No, my legs are too weak", Elaena replied.

"Bowl wash here it is then", decided Niwelyn.

Going over to her bag she opened it and took out a leather apron, "Have you eaten?" she asked.

Elaena shook her head, Paedur replied, "Only half an apple each".

Niwelyn nodded, "Go get some food then, the women are still down at the fire".

Paedur nodded and was about to carry out her order when there was a knock on the door, he crossed the room and opened it, one of the women handed him a basket of food and clean towels saying, "Násuin instructed me to deliver these to you".
Paedur bowed and replied, "Thank you for bringing it to us and thank him for thinking ahead for us, we are most grateful".
She nodded and left.
By the time Paedur had brought the basket to the table Niwelyn had already filled a large glass bowl with warm water, had seated herself at the end of Elaena's bed and was already checking her.
"There appears to be no damage done, all is as it should be. You are young so you will heal quickly", she said.
Elaena nodded.
Paedur replied "That is good". "What is causing her pain?"
"After effects of birth, nothing more", replied Niwelyn.
"That is what I thought", he replied. "Is there need for herbs to assist?"
"No, nature will do what needs to be done now", she replied.
Paedur nodded.
Looking into the basket he took out the towels and laid them on the table, under them was a selection of breads, fruit, grains and vegetables, there was also a small amphora of red wine.
"What do you suggest we eat?" he asked Niwelyn.
"Make up a pot of porridge", she replied. "We could all do with the fortification".
He immediately scooped up a cupful of oats into a pot, brought it over to the fire and put some boiling water into it, mixed it around and placed it on a smaller tripod over the fire. While he was waiting he went over to the dresser and took out three bowls and spoons. Niwelyn continued to work deftly, when she was finished she stood up and walked to the top of the bed, reaching down she gently took the baby out of Elaena's arms, Elaena squealed in distress.
"She needs to be checked and cleaned", Niwelyn said authoritatively, "and you need to eat".
Elaena looked beseechingly at Paedur, he nodded reassuringly and Elaena quietened down.

"Feed her", Niwelyn commanded and brought the baby over to the table. Holding her in one arm she spread out one of the new towels on the table and gently placed her on it, she inspected her from head to toe.

Paedur took the three bowls and spoons and walked over to the fire, scooped out a portion of porridge into one of the bowels and brought it over to Elaena she took it and slowly, with shaky hands, began to eat. Paedur returned to the fire and scooped out two more portions into the other two bowls, sitting at the end of Elaena's bed, he began eating. Niwelyn completed her inspection and wrapped the baby up in the towel and gently placed her back in her cot. She then walked over to the fire, took up her bowel of porridge and began eating. All three eat in silence while baby Elaena made cooing noises. When they were finished Paedur took all three bowels and spoons and began washing them. Niwelyn instructed Elaena to take her tunic off and assisted her to have a bed bath.

Turning to Paedur she said, "Go have a wash and change of clothes, I will assist Elaena now".

Silently he nodded, gathered up some fresh clothes and, wrapping his travelling cloak around him; he left the room and headed for the fort bathhouse. As he passed the fire the same woman who had given him the basket of provisions was finishing clearing up after breakfast.

"Diolch, you are most kind", he said.

She nodded and asked, "Is the Lady Elaena and her baby well".

"They are", he replied. "Thank you for asking".

"Thank the Goddess for that", she said.

"We already have", he said.

Walking past her he walked over to the bathhouse, just then Násuin came out of his dwelling and saw Paedur going in the door of the bathhouse. He contemplated following him then, decided not to, he figured Paedur wanted to be alone.

Making sure that Elaena was sitting up straight and propped comfortably Niwelyn handed the baby to her showing her how to hold her against her breast to feed her. At first Elaena winched but quickly got the hang of it and managed quite well.

Then bringing the baby over to the table Niwelyn showed her how to change the nappy using cotton clothes. Elaena looked on with amazement and committed the sequence and movements to memory. Once the baby was burped and changed Niwelyn dressed her and put her back into her cot.
Going over to Elaena she pulled the bed covers off her and commanded, "Get up and walk".
"I do not want to, my legs are weak", replied Elaena.
"Get up and walk", commanded Niwelyn.
"No".
"Get up and walk".
"No, I will not".
"If you do not walk you will remain weak and recovery will be slow".
"I do not want to I am too tired and weak".
"Then you will remain so and you will be of no use to anyone".
Elaena, realising that Niwelyn wasn't going to give in, swung her legs over the side of the bed and stood up. She wobbled and almost fell but Niwelyn quickly grabbed her and steadied her.
"Stand for a moment and find your feet", Niwelyn advised, still holding on to her.
Elaena stood holding tightly on to Niwelyn's arms.
Taking one step backwards Niwelyn made it possible for Elaena to walk forward, she took several more steps backwards bringing Elaena with her. Slowly Elaena got the feel of her feet and their pace increased.
Niwelyn then gently let her go and said, "Now walk towards me on your own".
Unsteadily Elaena did so and after a few paces reached out for Niwelyn's arm again and stood holding on to her breathing hard. Niwelyn gently turned her around and, putting her arm around Elaena's waist, patiently walked her back to her bed.
"Very good, well done, later we will try again, for now get some rest and sleep if you can. Remember, from here on sleep when the baby sleeps, that way you will rebuild your strength later you will be able to work while the baby sleeps", Niwelyn advised.

Elaena got back into bed assisted by Niwelyn, snuggled down and was asleep in minutes.

Paedur entered the foyer and went immediately to the apodyterium and, placing his clean clothes into his alcove, he noticed that number fourteen now had a tile with a candle design and Elaena's name on it. He smiled to himself and looking around the room noticed that number one had a sword design and Násuin's name on it, other alcoves had pictures but no names. He walked over to the press and took out some towels, removed his clothes and wrapped himself in the large towel. Holding the small one in his hand he walked through the archway into the tepidarium, dropped his towel at the side of the pool, stepped in and submerged himself totally. For several minutes he remained beneath the surface wallowing in the warmth of the water then, coming back to the surface, he swam several lengths of the pool. After a few minutes he lay on the surface of the water floating, his eyes closed his breathing calm and relaxed. He was alone so he surrendered to the feel of the water and the quietness of the room. Presently he swam over to the side and got out, wrapped himself in the towel and used the small one to dry his hair, returning to the apodyterium he dressed and left the bathhouse.

As he walked back to his room across the courtyard he put his hood up over his head indicating that he didn't want to be approached. Although the courtyard was rather busy everyone appreciated that he wanted space and honoured this.

When he returned to his room the Elaena's were asleep and Niwelyn was sitting at the table making notes. She looked up as he entered the room and smiled.

Walking across the room to the table he said, "Niwelyn, thank you so much for helping us today, we are most grateful".

Standing up she replied, "Croeso, I have shown Elaena how to breastfeed and wash and change the baby. I have also got her to take a few steps herself; she is weak and unsteady on her feet. Rest will help her strength to return but we must encourage her to move, at the moment she is not inclined to".

"Perhaps we should honour her wish to rest at first but I agree we should encourage her to move, I will see to it that she does. Now, go and rest and take care of yourself if we need you we will send someone to get you".

Nodding she looked at the Elaenas and then left. As she crossed the courtyard Násuin detached himself from his men and went over to her.

"How are the new family?" he asked.

"Well, thank you", she replied.

"Is there anything I can do to assist?" he asked.

"No, Násuin, I do not think so", she replied.

Looking directly into her eyes he said, "I want to be of assistance".

Looking directly back into his she took a deep breath and opened her mouth.

"...Please", he interrupted.

"Niwelyn closed her mouth and held his stare. He looked pleadingly back at her.

She sighed deeply and then nodded saying, "Alright". "I will put your request to Paedur and see how he is willing to integrate you.

"Can I not do that myself", he asked.

"Perhaps you can, but I am not sure how he will react. How much does he know of your love for Elaena"?

"Nothing", he replied.

"Good, let us keep it that way, if he does not suspect he will be more willing to allow you to help", she said.

"Now, Násuin, I am extremely tired, if you will excuse me, I am in need of rest", she continued.

"Of course, My Lady, forgive me I forget myself. Shall I escort you?"

"No, Násuin, I am quite safe, thank you".

He nodded and bowed and returned to his men, Niwelyn left the fort and returned to her roundhouse.

Chapter Ten

The following day Niwelyn checked in on Paedur and the Elaenas, Elaena was sitting up feeding baby Elaena and seemed to be coping quite well. Paedur had just finished washing up after breakfast and was tidying the room. One shutter was open allowing light and fresh air into the room, the other was closed allowing Elaena to have some shade when resting.

Going over to Elaena Niwelyn asked, "How are you today?"

"Much better, thank you, I am not in as much pain", Elaena replied.

"That is good, perhaps we can get you up and out for a short walk today", Niwelyn said.

"Is that wise?" asked Elaena.

"Very much so", she replied. "As soon as you are finished we shall wash and change you and get you down the stairs at least".

Elaena looked at Paedur; he nodded reassuringly and said, "We will assist you".

Elaena nodded.

"Give me Elna", Niwelyn said, "I will attend to her needs while you attend to your own".

Paedur smiled and quietly said, "Elna, huh, I like that one too".

Elaena handed Elna to Niwelyn and stood up, she was still cumbersome but steady on her feet this time. Paedur readied a bowl of hot water and towels for her and got a fresh gown, underclothes and boots and laid them on her bed.

Looking at Elaena he said, "We will leave you to wash. We will be outside the door in the corridor, if you need assistance call us".

Quietly she nodded. Slowly she took her clothes off and began washing and thought back to her first day here when she had done the same thing. Washing herself was a bit difficult, her abdomen was still extended and she found it hard to get to some parts of her body but she did and felt all the better for it. When she was washed she dried herself and put on the fresh gown, this one was dark brown with gold trimmings.

Looking down on the sleeping baby she fought within herself to describe her feelings. "*The pregnancy went well, there were no problems and I birthed safely, now I have this little...thing...this little creature that I am responsible for and I have absolutely no idea what to do with it*", she thought. "*Niwelyn has shown me how to feed, wash and dress the baby but I suspect there is so much more to it than that. I am hardly able to take care of myself, how...in the name of the Goddess...am I going to take care of this...thing*", she wondered.

"*My childhood is a blur, I can hardly remember it and any memory I have is only of bad things*", she thought. "*I did not know that there would be so much pain, I was not prepared for it, I do not think I can take care of her*", she agonised rubbing her abdomen.

She took a deep breath and closed her eyes she took several more deep breaths and then opened her eyes, looking down on baby Elaena she said, "I will give you a good life, I will give you all the things I never had...and I will make sure that no one... ever takes advantage of you". "I will be a good mother for you and I will love you like I wanted to be loved".

While they were in the corridor waiting for Elaena to wash Niwelyn said to Paedur, "Násuin is enquiring as to the health of the Elaenas, he wants to know if he can be of assistance".

"Why?" asked Paedur.

"As your friend...and protector...and, as Chief Warrior, he is concerned for all the dwellers within the fort walls. In olden times he would have been Chieftain and the welfare of everyone would have been his responsibility. In these modern times he is merely Chief Warrior, a role that has no real responsibility attached", she explained.

"So let him enjoy that", Paedur said flippantly.

Niwelyn nodded, "That is all very well, but as your friend, he wants to assist, he just does not know how and awaits your instruction", she continued.

"Is his concern genuine?" he asked.

"I do believe it is", she replied nodding.

Paedur nodded and thought a few moments then nodded again and said, "I will speak with him".
"Then go do so now", she advised.
Paedur nodded, turned and walked down the corridor, Niwelyn knocked on the door, awaited Elaena's permission to enter and went in.
Paedur found Násuin sitting alone by the open fire in the courtyard. He had dispatched some of his men to the weapons store and the rest of them to the stables. Holding a cup of hot brew in his hands he stared into the flames pensively.
Paedur approached him and looking down at him asked. "May I join you?"
Násuin looked up and replied, "Of course", and gestured to Paedur to sit on the next log beside him.
"Elaena is somewhat weak after the birth and Elna requires a lot of attention". Paedur began.
"Elna?" said Násuin quizzically.
Paedur smiled, "Baby Elaena, for some reason Niwelyn called her Elna this morning and we all quite like it, it distinguishes the Elaenas and seems more appropriate for one so small", he explained.
Násuin nodded.
"Elaena's training is incomplete; she still has much to learn but at the moment is weak and vulnerable. I will not always be able to be with them, I wonder would you be willing to keep an eye on them for me and look out for their safety".
Násuin closed his eyes and took a long silent deep breath, "It would be the greatest honour to do so", he replied. "When can I see them?" he asked.
"We will be taking them for a walk later, you can see them then", Paedur replied.
"I shall look forward to that", said Násuin.
"In fact I think they are probably ready to be presented now, I will go and get them", Paedur continued.
He stood up and walked towards the great hall. Násuin watched him.

Going into their room Paedur found Elaena and Niwelyn with Elna sitting at the table, “Do you think you are ready to take a short walk now?” he asked.
Niwelyn nodded, stood up and took Elna while Paedur assisted Elaena to her feet, carrying Elna she preceded them down the stairs. Paedur linked Elaena’s arm, walked her slowly across the room and down the corridor. When they got to the top of the stairs he said, “I will go ahead, put your hand on my shoulder and take one step at a time”. Slowly they made it to the bottom of the stairs where Niwelyn was waiting for them.
At the bottom of the stairs Elaena stood leaning against the wall breathing hard for a few minutes. She took a few deep breaths and, when her breathing had calmed down, Niwelyn handed her Elna and held the door open for her. As Elaena stepped through the door Paedur and Niwelyn fell into step behind her, one on either side.
As Elaena emerged from the hall everyone stopped what they were doing and there was a round of applause. Násuin stood up and waited for them to make their way to the open fire, everyone gathered around them and immediately started fussing over Elna. Paedur took her in his arms and held her protectively while everyone took it in turns to have a look at her. The children squealed in delight at her cooing noises and funny faces.
Elaena stood at the edge of the group and looked on.
Násuin went over to her, “My Lady, it is good to see you and to know that you are well.”
“Elaena...remember?”
“Bowing he replied, “Elaena...I was not sure I could still use your given name”.
“And why wouldn’t you”?
“Your...status has changed now”, he replied.
“That may be so, but I am still Elaena to you”, she said. “You are Paedur’s friend and protector, that means you are my friend too”.
“I am so glad to hear that”, he said inwardly smiling.
“Are you not interested in the baby?” she asked.

"No", he replied quietly. "I am more interested in you".
Elaena looked at him and saw him staring at her; quietly he said, "I was concerned for you".
"Well, as you can see, I am fine, I do not need your concern", she replied haughtily.
"So it would seem", he replied nodding. "Paedur has asked me to be your protector...is that your personal wish too"?
"Do I need one", she asked almost aggressively.
"Paedur thinks you do", he replied quietly.
"I cannot imagine why if, as you say my status has changed, then I am no longer fair game and therefore should not need any more protection than any other woman", she said haughtily.
"The other women are just women; you are...the Chief Druid of Cymru's woman...and therefore are a...prime target", he explained.
"Oh! I am tired of men making decisions for me", she said in exasperation. "Be my protector if that is what you have been... ordered to do", she replied impatiently.
"Not an order...more a request", he said inclining his head, "but one I am most happy to grant".
She looked at him and he looked back at her.
"Elaena, are you well", he asked with a slight edge of concern in his voice. "Did birthing go well for you"?
"It hurt. It has made me weak and I have difficulty walking and doing things", she replied angrily.
"I am sorry to hear that", he said quietly. "Is there anything I can do to help"?
Again she looked at him and he held her stare.
Just then one of the women came over to Elaena and said, "Congratulations, you have a fine baby and you are well".
Násuin quietly stepped back and stood behind Elaena, watching.

***

Over the next few weeks the days became warmer and longer, the trees burst into leaf, the flowers began to grace the town with colour and town life returned to normal. The men returned to their work and the children returned to their lessons. The women continued their home duties and work and the warriors continued their defence and surveillance of the town.

The last two months had been exceptionally busy for Niwelyn; three babies had been born in the month of February, the result of last year's Bealteinne festivities and baby Elaena in March. She visited each household every day instructing, treating and reassuring, she had very little spare time and less time to think, when she got a few quiet moments to herself, she slept.

At the Bealteinne/Ludi Florales festivities the ground was dry, the scent of flowers wafted on the breeze and there was a slight chill in the air. There was much to celebrate, no one had presented for hand fasting but there were four healthy babies and mothers to celebrate and there was much excitement in the town. The days had become quite long and warm, the birds sang loudly and the flowers were in bloom. The Romans danced around the area outside the temple decked in floral garments, their Goddess Flora was decorated with flowers and all around her statue tables were piled high with flowers.

Early on the morning of the festivities Niwelyn brought the children into the forest and together they collected the sweet-scented hawthorn which was bursting with blossom. Carefully she cut off the branches and gave one to each child then she cut several more and the children placed them in the basket.

At mid-morning one of the Druids and Niwelyn, both dressed in green gowns with soft brown leather sandals on their feet, began the parade at the Fort Gate. This year, representing the May Queen Creiddylad, Kerri dressed in a light green floral gown, a crown of flowers on her head and a basket of flowers in her hands, rode through the streets on a flower decorated cart pulled by a warrior on his horse. The warrior, dressed in dark brown bracae with a dark green thigh length tunic and soft brown leather boots, this year represented the Green Man, the God of Nature.

As she passed the townspeople followed behind the cart, when they arrived at the altar in the oak grove, it was decorated with flowers and the hawthorn branches that the children had gathered earlier in the day. Making their way to the altar and facing south-east the Druid and Niwelyn began the chant. One by one each person joined in and after a few minutes the forest rang with the sound of their voices.

When the chant stopped there was a moment's silence. The warrior dismounted his horse, assisted Kerri down from the cart and accompanied her to the altar; clumsily she placed her basket in the centre of the altar and stepped back. The women approached the May Pole and each one tied a coloured ribbon around it, Kerri danced self consciously around the May Pole. The Druid stepped away from the altar and lit the bonfire, the warrior ran towards Kerri and chased her into the forest, under the branches of the hawthorn he caught her and led her back to the altar.

Niwelyn called, "Goddess Creiddylad, bless us with abundance and health this year".

Paedur had been relieved of his duties on this occasion, standing by the fire with Elaena at his side and baby Elaena in her arms, he felt proud and content. Both he and Elaena were dressed in dark blue silk long tunics, presents they had received from his Order on Ynys Mon. Paedur's hair was loose, Elaena's was braided, baby Elaena was dressed in fine linen and lay cooing in her mother's arms, around her wrists were tiny garlands of flowers made especially for her by the children. Paedur stood with his arm protectively around Elaena. Násuin, dressed in plain brown bracae and yellow plaid hip length tunic under a leather breastplate with soft leather boots, stood beside Elaena protectively, his left hand gently on the top of his sword, his eyes watchful, his ears listening and his senses tuned to the slightest hint of danger,

Niwelyn dressed in a dark blue velvet gown, her hair loosely hanging to her waist called, "Parents present your babies for naming".

The four sets of parents stepped up to the altar and stood in front of it; Násuin became more alert and tightened his hold on the top of his sword.

Niwelyn asked the three sets of parents to name their child and then she turned to Paedur and Elaena. In a strong voice she asked, "How shall you name your child".

Together, Paedur in a strong voice, Elaena much quieter, answered, "Elaena".

"So shall it be", called Niwelyn. "May good health and strength be bestowed upon all parents and babies presented here today".

The Druid nodded to Kerri.

"Join me in song, feasting and dance", she called.

Immediately the women dished out the food, the musicians played their instruments and sang and the children played. Kerri returned to her friends and joined in the festivities.

As the festivities continued and the women fussed over the Elaenas, Paedur went over to the fire and sat quietly alone staring into it; Násuin joined him, placing himself so that he could continue to watch Elaena.

"There is much celebration tonight", he said sitting beside Paedur.

"Mmm, let them enjoy, I fear the excitement will be short lived", Paedur replied.

"I fear you may be right, Paedur", agreed Násuin. The barbarians grow ever more militant; they have now recruited several ex-members of the Roman Army and are being schooled by them".

He watched Paedur and continued, "The Roman Empire is in total disarray; Stilicho has been put to death and Honorius continues his exile in Ravenna. Alaric has threatened Roma and has tremendous support and, as expected, the Vandals have invaded Hispania".

He paused again waiting.

"The Christians grow stronger too", said Paedur, "they fill the people's heads with notions of a single male God and this Jesus Christ figure seems to have captured their hearts and minds".

He paused continuing to stare into the fire. "Their Priests preach repent and reform and encourage the people to take part in their new ceremonies involving the body and blood of Christ".

Both men sat in silence each in his own thoughts, shoulder to shoulder...equals, eventually Násuin turned and looked at Paedur, he noticed the deeper lines around his eyes and lips. His expression had become darker and more pensive, his eyes slightly harder and his hair flecked with more white.

Elaena, tired still from the effects of the birth, yawned and made her way over to the fire, both men stood up when she arrived. Násuin stood back a few paces his hands resting loosely by his sides, his eyes watching all around.

Paedur affectionately looked at Elaena and asked, "Are you well, Elaena"?

"I am, Paedur, but I grow weary, I think I will return to the great hall", she replied.

"I will accompany you", he said.

"No", Elaena replied, resting her hands on his right arm, "some of the women are also returning we will walk together and one of them will carry Elna for me", she continued.

Paedur nodded but continued to watch her in case she changed her mind.

"I will dispatch some of my men to accompany you", Násuin offered behind Paedur.

Elaena looked around Paedur at Násuin and replied, "No need to Násuin, though thank you, no one will attack us tonight, I know you have seen to that".

"Thank you for your confidence, Elaena", he replied bowing.

Still with her hands on Paedur's right arm she kissed him, "Nos da", she said softly.

"Nos da, sleep well, I will return soon", he replied.

They kissed and Elaena walked away.

Násuin returned to Paedur's side, together they watched her walk over to the women. One woman linked her arm around Elaena's, another fell into step beside her cradling baby Elaena in her arms. Three other women formed a protective arc around them and together they walked back to the great hall.

"Do whatever it takes to keep this place safe" said Paedur in a hard voice, still watching Elaena.

"I will guard it with my life", replied Násuin also still watching Elaena.
"Inform your men that the warriors and the Druids will meet next month, we will discuss tactics then", continued Paedur.
"As you wish, My Lord", replied Násuin bowing.
They shook hands looking into each other's eyes for a moment then parted. Násuin returned to his men noticing that Niwelyn was nowhere in sight. Paedur returned to the great hall, when he arrived in his room the Elaenas were already asleep.

***

Since the birth of baby Elaena Paedur had stopped all training with Elaena, he felt she had enough to do adjusting to taking care of the baby and herself. He helped as much as he could delighting in baby Elaena's squeaks and coos, learning how to distinguish the different tones of cry to establish her needs. Together he and Elaena grew in love with each other and baby Elaena.
The townspeople made sure their every need was provided for, clothes for the Elaenas, food and drink for them all. Niwelyn assisted by day, Paedur by night; sometimes it took all three of them to care for baby Elaena. Paedur was extremely protective of them both and constantly kept a watchful eye over them. When he and Niwelyn were unable to be with them he made sure one of the women would assist instead and that Násuin was keeping guard. There was no shortage of available women even the children came in and played with baby Elaena as often as they could.
....
May turned to June and the air became hot and sometimes oppressive everyone, both men and women, Roman and Cymru, took to the Roman custom of short tunics. Again the town started gearing up for the Solstice festivities, this year the children excelled themselves with decorations and gifts for all the new babies. Each one made an extra special gift for baby

Elaena; they now called Elaena Mama and baby Elaena Elna sister.

At mid-day Paedur and Niwelyn, both dressed in long blue silk gowns, conducted the ceremonies, both silently aware that the new religion was rapidly taking hold, facing south, they began the chant. One by one the townspeople joined in and the grove rang with the sound of their voices, the trees joined in too and a deep sense of calm and peace hung in the air the forest hummed with energy and everyone felt its effect.

When quietness returned Paedur lit a candle in the centre of the altar and called, "Beli Mawr, thank you for gracing us with your presence this fine day".

Niwelyn called, "Mother Danu", thank you for bestowing abundance upon our town this year".

She then gestured to the people in the front row; the farmers approached the altar and presented baskets of fruit. The women approached and presented flowers and the tradesmen presented tokens of their professions.

Elaena stood close by observing and waiting. Násuin stood beside her, on alert, watching.

Paedur then nodded to Elaena.

With a small candle in her hand she approached the altar and lit her candle from the main one, shielding its flame, she walked over to the fire and carefully lit it from her candle. As the flames began to form she returned to the altar, placed her candle on it beside the main one and joined Paedur and Niwelyn at the altar.

Niwelyn called, "Mother Danu, we present our gifts to you in appreciation for your abundance".

Paedur called out, "Beli Mawr, we thank you for your protection, we continue to live in peace and prosperity and we continue to improve our town".

Then, looking at the crowd, Niwelyn raised her hands and called, "Join us now in thanksgiving and celebration".

The ceremonies done, their duties attended to, Paedur and Niwelyn kissed lingeringly and hugged. Paedur took Elaena's hand and together they returned to the crowd that had gathered around baby Elaena. Násuin stayed close watching but not intruding, he had his men on high alert; the Romans had begun to get edgy and were making their presence felt. Niwelyn mixed and mingled enjoying the joyful atmosphere, proud that her work had been successful, she allowed herself to relax.

Presently Paedur felt he was being watched, looking up with baby Elaena in his arms, Elaena by his side, he saw Násuin staring at him, Násuin made a gesture with his head requesting Paedur to join him. Kissing baby Elaena on the forehead and handing her to Elaena kissing her full on the mouth, he stood up and walked over to Násuin.

Násuin, the warriors and the Druids sat together ignoring the crowd close by, they had selected a few members to keep watch and listen for the slightest provocation. Paedur joined them and sat among them.

Násuin turned to Paedur saying, "It is confirmed, Paedur, the Empire is in serious trouble, the Romans are desperate to launch an attack and make a last ditch effort to control all of Britannia..."

Another warrior continued, "The Barbarians march ever closer to Roma conquering as they go recruiting defecting Roman soldiers".

Yet another warrior took up the report, "Honorius grows fat in luxury in Ravenna which has now become a thriving area and cares little for the Empire".

As each one spoke Paedur turned and looked at them silently listening, nodding in acknowledgement.

Násuin continued, "The Vandals have conquered Hispania and are turning their sights on Italy and Roma. It is expected that they plan to attack and sack the great city, possibly very soon".

At this there was silence, all watching Paedur.

Taking a deep breath and blinking hard he said, "The new religion takes hold also..."

One of the Druids finished the sentence for him, "...and grows stronger every day".

Another Druid took up the report saying, "Fewer people attend our ceremonies and seek our advice".

Another Druid continued, "They now attend the new religion's services and seek advice from its Priests".

All sat in silence, the warriors stroking their beards, the Druids staring into the fire, Násuin and Paedur watching everyone their senses fully tuned and alert.

Násuin looking intently at Paedur said, "Defence becomes harder every day, conflict is inevitable. The Cymru are eager to rid Britannia of the Romans and the Romans are desperate to hold on".

Quietly, looking intently back at Násuin, Paedur replied, "Time is running out...for us all, that should bring us comfort, but it does not. The Cymru are strong...but the Angles and Saxons are even stronger and better equipped. I fear that when the Roman Empire falls...the Celtic Empire will fall with it".

Everyone sat in silence thinking of the implications of Paedur's words.

Quietly Násuin asked, "Paedur, do you really think that is so"?

Nodding Paedur replied, "Aye I do".

Then, taking a deep breath and pressing his thighs with his palms, he continued, "But that does not stop us fighting to hold on to what we have for as long as possible".

Násuin nodded, "Then let us do that. What is your advice"?

Paedur replied in a hard voice, "Double the defences, strengthen the walls, do whatever is necessary to turn this town into an impenetrable fortress. Protect the woman and children, recruit more men and train the men we have to the highest degree".

All warriors nodded.

He turned to the Druids saying, "Make extra sacrifices to Camalus and especially Macha. Remind your people of the old ways and strengthen their faith in the old ones in whatever ways seem appropriate. We will reclaim our lands and our faith, by whatever means possible".

The Druids nodded also.

Together they sat in silence, each one formulating their own plans. Paedur let out a deep sigh, raised his head and closed his eyes, breathing deeply he drew strength from the air around him.

Lightly Niwelyn, sitting beside him, touched his left arm with her right hand and said softly, "Paedur, you are tired, we have done what we can for now. Rest, your energy is low and we are all in need of your great strength, rest", she urged.

Paedur brought his head down, opened his eyes and looked at Niwelyn; resting his right hand over her hand he smiled and asked, "Where would I be without your great strength, My Lady".

Nodding he got to his feet asking, "Do we have anything else to discuss".

Násuin looked at each man in turn, all silently shook their heads, then turning to Paedur he said, "No, we are done for tonight".

"In that case I shall return to my family...and I suggest you all return to yours", he said tiredly.

Looking at each man in turn he said, "Diolch for...everything". They all silently nodded.

Násuin replied, "Croeso...My Lord".

"Do whatever it takes". Paedur repeated.

As he walked away all watched him go, each could see the tiredness in his step.

Elaena, seeing him return, handed baby Elaena to one of the women and went to meet him, as he drew closer she saw his tiredness.

"You are troubled, Paedur" she said, a look of concern in her eyes. She noticed the drawn skin and the deeper lines; she thought he looked almost sad.

She waited for his reply, eventually, taking her hand; he walked with her over to the trees. As they walked Elaena remembered the last time they did this and thought, "I*s it really only a year ago, so much has happened since then*".

"Is there bad news?" she pressed.

Paedur, not sure of what to tell her, eventually replied, "There is great unrest".

"Are we in danger?" she asked concerned.

"I think not, Elaena, I think we have things under control", he replied.

He leaned against an oak tree and remembered this time last year; he took her in his arms and kissed her deeply. He felt the strength of the oak tree behind him and the other ones around them and drew strength from them, Elaena's love reassured him. The kiss ended, a warm tingling feeling coursed through her, Paedur seemed calmer now so she relaxed.
Looking at her and stroking her hair affectionately he said, "You have grown up, My Lady".
"Aye, My Lord, that I have" she replied, nodding and looking into his eyes.
"You look lovely tonight", he continued.
"Perhaps My Lord is somewhat biased" she replied, coyly resting against him.
"Perhaps he is, but he also speaks the truth" replied Paedur, a hint of amusement in his voice. "Your figure has returned and you grow stronger every day".
"I am well cared for...and well loved", she replied.
Paedur nodded and leaned his head against the tree; he closed his eyes and breathed.
"You are tired", Elaena said. "Accompany me back to the hall".
He nodded.
Falling into step with each other they walked back to the fire, their arms wrapped tightly around each other. They retrieved baby Elaena from a dotting woman reluctant to let her go, and together they walked back to the great hall, both pulled their hoods up over their heads. Elaena, Paedur at her side, his arm around her shoulder, Elna in her arms, felt loved, respected and cared for. So many times she had walked home with Paedur; tonight there was one addition...their child.
From their positions at the fire, Násuin and Niwelyn watched them walking off into the night. Násuin, jealous that Elaena was with Paedur, took several deep calming breaths. "*She is Paedur's woman and mother of his child*", he reminded himself. "*But I still wish she could be mine. Paedur is much older than her so it is reasonable to expect that he will die long before her. When that happens, perhaps she will turn to me for comfort*

and that may give me a chance to take his place", he comforted himself.

He let out a big sigh.

Sitting close by Niwelyn observed Násuin and his reaction; she could almost hear his thoughts. As for her own...she too was disturbed. Paedur had been her first mentor and had also become her friend; she knew he felt strongly for her, he had shown her that many times, but he had never committed to her and so she accepted friendship was better than nothing. Now, seeing him with Elaena and how quickly he had committed to her, Niwelyn had to admit that she was...jealous.

Deeply she sighed.

She looked up and caught Násuin's eyes; they stared at each other both knowing what the other was thinking.

Chapter Eleven

July was hot, the days long and the breezes pleasant. The children progressed in their lessons with Paedur and played with baby Elaena giving Elaena some welcome time to rest and attend to her own needs. Paedur spent as much time as he could with the Elaenas, sometimes walking in the forest, sometimes just resting in the oak grove, baby Elaena lying on their cloaks beside them. The townspeople went about their business happy in their work content with life.

One day in early August Paedur called to Niwelyn she was sitting outside her roundhouse enjoying the warmth of the sun, her lightweight sleeveless tunic accentuated her slim figure. Resting against the side wall of her house her eyes closed, she felt his approach, she kept her eyes closed until his shadow fell across her. Tuning her senses to his mood, she felt he was troubled.

Sitting beside her he began, "Time is running out", he said taking a deep breath, "the Roman Empire is all but dead and the Celtic Empire is not far behind it. I fear...within the next year...there will be great unrest, maybe even war and both Empires will fall".

Niwelyn opened her eyes, turned her head toward him and watched, listening.

"The Romans move ever closer, when they come, you and I will be in great danger. The warriors will fight to the death but the women and children will be vulnerable" he said, his voice infused with worry.

"And your plan?" she asked.

"Get Elna safely to our Order on Ynys Mon, giving me time to make arrangements for Elaena and I to get to safety", he replied. "When I have suitable arrangements made I will retrieve Elna and get us all to safety".

He stared intently at the ground seeing his plan in action.

"Elaena will never agree to being parted from her baby", Niwelyn replied quietly.

"Elaena will do what I say is best for her", he said, his voice filled with determination.
"Elaena has a mind of her own and needs to be convinced", Niwelyn reminded him.
"Elaena has no say in this..." he said,
"...as the child's mother she does", interrupted Niwelyn.
They both sat staring at each other, Niwelyn searching inside herself for some inspiration.
Paedur, determined to convince her that he was right, said, "It is the best thing to do".
"And what if she objects?", asked Niwelyn. "As her strength returns so does her fiery nature, I have seen it emerge lately, her confidence grows and she is taking on more things".
Paedur remained silent, he too had noticed this.
Niwelyn continued, "If she objects strongly enough she will go into a rage and do something stupid".
"Do you think that is possible?" he asked,
"Knowing Elaena...yes I do", she answered.
Both sat silently, Paedur, his face in his hands his elbows resting on his knees, Niwelyn intently watching him.
"On Elaena's behalf, I object and refuse to let you go ahead with this plan", she said, quietly. "She will not co-operate, no matter what you say. A woman's new born baby is her first priority, taking her baby away from her now is like cutting her arm off. She will not agree, no matter what you say".
Breathing deeply Paedur said, "I have decided this is best...for all of us".
"Wait, a few days, arrange with the Order for you, Elaena, Elna and me to go to Ynys Mon together. As a group we will be stronger travelling and when we get there we will be under the protection of the Order which will give us all the safety you desire", she advised.
Paedur, breathing deeply, said with determination, "I have decided this is best...for all of us".
Niwelyn sighed saying, "At least discuss it with her first".
Paedur nodded, got up and left.
As he walked away Niwelyn felt a strange sense of foreboding.

As he walked back through the town he was unaware of the roofers retiling some of the houses, the hackers calling out their wares, the cats and dogs running between peoples' feet and the townspeople going about their daily business. His mind was intent on his plan and how he would present it to Elaena, he found her in the square with the children, baby Elaena asleep in a basket at her feet.

He went over to them and quietly to Elaena he said, "I have to go to my Order on some urgent business, can you stay with the children and help them with their lessons today"?

Looking into his eyes she replied, "Of course, if that is your wish, is there a problem"?

"No, do not be concerned, all is well, I will return soon", he replied.

"Then go, I will work with them today", she said.

Nodding he left her, went to the stables, mounted his horse and rode out.

Násuin, unnoticed, watch him leave.

In the village of Caerhun Paedur met the Mother Superior of the Order, dressed in a simple royal blue long gown and veil, she was already waiting for him, flanked by her two assistants. Chief Druids always met as a triad, Paedur was alone.

"Bore da, Mother" he greeted her, dismounting his horse; he knelt on one knee bowing deeply.

"Bore da, my Lord Paedur", she greeted him also bowing, "your journey was smooth"?

"Yes it was, all seems quiet", he replied.

"Sit with me", she commanded gently, patting the empty chair beside her.

Standing up Paedur nodded in turn to each of her assistants, also dressed in simple long blue gowns, and took his place beside her.

"Why have you summoned me?" she asked firmly.

"I am troubled for my family, Mother", he answered. "I wish to get the baby to safety as soon as possible, then I will make arrangements for Elaena and I to get to safety, when I have everything arranged I will return and retrieve the baby".

"Elaena agrees to this?" she asked, her face showing no emotion.
"She does", lied Paedur.
Mother sensed the lie but said nothing.
"Where do you intend to go?" she asked, her emotions firmly in check.
"South, perhaps Cornwall", he replied.
"I do not think that wise", she said. "The south is completely Romanised even the Order in Cornwall struggles to remain in control".
"What would you have me do" he asked looking intently at her.
"Stay where you are. Násuin and his men will protect Conwy, Niwelyn will administer to the people and you will be safe there", she advised.
"Conwy is vulnerable, I do not think we will be safe there", he said.
"If you are looking for safety, perhaps all three of you should come to Ynys Mon", she replied watching Paedur.
Looking down at the ground his eyes wide, he nodded in acknowledgement.
Mother superior waited patiently, her assistants watched silently.
"Will you take the baby into custody now", he asked looking intently at her.
"And Elaena", she enquired straight faced.
"Leave her to me, I will bring her with me later", he replied tiredly.
"No", she replied quietly.
Stunned Paedur stared at her then asked, "Why?"
"Because no good will come of it", she replied. "Elaena will never agree, no matter how you present it to her. On her behalf, I forbid you to take this course of action".
Taking in a deep breath Paedur said, "Mother, I have always done as you wished, but this time I ask this of you".
Breathing silently again she said flatly, "No".
Paedur desperate to get her to agree said, "I will speak with Elaena, I will tell her it will only be for a short while and we will join Elna here again in a few days".

Taking a deep breath she asked, “Is there someone you can trust to deliver her to us”.
“Yes...Niwelyn”, he replied.
“She will agree?” she asked surprised.
“She will if I ask her to”, he replied.
Nodding she asked, “There is great unrest, what if something goes wrong”.
“If I do not return, Elna must know who her parents are and why she has grown up in the Order”, he replied.
“As you wish, be it done”, she said resignedly.
Standing and bowing to all three women Paedur took his leave of them and returned to Conwy. He didn’t notice anything along the way; his mind was consumed with how he was going to get Elaena to agree.
Elaena, feeling the strain of taking care of the children on her own, gently dispersed them back to their homes. As she was picking up the basket with the sleeping Elna in it Násuin appeared at her side, “I have been watching you with the children”, he said.
Elaena jumped, “Násuin, I did not see you there”, she said surprised.
“Paedur is not with you?” he asked.
“No, he had to go to his Order on some important business”, she replied.
Násuin narrowed his eyes asking, “When did he leave?”
“Some time ago”, she replied.
“You are alone then”, he stated.
“I am”, she replied.
Looking at baby Elaena sleeping peacefully he said, “She grows big...and strong”.
“Aye, that she is”, she said.
“Like her mother”, he said.
“I am tired, I think I will return home now”, she said.
“I will escort you”, he said.
“No, there is no need to, I can manage”, she said.
“I insist...My Lady”, he replied bowing a slight smile touched the corners of his mouth.

Elaena glared at him.
"I insist...Elaena", he said bowing his smile getting more noticeable.
"I am quite capable of getting myself home alone", she said defiantly".
"My men may encircle you again and with the baby to contend with you will be vulnerable", he said smiling.
"You have not had any further lessons so your skills are not as they should be", he continued. "Allow me to escort you", he pressed.
"No, Násuin, I can manage", she insisted.
"Can Elna manage on her own?" he asked watching her closely.
Narrowing her eyes she replied angrily, "Escort us then, if you must".
"With great pleasure...My Lady", he replied smiling.
She glared at him again but said nothing.
Together they walked to the great hall, as they entered the courtyard the warriors stopped and watched, Násuin gestured to them to return to their duties.
"Have you eaten?" he asked.
"No, I have not", she replied.
"Come to the fire and eat then", he encouraged.
She nodded and he escorted her over to the fire, one of the women handed her a bowl of stew and a cup of beer, she sat on one of the oak logs and eat. Násuin placed the basket on another and stood protectively behind them. The woman busied herself around the fire but didn't intrude.
After eating she stood up, picked up the basket, and began walking towards the great hall. Násuin walked behind her to the bottom of the stairs.
Do you require assistance?" he asked.
"No, I can...please" she replied exhaling.
Taking the basket from her he allowed her to walk ahead up the stairs. Following her, with the basket in his arms; he watched her noting the confident way she held herself and her strong stride as she walked down the corridor. Opening the door she held it for him, he walked passed her, crossed the room and

deposited the basket on her bed. Turning around he looked at her, apart from the baby they were alone...in Paedur's room, taking a deep breath he drank in the quiet serene atmosphere. Paedur's presence hung heavily in the air and he remembered the night he had sat in this room drinking with him.

Quietly he said "I can stay...if you wish".

"No", she replied, "Paedur will be home any minute, I am safe now", she said.

Nodding he said, "If there is anything you need...come to me".

"Diolch, Násuin, I shall", she replied.

Násuin opened his mouth as if to say something but closed it again.

Noting his movements Elaena asked, "Násuin is there something you want to say"

Breathing quietly but rapidly he shook his head, "No...Elaena... all is well", he replied.

"You are sure", she asked concerned, stepping a little closer to him.

The lavender smell of her intoxicated him and he closed his eyes breathing hard to control himself. He could take her in his arms right here right now and there would be no one to stop him but then Paedur could walk in and witness it and he didn't know how Paedur would react.

Thinking better of it he again shook his head and quietly repeated, "No, Elaena, all is well, I will bid you a good night".

Taking a moment longer he walked across the room and at the door, drinking in her presence, said quietly, "Nos da, Elaena".

"Nos da, Násuin" she said, "thank you for escorting us", she continued.

Taking a moment longer than he should have he nodded and left.

After he left, Elaena stood for a moment thinking that Násuin's actions were a little bit strange.

Arriving back in Conwy Paedur first went to Niwelyn, it was a dry bright evening and the air was heavy with the scent of flowers. She was in her roundhouse writing, hearing Paedur's horse arriving; she put her work down and opened the door

for him, having greeted each other and kissed, they both went indoors and sat by the fire. Niwelyn poured wine for them both.
"I have just been to see Mother Superior", he began.
"You rode to Ynys Mon?" she asked.
"No, we met in Caerhun", he replied. "I have made arrangements with her for Elna and will now begin making arrangements for Elaena and me".
Niwelyn nodded, "So Mother agreed then".
"With a little persuasion", he said nodding.
Niwelyn waited.
Paedur continued, "I will distract Elaena with some task, get Elna here and you will bring her to the Order".
"So you have discussed this with Elaena then," she said.
"No", he said staring into the fire.
"No...I will not be a part of this", Niwelyn said firmly.
Paedur looked at her pleadingly.
Niwelyn stared back at him holding his gaze.
"Please", he begged.
"Go home and discuss it with her now, before you do anything else", she commanded.
Paedur looked at her, wanting to object, and decided not to.
"All right", he replied nodding.
"Will this be by day or night?" she asked.
"By day", he replied. "Night is too dangerous, even for you. When I return I will have Elna with me, be ready to leave immediately", he commanded.
He kissed her on the cheek and left.
As she watched him leave her sense of foreboding deepened, she sighed and shook her head.

Arriving back at the great hall he found Elna sleeping peacefully and Elaena folding clothes and putting them away. Her blue stola matching the colour of her eyes, her skin tanned giving her an appearance of health and radiance, her eyes shone with a new strength and confidence. The Summer had strengthened her and she was now a fully fledged woman.

She looked up when Paedur opened the door and, although she smiled, there was a look of concern in her eyes, she stopped and walked over to him noting his tiredness.
"Paedur, you have returned, what kept you, you have been away from us too long", she said.
Wearing brown bracae, a cream tunic and woollen jacket, he had the appearance of a weary traveller. Removing his jacket he greeted Elaena with a kiss taking her hands in his.
"Apologies, Elaena, the business took rather longer to conduct than I had anticipated, you are both well?", he enquired, a look of concern coming into his eyes.
"Yes, yes, all is well, Násuin escorted us home, it is just I expected you home much sooner", she replied.
He kissed her soothingly and asked, "You have eaten?"
"Yes, we ate with the women at the hearthside, we have been well nourished", she said. "You have eaten too?"
"I am not hungry, I do however require a wash", he replied.
Together they prepared washing facilities and after washing he changed into a long flowing light weight cotton gown and lay down, within minutes he was asleep. Elaena extinguished the candles, dampened down the fire and lay down; within minutes she too was asleep.

At breakfast the next morning Paedur asked, "Will you assist with the gathering of the harvest today, Elaena?"
"What about Elna?" she asked.
"I will care for her today, I will bring her with me to lessons the children will keep her company", he replied.
"But I do not want to leave her", she said.
"She will be safe with me", he assured her.
"No, I do not want to leave her", she said more firmly.
"She will be safe with me", he insisted.
About to object again instead, she said, "If that is what you wish, Paedur, then I shall do it".
After breakfast she put on a long grey canvass tunic and went out to gather the harvest, when Paedur was sure she was gone he put Elna into her basket, gathered some clothes, a leather

skin of milk and went down to the square to meet the children. Leaving Elna with them, he set them up making baskets for the harvest and went back to the courtyard. The girls fussed over Elna and were delighted that Paedur had left her in their care.
He went straight to the stables; Násuin was tending to his horse, "Get my horse ready", he commanded, "I have urgent business out of town to attend to" he barked.
Násuin, in mid stroke, asked "Anything I can assist with?"
"No", barked Paedur, "I must go alone".
Násuin put the brush down and walked down the stalls to Paedur's horse, bringing him to Paedur he asked, "Will the Lady Elaena be travelling with you"?
"No, she is gathering the harvest", he replied.
"And Elna?" Násuin enquired.
"She is being cared for", he replied.
Násuin handed the horse over to him and waited, Paedur quickly got on to the horse and without another word rode out of the stables. Násuin watched as he galloped out, he stood for a moment narrowing his eyes thinking that Paedur was acting rather strangely and then went back to tending his horse.
Paedur returned to the square, the children looked up, he dismounted saying, "I have business to attend to, continue your work we are in urgent need of the baskets".
He scooped the basket with baby Elaena in it up and mounted his horse.
One of the children asked, "Why are you taking sister Elna with you"?
"Because I need to", he barked.
The child shrunk back and said no more.
At her roundhouse Niwelyn was waiting, dressed in dark bracae and a dark tunic tied with a leather belt, a dagger, a sword etched with serpent designs and a leather bag hung from it. She had leather boots on her feet. Her hair was tied back and her hood covered her head. She had fashioned a leather pouch with carrying straps for baby Elaena which hung around her neck. Her horse stood beside her with a leather pannier strapped across its back.

Paedur arrived, a frown of concentration lining his face, his eyes intent, his voice determined. "Make haste", he said. "You know where to take her, the Order awaits return when you are rested", he said urgently.
"Elaena has agreed then?" she asked.
"Yes, yes", he lied, "hurry now" he continued.
Niwelyn saw the lie but chose not to acknowledge it, she may not always agree with him, but she did trust him. Taking baby Elaena from him she gently placed her in the pouch and secured it around her neck with the straps. Paedur handed her the bag of provisions which she put in to the pannier, she mounted her horse assisted by Paedur and, after making herself comfortable, she wrapped her cloak around her concealing the pouch.
They stared at each other for several minutes, eventually he said, "Godspeed, Goddess Druantia protect you both".
Nodding silently Niwelyn tugged on the horse's reins and headed off. Taking the empty basket, Paedur mounted his horse and returned to the stables, handing him back to Násuin offering no explanation. Silently he strode back to his room with the empty basket then returned to the children.
Násuin watched Paedur stride across the courtyard and wondered what was going on, it was unusual for Paedur not to discuss things with him but on this occasion he had chosen not to. Násuin knew that Paedur had a very good reason for everything he did and reckoned that all would be revealed in time.

Niwelyn rode hard, it had been arranged that she would meet Mother's triad in Caerhun and they would take baby Elaena on the boat back with them to Ynys Mon. All three women were waiting for her, the boatman stood close by ready and waiting. Niwelyn greeted them, "Bore da, Mother...Sisters; she bowed to each in turn.
"Bore da, Lady Niwelyn", they chorused.
"My Lord Paedur requests me hand the baby Elaena into your safe custody and sends his deepest thanks for your help", she said.

She handed the baby to one of the assistants and gave the bag of provisions to the other one saying, "There is a letter of instructions within, one for you, Mother, and one for Elna. If he does not return he requests that the letter be given to Elna at the appropriate time".
"His wishes shall be carried out", replied Mother and, nodding to her assistants, they got into the boat.
"Please, Mother...beseech Druantia to protect us...I fear for the outcome of our actions this day", Niwelyn pleaded.
"Have no fear, the baby will be safe", replied Mother and gestured to the boatman to begin their journey.
As Niwelyn watched them sail away she said in a low voice to herself, "It is not the baby I am concerned about".
After a few minutes she turned, mounted her horse and returned to Conwy, on her journey back she walked slowly calculating that baby Elaena was five months old. She wondered how Paedur would handle Elaena when she found out what they had done and figured that Elaena would partly blame her for helping him.

That evening Elaena returned home dirty, tired but in good form, the movement had been good for her and she felt a new strength in her body. She washed, put on a long emerald green velvet dress and brushed her hair leaving it out loose, when she was happy with her appearance she went down to the hearth to eat with the woman. A while later Paedur entered the courtyard, his hood pulled up over his head, his cloak pulled closely around him and, without acknowledging anyone, he went straight to his room, Elaena excused herself and followed him.
On entering their room Paedur removed his cloak and went over to the hearth, poured some wine into a golden goblet and waited for Elaena to join him. Standing in front of the hearth with his back to the door, he drank deeply calming himself so that he could transmit some calmness to her. A few minutes later the door opened and Elaena walked in, the hem of her dress gently swishing around her ankles as she moved, her cloak draped around her shoulders, her hair out loose flowing down her back.

Paedur turned to face her and silently looked at her, she looked around the room and saw no sign of Elna, her basket was empty and her clothes were gone. Turning her head from side to side, her eyes wide, a deep sense of disquiet welled up inside her.
Looking squarely at Paedur she asked "Where is Elna?"
"She is gone", he replied his eyes steady.
"Gone? Gone where? What have you done with her?" she asked.
"She is safe", he replied in a low voice.
"Where is she?" she asked, her panic rising.
"On Ynys Mon...with my Order", he replied.
"What is she doing there?" she asked.
"She is in safe custody, she will be well cared for", he replied.
"She is well cared for here", she said.
"There is great unrest, none of us are safe here now", he replied levelly.
"I do not care, I want her back...NOW", she said forcibly.
"You cannot have her now", he replied quietly.
"Get her for me", she insisted.
"No, Elaena, I have sent her away so that she will be safe, soon we will both go and get her and go into hiding together", he said.
"Why do we have to go into hiding", she asked forcibly.
"The Romans draw closer..." he said.
"...they are already here", she interrupted.
"Their governor is on his way here to secure Cymru in a last ditch effort to gain control over all of Britannia", he explained. "When he does he will seize control of the town. The warriors will pitch a battle against them but everyone will be drawn in, there will be bloodshed and death and I do not want us to be among them when it happens".
"I do not care what you want", she shot at him her eyes wide with anger, her hands opening and closing by her side, "I WANT MY BABY BACK", she shouted.
"Our baby", he said quietly.
"My baby, I carried her, birthed her and have fed her since, SHE IS MINE", she shouted.

"She is ours", he said quietly, "and it is my responsibility to make sure that you are both safe at all times".
He took a large sip of wine keeping his eyes on her, alert.
Pain rose in her chest, her panic grew; she didn't know how to describe her feelings. Not knowing what to say she said again, "I do not care about safe, I want my baby".
"No, Elaena", he said.
"Why not", she shot at him angrily.
"Because she is in the best place possible, in a few days we will both go and get her..."
"...Why can we not get her now?" she interrupted.
"Because it is night, the Romans are probably on the road and will most likely ambush us along the way", he replied.
"What have you to fear from the Romans", she asked, her anger growing.
"I have the most to fear from them", he explained. "When they come I will be the first they will kill, you will be sold into slavery and Elna will be adopted and brought up as a Roman child".
Steadily he stared at her hoping she would see reason, she didn't.
"I have been a slave all my life, so what is the difference", she said defiantly, shaking her head.
"Here you are respected and loved there, with them, you will be mistreated and probably raped", he said a slight shudder barely detectable.
"I have been raped all my life too, I am used to it", she continued defiantly.
"Think of Elna", he urged, "she is not and has not, nor do I want her to be, her best survival is with the Order, with her own kind".
"We are her own kind", Elaena replied, her voice rising.
"Think what is best for her", he urged.
"Here, with me, is what is best for her", she replied angrily.
"You cannot protect her", he said.
"The warriors can protect us, that is what they are there for, let them do their job", she said forcibly.
"And they will", he assured her, "but you, me and Elna are the first people the Romans will come looking for..."

"...You have magic, can you not use that", she interrupted.
"Yes I can", he replied, "but even magic may not be able to equal the might of the Romans, they will outnumber us and subdue us and probably put us all to death".
"Can we not escape and with your magic overpower them", she asked forcibly.
"Elaena", he said tiredly, "you do not seem to understand, with the townspeople they will show some mercy...but with us...they will show none" he explained.
"I do not care, I want my baby, get her for me", she insisted.
"I will, but not now", he said levelly.
Pouring wine into a golden goblet he extended it toward her gesturing to her to take it, she crossed the room hitting him forcibly on the hand knocking the goblet to the floor. The wine splashed out across the floor, a few drops falling on to Paedur's boots a dark stain appearing on the leather.
"I will not drink, you will not subdue me with wine", she said angrily.
He stared at her unmoving.
"WHY DID YOU NOT TELL ME", she roared.
"Would you have listened", he asked quietly.
"No, but you should have told me", she said angrily.
"That is why I did not", he said quietly, "you would have talked me out of it, putting us all in great danger, I did what is best... for all of us".
"You should have told me", she whimpered, then quickly changed her tone, "GET HER, GET HER NOW", she shouted.
Paedur took a deep breath and remained silent.
Below them music could be heard around the fire.
Elaena, breathing hard, paced up and down the room her distress very visible, Paedur waited silently sipping wine, watching.
"I want my baby", she moaned, "I want my baby".
Paedur took a deep breath and remained silent.
"She should be here, she should be with me", she sobbed. "Why did you take her away, why can I not hold her", she hugged herself sobbing. "My arms ache for her, my body yearns for her", Why, why", she sobbed.

Paedur stood silently watching her breathing calmly, Elaena sobbed quietly lost in her grief.
The music played below them.
"You should have told me", she sobbed, "You should have given me a chance, you should have discussed it with me, you should have asked", she sobbed, "you had no right to do that".
"I did what is best", he said quietly.
Elaena sobbed the pain in her chest growing, darts of pain shooting through her, "It is not fair", she moaned, then, her voice becoming stronger, "It is not fair", she said, anger welling up inside her.
She stopped sobbing; her cheeks were wet with tears. "You should have told me", she said, her voice becoming angry, "YOU SHOULD HAVE TOLD ME", she shouted.
Striding over to Paedur she began beating him on the chest, his goblet fell to the floor the remaining wine spilling out across the floor.
He stood silently, feet hip width apart allowing her to vent her anger.
"YOU SHOULD HAVE TOLD ME, IT IS NOT FAIR", she raged, continuing to pummel his chest.
He tried to put his arms around her but she slapped at his arms, eventually he put them down by his side and waited for her to calm down. She didn't. On and on she ranted, raged and screamed he remained silent, watching, his silence annoyed her and his quietness angered her, she couldn't understand how he could be so calm. She searched inside herself for some way to make him angry, some way to get revenge and then a thought struck her.
"I am going out", she said, in a hard voice her eyes narrowing, breathing hard her hair dishevelled.
"Where are you going?" he asked quietly.
"To the taberna", she replied.
She strode across the room her cloak flaring out around her; angrily she opened the door and strode down the corridor.
Paedur made no attempt to follow her or stop her; he stood in front of the hearth breathing hard.

Elaena rushed down the stairs, out the door, across the courtyard and out on to the street. She heard nothing. She saw no one and wasn't aware of anything, in a rage she strode across the square and down to the taberna. She knew that the one way to get him really angry was to go back to her old life.

Chapter Twelve

Standing in their room Paedur let out a long deep sigh and closed his eyes, he knew where she was going, he knew what she was doing and who she was doing it with.

The music continued playing below him; someone was singing a few others joined in.

He took several deep breaths his chest hurt, his head hurt too, slowly his breathing returned to normal. Looking around the room he noticed the two goblets and stains on the floor, slowly he bent down and retrieved them. Taking a cloth and dipping it into the cauldron he soaked it with hot water and, bending down, he cleaned the wine stains then, returning to the fire, he cleaned the goblets.

He poured another goblet of wine and drank deeply; his eyes deeply sunken in his head, took on a dark blue smoky colour. He breathed deeply several times calling upon his inner strength, his presence filled the room.

Slowly, deeply in thought, he paced the room goblet in hand sipping from time to time, thinking out loud he said, "I know Elaena is right, I should have told her. I did not tell her just how much danger we are in; I do not want to frighten her. Because she does not know she does not understand and now it is probably too late to make her understand. I know she is running away, I know she is shutting out the night, shutting down the sun and locking away a broken heart. Niwelyn warned me, she said this would happen and I did not listen to her".

In desperation he thought, "*Oh, Elaena, if only you knew how much I love you and cherish your love. I had intended showing you how to use that love but I waited until you were fully over the birth, now it is too late. I know you have been through the fires of hell and have experienced great pain. I know I have already helped you heal the scars but now I doubt if I will have the chance to help you turn your bad experience into constructive use*".

A sharp pain gripped his chest and his heart ached, he put his right hand over his heart transmitting some healing energy to himself. Continuing his dialogue as if she was there he thought, "*Oh! Elaena, I do not want to lose you I have forgotten how to live without you*".

Breathing deeply to calm and reassure himself he thought, "*All I can do is hope that during our short time together she listened to me. That some part of her will believe that everything I have taught her is true and that this will bring her back to me*".

He sipped some wine drawing its taste and strength deeply into him, his head hurt his heart ached; he could still feel her fists beating his chest. He couldn't remember ever feeling so much pain, breathing deeply he willed the pain away. On and on he paced unable to rest fighting to stay calm. Scenes of his life in Londinium with other women flashed in his mind recalling the feelings he had for them but none of them, not even one of them, had made him feel like he felt now.

In a low voice to himself he said, "I have had the richest, the most famous, the most cunning, the most daring and I have felt nothing for any of them. Yet here I am, emotionally devastated, and it is a teenage gutter rat who has brought me down".

He remembered Niwelyn's cruel statement "*That is it; that is the whole purpose of it, you are very much aware of your age, you want a child and she is the perfect age to give you one*". As if Niwelyn was in the room, he said, "I could never have a child with a woman that I do not love, AND I LOVE ELAENA".

Continuing his dialogue with himself he said, "Elaena asked me if my magic could not outwit the Romans, I have been a Druid for twenty years and a trainee Druid for almost twenty years before that. Although I specialise in academics I have also mastered all the other arts including healing, construction, battle, law, sacrifice and invocation. I can make anyone fall with a thought, with a wave of my hand I can turn night into day, I can heal – and I can hex too. I can win battles and wage war; I can change the minds of kings and make emperors do what I please. I can make every wish come through and grant anyone the sun moon and stars, but no one has made me feel the way

I feel tonight. Everything I know has meant nothing, nothing until I tried to teach Elaena.

Shaking his head, partly in disbelief and partly in sadness, he realised, "*I need all these things in order to love, but Elaena seems to be able to make love out of nothing. This is a magic I have not been taught and it is a magic that I do not understand*".

Racing through the streets that night Elaena's cloak billowed out around her, the hem of her emerald green velvet dress swished around her ankles as she strode in haste. Muttering under her breath, sobbing tears running down her cheeks, she felt anger, rage and an absolute desire for revenge. She heard nothing she saw no one, she was completely lost in her grief for Elna and her anger at Paedur. Her hair flew out behind her, her eyes were wild with rage and her feet pounded the pavement beneath her. When she arrived at the taberna she flung the door open and stood on the threshold breathing hard surveying the occupants. Some stopped and looked up, most took no notice, the noise of its occupants deafened her. She chose an insignificant Roman soldier about her own age strode over to him and stood at his side

"You", she said, "follow me".

She grabbed him pulling him out of his seat and led him up the wooden stairs and into the first room which she once worked in; it was empty and slammed the door behind them. She threw him down on the bed and, after removing her cloak, launched down on top of him straddling him. Roughly tearing at his clothes, she held him between her knees while she removed her dress. Viciously, ferociously she smothered his face in passionate kisses, grabbing at his body scratching and tearing at his flesh. Venting the full force of her anger on him, she lost control. Nothing mattered, no one mattered, not even this Roman soldier, as she drove him deeply inside her she gave in fully to her rage. She didn't hear his cries of panic she wasn't aware of the pain she was inflicting upon him, all that mattered was revenge. Eventually her energy waned; she couldn't sustain the physical force any longer. She slumped down on top of him breathing hard, her wild hair completely covering his face. When her breathing had calmed down a bit she got up, put her dress back on, flung her cloak around her and strode out of the room leaving the door wide open.

As she strode back through the town the air was cool and the streets were dry and deserted. Crossing the square she saw the bench were Paedur taught the children and she stopped. All anger, all rage and all revenge gone, she slumped down on to the bench and sat there staring into space. Her body hurt her mind raced and her breathing was erratic, she fought hard to control her breath her chest ached with the effort. Slowly her breathing calmed and she sat unmoving unable to feel. For several minutes she sat there lost within herself completely unaware of the town around her.

The taberna door opened and the revellers made their way home passing her and nodding to her. She didn't see them and she didn't hear them, no one approached her they quickly passed by. After a few minutes the streets became deserted again and still she sat there. Slowly the cold drew in around her; she pulled her cloak tightly around her and pulled her hood up over her head. The movement broke the spell and in a soft voice she said, "What have I done"?

Suddenly her body was racked by deep sobs that began in her toes and went right up through her body into her head, she sobbed and sobbed and sobbed, her whole body shaking. Eventually she calmed down; she was exhausted and unable to move, now that the anger had passed, it was replaced with fear. She remembered the childhood stories about the Druids and having spent almost two years living with one...she knew what they were capable of. She also remembered her earlier mental note to herself never to get him angry.

In a quiet voice filled with fear she said to herself, "What will he say...what is he thinking...what will he do to me?"

She gasped, the breath catching in her throat.

"Will he turn me into some hideous animal or will he send the plague upon me to rot away my flesh? Will he have me dragged out here to the square and have me publicly flogged"?

She looked around the square picturing the scene, the warriors jeering, the Romans laughing, the townspeople cheering...and she shuddered.

"Will he brew up some concoction that will burn my insides and poison me to death?"

Her fear grew, her panic increased.

Without realising it her breathing was changing, some part of her brain was kicking in, slowly, dimly, the thought occurred to her, "*but he loves me, or at least he did up until tonight*".

She held that thought in her mind and remembered his smile, his compassionate eyes, his strong gentle arms and his soft yet strong voice. She closed her eyes and breathed deeply. Inside her she felt the warmth of his kiss, the protection of his arm around her, the safety she felt in his company, slowly her courage awakened.

Quietly she said to herself, "I cannot leave him I have nowhere to go....but I am afraid to go back to him. If I do go back, is it possible that he would even take me back without punishing me? If I do will he forgive me...and love me"?

She felt desperate, her fear of him mixed with her dependence upon him frightened her, yet she felt there was nothing else she could do; all she could do was hope. She closed her eyes and took several deep calming breaths, in her mind she thought, "*He is my only hope...no one else has ever loved me...with him I am at least safe...I am respected, I am protected and no one will harm me*".

Breathing deeply she thought, "*Perhaps it is possible that he still loves me, in spite of what I have done...maybe I can apologise and seek his forgiveness and ask him to take me back*".

Having made her decision, slowly heavily and painfully she got to her feet, huddled deeply into her cloak and made her way back to their room remembering all the other nights she had made this journey.

Every step took her closer to him and to her fear but she hoped that love would be enough. As she climbed the stairs and walked down the corridor she desperately mustered every bit of courage she could find within herself, willing herself to remain calm.

"Whatever I am facing...whatever he will do...I will accept it... because I deserve it. I do not deserve his love but perhaps he will be gentle with me", she thought.
Standing outside the heavy wooden door, her hand in mid air ready to push it open, she hesitated and steeled herself.

***

Realising that he had over drank and that it hadn't taken the pain away, he put the goblet down and stopped pacing the room. He wrapped himself completely in his cloak; the hood pulled up over his head completely covering his face. He sat in his chair in front of his desk, rested his head against the back of the chair and slept; his senses fully awake.
After a while he woke up, he had sensed Elaena returning, he was still angry but he felt her fear. He remembered her childhood fears about the Druids and knew that coming back now required enormous courage on her part. He felt her panic and sensed her shame, he wanted to be angry but his love for her flooded him with compassion. He sat waiting, he knew she was outside the door, he felt her hesitation and he willed her to open it.
With one big deep calming breath, she pushed the door open and stepped into the room, the door closed behind her. Looking around the room she noticed its only light was the dying embers of the fire. She felt he was sitting beside her, just inside the door, but, when she looked at him, all she saw was a dark shape and the toes of his boots. She stood in front of him willing herself to be calm and waited, silently.
Slowly he lifted his head the hood falling back to his forehead, and stared at her, staring back at him she saw two flaming red eyes holding her in a cold stare. She quietly gasped, she wanted to run but fear and her defiant nature held her rigid on the spot; they stared at each other for several minutes then, in a low deep menacing voice he said, "Go to bed".

She was terrified, she was petrified but she was also exhausted. Wrapping her cloak around her, she ran across the room and flung herself down on her bed. Within minutes she was asleep.
Paedur continued to sit in his chair, slowly his eyes returned to a deep dark dusky blue. Lowering his head, his hood falling back over his face, he slept...totally exhausted.
The next morning when Elaena woke up she found Paedur at the fire stirring some liquid in a pot. Quietly he worked so as not to wake her and she lay quietly watching not letting him know she was awake.
In her mind she thought, "*Oh no, is this the potion to make my insides burn*"? She shuddered inside.
She noticed his eyes were their normal bright blue colour, his faced looked calm and relaxed. There seemed to be an air of peace and tranquillity about him, the atmosphere in the room seemed calm.
Slowly she moved and quietly gasped; her pelvis hurt, he was aware that she was awake but he didn't make it obvious. Slowly she sat up leaning her back against the stone wall behind her and watched him silently. He scooped some liquid from the pot into an earthenware cup, walked over to the bed and handed it to her. She hesitated before taking it; she looked deeply into his eyes the question obvious in her own. He nodded holding her in a steady stare silently reassuring her, she reached out and, with a trembling hand, took the cup from him.
Silently he watched as she raised it to her lips testing it first, her insides didn't seem to be suffering so she drank, it tasted awful and reminded her of home. She took a few more sips then held the cup in her hands, the liquid seemed not to be harmful and she began to relax.
"I know it tastes bad", he said quietly, "and you may experience some pain and blood later. Perhaps you should stay home and rest today", he advised.
His presence was heavy and disturbed her greatly, she still expected him to do something terrible to her. Inwardly she was afraid but tried not to let him see that.

"What have you given me?" she asked quietly, her eyes wide with fear.
"Caulophyllum Thalictroides, Blue Cohosh, an herb to prevent... consequences, it will do you no harm, let your fears be at rest", he stared at her reassuringly.
She nodded and took some more sips of the drink.
Quietly he sat on the end of her bed and observed her.
"Are you in pain?" he asked.
"Yes, some around here", she pointed to her pelvis.
He nodded "The herb will help that too", he said quietly.
"Paedur I want to..., she began,
"...No", he interrupted raising his hands, "...not now Elaena... we are both too tired and upset to talk...for now let us just rest".
He got up and walked over to the fire, scooped out some porridge into bowls, mixed it with some honey and brought them over to her bed. He handed her one of the bowls and a spoon and sat down.
Together they ate in silence, when they had finished he took the bowls over to the fire, washed them and put them away.
Turning to face her he stared at her saying, "I am going down to the children. Wash, change and rest, I will return later".
Staring at him with big eyes she nodded.
He turned and walked over to his own bed, his cloak was draped neatly across the bottom, picking it up and wrapping it around himself, he left the room.
She rested her head against the wall behind her, closed her eyes and let out a deep sigh. She couldn't believe her luck, it seemed he had, in his own way, come to terms with what she had done and was not going to punish her. A wave of relief washed over her, slowly she breathed, relaxing.
After a while she got to her feet, standing on the floor sent darts of pain up her legs and into her pelvis. She winched. Slowly and in pain she hobbled over to the hearth where she found a large glass bowl and filled it with hot water from the cauldron hanging on a tripod over the fire. There was a small bottle of herbs beside it, she didn't know what they were but she guessed

that Paedur had left them for her use so she put them into the water.
Carrying the bowl carefully over to the table, and removing her clothes, started washing. Her skin hurt, there were bruises and some dried blood around her pelvis, gently and tenderly she sponged herself from head to toe. She remembered the first time she had washed here, in some ways this felt the same but also it felt different. Then it was because she was a victim of her own life, now she was a victim of her own stupidity. After towelling herself dry she put on a long white cotton gown and tidied up.
Taking a comb she walked over to the window and opened the wooden shutters, standing at the window she began to comb her hair. Looking out she didn't take much notice of the courtyard below her, the sky above her and the sun streaming through the waves in her hair. She was lost in her thoughts.
After a while she sighed and, with the comb still in her hand, she turned and looked around the room and realised, "*I am comfortable here in my new home and I have become comfortable with Paedur...until last night*".
She sighed deeply; a wave of tiredness engulfed her, the effort of washing had tired her and she began to feel sleepy. Walking over to her bed she put the comb down on top of the press and, lying on her bed, she closed her eyes.

Paedur went down to the square where the children were waiting for him, they greeted him and asked, "Where is Mama and Elna sister"?
"They are unwell, they will not be joining us today", he replied.
"Can we see them?" they asked.
"No, they are sleeping; I do not want to disturb them".
"I too am unwell", he continued, "I think we will not have lessons today. Go back to your families and help them with their work, do not get in their way and do not upset them. We will meet again tomorrow".
Disappointed the children did as he said and he returned to the courtyard. On entering all continued their work but watched

him from the corner of their eyes. Násuin and the warriors were huddled together deep in conversation.

Tiredly Paedur sat on one of the oak logs; one of the women brought him a cup of beer and a piece of bread.

"Diolch", he said, "you are most kind".

Quietly she asked, "Is Lady Elaena well"?

"No", he replied, "but thank you for asking".

"There is talk", she said.

"What kind of talk?" he asked.

"It is not my place to say", she replied, bowing respectfully.

Just then Násuin detached himself from his men and walked over to Paedur, immediately the woman slunk away busying herself at the fire.

"Bore da, Paedur", he greeted his friend.

"Bore da, Násuin", Paedur replied.

"I do not wish to intrude upon your thoughts but, may I join you?" he asked.

Paedur nodded silently.

Sitting down beside him, Násuin began, "There is talk".

"What talk?" Paedur asked.

"Elaena", replied Násuin. "Apparently there was an incident in the taberna last night, it seems she raped a young Roman soldier and caused quite a scene".

"What are people saying?" asked Paedur.

"They say she barged into the taberna grabbed a soldier, took him to her old room and raped him", replied Násuin. "It seems she was brutal and word this morning is that he sustained injury", he continued, watching Paedur.

"Mmm, he is not the only one, Elaena is not too well herself", Paedur said.

"I am sorry to hear that, is she bad?" Násuin asked.

"No, minor cuts and bruises, I have given her something that will prevent consequences and aid her recovery", replied Paedur.

"Good", nodded Násuin. "I take it she is resting now"?

Paedur nodded.

"What are your men saying about her?" he asked.

"That she is a hooker, a whore, slut, harlot and a tramp, the more educated among them call her a scortum, a strumpet", Násuin replied shrugging.

"We both know that is not true", said Paedur.

"Aye, we do, but convincing them of that is not easy, I have just tried", said Násuin. "I have done my best but they still hold to their own opinions".

There was a few minutes silence then Násuin asked, "What happened between Elaena and you last night".

Paedur sat silently staring at the ground.

Násuin sat quietly, waiting.

Eventually Paedur drew in a deep breath, "We fought", he replied.

"Physical or verbal?" asked Násuin.

Paedur looked up at him for a moment questioningly, Násuin stared steadily back at him.

"Both", Paedur replied

A hint of a smile touched Násuin's lips, "Who sustained the worst injuries"?

Again Paedur looked at him, Násuin held his stare.

"Neither", replied Paedur.

"What did you fight about?" Násuin asked.

Paedur took a deep breath, "I sent Elna to Ynys Mon for protection...without Elaena's permission. When I told her she became very angry, pummelled me on the chest, ranted and raged and then stormed out down to the taberna", he replied.

Násuin nodded, thought for a moment and then said, "I believe that is the natural reaction of a new mother".

Paedur nodded, staring at the ground, "So I believe, I was warned but paid no heed", he said.

"Who warned you?" asked Násuin.

"Niwelyn", replied Paedur.

Násuin nodded, "She would know such things".

They both fell into a companionable silence, Paedur staring at the ground, Násuin watching Paedur.

"What should we do now", asked Paedur.

"You take care of Elaena, leave my men to me", replied Násuin. "As for the people they will adjust", he said shrugging.
Násuin stood up and quietly said, "Give Elaena my Lov...best regards".
"I will, thank you", said Paedur, still staring at the ground.
Násuin stood looking down at Paedur's bent head for a moment then turned and walked across the courtyard as he did so he thought, "*I wonder what the outcome of this will be*".
One of the women brought a basket of provisions over to Paedur and quietly said, "For your family, My Lord, give our regards to Lady Elaena".
Paedur silently nodded.

It was only when she heard the door opening that Elaena realised she had fallen asleep. Paedur entered the room with the basket of provisions in his hand and put it on the table. He took some plates out of the press, divided the food out between them, sat down and began eating. Elaena slowly and painfully got to her feet and sat with him picking at the food.
"Everyone sends you their love, the children want to come and see you" he said quietly.
Her lower lip quivered and tears came into her eyes, fighting hard to control them she whispered, "How much do they know"?
"Only that you are unwell, I gave them no details", he replied.
Elaena nodded, "And the women?"
"I have given them no details either though they have heard their men folk talk", he replied. "They gave me this food with their blessing and send you their best wishes".
"That is nice, thank you and thank them for me", she said quietly.
"I already have", he said quietly.
"And the men...what are they saying about me?"
Taking a deep breath Paedur replied, "That you are a tramp, harlot and a slut".
Elaena nodded, put her face in her hands and shook her head. "How am I going to face them?"

"Násuin has assured me that he has spoken to them defending your honour and insisting that they continue to treat you with respect".

"Do you believe him?" she asked.

"Aye, I do", he replied.

Nodding she said, "The townspeople never had much regard for me, the warriors and the soldiers had none and my family did not care about me. The only love I have ever known is that which you have shown me. I have ruined everything".

Taking a deep breath Paedur wanted to comfort her but his own anger prevented him from doing so, instead he sat silently allowing her to agonise.

They ate the rest of their meal in silence, Elaena returned to her bed and Paedur spent the day at his desk writing.

Násuin, having issued orders to his men to attend to the town's defences and their other duties, went to see Niwelyn. She was sitting outside her house quietly resting and looked up when she saw him approaching.

"Bore da, My Lady", he greeted her. "May I have a word with you?"

"Of course, Násuin, you are welcome", she replied.

Sitting beside her he began, "I have just been with Paedur; it seems Lad...Elaena is unwell. Paedur is somewhat disturbed about her; it seems there was an incident in the taberna last night which has got the town talking".

"Is she well?" Niwelyn asked.

"It seems some medical intervention was necessary but Paedur has attended to her needs", he replied.

"She is alright then", she stated.

"My Lady"...he said,

"...Niwelyn", she interrupted,

"Niwelyn", he said nodding, "I fear there may be...repercussions, there is already great unrest...this will play straight in to their hands...and they could use it against us".

Niwelyn nodded, "All we can do is wait and see what actually happens...and deal with it as best we can...when it does", she said.
Násuin nodded in agreement.
"Do they require my help now?" she asked.
"I do not think so", he replied.
Niwelyn cynically closed her eyes and went very silent.
Standing up Násuin said, "I have taken up your precious time. I will take leave of you, thank you for listening".
Niwelyn nodded.

Later that night Elaena became unwell, she was bleeding quite heavily and in great pain. Paedur gave her some more herbs and helped her to bathe and change into a long dark cotton robe. Gently he helped her into bed and, when he was sure she was comfortable, he urged her to sleep but she was unable to rest.
Leaving her momentarily, he went down to the courtyard and found Násuin, "Get Lady Niwelyn for me, I am in need of her advice. And tell her to bring her medicines", he said urgently.
Násuin nodded and immediately hurried away
Paedur returned to Elaena and kept watch over her, a short while later Niwelyn arrived. Násuin stood guard at the end of the stairs and waited for instruction.
Paedur greeted her when she entered the room but she ignored him and immediately went to Elaena. With her usual deftness she instructed, "Get her a short tunic".
Paedur immediately went to the press, selected one and handed it to her. She raised Elaena into a sitting position and exchanged the blood soaked tunic for the clean short one.
Elaena was distressed and Niwelyn cooed softly in her ear while she inspected her. After a few minutes she said, "I can find no lasting damage, there is bruising and some swelling but that will heal".
Looking at Paedur she said quietly, "You have treated her well, Paedur, she is lucky that you acted quickly. I suggest a few days bed rest".
"And the bleeding?" he asked.

"That is the herbs at work", she replied. "It will stop soon".
She packed her things away and walked towards the door; Paedur opened it for her and walked her down the corridor.
"Thank you, Elyn, as always your strength and skills benefits us, thank you, I am forever in your debt" he said.
"Paedur, you know what happened, you know there is talk around the town" she said.
He nodded, "Yes, I have spoken with Násuin and he has told me some of the stories", he replied.
"What will you do now", she asked.
"Concentrate on getting Elaena well again and then I will make arrangements for us to leave town. It is well that we do not do anything in haste", he replied.
Niwelyn nodded saying, "Things have already been done in haste. She is well for now, there should be no problem however if there is do not hesitate to summon me. The physical bruises will heal quickly...the emotional ones will take time, be gentle with her".
Paedur nodded and kissed her on the check, "Thank you, Elyn, Druantia bless you".
Niwelyn nodded and left.
Paedur returned to Elaena, she was now sleeping quietly, he kept watch over her, only when he was certain that she was in no danger did he allow himself to rest.
When Niwelyn reached the end of the stairs Násuin asked, "Is Elaena well, is there anything I can do...is Paedur well?
"Rest, Násuin, all is well for now. She has been given herbs and has had a reaction to them, a natural reaction. She will be unwell for a few days but she will heal and return to us shortly".
"That is good", he said relieved.
"I am tired, I need to rest and you should rest too", she said. "I will be safe returning home, Paedur and Elaena will be alright tonight. Go home and rest, all is well".
"I will at least walk you to the gate and lock it behind you, that way I will know that we are safe within and I will then be able to rest", Násuin said.
At the gate he said "Niwelyn..."

"...Not now Násuin, I am too tired. Nos da, we will talk in the morning", she interrupted.
Nodding he watched her leave, closed and locked the gate then turned and striding back to his dwelling he looked up to Elaena and Paedur room and sighed. In a quiet voice to himself he said, "I wonder what will be the outcome of this".

Paedur and Elaena settled into a rather quiet, sullen and uncomfortable life together after that, things were never quite the same for them, neither spoke of the taberna incident. Paedur was grateful that she had come back to him and made no further plans to leave the town. Elaena did not attempt to push the issue, she was grateful that he had not punished her and that he continued to care for her and protect her.
While she was with him the warriors continued to greet her with respect, the women quietly accepted her, the men avoided her and the children loved her. No one spoke of baby Elaena and no one asked about her. Elaena was content to wait until Paedur was ready, she knew he was keeping up to date with current events and that he would know when it was the right time to leave.

Chapter Thirteen

Autumn ended the harvest was in, the stores were stocked and the people began to prepare for the Winter months. The weather was still good for October and everyone was quite happy, the new babies were strong and healthy and the mothers fully recovered. Preparations began for the Samhain/Ludi Plebeii celebrations, the children made decorations for the altar and great hall and some extra presents for Elaena to help cheer her up.

The Druids began arriving the day before Samhain and, together with the warriors, spent many hours in the great hall discussing the current situation in the country.

Sitting together close to the fire Násuin began, "Friends, we can no longer wait the time to defend ourselves has come. We must strike now if we are to remain in control of our lands", his voice was strong and determined.

One of the Druids spoke in a strong but level voice, "Christianity has won the hearts and minds of the people, each day we lose more and more people to the new religion".

One of the warriors rose and spoke in a booming voice, "Let us rise up now and drive the Romans from our town and then drive them out of Cymru altogether".

The warriors cheered loudly stamping their feet.

One of the Druids rose to his feet and raised his hands gesturing to all to calm down and, in a soft but strong voice said, "Friends, tonight at celebrations let us make special sacrifices to the Gods to guide our actions and protect our people".

The Druids nodded and murmured.

Paedur, looking from one to the other as each one spoke, stood and waited for everyone to quieten, his presence filled the great hall, when all were silent he began.

"It is true that we must defend our lands but I say we wait, winter is drawing in and no move will be made during the cold months".

He turned to the warriors, "Recruit and train new men, gather your strength and resources".
To the Druids he said, "Beseech the Gods, brothers and sisters.
To all he said, "We will strike as Spring takes hold and the weather is more favourable, we will call upon our neighbouring tribes to join us and Násuin and I will lead you all in battle".
The Druids nodded in agreement, the warriors cheered and clapped, Paedur gestured them to calm down again, when they had quietened he said, "For now, let us celebrate the New Year and give thanks for the harvest".
Together they left the great hall and joined the townspeople.
On the morning of Samhain Paedur, Elaena and Niwelyn set up a small fire for the children just outside her roundhouse. They went into the forest to collect chestnuts, when they had a basket filled they brought them back to the small fire and roasted them until they burst. Laughter filled the air and the children's excited voices cheered Elaena. Niwelyn placed apples into a large samian ware bowl with clear spring water and Paedur and Elaena gently tied the hands of the children who had been selected to put their faces into the water and grab onto the apples with their teeth. The children not participating cheered and encouraged the ones who were, their excited voices cheered the hearts of everyone close by preparing the evening festivities
As evening drew near the children dressed up in costumes assisted by Paedur, Elaena and Niwelyn and when they were ready they were lead into the oak grove to join the adults.
That night all gathered around the great fire in the oak grove and as darkness descended upon the town Paedur, Niwelyn and the Druids took up their positions around the altar.
Tonight Paedur was dressed in heavy dark brown velvet bracae and a deep cream long sleeved heavy tunic. His winter cloak fastened at his neck with a gold clasp decorated with Celtic designs. His serpent pendent hung around his neck, his hair flowed loosely around his shoulders. Niwelyn wore a heavy dark brown velvet robe trimmed with gold at the cuffs and hem;

she too wore her heavy winter cloak her hair hung loosely down her back unadorned.

Násuin, at the edge of the crowd, dressed in heavy navy coloured bracae and long sleeved red tunic. Around his shoulders was his heavy winter cloak and on his feet he wore studded leather boots. His hair was braided, tonight he also wore leather armour – he was on high alert. He loaded his bow with an arrow, one of his men lit its tip with a lighted firebrand and he shot the arrow into the fire stack, immediately it burst into flames.

Paedur called the crowd to attention and when all eyes were on them he gestured to Elaena. Standing at the edge of the crowd, dressed in an emerald green velvet gown trimmed in gold with a full length cloak to match fastened at her neck with a gold clasp similar to Paedur's. Her hair was braided and lightly adorned with autumn leaves. Slowly she walked through the crowd carrying a plate of food in one hand and a glass of red wine in the other. When she reached the altar she handed the food to Niwelyn and the wine to Paedur and joined them at the altar.

In a strong clear voice Paedur said, "We give thanks for the summer abundance". Pouring the wine into an earthenware cup and raising it high above his head, in a strong booming voice, he called, "May the Gods protect us this winter and keep us from all harm", he lowered his hands placing the cup on the altar.

Taking the plate loaded with food Niwelyn carefully raised it above her head and, in a strong voice that carried on the air, she said, "Cerridwen, we thank you for your generosity and kindness, may your abundance sustain us throughout the winter months", she lowered her hands placing the plate on the altar beside Paedur's cup.

Paedur continued, "We honour our dead and ask that you keep the souls of all who have gone before us safe and close to you. Give each one comfort and rest according to their needs".

Together, hand in hand, their strong voices carrying in the wind they said, "We place our town and all who live in it in your hands this night, guide us, protect us and keep us safe".

Releasing each other's hands they both eat and drank from the cup and plate, Paedur gestured to Elaena to do the same.

He then looked at Elaena and nodded, loudly she called, "Join us in feasting, song and dance. Eat, good people, we have much to celebrate".
Immediately the feasting began. The musicians struck up their instruments and the entertainers performed for the crowd. As a special treat Paedur and Niwelyn performed a song written by Niwelyn, her high sweet voice complemented the deep rich timbers of his. Together in song they cast a spell over the town; it was a song of protection
As their song came to an end Paedur looked over at Niwelyn saying, "An excellent composition, Niwelyn, congratulations".
"It is my birthday present to you, Paedur, with the added bonus of being a song of protection...for all of us", she replied.
"Diolch then, it is a wonderful gift...from a wonderful person", he said quietly.
"You have made it", she said, "you are now fifty, that makes you an Elder".
Paedur nodded, "Aye, indeed I am".
Elaena, watching Paedur and Niwelyn felt jealous of their comfort in each other's company and the way they matched and complemented each other. Sadness moved within her lodging in her chest, she moved away from the crowd and poured some wine into a goblet and drank deeply.
Násuin detached himself from the group he was with and went over to her. Standing beside her he said, "It is good to see you fully recovered and well again, Elaena".
"Diolch, Násuin", she said quietly.
"I told you to come to me if you ever needed anything", he continued, looking at her intently.
"That you did", she said, her voice slightly shaking.
"But you did not come", he said quietly.
"No", she said.
"May I ask why?"
"It did not occur to me to do so", she replied, her lower lip quivering.
Standing protectively close to her he could see that she was upset and said no more.

After the ceremonies all four mixed and mingled, each watching each other but not being with each other.
As the festivities ended the town settled down into the winter.

***

On the last day of November Elaena went out on an errand for Paedur, as she crossed the courtyard Násuin watched her leave. Knowing that Paedur was alone, he seized the opportunity to speak with him. He went to Paedur's room knocked on the door and waited for permission to enter.
"Enter", called Paedur.
On entering the room Násuin found Paedur at his desk writing.
"Paedur, may I speak with you please?" he asked quietly.
"Yes of course, Násuin come in sit down, can I get you a drink", Paedur said.
"No, thank you, I will not stay long, I want to be gone before Elaena returns", Násuin replied.
"What troubles you?" asked Paedur.
"Elaena", replied Násuin.
Paedur instantly stopped writing and putting down his pen, got up and stood with Násuin in the middle of the room.
"Elaena, what do you mean?" he asked.
"I fear for her safety", Násuin replied. "The Roman governor has arrived, he is camped outside the town, about a half day's journey away, he is expected to arrive perhaps tomorrow", he stopped watching Paedur.
Paedur nodded, listening but remained silent.
Násuin continued, "You are aware that when he gets here he will seize the town and divide up the people, we cannot fight them off though we will do our best. The first person they will come for is you and, as your woman, they will take Elaena and do Macha knows what with her".
Again he stopped, watching Paedur closely.
Silently Paedur nodded, listening.

Násuin took a deep breath and said, "I have come to ask that you release Elaena into my custody, she has a better hope of survival with me than she has with you".
Paedur's eyes shot open wide, his mouth opened and he began to breathe heavily.
Násuin noticed the reaction and waited for a reply, there was none, so he continued, "As a warrior's woman she has a better chance of survival, I can protect her and..."
"...As a warrior's woman she has no better chance than as a Druid's woman, especially the warrior leading the attack", Paedur interrupted in a hard voice.
They stood staring at each other for a few minutes.
Eventually Násuin said, "My men will protect her and keep her safe".
"Your men have no regard for her, besides they will be too busy fighting the Romans to be able to protect anyone, let alone Elaena, and so will you", Paedur said hardly.
Paedur walked over to the fire staring into it, his back to Násuin. Násuin stood where he was staring at Paedur's broad, solid strong back. He realised he loved his friend and that what he was asking was difficult but he believed he had Elaena's best interest at heart.
"You know I am right, Paedur", he said quietly.
"And Elna"? Paedur asked.
"I am prepared to take both into my custody", Násuin replied.
Paedur shook his head and, in a low deep menacing voice, said "No, I will not allow it".
"Why?" asked Násuin.
"Because they are my responsibility", replied Paedur.
"You cannot protect them, even your magic will not save them", Násuin said.
"I will get her to Ynys Mon immediately, she will be reunited with Elna and they will both be safe there", Paedur said.
"She will be less safe there than she is here, at least here she has half a chance", Násuin said.
"No, Násuin, I will not allow it", Paedur said his voice becoming strong and determined.

"Please, Paedur", Násuin pleaded.
"NO", shouted Paedur, his eyes wide.
He turned to Násuin and held him in a steady stare.
Násuin had seen this look before, putting his hands up to his face and closing his eyes he took a deep calming breath. Letting it out slowly he said, "Paedur, I know you want what is best for Elaena, but believe me this is her best hope".
Paedur shook his head and closed his eyes releasing a deep breath. "No", he said, "if as you say I am dead anyway, then I would rather she be with me than with you".
"Why?" Násuin asked forcibly.
"Because I love her", Paedur said, equally forcibly.
"So do I", said Násuin, his eyes wide staring at Paedur.
Paedur stared at Násuin in disbelief, "You love Elaena", he said.
"Yes", replied Násuin quietly. "I have loved her for some time now".
"Have you been with her", Paedur asked his eyes narrowing.
"No, of course not, she is your woman but..." replied Násuin,
"...but what?" asked Paedur forcibly,
"...but if anything happens to you she will be alone...and unprotected...I have seen how the warriors and soldiers jeer her, as my woman I will be able to protect her better than if she were just another citizen of the town", Násuin continued forcibly.
In a way Paedur knew that Násuin was right but now that he was on the verge of losing her he realised he could not let her go.
"Does she share your love?" Paedur asked.
"No", Násuin replied.
"And does she know you love her?" Paedur asked.
"No", replied Násuin.
This time Paedur raised his hands to his face covering his mouth and, breathing into them, he closed his eyes. He shook his head and put his hands down by his sides.
"No, I will not let her go", he said quietly.
Násuin let out a sigh of exasperation, "Why?" he asked.
"Because she is mine and I WILL NOT LET HER GO" Paedur shouted menacingly.

They stood staring at each other, both breathing hard, defying each other.
Elaena walked in, saw them angrily staring at each other and felt the tension between them,
"What is wrong", she asked, looking from one to the other.
"Nothing, Elaena", replied Paedur quietly blinking. "We were just having a disagreement about some battle tactics".
"Oh!" she replied, "I thought you both agreed on all things".
"We do", he replied forcibly, his eyes wide.
Then, in a quiet voice, he continued, "That is the problem".
Násuin bowed, "My Lady, I will not take up any more of your time, Good day to you both", he said, his voice restrained.
Looking hard at Paedur he then turned and left the room.
Paedur stood staring at the floor.
Elaena went over to the fire, poured some wine for both of them and returned to Paedur.
Standing in front of him, she handed him one of the goblets, "Drink" she said.
"Do you mean to subdue me with wine, My Lady", he asked quietly, looking deeply into her eyes.
"Do I need to, My Lord?" she asked, looking back deeply into his.
"No", he replied, shaking his head.
"Then come sit with me I am in need of your company", she said quietly.

Paedur didn't tell Elaena about his conversation with Násuin, nor did he tell her how close the Roman governor was. He quietly planned to go to Násuin the next day and ask him to take on the attack alone while he took Elaena to Ynys Mon. For now, being in her company was all he wanted.
The next day Násuin was out training with his men when the governor arrived in Conwy, he went immediately to the garrison for a briefing with the Roman soldiers.
Paedur and Elaena were in their room writing. The fire-was lit the room was warm Paedur sitting at his desk working on his

history of the Druids, Elaena trying to master the art of writing. The room was quiet except for the crackle of the fire.
With some difficulty she formed the letters

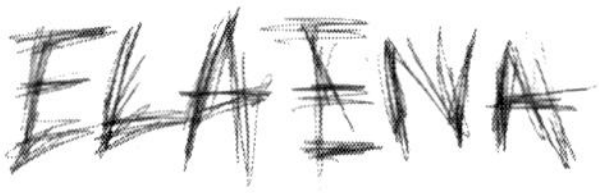

Suddenly below them there was the sound of hooves, Paedur thought the warriors had returned. Some of the women around the hearth screamed in fright, then there was the sound of booted feet coming up the stairs in haste.
The door burst open and four Roman soldiers entered, two flanked Paedur and the other two crossed the room and seized Elaena. The governor and the young soldier blocked the door; twenty other soldiers blocked the corridor.
Paedur stood up in front of his desk Elaena jumped up from the stool in front of the fire and shrieked, her work fell to the floor as they roughly grabbed her and held her between them. The two soldiers flanking Paedur stood silently beside him, not touching him, their swords crossed in front of him.
Pointing to Elaena the young soldier said, "There they are...that is her", the soldiers tightened their grip on her arms holding her tightly. Elaena looked at the young soldier in disbelief.
The governor stepped into the room; the young soldier continued to block the door.
Looking at Paedur he asked, "And so, Druid, it is you who plan to bring us down, is it?"
Paedur remained silent, Elaena whimpered in pain, struggling.
The governor continued, "We will see about that". In a large booming voice he said, "seize them, have them locked away and place them under heavy guard, let no one near them".
He turned and strode from the room; the young soldier stood aside. The other soldiers parted and formed a line along the walls when he reached the top of the stairs they fell into step behind him.
Elaena looked at Paedur a silent look of pleading in her eyes.

Paedur moved and the soldiers tightened their swords in front of him blocking his movement. He stood still, hands down by his sides, looking back at Elaena.

Roughly the two soldiers holding Elaena moved her towards the door, she pulled struggling and screaming, "NO, NO, NO", roughly they urged her on.

At the door they stopped. Paedur and Elaena were only feet away from each other, neither spoke, neither could. Elaena looked silently pleading with Paedur to forgive her, she recognised the young soldier who had pointed her out, he was the one she had raped that night down at the taberna. Silently with frightened eyes she begged, pleaded and beseeched Paedur to forgive her.

Silently he stared back at her unable to speak unable to move realising that he'd already lost her. The soldiers tugged on her arms encouraging her to move, she took one last look at him and on his face she saw a look of complete understanding, total forgiveness, deepest sadness and...LOVE.

As they dragged her out of the room and down the corridor she screamed, "Noooooooooo".

They hurried her down the stairs and into the courtyard.

Násuin and his men had just arrived back and stood talking to the women.

The soldiers formed a tight circle around her and hurried her out.

Násuin hurried over to them drawing his sword and lunged at the soldiers, "Let her go", he commanded as he clashed swords with one of them and fought with him.

The soldier slashed at him catching him on the arm breaking the skin then roughly the soldier kicked him in the chest knocking him to the ground. He got up and lunged again, crossing swords with another soldier and again he was kicked in the chest and knocked to the ground. This time the soldier kicked him in the kidneys, he curled up into a ball, his men rushed to his aid but they were blocked from getting to him.

Roughly the soldiers hurried Elaena across the courtyard and left along the street past the house where she used to live. Past the mill gate and along the street passing the square, where she first met Paedur teaching the children, then on along that street and turning left along the upper gate street. The few people on the street stopped what they were doing and stared. The Roman soldiers stared straight ahead not looking at anyone, intent on their mission to get Elaena to the villa as quickly as possible.

The entrance was a simple low stone wall painted white there was a small two storey detached building just inside the walls the other three walls had large buildings set into them. A large courtyard of hard packed earth served as the garrison and training area for the soldiers. At the end of the courtyard there was a high white washed stone wall with a single gate in the middle dividing the garrison from the house.

Roughly she was ushered across the courtyard and in through the gate. Square patches of tended lawn formed the inner gardens, statues of goddesses stood in the four corners. A fountain with a statue of the Roman god Apollo took up pride of place in the centre, a path on either side of Apollo lead up to the door of the villa. Surrounding the gardens were stone buildings, white washed with pointed terracotta roofs and in the centre back wall was a two storey villa with a balcony over the entrance. Roughly she was pushed through the door into a short corridor the floor of which was decorated with a cross detail mosaic. The doors to the rooms on either side were closed.

As Elaena was brought to the Roman villa, she heard nothing, saw no one and wasn't even aware of anything. She was thrown into a bare stone room and left there; a heavy guard was placed around it with strict orders not to let anyone in or out.

Násuin lay on the ground panting and bleeding. The women screamed, the children cried, the men stood by helpless. As each warrior tried to break the soldiers' ranks they were roughly pushed back and kicked to the ground, Elaena, under tight guard was lead away.

A few minutes later Paedur was ushered from the room, a tight guard of soldiers formed around him as he walked down the corridor flanked by the two soldiers. As they escorted him across the courtyard Násuin and his men lunged at the guards and were again kicked to the ground slashed and beaten by the

soldiers. Paedur, also under heavy guard, was led away. Násuin and his men lay on the ground dazed, breathless and bleeding. Paedur was escorted out of the courtyard and left along the street where Elaena used to live, past the mill gate and along the street passing the square where he used to teach the children, memories of such times flashed in his mind, then on along that street and turning left along the upper gate street. This was the quiet part of town mostly residential, he was aware that everyone was going about their life and as he passed them they stopped and watched silently. The Roman soldiers stared straight ahead not looking at anyone intent on their mission to get Paedur to the garrison as quickly as possible.
Crossing over the upper gate bridge Paedur was brought to the Roman manor house just outside the town. It was small by city standards; there were no Roman villas in Cymru so this was simply a provincial manor. He was marched across the courtyard with hard packed earth; the buildings on either side of it were stone, white washed with pointed terracotta roofs. He was placed under heavy guard in an empty store room and given nothing to eat or drink, the governor did not come to see him and no one was allowed in or out.

Násuin got heavily to his feet coughing and gathered his men in the courtyard, "Is everyone alright?" he asked, a fierce look of anger in his eyes.
Dusting themselves off they nodded, one of them asked, "Are you alright"?
Inspecting his injuries he replied, "I will heal".
Everyone stood by in shock. They had never seen Násuin bested. He had fought fiercely and bravely and he was visibly wounded but he was no match for the Romans. His men had never been beaten back with such ease.
"Gather the horses, arm yourselves", Násuin said fiercely, "we ride immediately to the villa and free Elaena and Paedur".
The warriors nodded and immediately jumped to his command. His horse was brought out to him; deftly he mounted and lead his men out of the courtyard and through the town. Everyone

stopped what they were doing and shrunk back behind their walls and gates as they passed. Násuin was aware of their frightened looks he contemplated shouting some words of reassurance but his whole concentration was on getting to the villa as quickly as possible and releasing Elaena.

When they arrived the Romans had already anticipated their arrival and easily fought them off. As dusk fell Násuin realised that it was useless to fight any longer and called his men off. Several were badly wounded and a few lay dead on the ground, they gathered the dead and returned to the great hall to rest and regroup.

Having checked that everyone within the fort was reasonably well he went to see Niwelyn. Banging on her door he stood impatiently waiting for her to answer, when she did so he said breathlessly, “Niwelyn, forgive the intrusion...there has been... an incident...can you come and bring your herbs...we have wounded...please come now we are in need of your help”.

Grabbing her cloak and medicines bag she left with him, “Násuin, what has happened”, she asked as he led her to the great hall.

“The Romans and their governor arrived while I was out training with my men”, he replied. “They have seized Elaena and Paedur and have taken them away under heavy guard. We tried to recapture them but were unable to do so; we have sustained many injuries and some deaths”

“Are you hurt”, she asked with concern, she noticed there was open wounds and fresh blood on his face, arms and chest.

“I will heal”, he shrugged, “my men are in need of your skills and the townspeople are in need of your strength and comfort”.

Together they arrived at the great hall and Niwelyn immediately got to work treating and healing, Násuin assisted as best he could. For several hours Niwelyn worked tirelessly to make the warriors comfortable. The women and children huddled around the fire rocking back and forth crying, moaning and whimpering, the men sat together helplessly.

When everyone had been attended to Niwelyn went over to Násuin, “You are injured”, she said. “Let me help you”.

I am fine I am not in need of help", he said sullenly.
"You have open wounds, if they are not treated they will become infected and you will be of no use to anyone", she insisted.
Nodding silently he relaxed and allowed her to attend to his wounds as she did so he looked around the courtyard and took in the distress of the women, the frightened whimpering of the smaller children and the frozen fright of the older ones. The men stood helplessly not knowing what to do; his men lay wounded and exhausted on the hard packed earth.
No one slept that night. Niwelyn brewed up a cauldron of Camomile tea and administered it to everyone. She sent a lone rider out with a message to her fellow Druids and backed it up with a message by carrier pigeon informing them of what had happened and requesting assistance.
When everyone had been attended to according to their needs she went over to the open fire and, raising her arms in the air she called, "Nemain, Goddess of Panic, grant us your comfort this night, sooth our fear and our fright and bring peace back into our town".
Turning to the warriors she commanded, "Someone give me a token of war".
Násuin immediately handed her a wooden sword.
Niwelyn took it from him, bowed and said, "Perfect, thank you Násuin".
She turned back to the fire, threw the wooden sword into it and watched it burn.
Loudly she called, "Take this token Nemain and grant us your peace".
Turning back to the people she said, "Rest as best you can, we all need our strength now".
At some stage during the night a Druid from Caerhun arrived, the others, realising that they too were now in great danger, secured their own towns and prepared for possible attack. Násuin, Niwelyn and her fellow Druid spent the night mingling, comforting, reassuring and counselling everyone.

***

Alone in the empty storeroom under heavy guard Paedur sat on the floor, his back against the stone wall, his knees pulled up his elbows resting on them, his face in his hands breathing deeply. There was only one wooden door and it had been fastened and bolted from the outside, there was one small window in the room.

In a low voice to himself he said, "Oh no, this is it, this is the end, I know I will survive the night but at first light I will be put to death".

A deep wave of sadness washed over him.

"Oh Druantia what will they do with Elaena? Should I fool the guards and release myself then go to her and rescue her? If I do will I make it before they kill me, will they hurt her all the more because I tried? Oh Druantia guide me".

In desperation he searched within himself for the right thing to do, after several agonising minutes he decided, "No, what is done is done, there is no point in angering the Romans any further".

He got up and paced the room several ideas came to him and, having given each one some thought, abandoned them. Slowly he paced unable to rest.

"I wonder how Elaena is coping; I hope they are not brutal with her. What will they do with her, no doubt they will rape her at least, perhaps even flog her. Oh! Druantia, this is what we feared most, especially Elaena, now it has come to pass. Why did I not get her to safety sooner", he asked himself angrily. "Did I really expect to be able to take on the might of even a small Roman legion? Others have tried, especially in Gaul, and failed, why did I think I could succeed? Maybe I will break free and then free Elaena but...no that would only make an already bad situation worse".

On and on he paced running his hands through his hair, "How did we come to this", he asked himself. "This is probably the result of the night Elaena went to the taberna, evidently the young Roman soldier was angry, went to his superior and told him what happened. The Romans must have made enquiries and discovered that we are planning a rebellion and naturally they discovered that I am leading it. The governor has obviously decided to move swiftly to quell the opposition and has moved in with immediate action".

Shaking his head he continued, "No matter how hard Násuin and the warriors fight, good though they are, they are no match for the Romans. Within days most, if not all, of the townspeople will be dead, there will be no mercy, there will be no peace making". He continued pacing breathing deeply.

Standing against the wall he took a rest and thought, "*Three short years we have known each other and I have seen Elaena turn from a scruffy gutter rat into an almost elegant lady. She had such wonderful fire which flared dangerously and now has been subdued, we have had such good times together boating, walking in the forest, the ceremonies and...that night on the beach*".

He closed his eyes remembering the night he had brought her to the beach, he breathed deeply.

"I wonder what will become of the children slavery at worst, death would be better. At least Elna is safe and well cared for, thank Druantia for that. How happy we once were and how uncomfortable and formal we have become with each other since the taberna night", he sighed.

"I hope Elaena will remember all I have taught her and use it to her advantage now. What will they do with her, will they put her to death, somehow I do not think so, more likely they will keep her imprisoned and mistreat her", he agonised.

"This is her deepest fear and worse nightmare and I am not there to help her, this time she is on her own. Is she strong enough, will she cope? Perhaps I will break free and rescue her but...no; if I do they will kill us both. Even if we do survive and get out of the town alive, they will hunt us down and kill us on the road".

He breathed trying to calm himself and then he reasoned, "Even if we do survive and get to safety, once Elaena has calmed down she will blame me for everything and then she will hate me for ever...and probably leave me in anger...for Násuin...but better him...than the Romans".

Shaking his head he agonised, "No matter what I do…I have lost her. Násuin offered me her protection last night and I turned him down now…if she is lucky…Násuin will find some way to rescue her and make her his woman, or the Romans will keep her and put her to death…either way…I have lost her".
Shaking his head sadly he paced and paced.
"What can I do, I have already lost her but I cannot let her go. At first light I will be put to death and she will blame herself, she will be totally devastated but at least blaming herself will secure her love for me…forever. I cannot lose her in hate; the best I can do is lose her in love and if blaming herself achieves that…then it is worth it. Allowing myself to be put to death by the Romans will secure her love for me…for all eternity", he reassured himself.
"As a Druid I know this is against the rules because I am trapping her soul but…as a man…it is the only way I can cope with her loss".
As if she was in the room he said, "Oh! Elaena, thank you for coming to live with me, for learning from me and helping me. Thank you for giving me my only child and for being there for me. Although I am the master and you are the student, in truth you are the master and you have trapped my soul. No matter how high I fly, you are always flying above me, no matter how much in control I believe myself to be, you can bring me down with a look or a single word".
As the night wore on and grew dark he wished he could tell her so many things.
"Oh! Elaena, I wish you could see me as a warrior who loves you, I wish I could tell you that since you came into my life you have made me whole. I wish I could hold you in my arms and wake up with you every morning. I wish I could tell you that I have loved no other woman but you. You have been my only love and there has never been a love like ours, I wish I could tell you how much you mean to me. I have waited so long to find you and now that I have…I cannot let you go. I hope Násuin will find a way to rescue you and get you to safety, at least with

him you will be with someone who loves you and will care for you".

He prayed that this would be so, it comforted him to know that Elna was safe and protected and that at least she would survive.

In the early hours of the morning a sense of calm returned to the courtyard and most people, now sufficiently comforted, drifted off to their dwellings to rest. Niwelyn and Násuin sat together by the fire exhausted her fellow Druid went to Paedur's room to rest. With a hot cup of Camomile tea in their hands both began to calm down.

"Are you in pain?" Niwelyn asked Násuin.

He shook his head, "No".

"I am told you took quite a beating", she said.

He nodded, "Yes...but I am strong, you have attended to my wounds, and I heal quickly...I am alright. My concern is not for myself but for Elaena and Paedur, what will become of them? What do you foresee"?

"I am not gifted with foresight, that is Paedur's gift, however I know that the Romans have been looking for a reason to drive us Druids out of this land and this will give them a perfect excuse to do so", she replied.

"What will we do now", he asked.

"Rest, if we can, the people seem to be comforted so we should take this opportunity to rebuild our own strength".

"May I suggest that you stay with me this night, that way we can rest and be on hand if something happens", he said.

Nodding tiredly she replied, "Yes, perhaps that is best, thank you."

"Come with me then you may rest on my bench for the night".

Together they went to Násuin's dwelling and Niwelyn slept on his bench wrapped in her travelling cloak.

Resting quietly in what was left of the night Násuin replayed the events of the day in his head. His body hurt and he was in pain but his thoughts were with Elaena, what would they do to her, how would they treat her, would they treat her with respect or would they abuse her? He figured that this had something to do with the taberna night; he had wondered what the outcome would be and thought that perhaps this was it. He contemplated getting up quietly and going to the villa alone but he remembered how he and his men had been so easily bested by the soldiers and decided not to. He ran several scenarios around in his head as to how he would gather his men and make another attempt at rescuing her and while he did so he fell asleep.

Chapter Fourteen

Elaena, alone in her cell sobbed, she was very frightened and wondered what was going to happen to her. This was what she feared most, caged with no freedom at the mercy of the Romans, and she knew they would have none. To distract herself she looked around the cell. It was small with bare stone walls and a clay floor; an iron gate on one of the walls and a small window type opening high up on another wall with an iron grill on it. There was nothing at all in the room; through the window she could see a small patch of sky, there was nothing to do and nowhere to go, all she could do was wait.
Presently the two soldiers that brought her here came for her; roughly they seized her and brought her to the governor. She was brought along another long corridor the floor was decorated in the Roman opus sectile mosaic pattern the centre panel was small pink and grey tiles with a white border. The outer section had pink, white, grey and brown triangle tiles. Roughly she was brought into the hall of the villa and made stand before him, he was talking to an assistant which gave her time to look around. The floor was decorated with the same mosaic as the corridor, around the edges where the floor met the walls was decorated with a panel of cross detail mosaic. In the centre of the floor was a large mosaic of the Roman Goddess Venus, the image was flanked by long-tailed birds. Big swaths of cloth draped the painted and decorated walls, a cornice with a bird and basket pattern ran along the top of the walls just under the ceiling. Expensive urns, tables, chairs and couches were placed around the room which was bright. Fire braziers stood in all corners, she had never seen anything like this before and it was in stark contrast to the cell she had been thrown into. Painted ladies in beautiful dresses sat chatting in groups eating and drinking; men also sat eating and drinking in long dresses which she remembered Paedur telling her were toga. In the centre of the room stood a large wicker chair with a high hard curved back,

bright patterned rugs covered the area of the floor underneath it.

The governor was dressed in a white toga trimmed with red; a red silk cloak was draped around his shoulders, soft leather sandals covered his feet. There were heavy gold rings on all his chubby fingers, his face had big jowls. His skin was puffy and red, folds of skin surrounded his eyes and his rather large plump body filled the cathedra completely, his hair was short and neat. Beside him stood a tall lean man wearing a knee length white tunic with gold trim around the neck, a gold rope holding a small canvas bag around his waist acted as a belt, he wore gold sandals on his feet, he was the High Priest.

After a while he turned his attention to Elaena and noticed that she was wearing a long emerald green velvet dress, soft leather boots covered her feet. She hadn't had time to grab her cloak before she was dragged away so all she had was the dress. She looked like a lady even though her hair was dishevelled and there was a dark angry look in her eyes. She wished she could manifest Paedur's red flaming eyes but didn't know how so instead she packed all her anger into her eyes and stared defiantly at the governor.

"Tonight...My Lady", he sneered, "You will dine with me and see what it is like to be with a real man".

The soldiers sniggered and nodded knowingly.

"Take her away, bring her to my chambers and have her made ready", he said dismissively to his High Priest standing beside him.

The man nodded and gestured to the soldiers to carry out the governor's orders.

As the guards reached for her she struggled and flapped at their hands but they quickly subdued her.

The governor took a large gulp of wine from a gold goblet and, standing up, said to his secretary, "See that we are not disturbed".

"And the Druid, My Lord?" asked the secretary.

"Have his armour brought to him".

"Yes, My Lord", the secretary said bowing.

The High Priest demanded that the soldiers release their tight grip on Elaena and immediately they let her go. Quietly and respectfully he escorted her to the governor's chambers, like the hall they had mosaic floors and painted walls. Wooden chests tables and chairs were placed around the rooms. In the middle of the bedchamber stood a large bed with satin sheets and big swathes of curtain surrounding it. A large window opened on to a balcony which had a commanding view of the town's upper gate.

Once the High Priest had got her safely to the room he bowed and softly said, "My Lady, the governor will be with you shortly", his manner was soft and respectful.

He turned and left the room.

While she was waiting Elaena contemplated escaping but when she stepped out on to the balcony she noticed a heavily armed guard of several soldiers standing below. There was a large drop to the ground and she figured either the fall would kill her or the soldiers would. She didn't fear death, right now it would be a welcome release, but she didn't really want to go to all that bother just to die. Leaning on the balustrade she looked around her; the house was the only two storey structure. Immediately to her right at ground level was a room, at right angles to it was a wall running along the right hand side of the garden it connected to the wall opposite her with the gate. On the left side of the gate was a wall with more rooms in it and it connected at right angles to a wall taking up the left hand side of the garden, it appeared that there were rooms with small windows within the walls. The door opened behind her and the governor entered, she stood up and walked back into the room. Looking her up and down, he said, "They tell me you are a prostitute".

"You told me we were dining, where is the food?" she asked sullenly, defiantly staring at him.

"I have already eaten, what need of food have you?" he asked sneeringly.

Somehow she figured there was no point in arguing.

"Well...are you a prostitute?" he pressed.

"Once was...am no longer", she answered sullenly.
"Once a prostitute...always a prostitute", he said dismissively. "Let us see just how good you are".
In spite of his plumpness he moved quickly and grabbed her before she had time to react, roughly dragging her across the room and throwing her on the bed. He pulled up her dress and rammed himself deep inside her mercilessly; gasping with pain she blanked her mind and waited for him to stop. On and on he rammed her, after several minutes he withdrew and, breathing hard, looking down at her with disgust, he said sneeringly, "Now you know what a real man is like Celt".
Turning away from her he clapped his hands, almost immediately the High Priest entered bowing.
"Take her away, I am done with her, have her returned to her cell", he said.
The High Priest bowed and walked over to Elaena, she looked dazed and dishevelled and seemed to be unable to move, blood trickled down the inside of her thighs and her dress was bunched up around her abdomen. Gently he pulled down her dress covering her and helped her to her feet supporting her while she steadied herself and escorted her from the room. As they reached the door she stopped and looked back, the governor's back was turned to her; he was drinking wine from a gold goblet. Angrily she stared at his back narrowing her eyes, she wished she knew one of Paedur's spells but she didn't so she just glared angrily at him.
Patiently the High Priest waited by her side observing; gently he touched her arm and gestured to her to leave the room with him. Silently they walked back to her cell; she was in pain and had difficulty walking, noticing her difficulty he slowed his pace to match hers making it more comfortable for her. Her head was in a spin her body hurt and she fought within herself not to show any emotion.
Just before they reached the cell she asked, "May I have some hot water, towels and some herbs please", her voice was shaking, she was fighting to remain in control, "and may I have a blanket

and some bedding", her voice faltered, tears stung her eyes, she fought not to cry.
The High Priest bowed replying, "Of course, My Lady, I will have them brought to you immediately".
"Thank you", she whispered.
When they reached her cell he opened the iron gate and stood back for her to enter, closing the gate after her he went away, the soldiers closed in around the area on high alert. Later a large bowl of steaming water, a small bottle of sweet smelling herbs, some towels, a blanket and a long cushion were brought to her. After she washed a wave of exhaustion engulfed her, she placed the long cushion along one wall and lay down. She settled herself as best she could, pulled the blanket up over her body and head, closed her eyes and slept.
In the early hours of the morning a squad of Roman soldiers were dispatched to the great hall to collect Paedur's armour, when they arrived everyone was too shocked and in pain to react, even the Druid in Paedur's room hadn't the energy to confront them.

As night turned to morning Paedur accepted his death and prayed for Elaena's protection. As dawn broke the Romans came for him, handing him his armour they waited for him to make himself ready and then escorted him out. Inwardly he was calm, relaxed and at peace with himself.
The High Priest greeted him, "Good morning, My Lord".
Paedur nodded silently.
The guards surrounded him and the soldiers formed a line behind them, they walked him out of the garrison, down to the upper gate along by the granary and store rooms down the traders' street and into the courtyard of the great hall. The town was just waking up, the women were working by the fire preparing breakfast. The warriors were getting themselves ready for another attempt to rescue Elaena and Paedur. All stopped when they heard the sound of heavy boots marching on the pavement. Paedur was escorted into the courtyard under heavy guard and placed in the centre in front of everyone.

The High Priest stood in front of Paedur and, addressing the crowd he said, "The governor has decreed that this man be put to death".
Turning to Paedur he said, "May our God, and your own, watch over you this day and deliver your soul safely, may you rest in peace".
Paedur listened silently.
The prayers said, the High Priest gestured to him to kneel down and as he did so he said a silent prayer of his own, "Druantia protect Elaena and keep Elna safe from harm".
Behind him a Roman soldier raised his sword above him, the first rays of sunlight glinted on the metal dazzling the eyes of all who watched. Quickly and cleanly he brought it down through Paedur's neck severing his spinal cord killing him instantly.
As his lifeless body fell to the ground Elaena, alone in her cell, woke up and screamed, "Noooooooooo".
Turning to the crowd the High Priest addressed them again, "Let this be a warning to all who are thinking of opposing us, be it known that we are in command and you cannot win".
Turning he marched out of the courtyard followed by the soldiers and the guards.
Niwelyn and Násuin instantly rushed over to Paedur's body, she fell to her knees beside him. Gently, taking his head on to her lap, she sobbed, Násuin stood silently beside her. Gently she stroked his head her tears falling on to his face, she rocked back and forth sobbing, Násuin gently placed his right hand on her left shoulder and together they grieved openly.
Slowly the warriors surrounded them and, gently lifting Paedur up, they carried him to the great hall. Násuin assisted Niwelyn to her feet, allowed her a moment to steady herself, and then together, with their arms wrapped around each other, they followed his men.
The women moaned and the children cried they could not believe what they had just witnessed, the men stood silently, helpless. There was a heavy sense of shock and sadness in the town, no one worked and no one was interested in food. Niwelyn and the women prepared Paedur's body for the ceremony. Násuin

locked down the fort and commissioned a boat for Paedur's burial. The men retreated to the taberna lamenting in their own way and the children began making good bye gifts for Paedur.
When the women were finished their preparations they placed Paedur's body on a wooden litter. Dressed in full battle gear, his sword lying on his chest, his staff lying at his side a pen in his right hand, his cloak wrapped around him, they left him lying in state for the rest of the day.
Niwelyn sat beside Paedur's body silent with grief; no one knew how much she loved Paedur except Násuin. Silently she stared unable to move, unwilling to be of any assistance to anyone. This was the first time in her adult life that Paedur was not there, they had been separated before but had been reunited, this time their separation was final. An empty space formed within her that she knew would never be filled. She sighed. Looking at Paedur's body a deep sadness welled up inside her and she hugged him. Tears streamed down her cheeks onto his face and then holding him, resting her head on his chest, she sobbed unwilling to be parted from him. Eventually she stopped crying and lay on the floor beside him wrapped in her cloak and slept.
Násuin in the short time he had known Paedur had come to love and respect him greatly, in an effort to hide his grief he barked out orders to his men but later, alone in his quarters, he could not believe what had just happened. He could not believe that Paedur had been paraded through the streets and into the courtyard and put to death in front of everyone. A warrior he may be and as such death did not upset him...but he was also a man who had just lost his friend through a cold callous act of murder. He had got over his father's recent death quite well and carried on; tonight he struggled within himself to remain in control. His grief for Paedur was something he had not felt before and, unable to comfort himself, he allowed himself to acknowledge the grief and sobbed helplessly.
As dusk approached the fort was reopened Niwelyn and her fellow Druid conducted a burial ceremony in the great hall. When all were gathered around the hearth the Druid began,

"Dis Pater, god of Death and the Underworld, accept our friend, Paedur".

In a faltering voice strained with emotion Niwelyn continued, "Arianrhod Goddess of time, karma and reincarnation...protect him and guide him...safely to Emania, the land of the moon".

Gulping and steadying herself, she continued, "Grant him safe passage and...may he rest...with you...in peace".

The Druid continued, "We pray for all here that comfort may be bestowed upon them".

Together they said, "We commit Paedur into your loving care".

The ceremony completed six warriors took up positions around the litter and gently raised it onto their shoulders. Násuin led them down to the bay; Niwelyn and her fellow Druid followed behind, the warriors formed a protective circle around them and the townspeople fell into step behind them. There should have been singing, there should have been drumming but there was only silence; everyone was in shock and no one could muster up the energy to sing...not even a lament.

Later that day, while the townspeople buried Paedur, the Romans returned to his room and, taking all his writings, they threw them into the fire in the courtyard. When Násuin and the warriors returned to the courtyard and realised what the Romans had done they were too much in shock to object or retaliate.

As Paedur's body was brought down to the bay the High Priest came for Elaena, the iron gate was opened for him and quietly he said, "My Lady, the governor requests that you dine with him".

As they walked to the governor's chambers Elaena said quietly, "He is dead, they have killed him".

"Yes, My Lady, this morning at dawn", he replied.

"Was it quick?" she asked

"And painless", he replied nodding.

Elaena nodded in silence, the High Priest noted that she slumped a little, that her bottom lip quivered and that she fought not to cry. She had hoped in her sleep that somehow Paedur would have found a way to rescue her, now she knew this hope was gone. The fight left her and she steeled herself.

As she entered the governor's chamber he was waiting for her just inside the door, he grabbed her knocking her to the floor giving her no chance to react. As she hit the floor and felt him tugging at her dress she blanked out. When he was finished he got up and left the room.

Silently the High Priest entered the room and found her on the floor unconscious, he revived her and assisted her to sit up covering her. Dazed and weak she clung to him, she felt nothing she was completely numb. After a few minutes he assisted her to stand up and escorted her back to her cell, she rested on his arm willing herself to walk without faltering. When they reached her cell he gently walked her over to the long cushion and assisted her to lie down. Within minutes he had hot water, towels and herbs brought to her, this time he also included a small plate of food.

She lay exhausted in her cell unable to move, inwardly she was crying, outwardly she showed no emotion. Slowly, painfully she got up, washed and eat the food, after she had finished she lay back down and stared at the ceiling.

At the water's edge the warriors carefully placed Paedur's body into the boat, his staff, javelin and writing implements were placed around him. Násuin placed his sword on his chest and kissed his forehead, tears stung his eyes. The children placed their presents around him and kissed his forehead, the women placed holly and ivy around him; there were no flowers at this time of year.

In as strong a voice as she could muster Niwelyn said, "Druantia, take Paedur and grant him safe passage". She lovingly placed a bare branch of oak and some mistletoe on his chest; she kissed his lips, tears rolled down her cheeks as she did so.

Her fellow Druid and Násuin stood on either side of her and the final farewells were said, the boat was pushed into the sea and began its journey.

Násuin raised his bow and loaded it with an arrow one of his men touched a firebrand to its tip and, with precision aim, he shot it into the boat which immediately caught fire. Everyone watched in silence as the boat faded out of sight.

One by one the crowd dispersed leaving Niwelyn, Násuin and the Druid standing side-by-side, shoulder-to shoulder. All three turned at the same time and as they began their journey back to the great hall Niwelyn stumbled; the two men steadied her and then, each holding one of her arms, walked with her supporting her. The Druid retired to Paedur's room.

Násuin walked Niwelyn to her roundhouse at the door he said, "I can stay if you wish".

She shook her head, "No thank you, Násuin, I need to be alone", she said quietly.

Nodding he said, "Nos da, Niwelyn".

When she was alone she allowed herself to give in to the grief and sobbed uncontrollably, eventually she sobbed herself to sleep. Násuin returned to his quarters and when he was sure he was alone he too gave in to the grief and sobbed.

Alone in her cell, Elaena knew that Paedur had just been buried; she closed her eyes and breathed, quiet hot tears coursed down her cheeks and burned her skin. She didn't have the energy to move or to cry, she knew now all hope was gone. The only man who had ever loved her was dead and she was doomed to a life of sexual slavery, slowly the tears stopped and she drifted into sleep.

The next morning at dawn Niwelyn awoke and lay in her bed thinking about Paedur his face...his voice...his eyes haunted her. She breathed as memories of their time together presented themselves to her...*the recent conversation they'd had about Elaena and how she had helped him get Elna to Ynys Mon*. She was glad now that she had because at least his legacy would live on through her no matter what else happened.

Slowly she got up washed and put on her dark blue velvet gown, going over to her dresser she took the cup Paedur had used at the Samhain celebrations, his fiftieth birthday, and putting on her heavy woollen cloak, she quietly left her roundhouse. Numb with grief she walked in a dreamlike state down to the stream in the forest and stood silently staring into the water, normally the sound comforted her, today it didn't.

Breathing deeply, drawing strength from the air and the trees around her, she raised the empty cup to the rising sun. Quietly she said, "Druantia, accept this cup on behalf of your devoted Druid Paedur. May you reward him for his achievements and may he rest with you in peace for all eternity".

Lowering the cup and slowly bending on one knee she gently placed it in the water; silently she took several deep breaths. After a few minutes she slowly stood up, watched it floating down the stream then bowed to the trees and returned to her roundhouse.

***

For the rest of December the townspeople came to terms with their grief, slowly life returned to normal, the children were affected the most; they had lost their beloved teacher and were not sure how to cope without him.

For Elaena the month passed in a blur of rape by the governor, jeering and taunting by the soldiers. The only thing that made it bearable was the kindness and respect of the High Priest, he seemed to anticipate her every need and within minutes of returning to her cell her requirements were sent to her.

One day towards the end of December on the way to the governor she asked, "Do you think it possible that I could have another dress, this one is smelly and dirty and has brought me nothing but bad luck"?

"Yes, My lady, I will see what I can do", he replied.

When she returned to her cell later that day, exhausted and in pain, she found a long grey canvass dress lying on her long cushion, it wasn't new but it was very much better than the one she was wearing. After washing she put it on and ate the food that had been left for her, she was very grateful to the High Priest for his kindness.

Násuin and the warriors doubled their defences, several times they made attempts to rescue Elaena but each time they were beaten back sustaining injury and deaths, eventually he decided he needed every man for the coming revolution and so he abandoned all attempts at rescue knowing that she would be released when they were victorious.

The Order on Ynys Mon, on hearing of Paedur's death, appointed another Chief Druid and dispatched him to Conwy giving him custody of the town. Niwelyn's fellow Druid returned to Caerhun and prepared his people for the coming battle.

The winter Solstice celebrations were quiet, subdued and solemn, in her roundhouse Niwelyn and the new Chief Druid conducted the ceremony half-heartedly. Very few people turned up, the Christians had replaced the Solstice with a new celebration they called Christmas celebrating the birth of their new Son of God. A new feast was created on the twenty-fifth of December, four days after the Solstice, to commemorate this event, and the ceremonies were conducted in buildings they called churches. Only a handful of people stood around the fire that night and left soon after.

Násuin hung back and asked, "Are you alright, Niwelyn?"

"As alright as I can be", she answered.

"I can stay if you wish", he said.

"No, Násuin, thank you, I need to be alone", she said.

"You will come to me if you need assistance", he pressed.

"Yes, I will, but for now I need to be alone".

Nodding he made his way to the door as he opened it Niwelyn said, "Forgive me Násuin, I did not ask about you, how are you coping"?

"As well as can be expected", he replied. "It is hard to believe Paedur is no longer with us".

Niwelyn nodded.

"At least they gave him a warrior's death", he continued.

"Aye that would have pleased him", she said nodding.

"Are you sure you do not need company?" he asked.

"I am quite sure, thank you", she replied.

"In that case, Nos da", he said and left closing the door softly behind him.

***

Niwelyn still missed Paedur; she found it hard to adjust to not having him around and conducting the ceremonies without him seemed empty and without meaning. She fought hard within herself to control her emotions and her Druid training didn't seem to help her much. As a Druid she knew she should have adjusted immediately...but as a woman she couldn't. He had meant too much to her and she missed him too much to adjust without great difficulty. She also began to question her beliefs, it seemed that her Gods and Goddesses had deceived and abandoned her; they had not protected them as she had expected them to and all the invocations didn't seem to bring the desired result. She understood the new religion and saw its many comparisons with her own but she was not prepared to change her ways and to defect from the ancient religion of her people.
Násuin also fought hard within himself to remain in control, death was no problem to him; he saw it all the time, he had no feelings about it at all, but losing a friend as special as Paedur did affect him greatly. He remembered when Paedur had come to Conwy first and how they had fought in the mock battle to introduce him to the people, he rubbed his arm where Paedur had cut him. He remembered their night drinking together in Paedur's room and felt that it was on that night that they had become friends. He recalled the night outside the taberna when he had broken up the fight between Paedur and Medwyn and the times he sat in conference with his men and the Druids. He also missed Elaena and thought of the few short moments he had spent close to her especially the night he had walked her home right into Paedur's room. He wished he could break through the Roman defences to rescue her but all attempts so far had failed.

***

On the night of the Winter Solstice the governor sent for Elaena, knowing it was an important date for her and her people; he cruelly assaulted and raped her. She blanked her mind and was only dimly aware of what he was doing to her; she was in so much pain afterwards that, for the first time in her life, she prayed for death. She knew now that she would never be released and that no one would come to save her. All hope now gone, she no longer had any reason to live. As the High Priest escorted her back to her cell he saw her dejection and felt her despair. He took pity on her and ordered that a hot bath with herbs be immediately prepared for her. While she was wallowing in the hot scented water he procured a small plate of food and hot wine for her, he also insisted that a large soft towel, hair brush and fresh clothes be brought to her.

Elaena took her time bathing, breathing deeply to calm herself, she tried to will the pain away, unable to do so she distracted herself by looking around the room. It was a small room with white tiled floor and walls, a strip of small emerald green tiles at eye level were the only decoration in the room. The white ceramic bath lay against the wall opposite the door under a small window and the ceiling was painted plain white. Her breathing began to change and she began to relax a little. Presently she slowly got out of the bath and, grateful of his kindness, she snuggled into the towel and took her time drying. Putting on the clean dress and brushing her hair, she felt calmer and more relaxed. When she was finished the High Priest escorted her back to her cell and made sure she was comfortable, she ate the food he had provided for her and lay down.

The forest was lush and green and very silent, a heavy stillness hung in the air, Paedur came towards her, he seemed to be surrounded by a shimmering light. He took her hands in his and looked deeply into her eyes; in his own she saw pure love and compassion, he kissed her gently on the lips filling her with a sense of calm and peace.

The iron gate opened with a loud bang, a guard came in to take the plate and cup away, Elaena opened her eyes with a start, gasped and stared at the ceiling. Slowly she began to realise she

had been dreaming, she turned her face to the wall and cried softly, eventually she fell asleep.
She celebrated her birthday alone in her cell, the month of imprisonment had begun to take its toll, she had become very much slimmer and there were dark circles under her eyes. She was still recovering from her last encounter with the governor and was still in a lot of pain. Her bruises and the wounds had been slow to heal; she slept a lot and was grateful of its oblivion. As the Roman year 409AD drew to a close Elaena was twenty.

Chapter Fifteen

410 AD

In the cold dark months of January and February Elaena nearly froze in her cell, the High Priest acquired a woollen cloak for her and an extra blanket, he also brought her hot drinks and stew, to the best of his ability he made her life as comfortable as possible. At first she had been raped every day but events in Roma were escalating and the British Celts were not as co-operative as the Romans had expected them to be. The governor had been called upon to settle disputes between the Romans and the Celts, Násuin and his band of warriors were proving to be quite a nuisance. He was also receiving disturbing news from Roma of an imminent attack. He had Elaena brought to him a few times a week and his encounters with her were short, disrespectful and painful. He had no personal interest in her other than self-gratification and the use of her as a deterrent for her people not to offend the Romans. He didn't engage her in conversation nor was he interested in her welfare. The High Priest continued to assist her in every way and they developed a friendly respectful manner with each other.

One day when they were returning to her cell she asked him, "Why do you help me"?

"Because if my woman was in the same situation as you, I would hope someone would help her in every way", he replied.

"You are a good man and I deeply appreciate your help", she told him.

"You are welcome, My Lady. Is there anything else you require?" he asked.

"Other than getting me out of here, no, thank you, I am quite comfortable now", she replied.

Násuin and the warriors continued to work on their battle plans, without Paedur they were not as well informed and they had to find out what was going on from other sources. Niwelyn assisted as best she could but battle tactics were not her forte and she was rather busy attending to the health needs of the townspeople. The neighbouring tribes who had pledged their support to Paedur and Násuin were now called upon to honour that promise and in the great hall he convened a meeting.

When all were seated Násuin addressed the gathering, "Before I give my report Niwelyn will be our voice for the Druids today". He turned to her and nodded.

Niwelyn stood and spoke, "The Druids are worried; small Christian churches have begun to spring up everywhere, usually on or near one of the well established Druid sites of worship. Many oak groves have been cleared to make way for churches, and in the cities very large stone structures are being placed in key areas. New religious services are being introduced with strange practices and their ceremonies are being conducted in Latin with very little involvement or interaction from the people. The Christian Priests are spreading messages of doom and gloom and telling the people to repent and be baptised into the new form of worship with the threat that if they do not their souls will be sent to eternal damnation in hell. Less and less people are turning up for the seasonal celebrations and fewer people are consulting the Druids and all the Druid advisors have been replaced with Christian Bishops. Worship of the Goddess has been discredited and all female Druids are now classed as witches and have been cast out of society to live, unsupported, in what is left of the forests".

Everyone round the fire listened intently in silence.

She drew a breath and continued, "The Druids are being given the choice to convert or die, many have converted and become Christian Priests and the higher ranking Druids have been relegated to the Christian rank of Monk. The Monks are now healers supporting themselves by farming and some of them are scribes copying and translating ancient books from Latin and Greek and compiling histories".

She paused remembering Paedur, noting that this is the category that he would have fitted into.

Taking a deep breath, she continued, "The Priests and Monks have been sent out among the people to convert others and officiate in the services. The Christians have taken over the roles of the High Druids with their Bishops and Arch Bishops are now their advisors, philosophers and writers. Those who do not convert are being given an honourable death and returned to their people for burial".

Again she stopped, thinking of Paedur and the last time she saw him.

"In this way the Druid religion has integrated into the new religion and is dying out". The few Druids who refused to convert and who have avoided being killed are gone into hiding, particularly on Ynys Mon and Iona in Scotia and are continuing to observe the old religion there to the best of their ability".

She paused exhausted, Násuin looked at her reassuringly.

Násuin stood and addressed the gathering "There is talk of an imminent attack; it seems the Roman Empire is breaking down and is in chaos. High taxes have been imposed upon the people and the economy is buckling, infrastructure has collapsed and trade is returning to the barter system".

He stopped and drew a breath; everyone listened and waited for him to continue.

"Quintis, the Celtic/Romano chieftain, is struggling to amass an army big enough to take on the Romans. The Roman army has seen their pay withdrawn and have been told that they are to fend for themselves by whatever means they can consequently they have lost the run of themselves and are grabbing at whatever they can get".

He stopped and took a deep breath; there was silence in the room.

"The Romans fear their world is collapsing and have become mad and totally unreasonable, they will not negotiate with anyone and they repel every effort to take them down, as we have seen".

He stopped and breathed, then continued.

"As Niwelyn has just said, Christianity is being imposed upon all peoples and all practices other than their own are being banned".

He stopped, took a deep breath and continued.

"The governor is planning to overrun us and give us warriors the same choice as the Druids."

He paused for breath.

The warriors mumbled and the Druids nodded sagely.

He continued, "I say we fight to the death by whatever means we can and we keep Conwy".

The warriors cheered and stamped.

"Go now", he urged, "and prepare for battle it seems it will come sooner than we had all anticipated".

The meeting came to an end and the group dispersed.

***

In the month of March Elaena became aware that it was Elna's first birthday, she wondered what had become of her and how she was. Since her capture she had pretty much lost sense of time except when the High Priest informed her of something going on. She had difficulty believing that a whole year had passed since Elna's birth, in many ways it had flown but in many ways it had dragged, especially lately. Remembering made her sad and she hung her head and cried.

At some point during the month the governor became aware that his High Priest had been helping Elaena and making her comfortable, he approached him about it, "Are you helping the slut?" he asked.

"The Celtic woman, you mean", the priest replied.

"The slut, yes," the governor replied.

"Yes, My Lord", said the priest.

"Why", asked the governor, "are you making use of her too?" he asked.

"No, My Lord I would not intrude...I have no need to", the priest replied.

"Then why?" pressed the Governor.

"She is in a difficult situation, through no fault of her own", replied the priest, "I mean only to make things a little easier for her".
"It is rumoured you have become her friend", the governor said.
"We have a respectful friendship", the priest replied nodding.
"Respectful", the governor sneered, "what respect is due to her, she is a Celt, a woman and a whore", he said with disgust.
"She is a human and a High Priest's woman and therefore demands respect", the Priest answered.
"She is a subject, a foreigner, a pagan and a harlot, she deserves no consideration whatsoever", the governor said dismissively.
The High Priest bowed and remained silent looking at the floor.
"You are relieved of your duties...immediately", said the governor. "Make haste to Londinium, they are in need of you there".
Quickly the High Priest looked up horrified, opened his mouth to protest but could see that the governor had already dismissed him so he closed it again.
The governor called in some soldiers, "Have his Grace escorted to his chambers and he and his belongings sent to Londinium... immediately", he commanded.
"Yes, Sire", they replied and escorted the High Priest out of the chambers, he was given no time to tell Elaena or prepare her.
The next day a new High Priest came for Elaena and while she was with the governor all her comforts were removed from her cell, by the time she returned the cell had been stripped bare. Horrified she looked around the cell and a new sense of despair descended on her, she was thankful that the weather had changed and begun to warm up.

As Spring progressed she wondered how the townspeople were faring out and how the children were. She thought of Paedur often and of the few short years they had spent together, the time since his death had been a blur and lately it seemed she was either with the governor or she was asleep. Spring progressed into Summer and her imprisonment continued to take its toll, she had become thin, gaunt and tired. Her hair was matted even though she had tried to comb it with her fingers, since the High Priest had been taken away she had no washing facilities and her dress had become dirty and smelly. The new High Priest made no efforts to help her and when she asked for a new dress he grunted. One of the soldiers on guard managed to slip her a thin second hand stola and thin cloak which was an improvement, when it was discovered what he had done, he was relieved of his duties.

As the days wore on Elaena began to piece together the events of the last year. Sitting on the bare floor, her face in her hands, she said to herself, "This is all because of the taberna night the young Roman soldier must have gone to his supervisor and sought revenge. He is probably enjoying the fact that I am now in the custody of the Romans".

Her whole life had been a life of custody; first with her father then with Paedur and now the Roman governor.

For the first time she realised, "Custody with Paedur was the closest I have ever been to freedom and certainly the only love I have ever known". Quietly she whimpered.

"Because of me and my stupid anger and need for revenge, he is now dead. I am in prison the sex slave of a cold hearted Roman governor taken away from my people and worse...taken away from my baby".

A wave of deep regret, remorse and self-recrimination washed over her.

"I wish I had not gone to the taberna that night, if only I had not gone things would have been different. All I wanted was to make Paedur angry and to show him how I felt about Elna being taken away from me. I did not intend anything to happen because of it, there was not supposed to be any consequences. I thought I had got away with it, but I have not, this is worse than any punishment Paedur could have given me. Paedur forgave me, that is clear, but the young Roman soldier has not, he has sought his own revenge against me and now I am here living the consequences".

Until this moment she had lived only in the present with no thought for the past and no concern for the future, dimly she tried to look ahead and found that she couldn't. She had no hope of release that was for sure, all her comforts were gone and now she had nothing. Being inactive was beginning to cause her pain so slowly she got to her feet and walked around the cell. Her thoughts turned to Paedur, "*With Paedur I had everything, all I had to do was ask and he provided it for me. He had tried to teach me and I would not listen and all the time he was patient with me*".

Another wave of remorse swept over her and she missed him, she felt lonely and frightened.

"If only I had not gone down to the taberna that night", she moaned. "If only I had listened to him and allowed him to comfort me, then I would probably not be here and he would not be dead".

She felt grief and it hurt, a deep pain shot across her chest and she fought for breath. She felt a sharp pain in the back of her neck which shot down her spine; she rubbed her neck trying to ease the pain. A wave of deep sadness washed over her, engulfed her and she started to cry. A deep shudder escaped from her and she fell to the floor sobbing, deep heart wrenching sobs engulfed her and all the sadness of the past seven months were released. The sobs came up from her toes right up to her head and her whole body shook with emotion.

"It is all my fault", she sobbed, "if only I had not gone...if only I had listened...if only..." Her sadness deepened.

She remembered the last time she saw him and the look of pure forgiveness on his face, he may have forgiven her, but she could not forgive herself. At that moment she hated herself for what she had done and she could not forgive herself for killing the only man who had ever loved her. The pain, the loss, the grief, the remorse crushed her, she had never felt this much emotion and she had no idea how to cope. She sank into deep depression and remorse.

As the night wore on she stopped crying and leaned against the wall exhausted drained and feeling watery inside. She stared up at the little bit of sky that she could see and realised it was mid-summer; her people would be celebrating the Solstice. She remembered last Solstice and how great she had felt being with Paedur and their baby and how the women doted over them. How he had taken her to the edge of the forest and kissed her with such love. She remembered the previous solstice when he had taken her down to the beach, the night she had become pregnant. How things had changed since then, how far she had come.

She shook her head and looked down at the ground, after a few minutes her eyes shot open and a deep gasp escaped her. For the first time she realised she had not bled for months, a horrific thought crossed her mind and she moaned, “Oh no”.

Since the High Priest had left she had no herbs, she realised now that the ones he had been giving her were not only cleansing herbs but were also preventative ones. She calculated in her mind the dates and again moaned, “Oh no”.

She raised her head, leaned it against the wall and deeply sighed, she had just realised she was pregnant and this one was the governor’s.

She realised she had not been feeling too well lately, she put it down to the lack of food continual raping and the coldness of the cell. Now she realised it was because she was pregnant.

A deep sense of revulsion engulfed her and she felt contaminated, she noticed she had lost weight and had become bony pale and weak, again she had put this down to imprisonment. Now she realised it was the baby taking from her all it could get.

“I am not well enough to carry a child and I cannot ask for herbs and more food” she reasoned. I cannot let the soldiers know that I am with child, they will taunt and jeer me even more than they already do and the governor will use it to enslave me even more”, she moaned.

Any energy left in her drained away. The grief, the remorse, the self-hatred, the self-recrimination was crushing but she was strong, she could possibly cope with all of that if she had to. The self-blame for Paedur’s death was enormous, but even that she could cope with if necessary. The knowledge that she was pregnant by the Roman governor and that she was carrying a Roman baby, the product of rape, was too much. That she couldn't cope with – on any level. That completely crushed her. Staring at the opposite wall she envisioned him finding out and how he would use it to exert even more control over her. She pictured herself being brought up to his hall and he making the announcement to the painted ladies and the men in togas that the Celtic prostitute was with child, a Roman child, his child. He could have her ridiculed jeered and laughed at, she could see him wallowing in the glorious victory of a Celtic woman carrying a Roman child. This would be the ultimate victory, the ultimate prize.

She shook her head and shuddered, she thought of damaging herself but as she looked around the cell she realised, "I have no implements and I have no herbs and even if I did, I do not know how to use them. I never bothered to ask Paedur what he had used the night after the taberna and if I were to ask for some now I would probably not be given them. While the other High Priest was here he was secretly giving me the right herbs, but now with the new High Priest he gives me nothing and so I have been unprotected for the last few months. If he were here he would understand and give me the right herbs, but then if he were here, I would not be with child because he would have taken care of that automatically. Oh! Dear, what am I going to do", she asked herself in desperation shaking her head.

A momentary glimmer of hope dawned, "Maybe if I go to the Governor and tell him he will take pity on me, after all it is his child and perhaps he will move me to a nicer room until the baby is birthed".

She thought about the possibility of this and then her hope died. "No, he will not, he cares not for me nor for this child. He will probably hope that I die in childbirth and the baby with me and then he will be rid of me".

This thought brought back her childhood fears of childbirth, with Paedur he had taken every care to make sure she had birthed safely; she knew she would have no such care this time. She knew there was no hope of release and even if there was, she knew she couldn't go back to her people without Paedur. She knew they would blame her for his death and, being pregnant with the governor's child, they would ostracise her and probably drive her out of town. Even if they were to allow her to stay they would make her life miserable, the warriors would jeer and taunt her again and she would be regarded as fair game for any man, and this time she wouldn't get paid for it. The only time she had been safe in the town was with Paedur and as his woman she had been treated with respect and left alone. She sank deeper into depression, she started breathing desperately trying to think what she could do but all she could do was cry. Placing her hands on her abdomen she moaned, "Once I carried a baby of light, now I carry a baby of darkness. Once I was loved, now I am just used".

The tears flowed down her face and her shoulders shook with emotion, she put her face in her hands and cried, "Oh! Paedur I need you now, I need your strong gentle arms around me. I need you to kiss me and tell me all is well, I need you to take the pain away. I need your compassionate eyes and your soft voice to reassure me".

She shook her head and, sadly, to herself said, "But you are not here and it is all because of me".

Tears engulfed her again and she sobbed, holding herself, rocking back and forward.

"If only I had not been so stupid, if only I had listened. If only I had realised he did know best and he had my best interests at heart", she deeply sighed and sniffed.

"Once I was loved, once my heart was open, now my heart is closed and it has been eclipsed", she moaned.

The remorse, the grief, the reproach and recrimination set in deeply.

"It is all my fault, I am a horrible person and I do not deserve to be forgiven. He may have forgiven me but I cannot forgive myself for causing the death of the only man who ever loved me".

She shook her head and lapsed into silence.

Sitting in the dark that night the cold stone floor beneath her, the cold hard walls around her and the full moon shining down on her, she reviewed her life. She shivered and looked around the cell for something warm but there was nothing. It was the middle of June and the previous weeks had been hot, all she had now was a thin dirty stola and a thin cloak, she drew them both closer to her trying to gain some warmth. She sat with her back against the wall facing the small grill in the opposite wall watching the moon; she drew her knees up to her chest and hugged them. She tried to remember what her life had been like but she had forgotten, the last seven months had been a blur and she remembered nothing. Trying to remember made her colder; she hugged her knees more tightly and drew right in on herself.

Slowly, dimly scenes began to emerge, *a child's laughter playing in the fields embracing the sun, embracing the wind, embracing the air, embracing the moon, playing in the water, dancing on the earth.*

The laughter grew louder and she smiled to herself.

She saw a teenage girl crossing the square huddled in a cloak in a hurry exhausted, she saw a man beating this girl and saying nasty things to her.

Pain shot through her body making her gasp, she woke up with pain in every cell of her body. She sat frozen unable to move. She closed her eyes and blocked out the pictures, remembering was too painful. Breathing deeply she tried to calm herself.

Those eyes, that voice, those strong gentle arms...the warm solid presence, the calmness, the quietness...the protection, the respect, the compassion...the love. Walking to work with him, he waiting at the end of the evening to walk her home... the lessons, the stories, the laughter and the playfulness...the walks, the boating trips, the beach, the forest...the great hall, the music, the laughter and the warmth.

Again she woke up visions of the warm fire in her eyes, the songs and laughter ringing in her ears. She looked around her but all she saw was four bare walls and all she heard was silence. She slumped into herself, her skin so cold now that it hurt the pain so deep that she couldn't move. She closed her eyes again breathing deeply willing her body to warm up.

The warm room, the angry words, the girl running from the room crying and shouting as she left, running down to the taberna, grabbing the young Roman soldier, laying with him venting all her passion, anger and revenge on him then grabbing her cloak and striding out again.
She gasped and woke up again, it was dark it was cold and she was in pain, she closed her eyes breathing deeply.
The corridor...the dark heavy door...the quietness...the creaking of the door as it opened...those flame red eyes.
She shivered and opened her eyes, the pain reaching into the deepest part of her; with great difficulty she closed her eyes.
The warm room Paedur quietly writing at his desk, she sitting in front of the fire trying to master the art of writing, the door flew open the Romans grabbing her surrounding Paedur and dragging her out screaming.
She woke up with a start her eyes were damp her bottom lip quivered, slowly, painfully, she closed her eyes again breathing with great difficulty, her chest rising and falling. She whimpered. Breathing to calm herself, she blocked out the memories.
Paedur standing quietly the Roman soldiers on each side of him, their swords crossed in front of him, the look of complete understanding, deep compassion and tender love on his face, the look of regret in his eyes, pleading with her to forgive him. As they dragged her away, out of the corner of her eyes, she thought she saw those beautiful eyes moisten.
She woke up; a shuddering breath welled up inside her and exploded, she sobbed with every nerve, cell and fibre of her being. The pain intensified, like a thick black cloud the remorse, recrimination, guilt, grief, loss and bereavement descended upon her and she moaned.
"It is all my fault", she shook her head.
"If only I had not got angry...if only I had listened...if only I had not gone down to the taberna, then he would be alive today and we would be together".
She sobbed totally giving in to the grief, the coldness drew in around her, the moon shone on her face and the pain filled her

head. All strength left her and she lay down, lying on the cold hard ground on her left hand side, she started breathing deeply. She remembered Paedur teaching her a special form of breathing which she had not been able to master, at first the breathing was difficult, she was sobbing uncontrollably.
The first breath was almost impossible.
The second breath was painful.
The third was hard and gasping.
The fourth was shuddering, she fought to gain control.
The fifth breath caught in her throat and she coughed.
The sixth breath was shuddering, she sighed.
The seventh breath came a bit easier and the eighth was easier still.
The ninth breath was slow and deep.
The tenth, eleventh and twelfth were deeper still.
She began to feel calmer, the sobs had become soft and light.
The thirteenth and fourteenth breaths brought a deep feeling of calmness and she stopped crying.
The fifteenth breath was slow, deep and calm.
She relaxed and let go.
The sixteenth breath brought deep calm and peace.
She felt like she was floating, she no longer felt cold; she felt light, calm and peaceful.
She took a deep, deep breath and floated on air, completely calm and relaxed.
She took one more very deep breath and as she did so she sank into a gentle peace, tranquillity and calmness.

It was the night of the 21st June 410AD, the night of the Summer solstice.

Chapter Sixteen

The next day when the High Priest came for Elaena he found her lying on the floor with her back against the wall, several times he called her but there was no answer. He bent down to rouse her and found that she was cold, he shook her but there was no response, he checked her pulse, there was none. Immediately he rushed to the governor and informed him that she had died.

"My Lord...the Celtic woman...she is dead", he said breathlessly.

"DEAD, HOW?" the governor roared.

"I do not know, My Lord, it appears she died in her sleep", he replied.

The Roman governor thought for a few minutes then nodded, "Have her sent back to her people, she is of no further use to us", he said dismissively.

"Yes, My Lord", the High Priest replied bowing and hurried away.

Later that day two Roman soldiers brought her body to the town gate and handed it to the warrior on duty, recognising her he instantly sent word for Násuin to come quickly to the gate. When he arrived he looked down at her emaciated body and tears formed in his eyes, he remembered her as full of figure, radiant with vibrant chestnut red hair. Now she was thin, gaunt and bony, her hair was a dull red, her skin bruised and bloodied, her clothes dirty and smelly. He stood over her looking down at her not believing what he was seeing. Quickly he gestured to his men to place her on a litter, the same one they had used for Paedur. Six warriors surrounded the litter and placed themselves around it raising it on to their shoulders. Led by Násuin, they carefully carried it down the tradesmen's street, everyone stopped what they were doing and stared, silence engulfed the street. They walked on down past the postern gate, into the courtyard and over to the great hall. By now a crowd had gathered behind the cortege and stood in the courtyard, no one thought of work the shops, booths and stalls were left open and unmanned and no one thought to care.

The women immediately began cleaning and preparing her for burial one of them keened - a mournful sound that froze the blood of all who heard it.

Násuin excused himself and went to his quarters, when he was alone he broke down; hot tears flowed down his cheeks, he sobbed uncontrollably shaking from head to toe. Since her arrest and imprisonment the thoughts of her eventual release kept him going; now he knew that hope was gone, after a few minutes he vowed to avenge her death and Paedur's. Grief turned to cold hard determination. He went out to his warriors and barked orders to them to surround the fort and strengthen the defences of the town, he knew now that time was against them and confrontation was inevitable. While they were engaged in this he went to see Niwelyn.

"Forgive the intrusion, Niwelyn", he said bowing. "Lady Elaena has been returned to us...she...is dead", he gulped, tears stung his eyes but he kept tight control of his emotions.

"Do we know how, Násuin?" she asked quietly.

"No, no details were given", he sank a little.

Niwelyn noticed him fighting for control and handed him a goblet of wine into which she poured some Chamomile, "something to quieten and strengthen you", she said.

"I am strong", he said in a determined voice.

"I know, Násuin, but the next few hours will be challenging, you may thank me yet", she said quietly.

"I already do, Niwelyn", he said quietly.

Taking a deep breath he shuddered.

"You are not well", Niwelyn said.

Silently he shook his head.

"You had feelings for her" she stated.

Násuin nodded, "I loved her", he whispered.

"I suspected that", she said nodding.

"Will you come and attend to the...Elaena", he asked. "The women are preparing her now".

"Yes of course, let me get my things", she replied.

Gathering her cloak and medicines bag she left with Násuin, he carried her bag for her.

When they arrived at the courtyard Niwelyn went immediately to Elaena, the women stopped what they were doing and stepped back reverently. Deftly she inspected her and when she was finished she allowed the women to continue to clean her and dress her in a long emerald green velvet dress trimmed with gold. They washed and brushed her hair, they painted her skin to cover the bruises and they clad her feet with soft brown leather boots. The children were crying and sat around her litter, some of them had already begun making things to adorn the litter and this helped them to cope with the sadness. Some of the other women busied themselves getting food, some just stood hugging each other trying to offer some comfort. Elaena may not have been popular, but she was one of them and what happened to her could have happened to anyone of them, they were glad it was her and not them. The women clung on tightly to their daughters especially the older ones.

Niwelyn and the New Chief Druid began some incantations, Niwelyn started, "Druantia we thank you for the return of Elaena; we present her now to you".

"Accept her into your tender loving care", intoned the Druid.

"Dis Pater, God of Death and the Underworld, grant her soul peace and safe passage", continued Niwelyn.

"Bless all here who knew her and comfort them in their sadness", continued the Druid.

Niwelyn looked over at Násuin and nodded holding him in a long stare trying to transmit some comfort to him.

That night Elaena's body lay in open view in the great hall so that the people could mourn her in their own way, the warriors stood guard, on full alert, and Násuin was very quiet. Medwyn and her brothers spent the night in the taberna drinking heavily, her mother sat silently alone, crying.

When everyone had gone home Násuin sat beside her body, memories presenting themselves to him.

The night at the taberna when he broke up the fight between Paedur and Medwyn...the time he walked her home and carried baby Elaena up the stairs for her and lingered in the room offering to stay with her until Paedur returned. The time when she and Paedur had slunk away unnoticed at the Summer Solstice...the times they chatted by the fire and how he had comforted her after his men had jeered her and...the time she had come to him for training...and he...had her in his arms pinned against him.

He closed his eyes and savoured that memory.

The night he went to Paedur begging him to release her into his custody and Paedur's anger.

He shook his head and took a deep breath.

Now she was lying next to him cold and dead, he bowed his head and allowed the tears to flow. Standing up he double checked that he was alone then stood beside her body and leant down placing his forehead on her chest. Hot tears flowed staining the cloth of her dress, he wrapped his arms around her and hugged her, she was in his arms only this time she was cold and dead. He shook from head to toe sobbing. After a few minutes all energy drained from him, raising his head and stepping away from her he lay down on the floor beside the litter and fell asleep.

The next day Niwelyn and the Druid prepared the funeral pyre; the children helped and decorated the altar for her. They decorated her litter with the things they had made and the girls put a crown of flowers around her head. She looked beautiful but Niwelyn, looking down at her, sensed that her soul was not at peace. She didn't know what actually happened to Elaena once she had been taken but, from the state of her body when it was returned, she suspected she had been raped, many times.

As dusk drew near everyone gathered in the great hall around Elaena, in a strong clear voice

Niwelyn said, "Creiddylad, May Queen and Goddess of Love, in life Elaena represented you in our ceremonies, we pray tonight for Elaena that she be released from her bondage and may her soul now be at peace".

The women and children kissed her cheeks, the men stood by silent - the warriors were on high alert.

Násuin stood silently, watching, slowly he approached the litter and, as he bent down to kiss her on the lips, his eyes filled with tears. His lips quivered and his hands shook, gently he placed a single red rose in full bloom between her hands. Fighting to control his emotions he stepped away and gestured to his men. Six warriors instantly took up positions around the litter and carefully raised it up and placed it on their shoulders. They carried it out to the pyre followed by Niwelyn and the Druid, her family walked behind and the townspeople fell into step behind them. Gently the warriors placed her litter on the pyre and stepped back. Násuin, his hands shaking, took a deep breath and calmed himself, slowly raising his bow up he loaded it with an arrow, one of his men touched it with a firebrand.

As he shot the arrow into the pyre, he said quietly, "Farewell My Lady...Elaena...my love".

The arrow whistled as it shot through the air and landed in the middle of the pyre, instantly flames shot up and engulfed it. Niwelyn and the Druid stood on either side of him and all three stayed while the crowd dispersed. Niwelyn turned to Násuin and touched him gently on the arm; both knew that the other was thinking of a similar night not so long ago, he had supported her then and she supported him now. The Druid moved away leaving Násuin and Niwelyn alone standing by the flaming pyre.

"She was with child...the governor's child...the product of repeated rape", Niwelyn said, watching him out of the corner of her eye.

Násuin blinked and nodded, "I thought that would happen", he said quietly.

"I went to Paedur the night before they were taken and asked him to release her into my custody...but he refused. If only he had...things could have been different". She did not know I loved her...perhaps if she had she...but she did not...and now she never will", he said sadly fighting to control his emotions.

"Will you be alright?" she asked.

Nodding he said, "Of course I will, I am a warrior, I have no feelings".

"We both know that is not true", she said quietly.
Násuin nodded silently keeping his gaze firmly fixed on the flaming pyre.
"What will happen to Elna?" he asked quietly.
"She is with the Order on Ynys Mon, they will take care of her", she replied.
"Will she know who her parents were?" he asked.
Niwelyn nodded, "Paedur left instructions with them to do so", she replied.
He took a deep breath, "Good", he said, "that is as it should be", he continued nodding.
"What will you do now?" he asked.
"I have not decided yet", she replied.
"What will you do now?" she asked.
Taking a deep breath he replied, "Paedur and I once spoke of rising up and ridding Britannia of all Romans, I intend to do just that. We were supposed to do it together...now I will have to do it alone".
"You are not alone, Násuin, you have your men".
"Aye that I do, but their numbers have been depleted and they do not have the knowledge, courage, strength and vision that Paedur had. On his and Elaena's behalf I will do everything in my power to claim back what is rightfully ours", he said.
Eventually they moved away and as they did so they noticed Elaena's family standing a little way off staring at the blazing pyre, together Násuin and Niwelyn went over to them. Her mother stood crying, wringing her hands, Ioan, Gruffudd and Dafydd stood staring at the fire. Medwyn stood silently showing no emotion at all.
Taking her mother's hands in hers Niwelyn said compassionately, "Branwen", please accept our deepest sympathy", may Danu comfort you in your loss".
Turning to Medwyn she said in a hard voice, "Pray that your daughter is now at peace".
Staring at each of the boys, she said, "Learn from this".
Silently Násuin nodded to each in turn.

Násuin returned to his quarters and spent the night alone trying to busy himself but stopping every so often as the grief engulfed him. Exhausted with grief he had no more tears, dejected with loss he stood in the centre of his dwelling beside the hearth unable to move. Shaking his head he went over to the press and took out a jug of wine and a glass and, carrying both over to his bed, he drank himself to sleep.

Niwelyn returned to her roundhouse and busied herself tidying an already tidy house. A deep sense of shocked calm descended upon her and, having no reason to stay awake any longer, she lay down and slept.

***

At dawn the next morning Niwelyn, dressed in a lightweight stola, went to Paedur's room and retrieved one of his pens that he had given to Elaena. She was in an altered state of awareness and was acutely aware of the dew on the grass and the scent of the forest. Taking it down to the stream she raised it to the rising sun and quietly she said, "Arianrhod, accept this pen on behalf of Elaena, although she was not yet a scribe, she was in training as such. Grant that in her next life she may be given the gifts of wisdom, knowledge and writing". Bending down slowly on one knee she placed the pen into the water, standing up she watched it bob along the top of the water then bowed to the trees and returned to her roundhouse.

Later that day Niwelyn rode to the fort on her horse, Násuin was in the courtyard with his men discussing how they were going to defeat the Romans, on seeing her enter the courtyard he detached himself and went over to the open fire to her.

"Good afternoon, Niwelyn, are you alright?" he asked.

Nodding she dismounted and replied, "I am, Násuin, however I need your help".

"Anything I can do for you, I will", he said.

"Násuin, could you procure a cart or carriage of some sort for me so that I can bring Paedur's belongings back to Ynys Mon with me", she asked.
"Absolutely, let me do that for you immediately", he said. "What size cart do you need?"
"I want his desk and two chairs, his harp and his chests".
"A large one then", he decided nodding.
"Could you also help me load it", she asked quietly.
"It would be my pleasure", he replied bowing.
Immediately he went over to the stables and chose a rather large cart and, bringing it into the courtyard, he attached it to her horse, gently, guiding the horse he walked over to the door of the great hall. Niwelyn immediately went to Paedur's room and began putting his writing equipment into the chests. She covered his harp with a black leather cover with a serpent design on it and took his cauldron and herbs.
Násuin came into the room and stood remembering the various times he had been here before, he watched Niwelyn as she gathered Paedur's things up and waited for her instruction. Some of his men followed him into the room a few minutes later
"Ah! Násuin, can you get the desk, chairs, harp and chests down the stairs for me", she asked.
Násuin gestured to his men to carry out her request.
"What do you want to do with the dresser, chair and tables", he asked.
"Have you any use for them?" she asked.
"No", he replied.
"Give them to Elaena's family then, perhaps they will make use of them", she said.
He nodded.
When Paedur's room was empty and the warriors were loading the cart Niwelyn said, "Thank you for everything...we were a good team and could have achieved so much if we had been given more time".
"You are welcome, Niwelyn, it has been an honour and a privilege knowing you and working with you".
Niwelyn nodded.

"Do you want an escort back to Ynys Mon?" he asked.
"No, Násuin, I am happy to travel alone, thank you". "I will have the cart returned to you as soon as possible".
"No need", he replied, "keep it as a memento of us".
"Thank you", she said quietly.
"Be safe then and may Druantia go with you", he said.
Together they took one last look around the empty room, nodded and went down to the courtyard, the cart had been loaded and everything made secure.
Niwelyn rode out of the courtyard back to her roundhouse loaded her own things on to the cart and began her journey back to Ynys Mon.

Epilogue

Once the townspeople had got over the sadness of Elaena's death they returned to normal life.
Niwelyn left Conwy and went to the Order on Ynys Mon.
Násuin and the warriors banded together with the neighbouring tribes and, together with the Druids, planned to join Quintis army. Before they could do anything significant word came from abroad that Alaric had sacked the city of Roma.

***

On 24 August 410AD, two months after Elaena's death, the Roman Empire fell and the troops were recalled from Britain to defend the shrinking Empire.
The Druids and warriors strengthened their defences around their towns and sought to regain control in the wake of Roman rule.

***

Christianity finally took hold that same year in Britain.
As Paedur had foreseen...both the Celtic and the Roman Empires fell...together.

Places and Names

Paedur	*pronounced*	Pay-dur
Elaena		El-ay-na
Násuin		Naw-soon
Medwyn		Med-win
Ioan		Ian
Gruffudd		Griffith
Dafydd		David
Camalus		Celtic God of War/Sky
Macha		Celtic Goddess of War/Life/Death
Mebh		Celtic Goddess of Earth/Fertility
Cymru		Cum-ree (Wales/Welsh people)
Cymraeg		Cum-ray-ik (Welsh language)
Conwy		Con-wee
Paedagogus		Pay-da-go-gus (Teacher/child minder)
Blitidae		Blee-tee-day (Taverna Prostitute)
Taberna		Taverna (Bar/Pub/Inn)
Oppidum		O-pee-dum (Celtic town)
Diolch		Die-ulk
Croeso		Croy-so
Iawn Diolch		U-in-die-ulk
Sut mai		Sit mai
Triskele		Tris-cal
Bracae		Bra-kay

Cornucopia	The horn of plenty
Apodyterium	Bathhouse / changing room
Tepidarium	Warm water bath room (bathhouse)

Where the places are

Roma	Rome
Britannia	Britain
Scotia	Scotland
Mona/Ynys Mon (Inis Mon)	Anglesey
Deva	Chester
Conwy	Conway, North Wales
Londinium	London
Hibernia	Ireland
Gaul	France
Caerhun	near Conway
Hispania	Spain